DESIGNS

ALSO BY JAMES BRADY

Superchic
Paris One
Nielsen's Children
The Press Lord
Holy Wars

DESIGNS
A NOVEL BY

James Brady

Crown Publishers, Inc.
New York

Published by Crown Publishers, Inc. 225 Park Avenue South, New York, New York 10003 and represented in Canada by the Canadian MANDA Group. CROWN is a trademark of Crown Publishers, Inc.

Manufactured in the United States of America

Book design by True Sims

Library of Congress Cataloging-in-Publication Data
Brady, James, 1928–
  Designs.
  I. Title.
PS3552.R243D47   1986   813'.54   86-6369
ISBN 0-517-56284-7

10 9 8 7 6 5 4 3 2

For Susan and Fiona. And for Coco.

Everyone's got a label sewn on somewhere ... inside the collar, the seat of your pants, right there on your face. Nobody goes unlabeled.

Lincoln Radford, *Mode* magazine

Prologue

Chelsea West has everything. But is it enough?"

Adam's bitter and resentful line enjoyed a certain season in Manhattan and Beverly Hills before being picked up by *People* magazine.

The remark was not only bitchy but inaccurate. Chelsea West at twenty-five years old knew with precision that she didn't have everything, that nobody did. She was very tall and quite beautiful, and the *Wall Street Journal* said that, depending on whose accounting you believed, she was now either the third or the fifth richest woman in America. She was also famous, for reasons that had nothing to do with money.

Despite all that had happened during the last year, she didn't yet have a philosophy. "Settle your debts." That was Marc Street. "Ante up and pay off." That was her grandfather. Maybe it was the same thing. She wished they were here now, both of them, either of them. This was New York the week before Christmas, a rotten time to be alone.

The small plane had brought her into Denver that morning from the West ranch. Winter was still a few days off, but already there was snow on the peaks, and Independence Pass, 12,095 feet up, was closed. December, an equivocal month, unable to make up its mind between autumn and winter. When her United flight left Denver at noon Chelsea West could see the storm coming off the hills, chill and menacing, tiny spits of snow whipping horizontally across the tarmac and past the jet's windows. The day before up at the ranch above Aspen had been sunny, nearly warm, and she had gone riding in a flannel shirt and a sweater. She loved the mountains but she was glad to be getting off early. You never knew with Denver in December. New York, four hours later, was another country.

The big plane banked over the Hudson and Manhattan, dropping smoothly toward LaGuardia and the twilight city. There were no reporters at the gate, no reason for them. She was traveling under another name, routine procedure by now, routinely arranged by West Industries. The limo, histrionically stretched and vulgarly silver, was waiting.

"Any checked luggage, Miss West?"

No, just what she carried. There were closets full of clothes in New York and closets in Colorado, other closets in other places, and what she lacked she could always buy.

Just before eight o'clock the car rolled up to the canopy of her building. The doorman, a familiar Irish face, took the small bag and offered genial blather. Sutton Place equals Sutton Place. Worlds change, lives begin and end, careers soar and crash, and the canopies and the doormen of Sutton Place are always the same. In the elevator she shrugged off the coyote coat. The operator stared straight ahead at the polished door, watching her in its reflection.

The apartment looked fine, with fresh flowers in the vases. A telex had alerted the maid she was coming. Chelsea walked through to the windows on the river side. A small chopper swung north toward the bridge, navigation lights blinking and low to the water. Just beyond, silhouetted against the lights of Long Island City, a tug towed a garbage barge seaward against the flooding tide. She dropped her coat on a couch and went into the bedroom and through it into the bathroom, hardly glancing into the mirror. Some people need mirrors.

When she had washed her face and brushed out her long hair, she undid the calf-length leather skirt, kicked off her boots, pulled off her blouse, and slipped into a terry-cloth robe. She

2

walked through to the second bedroom, sterile and neat, void and silent. In the kitchen she found a cold Rolling Rock and drank it from the bottle, wandering through the empty rooms, lighted only by the moon and the river. On a small table in the foyer phone messages were piled, and the mail.

Barbara Walters. Miss Walters called again. Miss Walters's producer. Call Barbara Walters. Please call . . . The messages had different dates, different hours. She knew what they meant. The same messages had come to the ranch, to the offices in Denver.

"No, thank you," she said aloud. "Miss Otis regrets." She did not trust herself.

It was still early, Colorado time, and Manhattan would be coming to life. She could get into an old pair of Adam jeans and wander over to First Avenue or to Second and have a couple of beers and a hamburger, or go up to Elaine's. There were always pretty girls hanging out, and she could go unnoticed. Instead, she went into the bedroom, propped herself up on pillows, and punched out a Denver number on the cordless white phone.

"Walter? I'm in New York, at the apartment. You getting snow?"

Felton told her about the snow, and they talked for a few minutes. No, he said, there was nothing from the detective in Paris. Not a damned thing.

"I'm sorry, Chelsea."

"Sure."

"He's a good man, Chelsea. He'll keep at it. He'll find him."

"Yeah," she said.

Felton, too, was a good man. If he said there was no news, then there was none. She thanked him and hung up.

In Paris, Marc would be asleep now. That is, if he was still in Paris. He could be anywhere.

Restlessly she made round trips through the apartment until, in the living room, above and to the left of a fireplace that smoked and was rarely lit, her eye caught the large old photo in its sterling frame, now dulled and tarnished (no maid was perfect). Chelsea stopped to stand in front of the photo, hands on hips, head slightly cocked, regarding it with mingled wonder and resentment.

It was the picture of a woman, not young, but dark-haired, dark-eyed, slender, wearing a white linen jacket with three buttons, over a black or navy dress. The woman's left shoulder leaned against the wall of a rather formal room. Her right hand, low and tense, braceleted, brushing her slim thigh, held a cigarette. The Sutton Place living room was rich with color and pattern, but this old black-and-white photo, static and marginally grainy, dominated the room, muting color. The woman's narrow face focused on hers.

Chelsea moved, but the woman in the photo did not. This did not diminish her authority, and Chelsea felt it even now, more than fifty years after the photo had been taken. She stared at the face, the arrogant posture, the unheeded, unlighted cigarette, and then wheeled, annoyed and disturbed. How unfair to be compared to her, to have to compete, to be asked to do again what she and only she had done. How do you contend with the dead?

The photo belonged to Marc, and he had hung it there the night before her first show, as a loving, supportive gesture. That was his intention, that was how she had seen it. Now this portrait of a woman long dead hung there oppressive and mournful, tangible evidence of the obsession that had caught them up, Marc and Adam and Chelsea herself. If she had known then what she knew now, she would have pushed the frame back into Marc's hands and refused ever to see it again, ever to hear her name. Coco Chanel.

In the bedroom she shucked off the robe and slipped into an oversized man's blue Brooks Brothers shirt. It came to the top of her long legs; it was one of Marc's shirts, freshly laundered. Irrationally, she thought she could still catch his scent in it. She stood for a time by a tall window in the darkened room, looking at the river, now turned and flowing toward the sea. Soon, in France, Marc would awaken, alone, or perhaps with someone else, descending to the newly swept and watered Paris streets for hot croissants fresh from the bakery oven, and for the morning *Herald Trib* and the *Figaro*. She remembered mornings like that, lying in bed watching him through the half-open door as he shaved, the bed-tousled hair still wet from the shower, the thick brows close-knit in concentration, the big, powerful body naked but for a damp towel knotted at the waist.

"You ought to exercise, you know," she nagged, "or one of these days you'll have a belly and I'll hate it. At least you could jog."

"I'll leave that to your football player," he said, continuing to stare at himself in the steamy mirror. Sometimes she wore to bed a football jersey given her by a halfback on the Broncos, and he teased her about it, calling her a groupie.

"Jealous," she said, and got the towel thrown at her for her trouble. She remembered that, and the laughing, tumbling happiness of love that followed. She could see him now, big, strong, grinning, his pleasant brown eyes set deep beneath their brows. She could hear his voice, bass but not solemn, recounting stories of the strange and wonderful people he worked with, stories she wondered if she should believe.

"Tell me more lies," she would urge playfully as they lay there after morning love, "I don't care if you make them up."

Even now she could hear his voice, low and murmuring, could remember the faded roses of the wallpaper behind him in that first bedroom on the rue Jean-Goujon, and his stories about France and about fashion: about Dior, who died of overeating on a voyage his astrologer had warned him not to take; about Marron, whose accounts were in such disarray that an embezzling bookkeeper could not be prosecuted; about Balmain, whose lover was reputed to be a Catholic monk; about Saint Laurent and Givenchy and the Lanvins, and about Chanel, always about Chanel.

Sometimes he talked seriously about it.

"They asked Saint Laurent one day, what is fashion? is it an art? and Yves said no, art was too important a word. It was 'un métier poétique' . . . a poetic craft. I like that," Marc said. "I'd like to think that's the work we do."

Now, alone in Sutton Place the week before Christmas, she recalled such moments, clutching them to herself like a child's letter to Santa Claus until, annoyed, she shook her head angrily and tried to close out memory.

Finally she climbed into bed, pushing the down comforter

away and pulling up one of the flowered Porthault sheets. She was not an indulgent person, and she tried not to wallow in useless regret. It was all so damned unfair, and there was nothing she could do about it except wait and hope that Felton's man was as good as Walter said he was and that somehow, somewhere, he would find Marc. And that Marc would come home.

Nothing else was important, not Adam, long cast out, not Stanley Baltimore, hated and feared. It was tempting to blame them for what had happened, tempting but too simple. Much of it was Marc's own fault, Marc who loved her and whom she loved, Marc who had built a cottage industry into a fashion empire and in the doing changed her from just another rich bitch into a name Barbara Walters and the world would know.

"So damned stubborn!" she cried aloud. He had thrown away everything he had, they had—his work, their company, the entire future—all because of a gangster like Lazer, to whom he owed a debt. She had debts of her own, she knew, and carried them with her even now, as she always carried a valid passport and an open airline ticket to Paris, waiting only for the word that Marc had been found, that he had stopped running.

How did everything that was so good go so wrong?

At last Chelsea slept, alone and restless. She dreamed wildly of Paris, where she first went as a schoolgirl holding tightly to her grandfather's hand, where she had first seen Marc; Paris, where it began with a funeral.

BOOK ONE

COCO

1

Chanel remains, at her age, the *monstre sacré* of Paris.
More monster these days than sacred.

Mode, January 3, 1971

Mademoiselle! *Votre Cadillac est arrivé!*"

A January morning in 1971, Sunday, a day for church or for driving into the country to lunch with friends in a smoky inn tucked into an elbow of the Seine. It was all the same, really, communing with God or with friends.

"*D'accord*," Gabrielle Chanel muttered impatiently to the maid. Let the car wait; chauffeurs were paid to wait. At her suite in the Ritz, Chanel lay in bed facing the window, beyond which Paris lingered under a thin sun, brightening but not warming, the day damp and struggling with cloud. The maid bustled about the bedroom. Under the covers Chanel's slim legs lay locked together, as if protecting dry loins. Ha! she thought, little danger there. A half hour later she was dressed, and the maid settled a flat-brimmed hat atop her wig while Chanel regarded herself in a full-length mirror, frowning at the image staring back at her, slender, chic, still erect, but hardly young. Well, she thought, laughing silently, how could it be else?

The car, an old, immaculately polished sedan, waited at the curb. She preferred American cars. These little French cars were ridiculous, like France itself, pretending to be important. The Cadillac whispered its way down the rue Cambon to turn into the rue de Rivoli, the cobbled streets full of Sunday motorists and cyclists. Chanel, muffled in a fur lap robe, watched through the side window as they crossed the Seine and the car rolled onto the autoroute, picking up speed. Trees and open fields and hedge and small châteaux sped by. How green it is, she thought, even in January, even through old eyes. By now the snow would lie deep about her chalet above Geneva. It would be pleasant to be there now, but the collection came first: the wonder, the splendor, the drama, the adulation, the bitchery; the twice-a-year orgasm of fashion.

She was now eighty-seven years old, and she had worked all day Saturday. The new collection was going well. Chunky, rough Irish and Scottish tweeds, skirts weighted with fine chain to hang straight, the jackets over Italian and Swiss silk blouses creamy as milk, evening dresses with no back and courtesy front, dresses for the rich, the sleek, the decidedly flat-chested. Nothing here for little Bardot, she thought, smiling maliciously as she recalled B.B.'s bosom. Flannel slacks for country weekends, wonderful sweaters for the patios of Montfort l'Amaury and Lago di Como, for the gardens of Kent and Surrey, and wherever it was wealthy Americans had their places. Suede coats with mink lining. Only the vulgar wore furs except as lining. New silk prints from Amtorg, the Zurich "fabric genius," or so the magazines had anointed him. So far as she was concerned, the man was too chummy by far with M. Saint Laurent.

The countryside had gone dull now; dusty gray quarries and small factories lined the autoroute, while the Seine, muddy and sluggish, curved in and out of sight. She stopped watching through the car window and her eyes, without closing, turned inward, seeing not the grays and duns of the industrial suburbs but the pastels and brilliant greens and navys and fiery scarlets and rich oatmeal tones of new clothes, saw not the quarry or the mill but the sunlit blond hair of her mannequins, tall, slender girls chosen not for their intelligence.

"You have to be a bit of a cow to be good at it," Coco once remarked to a friend who had asked how she selected her models, "so much standing around with your tail twitching."

She knew intimately about such things. She had been in the fashion business since 1914, when her lover, determined to keep her out of mischief, set her up in a milliner's shop before going off to die on the Marne. She wept and lighted candles and then, sensibly, freshened up the hats in her shopwindow with feathers and tulle. It turned out that she had a flair; the improbable worked. After the war, bored by the provinces, she came to the capital to open her couture house, soon to become a staple of Paris in the twenties, as flamboyant and even more enduring than Hemingway, Gertrude Stein, Josephine Baker.

Her new lover was the Duke of Westminster. The duke had two yachts, one of them a converted British destroyer painted dead white and with a crew of 180. She disliked the sea, suffered *mal de mer,* and rarely went with him to England. And of course, there was his wife, understandably part of her reticence. When Diaghilev died she and Westminster were sailing near Venice and put in for the funeral. Serge Lifar and other Russians, all of them dancers, made up the cortege. In tribute to their dead master, they vowed to follow the casket on their knees all the way to the cemetery. Weeping and groaning, they made their way painfully, inch by inch. Chanel could take only so much of this. Impatiently, she snapped her fingers and ordered the mourners to their feet. Grateful, they all walked the rest of the way.

In 1938 she closed her house. Another war was coming, a time for khaki and not for satin. During the Occupation there was a new lover, this one German. People sneered, but she was hardly the only one. De Gaulle, she announced, was a criminal. It had been the French who requested the armistice; it was for the French to respect law and not to shoot Germans or derail locomotives. The "soundness" of her politics did not stop Marshal Pétain from warning that if she wore pants on holiday in the south she would be arrested, Occupied France being a seemly place where women wore skirts.

After the war she reopened the *maison de couture.* The Swiss who marketed her perfume insisted. They needed the publicity, the controversy, the talk her clothes inspired. Dior came and went, exploding his "new look" in 1948, dying nine years later of gluttony. Fath came and went. Molyneux retreated to the Midi to grow roses. She feuded with Balenciaga, cackling with delight when he was hoaxed one season into hiring as his star mannequin a tall, leggy beauty who turned out to be a young French paratrooper smuggled into the models' *cabine* on a lark. "Pederasts!" she demanded. "What do they know of women?" Over lunch she confided to Mme. Bousquet of the *Bazaar* that the incident proved dear Cristobal was "too old," and Mme. Bousquet picked up her skirts to hurry across town to Balenciaga with the remark. Ever after Chanel said of Marie-Louise Bousquet, "the face of a monkey, the mouth of a sewer," and applauded in glee when, during a show at Dior, Mme. Bousquet, her hand trembling, dropped a cigarette and, briefly but spectacularly, set her own lap on fire. Overlooked in all the fuss was the fact that Chanel was a decade older than "old" Balenciaga.

She rejected the Duke of Westminster's proposal of marriage by reminding him, "There are many duchesses. There is only one Coco Chanel."

Other lovers were used and discarded. By now, she spoke in aphorisms, appreciating the value of a good quote, contributing consciously to the construction of a legend. "You can have love or you can have success," she told an interviewer. "Choices must be made." If it was a lonely life, it was of her choosing. There were rumors of a lesbian attachment with one of her mannequins, an exquisite Swiss girl. She did nothing to discourage the talk. Better to be gossiped about than to be ignored. She played the press as deftly as a pianist the keys. When an American writer friend brought Barbra Streisand up to pay brief homage, Coco professed confusion as to just who the singer was and then remarked, rapidly and in French, knowing that the remark would be repeated, "She is very nice, but the poor girl really must do something with that nose." She took Bardot out of blue jeans and T-shirts and skintight sweaters and forced her reluctantly into real clothes, admiring her legs, her curving and provocative little bottom (*"Très jolie, tu sais?"*), if not the rest of her. "Up here it is too much," Coco informed anyone who would listen, as she cupped and lifted her own minimal breasts.

Young Saint Laurent came under her spell. "She is the godmother of us all," he reverently informed a journalist. Chanel meowed her response: "M. Saint Laurent has good taste. And the more he copies me the better taste he displays." She feuded with

Antonio del Castillo, sending him into stuttering rages, and with Courrèges and Cardin, scheduling her January and July fashion shows at hours that would precisely compete with theirs, forcing editors and retail buyers into agonizing decisions. She blessed Alan Jay Lerner's efforts to create a Broadway musical about her, listening to him pick out the tunes on a piano moved into her salon for the occasion, but she vetoed Rosalind Russell in the lead. "The woman never draws breath," she remarked cuttingly after the two took tea on a suede couch in Chanel's suite. She approved Katharine Hepburn. Miss Hepburn, intelligently, had let Chanel do the talking.

The big car turned now from the autoroute into a secondary road that bent downhill through meadows toward the Seine. Coco hoped lunch would be amusing. Winter in the damp, gray north could be dull; dinner the night before had been dull. All that talk, talk, talk. It never occurred to Chanel that she had done most of the talking. Her own conversation never bored her. Thank God for Marie-Hélène de Rothschild, who at least had wit.

The Jews were to blame for most things, Coco had long been convinced: a fall in prices on the Bourse, a rainy autumn, a mediocre vintage in Bordeaux. Like most French men and women of her generation, she was an anti-Semite, yet the Baroness Rothschild was her closest friend. Her life had always been a series of brilliant, blinding contradictions. Everyone saw that except Chanel. She considered herself the very model of consistency.

Blacks. The same thing. Only the other day Liliane, her secretary, had taken her to the movies. That night she complained to her dinner companions, "This black man came and sat near us. We had to get up and move. He smelled so."

A friend wondered mischievously at that. "But, *chère* Coco, you used to have a friend, that American Negro boxer, what was his name?"

Coco smiled in memory. "Ah, yes," she said rapturously, her eyes glazing, "that man. How we danced."

It was left to her friends to speculate whether the relationship had moved from dance floor to boudoir. Chanel did not enlighten them, nor did she remark her own, mysterious, unfathomable contradictions.

The big car rolled heavily onto the graveled drive of the Seine-side inn, and she shook off reverie. Lunch, she hoped, would be amusing. The collection, two weeks hence, would cause talk. Her young protégé, the American Street, with whom she had worked so long, whose every professional step she had guided, who had learned his trade at her knee, would soon be here again. They would lunch together, dine, talk. She thought of Marc Street and smiled. Old women valued the company of attractive men, men like Street, who knew the difference between solicitude and patronizing.

"Coco, *chérie,* how splendid that you could come."

"Ah, well," she said, laughing, "old birds are offered few seeds."

It was an excellent lunch. The owner of the place, honored by her presence and hoping that one of the Paris newspapers might mention his establishment, hovered. There was a crisp, chilled vegetable salad, *crevettes,* pheasant peppered generously with birdshot, and *flageolets,* a Château d'Yquem to start and then a rather heavy Leoville Barton with the entrée. She snubbed the cheese, toyed with dessert, and refused brandy. Monday, after all, was another workday.

"Coco, did you see that photo of Jackie Kennedy? The one in New York, in a mini-skirt?"

Chanel made a face. "Mme. Kennedy? Ridiculous! A woman who wears her daughter's clothes?"

She got the appreciative laugh she expected.

Her driver wheeled the big Cadillac into the rue Cambon at six that evening. How pleasant it had been to spend a day in the country. Too bad the conversation had been so dull. That was the trouble with growing old, she mused. You remained fascinating yourself; it was the world that paled, became matte and tiresome.

At six-thirty she felt nauseated. It was the pheasant, she concluded in some irritation. At seven she phoned her secretary. "Liliane," she whined, "I'm not feeling well, not well at all. Come over."

She lay there, waiting, and felt awful, sickening things happening within her body.

Pain was no novelty. She remembered other, early pain: the physical pangs of childhood hunger, chill nights in an unheated house, the splitting loss of virginity as a teenaged girl in a plowed field behind a hedge in a thin autumn rain, the death of her lover on the Marne, other lovers lost.

She cried out once, not for a dead lover or childhood neglect. "Marc!"

A frightened maid looked toward her, wondering if she would say more.

But there was nothing else. Coco realized that calling his name was an odd thing to do. He had not even been a lover. Hardly that. Only a protégé, a friend, her last friend.

At eight o'clock that night, having rather cleverly avoided the sort of lingering illness that would have annoyed her intolerably, Coco Chanel died.

2

Nothing goes on forever. Fashion is change.

Mode, January 10, 1971

On a filthy corner of New York's Seventh Avenue
the next morning an old Jew in a yarmulke and a long, shiny gabardine coat blew his nose onto the pavement, pulled a handkerchief from his sleeve to tidy up, and hurried around the corner
against the winter wind to enter the lobby of a Thirty-eighth
Street loft building where a coat and suit house called Majesty
Fashions had made something of a reputation with its line-for-
line copies of Chanel's classic tweeds.

They always wanted you in early when there was trouble.
He was a patternmaker, a respected specialist at his trade. He had
never met Chanel, never even seen her. But his hands had
touched cloth she had touched; across an ocean a Paris designer
and a Manhattan technician had worked together to create
beauty. Now she was dead and something had ended. Something
else, the old man suspected, would begin.

In the editorial offices of *Women's Wear Daily* on Twelfth
Street they had worked all that night. The *Times* updated a long,
glittering obituary. At *Vogue* whole pages were remade. The Swiss
Wertheimer, who had grown rich marketing her perfumes, pondered a bleak future without her. Rival designers gloated or
mourned, depending on their degree of malice. Great retail store
executives at Saks and Neiman-Marcus and Marshall Field and
Bergdorf's wondered where they would spend their money next

season. And in a hotel room in Cleveland, where she had taken the Broadway musical on the road, Katharine Hepburn recalled their only meeting, amid the chinoiserie of Coco's sitting room in the rue Cambon in Paris. Now the real Chanel was gone; only the stage Chanel lived on.

Upstairs in the offices and showrooms and studios of Seventh Avenue and along Broadway in Manhattan, serious men spoke with their hands in discussing her death over bagels and bialys. Famous houses had made fortunes with their tastefully crafted copies of Chanel coats and suits. Arthur Jablow and Seymour Fox and the Davidow brothers had grown rich, and less famous houses had leeched off her with their cheap knockoffs. In the ladies' rooms, bored showroom models gossiped about her fabulous life, her jewels, her wealth, her lovers. Italian tailors lifted gnarled hands in tribute to her craftsmanship. Along the dirty, windswept sidewalks of the Avenue young black men who never heard of her clutched want ads and queued up for menial jobs they would probably not get. And Puerto Rican boys pushing wheeled racks of housedresses made smutty remarks to pretty seamstresses, ignoring Chanel's death as they ignored any event that did not immediately concern them.

Others mourned, in other places.

Lincoln Radford did not mourn. Radford was the publisher and editor-in-chief of the most powerful fashion weekly in America, *Mode* magazine. Radford had created *Mode,* and *Mode* created fashion immortals. He did not believe that his job as an editor was to print the news. His job was to discover, tutor, promote, and in the end canonize designers in whom he believed, designers who in their own turn believed in Radford and in *Mode.* Those who did not found their collections going unreported, their successes ignored, their failures recorded in lip-smacking detail.

Chanel had never permitted herself to be bullied.

Now, on the morning after her death, in a mansion on lower Fifth Avenue, Radford summoned his staff to the third-floor sitting room that passed for his personal office. Wielding his gold Cartier pen pedantically, as a pointer, his high-pitched voice occasionally cracking and from time to time whirling away entirely into an uncontrolled giggle, he informed his editors and art directors what *Mode*'s party line on Chanel's death was to be: "She was old, old and tired, repeating herself endlessly, a pastiche of what she had once been. People applauded out of ignorance or out of sheer . . . kindness.

"A mean, spiteful old woman. I advised her long ago to quit, to take a decent retirement and permit the world of fashion to get on with its renewal. Did she thank me for my counsel? She did not. She blackguarded me and this magazine. And I was not the only one. Poor Mme. Vreeland . . . "

They knew he despised *Vogue*'s editor and wondered what was coming.

"Poor Diana," Radford went on, "when she first left the *Bazaar* and took over *Vogue*, she visited Paris, sending before her like a flock of little doves letters to the couturiers, heralding her visit. Coco received her, of course. How could she not? *Vogue* was not to be snubbed. But when I asked Chanel what she thought of Diana, she made a face. 'The most pretentious woman I have ever met.' "

Radford paused for effect. Then, in a throwaway line, barely audible: "Not that she was wrong, of course."

When the requisite laughter had stilled, Radford threw himself down behind the Louis Quinze desk. "Our position is that a once-great talent, fallen recently on slim times, has passed from us. We regret her death, but we celebrate in the pages of the next issue of *Mode* the booming health of world fashion. And the magnificent opportunity for younger men and women to prosper now that the old hulk has been swept aside to make room."

Then, as if in afterthought, Radford whispered, "And we shall ask in our columns just who will be the next Chanel?"

Stanley Baltimore rarely wept, and he remained dry-eyed now. His fortune derived originally from the creation and sale of an adolescent acne remedy. Once dubbed "the pimple man," he now presided over a worldwide cosmetics and perfume empire. Success had done little to mellow him, and at the age of fifty he was the same brawling tough he had been at twenty. Only the externals had changed; there was only so much a famous art collection could improve a personality, only so much that Savile Row tailoring and silk shirts and Charvet ties could do for a longshoreman's body. On the morning after Chanel's death he reclined in his office high above Fifth Avenue while a barber and manicurist prepared him for the working day.

Baltimore resented rivals, ridiculed their work, danced in celebration at their misfortune. Years earlier, he had bid to become the American distributor for Chanel cosmetics and had been rejected. The decision was not hers, but that of the Swiss. No matter, she was added to his list of enemies. When he thought now of her death, it was with satisfaction, even pleasure. When his morning grooming was completed and he was again alone, he stood for a time at one of the picture windows framing the great city, absent-mindedly rubbing at a deep scar at the right corner of his mouth as he wondered how to wring commercial advantage from her death.

"Bitch!" he said, half aloud.

He paused for a moment to recall last night and the exquisite child Lester had arranged for him, the soft blond hair, the sweet smell of her, the slender arms and legs, the fresh taste of her mouth.

But in his satisfaction over the death of Coco Chanel, even the thought of pleasure was pushed aside. He briskly crossed the vast office to where a pink Carrara marble sink was built into the wall, sited between two lovely sketches, a Dufy and a Braque. Stanley Baltimore stared into the mirror above the basin for an instant, avoiding looking at his scar. Impulsively, he decided to attend her funeral, "just," as he later snarled, "to be sure the bitch is dead."

The idea pleased him as, ignoring the private bathroom just a few paces away, he unzipped his fly and urinated into the marble sink.

"I should piss on her grave," he told his mirrored self.

It took a day for the news of Chanel's death to reach Will West in Aspen. He had been out at dawn with his foreman, driving in a four-wheeled off-the-road vehicle up into the hills to where a cougar had been killing cattle. They'd found a disemboweled calf, lying in a snowdrifted gully cut across the shoulder of West Mountain.

"Goddamned cat," West muttered.

The foreman said, "Yessir." Old man West had no great love for his cattle. They were assets, bred for market. He felt no more emotion for the dead calf with its frightened, bulging eyes than he felt for a lump of coal from one of his mines, for the oil that gushed from his wells. Money.

Will West turned from the calf and slogged back through the snow toward the truck. "I want that cat killed, Jesse."

"Yessir."

Their breath hung like smoke in the cold Colorado air.

"Grandpa? Where've you been?"

The girl was thirteen years old, already tall, long legs scampering in faded jeans, small breasts barely disturbing an old khaki shirt, pony-tail flying as she ran to the old man and threw her arms around him.

"Jesse and I went up on the mountain," he said. "Damned cougar killed one of my calves. Didn't even bother to eat the animal. Just killed it for sport."

The girl's face screwed up. She loved the eyes of calves, the musky smell of their damp coats in the rain, the stupid, loving way they nuzzled against her. "Oh," she said.

He threw an arm around her, and they went inside the big house, unmindful of mud and melted snow on the polished hardwood floors. A Mexican maid scurried before them.

When the breakfast steak and eggs and coffee and hot breads were served, he picked up the newspaper.

"Grandpa?"

"Yes, Catherine?" He refused to call her "Chelsea," reminder of his dead son's folly.

"Didn't you know her, Coco Chanel?"

His gray, arched eyebrows rose. "Why, yes, I did. In Paris, a long time ago. Why?"

"Didn't you see it in the paper? She died."

Will West said nothing for a moment. He raised a fine china coffee cup to his lips and then, without having drunk from it, put it down again. His granddaughter saw the lean, tanned hand tremble slightly.

"Catherine," he said, "I am aggrieved to hear that. Sorely aggrieved."

His old man's face clouded, remembering Paris and an ivory silk dress, a gold necklace, a lovely, lingering scent, and the slim young woman who had once been his wife, and whom he had lost. It was all so long ago, when Chanel had greeted the two of them in her shop, rich young Americans who were the first of her clients from across the sea. He recalled her graciousness, the care she lavished on his bride, the enjoyment Coco took in his proud, possessive pleasure. And he thought too of other times in Paris, when the marriage was over.

He got up then and left the dining room to make a telephone call. Alone at the end of the long table, Chelsea West sipped freshly squeezed orange juice and wondered if it was possible that there had been tears in her grandfather's eyes. A few moments passed and he returned, clear-eyed, decisive.

"Catherine," he said, "I am going to Paris for a few days."

"Yes, Grandpa?"

He nodded. "Yes. And I think you might come along. It's time you saw something of the world."

On Monday, at his office at Majesty Fashions in Manhattan, Marc Street told his secretary to get him a plane ticket to Paris. Sydney Heidler thought he was a fool to go.

"All that way, Marc? For a dead person? New York to Paris for a funeral? She wouldn't expect it, you know."

"Well, I ought to go. I owe her something, I guess."

Old Heidler, who had seen too many deaths, moved his hands. After a moment, he nodded. "And you always pay your debts?"

Street paused. "Yes," he said quietly, "always."

Heidler said nothing more. He had known Marc since he

was a boy and had led him through the business by the hand. Heidler was a sensitive man who loved Marc Street, and he knew there was a time to argue, a time to go mute.

Heidler knew one other thing too, the burden that Street was carrying, the baggage his father had left behind, borne uneasily by this company, by this young man, none of it of his making and all of it the curse of his patrimony.

"Yes," the old man said, "yes, you must go."

Street flew out of JFK for Paris the next morning, a man with debts to pay.

3

Black is not necessarily for mourning.

Mode, January 17, 1971

The Madeleine was no typical church: a great, echoing marble barn Napoleon ordered built in deference not to God but to himself. Busloads of Belgian and German tourists in loden coats wandered through during services, their guides describing the place in loud, Baedecker monotones. Chanel's requiem mass was to begin at eleven. Marc Street walked up from his hotel, the San Regis, trying to clear his head in the sharp wind that came off the river and followed him along the avenue Franklin Roosevelt and across the Place de la Concorde. He had not slept well. He stood now on the sidewalk at the foot of the stairs that led endlessly upward to the porch of the Madeleine, his old pigskin trenchcoat belted snugly against the wind, a slouch hat by Lock pulled low on his forehead, a big man, dark-haired, hawk-nosed, with deep brown eyes.

Television crews had set up their cameras by the church doors at the top of the long, broad flight of stone steps. A dozen reporters loitered there, jotting down names in notebooks as the mourners arrived, occasionally having to step aside to let another covey of tourists pass. Large flower arrangements were carried up the steps and into the church. One of them was from Freddie Brisson and Rosalind Russell. Marc wondered just how sincere were Miss Russell's condolences. Then the Rothschilds arrived. He could hear Coco's voice now, railing against Jews.

Street stood with the reporters, unrecognized, assumed to be one of them. Some of the mourners he knew. Stanley Baltimore, a surprise, not the sort you expected to see at funerals. Perhaps he and Chanel had once worked together. A tall, lean, elderly man incongruous in a black chesterfield, western boots, and gray Stetson emerged from a limousine to climb the church steps with a young girl at his side, the child wide-eyed, long-haired, looking like a drawing out of an early edition of the *Alice* books, white-gloved, with white knee socks under a light blue melton coat. As they neared the reporters at the top the old man reached down to grip the girl's hand. When they passed, the girl's eyes flicked quickly, curiously, over the ranks of the journalists, among whom she included Street, even as her face maintained its solemn, childish dignity. He wondered who the old man might be, who this lovely child.

Régine, a red-haired woman who ran discotheques, got out of a car and began, heavily, to mount the steps. Then Yves Saint Laurent, pale, distracted, his eyes bright behind his glasses, and Lifar, Chanel's old friend from the ballet, painters, writers, and the man who was the French Johnny Carson. Just before the chimes struck the hour Dali bounded up the steps, mustaches aquiver, his cane brandished like a sword, eyes darting as the flashbulbs popped.

Street followed Dali inside and took a place in one of the rear pews.

Then there was a stir at the back of the church. Chanel's mannequins had arrived, eight or nine tall blonds, very erect, dressed not in black but in the latest Chanel suits, pinks and greens and bright yellows and familiar oatmeals and navys. They walked slowly down the center aisle with great dignity, unsmiling, genuflected, and took the pews in front usually assigned to the family of the deceased. It was a moment Coco herself had choreographed, for they were, these tall, slender, beautiful girls in their Chanel suits, all the close family she really had.

The service began; Street made no attempt to follow it, preferring to recall the living Chanel and her world, wormy with rivals and enemies and intrigue, stories told as she sat on a footstool and poured him neat Scotch in the sitting room above her salon: about the executive, for whom she had lobbied a membership in the Légion d'Honneur, and who repaid her with larceny, cutting a hole right through the wall of her ateliers into the next building, where seamstresses sewed up "false Chanels" from cloth and linings and even labels stolen from her storerooms; about Castillo, the Spaniard who stuttered in three languages, who she claimed had once tried to steer her, in her flowing chiffons, into the lighted candles of a chic garden party near the Étoile; about her directrice, who, having been sacked, drove round and round the Maison Chanel "shouting filth up at me through the windows"; about her transvestite secretary, who wore three-piece men's business suits by day and hand-me-down Chanel dresses by night.

There should have been anecdotes and emotion, tribute and laughter. Instead, an old priest droned on. Chelsea West sat there, alert, next to her grandfather, understanding only a few words from her schoolgirl French. Will West remained stiffly erect, standing or sitting, following what others did in the congregation, staring straight ahead, lost in the solitude of memories half a century old. Chelsea, respecting his reverie, contented herself with looking at the altar, strange and mysterious, the great baskets of flowers, the mannequins seated twenty rows ahead. She could see only their hair, and when they stood, their slim backs, eloquently flat. Occasionally she stared at the coffin, starkly alone at the head of the center aisle, and wondered what sort of person Mlle. Chanel had really been, whether she was aware of what was being said about her and of those who came to bid her farewell, and why her life, and death, seemed to mean so much to her grandfather.

Stanley Baltimore pondered no such mysteries. He already regretted the trip as a waste of time. He wished he could stand up now, turn his back on the coffin, and walk out into the fresh air, away from the cloying scent of incense and flowers, one final silent insult speaking volumes. Such a thing would of course bring contempt not on her but, unfairly, on him. At two that afternoon he had an appointment at the Galerie Maeght. There was a Degas drawing they thought he might like. He hoped so.

When it was over they all stood to watch the coffin pass. In its wake the mannequins came, somber, unsmiling, walking in perfect cadence like guardsmen at the slow pace of the dead march. Then came the others up the aisle, starting with those from the forward pews. Marc waited as they passed, watching the faces. When the lean old man and the blond child passed, the girl's eyes caught Marc's for an instant. Then they too were gone. Finally, in the dregs of the crowd, Street slid from the pew, genuflected in a gesture he had half forgotten, and turned from the altar, where a boy in vestments was already snuffing out candles.

People stood crowded together on the porch of the Madeleine watching the coffin being tucked into a hearse while the mannequins and a handful of other mourners got into the line of waiting limos. The crowd began to melt away as the brief cortege moved slowly into the flow of midday traffic of the Grandes Boulevards. Street lighted a cigarette and stood there for a last moment, alone at the top of the steps, thinking about Chanel. How odd to be in Paris and not to be going to her apartment for lunch, while she tutored him about fashion and beauty, punctuating the air with the crabbed talons of her twisted hands, the wise, warped judgments of her words.

He was still there when a skinny young man came up.

"Mr. Street, isn't it?"

"Yes."

"I'm Adam Green. I was at FIT when you spoke." That had been three or four years ago.

"What are you doing in Paris?" Marc asked, slightly pleased, mildly surprised anyone would remember a routine, pedestrian lecture given a class of students at the Fashion Institute.

The boy shrugged. "For her. I flew over for the funeral."

"You know her?"

"Nope. It's just what she meant to all of us."

A spatter of rain lashed across the *place,* and they both began to run. A café beckoned. The *poules* who worked the quarter had already taken shelter, saving their beehive hairdos from the wet. Street bought the coffee, steaming espresso.

Adam Green said he had a job in one of the cheap knockoff houses along the Avenue. He'd apprenticed for Max Mannerman for a few months, "shining his shoes and making the coffee." At the knockoff house he did the sketches for the Italian pattern cutters to copy. The sketches were hardly original. He stole the ideas from the Fifth Avenue retail display windows, from *Vogue,* from the J. C. Penney catalogue—stole wherever he found an idea worth stealing. There was nothing shocking in this. Half of Seventh Avenue prospered in precisely the same fashion.

"They didn't pay your way here," Marc said over the coffee, watching the rain slap against the windows.

"No," said Adam Green, "I borrowed the money."

Street had not expected candor. Young designers gave themselves airs. He and Green stood there sipping their coffee, Adam tall, nearly as tall as Marc, but with narrow shoulders, a slim waist, and none of the bulk. There might have been four or five years between them, but Marc felt much the older man. Adam was boyish, dark, delicate, even vulnerable in appearance. He was also, Street admitted to himself, one of the best-looking young men he had ever seen.

Adam jabbered on, about himself, about Paris, about fashion. Street grew skeptical. Suddenly resenting this intrusion into his private grief, he wheeled on the boy, having had enough of this Adam Green. "You borrowed money to come to Paris to mourn a woman you'd never met, never even seen?"

The cynicism in his voice was palpable, intended to drive the boy away. Adam nodded, not permitting himself to be insulted. There was a false naïveté about him that Marc mistrusted.

"Well?" Marc demanded.

Adam remained silent for another moment and then, with a dignity, even a grandeur Marc did not expect, he said quietly, "Yes, because I want to be like her. Because I want to be a great designer."

Street softened. Neither of them said anything more for a time, and the counterman refilled their cups with espresso. Why cross-examine the boy? None of his business, really. And even on Seventh Avenue there were a few honest people.

"So who lent you the money?" Marc asked.

Adam Green blushed. "A man."

Marc smiled to himself. Adam, like many designers of any age, was clearly gay—not because of his demeanor, which was at once masculine and intense, but because of a natural, youthful grace few of the straight men Marc knew possessed. Adam had probably gone to bed with the man who lent him money. Still— or perhaps because of this—he seemed honest; men had sold themselves for less than Paris and the funeral of Coco Chanel.

The rain stopped, and people were leaving the café to go back into the street. Marc, wanting to be alone to think about Chanel, spoke more gently. "Look, here's my card. Give me a call in New York. I'll look at your sketches."

"But you don't do knockoffs," Adam said, obviously puzzled.

"I don't want to see what you steal," Street snapped, "but what you design."

The boy smiled. Be careful of that smile, Marc told himself; charm and ambition are a dangerous combination. Then they shook hands, and Marc left the boy at the bar of the café to walk up the boulevard to the rue Cambon, where he turned right.

He wanted to see Chanel's place one last time before it faded in memory; her face and voice were already growing dim. He stood there for a moment looking up at the second-floor windows, where she showed the collection, the third-floor window, where they sat so often, talking and smoking and dining together. Then the rain began again, and he tugged his collar high against it and walked away, not noticing the limousine parked across the rue Cambon, where Will West and his granddaughter held a brief vigil of their own.

4

All designers hate one another.

Lincoln Radford, *Mode*, January 17, 1971

T*iens,* so your heroine is gone."

"Yes," Marc said in French.

"Well," Jimmy said, blinking through his glasses, speaking rapid, precise French. "You are not the only one. Perhaps you should not be so selfish. She belonged to all of us. She was my heroine as well, you know." There was resentment in his voice. But Marc knew he had not attended the mass.

They were having a late supper Chez l'Ami Louis. Brugère was with them, Jimmy's partner, manager, lover, and (some said) his brains. Dinner was *gigot d'agneau,* the legs of baby lamb so small they roasted two of them for the three men. Brugère interrogated the waiter. "How old is the lamb?" he demanded imperiously. "How many weeks?"

The old man smiled. "Days, monsieur, three or four days old."

Bottles of a young Fleurie kept arriving, unasked, at the table. There was no coatroom, only racks above the table, where the garlic reached for their coats. The meal was superb—this was one of the truly great restaurants of the world—but Street had to keep reminding himself to enjoy the food.

"Come, Marc," Brugère said, "she had a long life. A rich life. How can you mourn?"

Brugère was right. Marc should be able to shrug off death.

He could not. Brugère rattled on, seeking, with gentle malice, to distract him from grief, while Jimmy de Bertrand retreated behind pursed lips and the milk-bottle lenses of his glasses. J.-P. Brugère, small and vital, leaned forward, gesticulating with his hands, telling stories. Marc was unsure which would dominate in bed; in conversation it was surely Brugère.

"The night she died," J.-P. said, "Liliane was there with her, the secretary. There was a nephew and his wife, the only relatives. They'd been summoned, country people, totally out of place in the Ritz. But they came and sat over the body. Finally, about midnight, Liliane left. After all, she had a husband, a child, she was fatigued. She went home to bed, leaving the nephew to watch over Coco, to keep the vigil.

"About two o'clock in the morning, right out of sleep, Liliane sat up in bed. The ring! She had forgotten the ring! She got up, dressed, called a cab, and came across town. She mounted to the fifth floor and burst into the vigil. The nephew was there, half asleep in a chair. The wife was there. Coco was there, hands clasped across her breast in the bed. 'Excuse me,' said Liliane, and went directly to the body. She took Coco's hand, cold, *evidemment*, and, with an understandable difficulty, stripped off an emerald ring. Then she turned to the nephew. 'She promised me this. Long ago. It was always to be mine.' Then she left, the ring in her pocket." Jimmy de Bertrand tittered, and Brugère lifted an elegant eyebrow.

Brugère and Jimmy had been together more than ten years. Marc had known them nearly as long. During the Algerian War, when J.-P. was drafted, his uniform was hand-tailored by Jimmy, making him perhaps the only private in the French army with a couture-crafted uniform. Once when a collection flopped and the money was short Marc had gotten his American connections to help them with a little financing. Now there was plenty of money and the loan, long since repaid, was never discussed. Neither was Marc's help forgotten, just not talked about. What was talked about was Coco and Cardin and their other rivals, this slander over meals not especially original or shocking but cheerfully malicious, entertaining.

"What happens to Paris now that she's gone?" Marc asked.

Coco

The question had been gnawing at him since he left New York. Jimmy shrugged, too modest to make his claims aloud.

Brugère, clever, twisted the question. "My dear, the Paris couture will endure. But what of Seventh Avenue? For years you've lived off Chanel suits."

True enough, and something Marc knew he would be soon forced to confront. But not now, not on the day she was buried. "I know that. But what of Paris itself? Hasn't something gone out of the heart of it, Chanel dead, Dior dead, Balenciaga retiring?"

"There is Jimmy de Bertrand," Brugère said with a flourish.

"Sure, and Saint Laurent and Ungaro and Courrèges and—"

"That imbecile!" Brugère shot back.

Marc shrugged. He liked Courrèges and the French didn't. But this wasn't the moment to argue it. "I know about Jimmy and the others. Haven't I been Jimmy's biggest supporter? And you know how I respect Yves. But you guys are all so young. Chanel was on top for half a century. Within a couple of years the entire front rank of the couture is gone or going. Maybe Jimmy will inherit it all, or Yves, or someone we never heard of. But maybe it's time for someone else to dominate world fashion. Maybe the time of Paris is over, at least for now. Isn't that possible? Nothing goes on forever."

Brugère leaned forward on the table, all tension and flashing eyes.

"My dear, do you seriously believe Signor Valentino is going to teach us our trade?" There was venom in his pronunciation of the Roman's name. Nineteen forty had not been forgotten, and in Paris they still hated the Italians.

"Maybe not," Marc conceded, "but what about the Americans? There's a whole crop of talented young kids coming along. Ralph Lauren, Calvin Klein, Halston . . . "

Jimmy laughed contemptuously.

Brugère stared at Marc. "Dear fellow, you cannot be serious. Are any of these people giants? Don't forget, we know your Seventh Avenue. The best ready-to-wear in the world, superb machine work, sizing, volume, automation. We know that. But creativity? Ideas? Originality? You jest with us, you of all people, taught here in Paris, practically raised at Chanel's knee."

Jimmy smiled slyly. "And half a Frenchman, at that, *tu sais.*"

True. Half a Frenchman, half a German, half a Roman Catholic, half a Jew. No wonder out of such confusion came wild, romantic notions. But Marc was stubborn. "Look," he said, suspecting he was making an ass of himself, "anything's possible. Maybe I could do it myself. Find the right young designer, some brilliant kid out of nowhere, a real designer and not just a copyist. Why, with the workmanship we have, the technicians, with a little luck we could—"

Brugère snorted rudely. "Marc, you are my best of all friends, I assure you. Long ago when Jimmy was in a difficult time, you hastened to his side. We love you. But I must also assure you, my dear, that you are ga-ga."

It was so, Street realized with reluctance. Majesty didn't even employ a designer, just an efficient sketcher without a hint of creative juice. They copied what others designed, pedantically, precisely, professionally. Even to talk of finding a "new" Chanel in America was crazy.

Marc threw up his hands and called for the check. He'd not flown an ocean to debate French chauvinists on their own turf or to float improbable schemes. He had come to mourn a friend. "Forget it," he said, "it's the wine talking."

He lay awake in his hotel bed at the San Regis for a long time that night, the windows slightly ajar in the chill, listening to the traffic and wishing he'd gone along with Jimmy and J.-P. to Castel's, the music pounding, the smoke rising through the air, young women dancing, the taste of the brandy, the mingled scents of perfume, sweat, and money. He suspected that Brugère was right and that during dinner he had been talking rubbish. It was the wine and the emotion of the funeral, jet lag, fatigue, and loss.

And what of his own future, so long pinned to its precise copies of Chanel's designs, living on its line-for-line reproductions of what Coco created? How could there ever be another Chanel? What he knew he had learned from her, not only about fashion but about life.

Coco was with him now, with them all. The funeral proved that, drawing people as disparate as Stanley Baltimore and the Rothschilds, Dali and himself, this ambitious young designer Adam Green, an elderly man in cowboy boots and a beautiful child in knee socks, wealthy women and journalists, mannequins and rivals. In the morning they would scatter, iron filings without a magnet. Trying to sleep, restless and tossing, he rejected the notion, romantic, audacious, impertinent, that anyone could replace her.

And yet.

BOOK TWO
MAJESTY

5

And why shouldn't America be red, white, and blue this
week?

Mode, July 2, 1976

M arc woke to the dull crash of the surf and the
slash of low sunlight through the blinds and across the bedroom.
Carefully, so as not to wake her, he slipped an arm from under the
girl's shoulders and padded silently into the bathroom. It was
then, through the window, that he saw the jeep.

It had arrived, miraculously, on the graveled driveway of his
rented house during the night, a battered, olive-drab vintage jeep
with a huge red bow tied around it, incongruous and tantalizing.

"I'll be damned," he said, half aloud. He pulled on the plaid
bathrobe and went downstairs and outside, the velvet lawn wet
under his bare feet, then treading gingerly on the pebbles. A large
red envelope was taped inside the windshield.

"Congratulations!" the card read. "Five years ago today you
assured yourself of fortune and me of fame by hiring me. Love,
Adam." There was a postscript: "The girl to drive it arrives later.
Also wrapped in a red ribbon and little else. A."

Five years! Impossible to believe, but it must be so. Adam
had a mind that catalogued dates, names, faces. July 1976, the
weekend of the Bicentennial celebration, and Coco died in '71.
Five years!

The skinny kid named Adam Greenberg who'd borrowed
the money, no one knew where, to fly to her funeral was now

himself one of the most influential fashion designers in America. Skinny no longer, Greenberg no longer, not even "Green," now he was simply . . . "Adam." At a certain level of celebrity last names become superfluous. Ask Farrah, Liza, Halston.

Marc slid in behind the wheel. He turned the key and pumped the gas with a bare foot as the motor coughed and then caught. Grinning like a child, Street drove round and round the driveway, occasionally gunning the motor and spinning the wheels in the loose gravel. How did Adam remember everything? It must have been last summer, when he first rented a place in East Hampton, that Marc mentioned the only sensible car out here wasn't a Caddy or anything fancy but a four-wheel drive, an old jeep. Marc parked the jeep and reread the card. Funny, sassy too, just like Adam. He liked that part about his making the fortune and Adam's getting the fame. What the hell, it was true. Let Adam get the headlines, let the company make the money. Not that young Adam was doing badly. Then he sobered. He hoped Adam was just kidding about sending a girl to drive it. There was the girl upstairs in Marc's bed, still asleep in the coolness of the July morning.

Five years.

Their company was called Majesty Fashions. Few people on Seventh Avenue were conspicuous by their modesty. Exaggeration was the language of the street. Maybe it had *become* majestic. Fifteen years ago, when Marc took it over, it was hardly that. A sample-making room with a few seamstresses and pressers and the Italian production man, Sasso, old Sydney Heidler doing the buying and just about everything else, a showroom model fresh from her latest abortion, a bored saleswoman who spent her time reading movie magazines. There was not even a factory, just a few casual arrangements with plants in New Jersey that made the stuff on a subcontracting basis. Majesty was housed in a crummy loft building on Thirty-eighth Street, where lunch came from the Sabrett hot dog stand on the corner of Broadway, and the cockroaches that went with noshing at the desk. They were still in the same building, but everything else had changed.

"Marc?"

He looked up, saw the girl standing in the kitchen doorway, a white T-shirt barely reaching the tops of her tanned legs. He'd met her a few nights before at Elaine's.

"What are you doing out there?"

"Nothing," he said, "just thinking."

She stared at the jeep. "Do you know where it came from?"

"Yes, it's a present. From Adam."

"Hey, the guy you work for?"

"Yes," he said. It was easier to keep it that way than try to explain.

She continued to look dubiously at the old jeep. "Couldn't he get you a new one?"

He grinned and said nothing, and then she took his hand and led him upstairs to bed. She might not understand a gracious gesture, but he had to admit she had energy.

There had been girls like this one before, not too many but enough. Street had a capacity for self-entertainment; he was a man who could be alone without being lonely. He was bored by the ritual dance of the singles bars and disdained the model-bedding that was the Avenue's favorite indoor sport. And he had his work, which provided him with order and constancy, if not love—he owed that to Chanel.

Now, in a rented house in East Hampton, he slept with a picked-up girl. Both house and woman were indulgences. Fifty weeks of the year he worked, fifty or sixty hours a week. He had money but he owned nothing. He lived in an old rented flat on upper Madison Avenue, just below Seventy-second Street, on a nice block of booksellers and delis, a newspaper store, and small shops. He lived above the bookstore, in a big, echoing apartment filled with old furniture bought from the previous tenant for $1,400.

The job was his real home. He'd begun learning it at nineteen. It was simple then—cutting and sewing and buying cloth and wooing buyers and sending out bills. Now it was more complicated; even Majesty was getting complicated, going into offshore manufacturing. The big boys were all doing it. It gave them the edge, and Street hated to give anyone an edge.

He slept on jet planes, used hotel rooms to bathe and change his shirt and steal a quick nap, bribed officials where it was the custom, picked brains, and learned. He passed it on to old Heidler. "We've got some good plants over in Jersey, Sydney, nice, decent American workers who give us an honest day's work on a dress or on jeans. But let's face it—they take their sick days, they take a vacation, they want Christmas off. In Taiwan, they don't take sick days. You're sick? Come in anyway. Sit in the corner against the wall and we'll toss you some piecework. That's where to make goods. They graft, but it's controlled graft; you know who to pay off."

Heidler looked bleak. "Marc, you sound like a fascist."

Marc laughed. "A good fascist," he said, "like all those Germans who were always against Hitler and now they make BMWs."

"Where else, Marc?"

"Haiti, Mauritius, the Sudan, anywhere they sit and shit in the grass. They're fast learners. They've all got American experts there telling 'em how to do it, how to undercut Seventh Avenue and put us out of business. Listen, there are big U.S. companies waving the flag back here and singing 'Yankee Doodle' and they're all secretly investing big money offshore. You wouldn't believe it."

"You tell me, Marc, I believe it."

Heidler was dazzled. He had been in the trade forty years and he'd never seen anyone like this boy. It was too bad Ange Streit hadn't lived to see it. She would have been proud. It would have made up in some measure for what they did to French Jake. Ange was Marc's mother, French Jake his father.

That October Adam won his first Coty Award, the "Oscar" of American fashion. "From now on," he announced in jubilation, "I am to be addressed as 'Your Majesty,' get that?"

Sydney Heidler shook his head. Sasso, the production man, attended morning mass on the basis of it. The showroom models got drunk on New York State champagne. The salesmen called their best customers in the stores and demanded heavier orders next season. Heidler doubled the fabric orders and inquired as to the availability of additional subcontracting in the South. And Marc Street authorized full-page ads in *WWD* and in *Mode*.

Heidler inhaled sharply. Full-page ads! A few years ago Majesty was just another line-for-line house. Whatever models they bought from Chanel or Dior or Ricci or from the Italians were copied, as accurately as possible, in cheaper but similar cloth, and reproduced in the hundreds by machine. Then Marc brought Adam into the firm, their first creative designer. Now they were manufacturing from their own original designs, not just buying the rights to copy someone else's. That was what Adam Green had done for them; that was why this first Coty Award was significant.

Adam tapped Marc for ten thousand dollars out of petty cash and flew off to Bermuda. "I love the English," he said smirking, "just like Ralph Lauren." Ralph came from the Bronx and his name had originally been Lifshitz. Now he wore tweed jackets, rode horses, and subscribed to *Punch* and *Tatler*.

When Adam came back ten days later, suntanned and cocky, he and Marc lunched together at La Grenouille. Marc had been going there for several years, entertaining buyers, but always before there had been a table in back. Now the headwaiter, Jean, greeted him like an old friend and steered them to a good banquette up front. John Fairchild was there with Bill Blass; Mildred Custin of Bonwit's, who had bought Calvin Klein's first coats, which Calvin had wheeled uptown himself lest they get creased; the Duchess of Windsor with Brooke Astor; Alex Liberman from Condé Nast.

Over the smoked salmon and capers, Adam jabbered about Bermuda. He had taken a friend along. "You've got to admit, it's romantic."

"No argument there," Marc said. "I was there once with a girl."

Adam nodded. They understood each other without having to say much. It had been that way almost from the first. They were employer and employee, but quickly they had become more than that. After a few years someone christened them "Butch Cassidy and the Sundance Kid." Cannier, older, jealous of his privacy, Marc grimaced at that, while Adam, talented, glamorous, dashing, delighted in the label. "When they make the movie," he said, "Robert Redford is me."

"Hell," Marc said caustically, "I'll settle for Walter Matthau."

Some people assumed they were lovers, but that was just Seventh Avenue and they ignored it. Theirs was the intimacy of work, of solid achievement. Only when it came to their personal lives was there a disparity, Marc closemouthed, taciturn, Adam going on endlessly about his latest love, who was certain, of course, to be the real thing. Adam was always enthusiastic, Marc inevitably skeptical.

"Adam, tell me one redeeming quality this kid has outside of bed, just one!"

Adam thought. "He's a terrific dancer," he said finally.

"A dancer, a terrific dancer," Marc responded sourly.

Adam persisted. "Listen, if he were a girl, he'd be a goddamned Rockette."

Marc laughed. It seemed natural to both of them that Adam would come to him for approval, for advice. It never occurred to Marc to ask Adam about a woman. You don't seek counsel from younger brothers.

The waiter brought the *poulet grandmère* and a bottle of Château de la Chaize, and they concentrated for a while on the food. Adam was strangely edgy. Then he blurted it out. "Marc, not just because of the Coty, but don't you think we ought to re-negotiate my contract? I mean, I'm always broke, always having to borrow. And I really think I'm worth more."

"We don't have a contract, just a handshake," Marc said flatly. Adam's face clouded.

"I know," he said somberly, "I never thought we needed one."

"Well, maybe we do."

Adam looked hurt. Marc waited an instant, and then he rapped the back of his hand against the boy's upper arm. "Hey, I'm needling. Of course you're worth more. In fact, I don't think you should be an employee anymore. I think you rate a piece of the business."

Adam put down his fork, and very seriously he said, "Marc, I'll never forget this. Never."

"Come on," Marc said, "I'm just being selfish. You think I want to lose the best designer on Seventh Avenue to the competition?"

Adam's handsome face took on a childlike glow, splitting into a grin, his eyes widening. Then, just as suddenly, he sobered: "Marc, you remember that day we met in Paris? At Coco's funeral?"

"Sure."

"Well, I wasn't there just to say good-bye to the old lady."

"No?"

"No. Part of it was that. But part of it ... well, I figured some heavy hitters like you would be there. The fashion press. I thought people would notice a kid from New York without any dough who had gone all that way for Chanel. That I'd be noticed."

Marc said nothing.

Adam, self-conscious and nervous, went on. "You understand what I'm saying? That I lied to you. I was there pushing myself, making myself important. It wasn't just a selfless, loving gesture."

Marc laughed. "I figured that out a long time ago, Adam. One reason I liked you. I realized anyone who wanted to be a designer that badly must have something."

Alan sagged, relaxed and smiling. "Butch, I love you."

Marc Street nodded his head. "I know you do, Sundance."

They understood that men can love without being lovers.

It was a week later that the summons came from Lincoln Radford of *Mode*. For Marc it was an uncomfortable session, Radford doing most of the talking. They met in his mansion, with Radford bulwarked behind his desk, surrounded by books, good pictures, and framed copies of magazine covers, photos of Galanos and Dior and Norell, Balenciaga, even Chanel. Marc sat on a leather couch and listened. Most of it was about Radford, his view of fashion, of what *Mode* was and did. Then, after perhaps a half hour, he said: "Your boy Adam. How good do you think he could be?"

Marc wasn't going to be bullied. "He's pretty good now. The Coty jury thought so."

Radford's look was disdainful. "A motley assemblage of hacks, a process rife with politics. You vote for my designer this year, I'll vote for yours the next. They hand it around."

Marc let him talk. People rarely won arguments with Lincoln Radford.

"I'll concede he's not bad. Nice touch with some of the sportswear. He has taste, and if you have that, you can be taught the rest." He waited. Marc said nothing. "I'll try to help Adam if I can. At this stage of development, a little encouragement doesn't hurt."

"That's generous of you," Marc said, not really meaning it.

Radford had a sensitive ear. He caught the reservation in Street's voice and didn't like it. "Of course Adam will do very well without me, I'm sure. But it's always pleasant to work together, to cooperate." He used the gold pen to shove a fashion sketch across the table and then over the edge. It fluttered to the carpet. Marc wondered if he was expected to retrieve it. He didn't. Radford stood up.

"Well, Mr. Street," he said, with an enthusiasm he clearly didn't mean, "this was most helpful. So good of you to come. I'll be watching Majesty Fashions very closely. Very closely indeed."

Out on Fifth Avenue Marc was surprised to find he was sweating. What the hell, Radford was just a nosy old queen. But there was something in his voice that implied threat.

Marc Street didn't want anyone looking too closely at Majesty Fashions. The company had come a long way from its violent beginnings, and he did not like the idea of retracing that passage. Nor did he want Lincoln Radford digging into his life, or Adam's. Their future shone with bright promise. Let the past remain buried.

If Radford and everyone else just left them alone, he and Adam could do anything they wanted with Majesty. They didn't need anyone else; they didn't need strangers.

6

The American cowboy was the first male model.

Mode, May 4, 1977

The Colorado spring had come late. In the great mountains high above Denver and Salt Lake and Cheyenne, killing blizzards swept down cruel and fierce over the Canadian border through April and into May. Cattle froze to death standing up.

Will West blamed it all on the Democrats. "Damned Carter, damned redneck," he snapped over telephone and by telex to his offices in San Francisco and Denver and New York.

The blizzards stalled freight trains and buried roads and brought down overhead wires and grounded airliners. In the East, where the snows became rain, roads washed out, levees collapsed, good bottomland flooded out. Textile mills slowed their looms, factories went over to one shift from three, shopping centers failed to make their figures, and commerce and the economy stagnated, hostage to the wind. Will West cursed fate and the newly elected Jimmy Carter.

"Grandpa?"

Chelsea was nineteen now, tall, long-legged, and as beautiful, old man West admitted to himself, as her goddamned whore of a mother. He looked up at her from his old rocker. She stood in the doorway, silhouetted against the light, jeaned and booted and silk-shirted under a down vest, her long hair shining. The West line would end with her. He loved her.

"Yes, Catherine, come in."

She threw herself into one of the big leather armchairs, under a moose head that had frightened her as a child and was now as familiar and comfortable as the fireplace crackling behind his chair, as the portrait in oils of her father as a child. There were, of course, no portraits of her mother.

Chelsea, Catherine, knew her grandfather. She had known him from the first time she saw him over her bib, staring down, unbelieving and skeptical. She knew him from the first time she rode horseback. Or skiied. Or drove a pickup truck at the age of eleven. He taught her those things. She remembered his rages as well as his birthday cakes and hired clowns. She remembered strange men who came to the house to counsel with him. She remembered her father's death and her grandfather's impotent, tearless fury.

She remembered as well a cover story in *Fortune* magazine, reprising what her grandfather had told a Senate committee forty years before, a committee probing the brutal busting of trade unions. Her grandfather, not gray then, but just as lean, as hard, as intense, had informed the senators, in an incredulous tone, "But, gentlemen, you can't *run* a mine without machine guns."

Not even a teenaged girl could ignore such things. Now she was not afraid, but she was careful.

"Grandpa, I want to go to New York."

He stared at her. How lovely she was. "New York? This isn't the season for New York. Wait until fall. We'll go together."

"Fall is too long. I want to go now. This damned snow . . ."

"Well, you can't go," he growled, "and that's it."

"You know what I love about you, Grandpa?" She kicked her booted feet up onto a hassock. "You're so damned reasonable, so easy to talk to."

He laughed, a large, rasping laugh. "And I love you too, honey."

He did, too. She had balls. That was the irony of it. His son, her father, didn't. Her mother, the bitch, who had run off with God knows who years before, leaving the child, leaving her husband, had balls. She'd hated her father-in-law, fought with him, cursed him out, driven him into quivering, murderous anger. If Will West thought he could have gotten away with it, he would have had her killed. His granddaughter was like her, and he adored her.

"I've got a few bucks. Suppose I go anyway?"

"Go," he said, "and to hell with you."

"Hey, Grandpa, why don't you come with me? We could have a ball."

He shook his head. "Now *there*, Catherine, you are absolutely right. We would have ourselves a ball and a half."

"But you won't."

"No, I won't. I go to New York now and the *Wall Street Journal* and the damned newspapers will read something into it. In a market like this one it doesn't take much to start a panic. A Chinaman sneezes in Peking and you have a flu epidemic in Chicago. You know what I mean?"

"Nope."

"Good. Everyone knows too damned much. Why don't you go back to college?"

"They threw me out."

He laughed. "And not without reason."

"In New York, Grandpa, I'm told . . ."

"Yes?" he demanded, sulfurous, bristling.

"I'm told there are great libraries and bookstores and publishing houses and . . ."

He laughed again, admiring cleverness, but not to be charmed. "Are there, indeed?"

Beneath the banter, there was purpose, a reason to get away that had nothing to do with snow or boredom, something she couldn't tell the old man. Now, thinking she sensed an opening, she tried again.

"That's why I ought to go to New York. Maybe I could get a job."

"Doing what?"

"I dunno."

"Well, you'd think of something, I grant you that. If they took you up in one of those rockets and marooned you on the moon, you'd find a way."

"Grandpa, you're sexy."

He thought for a moment. "Catherine," he said, "once upon

a time you would have been right." He remembered Paris, fifty years before, and the sensuous, spirited Gabrielle Chanel.

That night Chelsea drove into Aspen. The Maserati stayed in the garage at the ranch. A foot of fresh snow on the roads suggested four-wheel drive, and she took one of the small trucks. Competently, she steered through a series of controlled skids that ended briskly in a snowbank in front of the Paragon.

They all knew her. Eastern skiers here for the late-spring powder, ski instructors, cowboys, local shopkeepers and professionals, boys and girls she'd gone to high school with, men she'd dated, waitresses, the barkeep, the piano player. The Paragon was fun, not like André's, a self-conscious joint, working hard at being picturesque. She did not make such distinctions. To Chelsea it was all neighborhood. Tourists came to Aspen the way they went to Sausalito or to the Bahamas. Chelsea lived here.

At the bar the barman slid a cold bottle of Dos Equis toward her.

"Evenin', Chelsea. Got a little snow up your way?"

"Oh, man," she said. She drank from the bottle, enjoying the sounds and the laughter and the talk, the bright look of people at play. But this life was claustrophobic, especially when winter hung on as stubbornly as this one did. New York wasn't so much a destination as a symbol.

Then Raker came over and touched her shoulder. "Let's have one more," he said, "and then let's go play."

His arm was around her waist, pulling her toward him, his posture, his voice communicating possession. For an instant, resentment flared. Then there was the feel of his body, hard and lean, and she shrugged.

Raker taught skiing during the season and worked summers as a cowhand. He'd spent a couple of months working at the West place. Jesse, the foreman, hadn't liked the way he hung around Chelsea and had paid him off. Raker didn't seem to care. Men like Raker could always find a job somewhere. In Aspen there would always be women anxious to spend money on a man like

Raker. Chelsea knew what he wanted from her, what she wanted from him.

They were in bed in Raker's furnished room in one of the old frame houses on Regalo Street, a long way from the posh hotels and the condos and the boutiques the tourists knew. There was only a straight-backed chair and a battered bureau, and her clothes and his were tossed on the floor and across the back of the chair. The ceiling light was off, but light came in from the street-lamp, shattered by the venetian blinds, striping the bed and their bodies. Raker was naked; Chelsea was wearing the silk shirt, un-buttoned.

"Leave it on," Raker told her, "I like to feel your tits through the silk."

"Oh, yes," she said, liking it too.

She was still too young and too candid to be coy, but not so young that she didn't know about her body and about what ex-cited it. Sometimes when she was alone she played with her nip-ples, nearly as sensitive as her clitoris. Raker somehow always knew how to reach a woman, even a girl like this. They lay en-twined, his rawhide body close, his big hand slowly caressing her breast, slick with sweat, the nipple leaping in response.

"Oh, yes," she said again, "don't stop."

Now, knowing he had her, knowing that whatever he asked now she would do, he said something and, sleepy and drugged by sex, she murmured, "what?"

"I said I could use a little loan. If you've got a hundred bucks that's not working . . ."

"Oh." He'd borrowed money from her before. Sometimes he paid her back.

"Well," he said, propping himself on one elbow to look down at her face, "can you?"

"Sure," she said, "sure."

His face lowered to hers then and they kissed, squirming against each other. She felt wanted, she felt used. Surely this wasn't what people meant when they spoke of being in love.

When she left at one in the morning, leaving the money on a

dresser, tucking a shirttail into her jeans and running from the room before he woke, she'd still not told Raker what she had driven into town to tell him. Two days later the roads were clear and she drove the Maserati into Denver. She had been sleeping around since she was sixteen, and finally it had caught up with her. Maybe it was all part of growing up, she tried to console herself. But it didn't help.

Dry-eyed but grieving, she checked into a hole-in-the-wall clinic under another name, and on a chill, antiseptic table of backroom Denver, she had the damned abortion.

7

I know personally very few saints on Seventh Avenue.

Lincoln Radford, *Mode*, September 15, 1977

His name had been on his schoolbag, Marc A. Street.

"That's a bullshit way to spell your name. It's got a 'k,' not a 'c.' "

Marc stared at the ginger-haired boy lounging on the sidewalk at the exit from the subway. The boy was small, pug-nosed, fierce. Every thirteen-year-old in the neighborhood knew Bobby Swaggerty. Marc was half a head taller and pounds heavier, but kids who lived on Central Park West didn't get into fights with the Irish from Ninth Avenue.

"Hey, you deaf, too? You can't spell and you can't hear?" Swaggerty had fallen in step with him, walking north, obviously bored and seeking diversion. "Can't talk, neither?"

"Sure, I can talk," Marc said, continuing to walk toward home and a protective doorman.

"Then why can't you spell your own name?"

Not sure whether he was angry or scared, Marc stopped and put down the schoolbag. "It's French, that's how the French spell 'Marc.' With a 'c.' "

"French? *French?*" Swaggerty put a hand on one hip and minced.

"First time I ever heard of the *Irish* teaching anyone to spell," Marc retorted.

Bobby hit him three times in the face before Marc could get his hands up.

The next time Bobby stole his new baseball glove, a present from his father, who knew nothing of baseball. Marc fought for the glove, and lost again. They fought a dozen times after that. Sometimes it occurred to him to get off the subway one station farther north and walk south to his family's apartment, avoiding the corner where Swaggerty hung out, smoking cigarettes and looking for trouble. But he never did. Swaggerty seemed to expect him. They fought. Swaggerty won, but the fights were getting better, with Marc learning to use his size. Then one afternoon there were three other boys with Swaggerty. Marc's stomach felt empty, nearly sick.

"This the sucker?" one of them asked Swaggerty.

"That's him," Bobby said, sounding almost proprietary. Marc put down his bag. He could never outrun them all.

But when two of the boys started toward him, Swaggerty shouted. "Hey, leave him alone. He's okay, for a Jewboy that can't spell."

That winter and spring he ran with them. Swaggerty's gang. His mother hated them. Why couldn't he find some decent boys to play with? Marc shrugged. He had friends at school, and there were boys his own age in their building and on the block. Compared to Swaggerty, they were predictable, dull. Swaggerty's gang attended school only on a whim, stole from candy stores and supermarkets, traded dirty pictures, fought with other gangs, and had their own pantheon of heroes, adult members of the notorious "Westies." That year's particular role model was Mickey Noonan, a local thug and small-time gangster who achieved fame when he killed a competitor easing in on his own protection racket. He cut off the man's head with a butcher knife, and went in and out of the Ninth Avenue bars he "serviced" with the head in a shopping bag, pulling it out by the hair at each stop as a cautionary gesture to his "clients" that they should stay in line.

When Noonan was arrested by the feds on a gun-trafficking rap, the Swaggertys went downtown to Foley Square for the trial. None of the witnesses showed up to testify against Noonan, such was the menace of the "Westies," and when Noonan strutted away a free man, Marc Street was one of those who celebrated.

That fall he went out for football for the first time, playing halfback on offense and linebacker on defense. Swaggerty took the subway to Riverdale one Saturday afternoon to watch him play and spent most of the time looking at the girls in the stand, teenagers in soft sweaters, knee socks, and kilted skirts, clean blond hair bouncing as they moved, their young faces already feigning sophistication.

"You guys oughta see the chicks Marc's got at that school of his," he informed his gang. "Man!"

But if Marc's prep-school girls were teasingly, achingly untouchable, the same could not be said of some of the girls Bobby Swaggerty knew. It was with one of these girls that Marc Street came of age.

She was Bobby Swaggerty's cousin, with the same red hair, the same tough little Irish face, the easy laugh, the quick anger. Only the body was different, nothing like Bobby's taut, skinny, sharp-boned fury. During Christmas vacation Marc screwed courage sufficiently tight to ask her to the movies. They went to one of the old barns on Broadway and sat in the balcony. He slipped his arm around her, awkwardly. He could feel the bra straps through her sweater. He was certain he was doing this all wrong, kneading her back and unsure of what to do next, when the girl turned suddenly in her seat, swung toward him, and raised her small face to his to be kissed. When he hesitated, she lifted her head and pulled his down so their lips met. They necked for a few moments, her tongue darting, and then, just as abruptly, she jumped up. "Right back," she said. He must have been doing it wrong. Maybe she wouldn't come back at all.

But she did come back, the down jacket swung over one shoulder, and she bounced back into the seat next to his, pulling her jeans-clad legs up under her and turning to him again. "I went to the ladies' room and took my bra off," she announced, taking his hand and sliding it up under her sweater to where her nipples waited, hard, erect, jutting dramatically from the young, near imperceptible swell of her breasts. She leaned toward him again, and this time it was he who yanked her close and clamped his mouth on hers, suddenly sure he was doing it right.

A few nights later, in her parents' living room, on a threadbare couch, with a colorful print of the Sacred Heart of Jesus gazing down, they made love. The parents were at the movies, Marc was terrified they'd come back, and it was the girl who had thought to buy the condom. That spring he took her to a Riverdale dance and realized, snobbishly, how wrong she was. But all summer and into the fall, knowing she was wrong for him, he continued to make love to her. Then a "proper" girl from Spence made herself available, and he realized for the first time that sex and class were not mutually exclusive.

Halfway through his junior year at Riverdale, school and football and the Swaggerty gang and even girls turned suddenly unimportant.

Marc's father, Jacob Streit (only Marc's name had been anglicized), was summoned to testify in Washington. Estes Kefauver's Senate investigating committee, having worked its way through the Frank Costellos and Bugsy Siegels and Frank Ericksons, had gotten down to the second and third levels of American criminality, where it reached French Jake Streit. Marc's mother, being French and having already fled one persecution, was all for flight. She was sure they could reach Canada, where, her grasp of international law being somewhat flawed, her husband could demand political asylum, and perhaps open a ski lodge. Senator Kefauver, she was convinced, would accomplish what Hitler had not. "Just don't talk about it at school," Jake had told his son.

That, of course, was the reason for the change in names. In Jake Streit's line of work, bad publicity was part of the cost of doing business. If you could shield your family with a simple change of name, why not? Marc asked questions, got grunts and evasions in response. He knew his father worked in the garment district, knew he made good money. They had yet another new apartment overlooking Central Park. Riverdale School wasn't cheap. Every summer there was a bungalow somewhere, a beach house, a cottage in Connecticut. They never owned a place, but they always took a holiday. Ange Streit dressed smartly. But just where the money came from, precisely what his father did to earn it and why he had been subpoenaed, was vague. French Jake kept it that way.

Then came the day. Of course Jake pleaded the Fifth Amendment. By this time, if someone hadn't pleaded the Fifth, Senator Kefauver would have been disappointed. The committee's assistant counsel, a thin, balding WASP with a prosecutor's eyes, read his record into the transcript. Born Jacob Streit in Potsdam, 1910, Jewish, left Germany in 1938. Kefauver looked up snappingly.

"Were you a victim of Nazi persecution?" he asked.

Streit's lawyer rapped his elbow and pointed, for the dozenth time, at the printed Fifth Amendment response. Jake began reading it in the same monotone he had adopted at the start. Kefauver interrupted.

"Come now, Mr. Streit, you can't incriminate yourself by telling us that. I think most Americans would think more highly of you were that the case. I think the *committee* itself would."

Streit again pleaded the Fifth.

Kefauver threw up his hands. The assistant counsel picked up the record.

Arrived Paris later that same year. Got work in the French fashion industry. Met his future wife, Ange de Melun, a fashion model. In 1940 they married. That spring the Germans invaded France and the couple got out. No details as to just how. In 1941 they were in New York, legal entry as wartime refugees. Mr. Streit apparently had friends. In 1942 a son was born, Marc Alain. Only child. The voice droned on. In the committee chamber spectators dozed or chatted in muted tones. To every question, Streit recited the formula response. In his room in the family's apartment on Central Park West, Marc Alain Street, son of French Jake, listened and watched the small black-and-white screen as he learned, for the first time, just who his father was and what kind of work he did, a man's life, a man's secrets, laid bare before his only son.

Wasn't it true that he fled Germany not to escape persecution as a Jew but to avoid arrest by the police as a strong-arm man for a protection ring that preyed on the garment manufacturers in the Alexanderplatz district of Berlin? Wasn't it true most of his victims were themselves Jews? Wasn't it also true that once he found sanctuary in Paris he demonstrated his gratitude to France by diving immediately into the Paris underworld and the same sort of criminal work he'd done in Berlin, extorting money from French ready-to-wear manufacturers and the great houses of the *haute couture*? Wasn't it while engaged in such criminal activity that he met his future wife, who was a fashion mannequin for the Maison Chanel? Hadn't they been assisted in their escape from Paris in June of 1940 by certain influential criminal associates? Hadn't Streit wasted little time after having reached America before hiring himself out to the same sort of criminals with whom he'd associated in Europe? Wasn't there a pattern to his career, to his life, that . . .

At the witness table Jake listened, conferred with his attorney, jotted the occasional note, and was tempted to go against his lawyer's advice. There were so many things he could have said and didn't. What did the Senate's counsel know of the Alexanderplatz in the thirties? Yes, he had been a strong-arm man. Were job opportunities for young Jews all that splendid? When gangsters ran the state, was it a crime to be a criminal? By God, he survived. And when, finally, the steel gates slammed shut, he was able to bribe and scheme his way out. There were already terrible, racking stories of the camps.

Jake Streit was twenty-eight when he arrived in Paris, with no visible means of support. Yet within a few months he had a small car, an apartment on the rue François-1er, and a girlfriend, Ange de Melun, twenty-two years old and one of the most beautiful mannequins in the couture. She sat there now in the hearing room, listening to lawyers and senators destroy her husband, herself, their life together. She closed her eyes, wished that she could cover her ears and shut out the words, remembering Jake as he was then, slim, sleek-haired, alive . . . oh, how alive he'd seemed in contrast to the soft, pallid men of the couture. She knew what he was, the work he did; how could she not? But she had fallen in love. And when the Germans came, he had gotten them out, bribing and scheming and threatening, a determined, brashly confident figure in a season of fright and panic and national collapse.

Young Marc, who had seen his father stripped naked on a

television screen, stayed home from school two days, pleading an upset stomach. On the third morning after his return to New York, Marc's father came to his bedroom.

"Marc, what I've done had nothing to do with you or your mother. Go back to school. There is no reason for shame."

He was still sleek, the black hair combed straight back, graying now at the temples, the trim waist softening, deep lines around his mouth and eyes. For the first time Marc realized his father was getting old.

Marc smiled. "Yes, Papa, I'll go. I'm feeling better."

At Riverdale, no one had noticed anything. "Street" for "Streit" might be crude; it was also effective. But Bobby Swaggerty knew. How, Marc never knew. The Irish boy was not a television viewer. But that afternoon, meeting Marc at the subway, he enthused, his small, freckled face beaming: "Hey, hot shit. Your old man on the television!"

A year and a half later Marc Street, more than six feet tall, weighing nearly two hundred pounds, said good-bye to Central Park West and the Swaggertys and to his father and mother and went off to Cornell University to play football and get an education and meet a nice girl and enroll in that most ferocious of American struggles, society's mainstream.

The following spring, in an incident the New York City police would never solve, his father was shot to death in a Cadillac parked on West Street. Marc left college forever to return home to mourn, to comfort his mother, and to learn that he was now the owner of a small Seventh Avenue coat and suit manufacturing house called Majesty Fashions Inc., which had been owned, through anonymous nominees, by his dead father.

8

In fashion, spring begins in November.

Mode, November 7, 1977

Abeautiful young woman, nearly six feet in height, with long blond hair, legs that seemed to have no start or end, high breasts that punctuated the gauzy blouse she barely wore, undulated from one end of the long room to the other. Behind and around her the deafening rock music pulsed and beat, the strobe lights flashed, the buyers watched, and the fashion editors took their notes. At the end of the runway the girl spun, paused, and, preceded by her hips, swayed back through the room, buttocks, legs, and breasts moving to the music.

The spring collection of Majesty Fashions, designed by Adam, had actually begun in their Thirty-eighth Street showroom before dawn.

There was a crisis about shoes that didn't arrive and then, when they appeared, didn't fit three of the twenty models. A couple of hemlines were still hanging, and Sydney Heidler harried and hustled the seamstresses, painfully kneeling on the carpet to keep the models from moving while they were pinned and basted. An assistant designer, his shirt cuffs dramatically turned up to cover his jacket sleeves, raged and cursed. "Cows! Clumsy cows!"

Marc was inured to backstage hysteria. He'd been through it often enough with Adam and before that with Chanel. One of the models threw up, messing her bodystocking and pantyhose, and they were treated to the spectacle of courtly old Heidler helping a totally nude teenaged girl into fresh bikini pants. Perhaps Adam was the calmest of them all. When Marc remarked on it, he grinned. "Compared to a tea dance on Fire Island, this is nothing." Adam was a competitor; Marc had to give him that.

One of the models chose that moment to begin her period, and a tampon had to be fetched. Old Heidler held his hands in the air, imploring heaven. He was not about to assist in *that* particular operation.

Marc himself threw out a photographer from the *Post*. Later, they would want the press, but not now; not until he knew just how good Adam was going to be this time, and precisely what they had to sell.

The jewelry was parceled out. Which girl would wear which bracelet, which necklace—selections everyone thought had been decided the day before at the dress rehearsal—suddenly became muddled and confused. Two models screamed at each other and exchanged stinging slaps, a man, not a jewel, the source of their fury. The showroom manager, a hard, bleached woman who had known her own jealousies, yanked at one's arm and told the other to shut up. Christiaan, the Dutch hairdresser, long-haired and intense, darted from girl to girl, teasing comb and spray can at the ready, vigilant for an errant curl. Marc found a black model sobbing.

"What's the matter?" he demanded.

"I'm having an abortion this afternoon."

"Great," he said sourly, "just don't have it this morning."

If everything were going smoothly, he would be worried.

Just before eleven he peeked out through the pearl-gray drapes. The long, narrow room was packed. He tried to gauge the audience's mood. Anticipatory, certainly, but like the mob in the arena, eager to turn thumbs down, or like a homecoming crowd at football, wanting the team to win? He didn't know the answer and, in a way, didn't want to know. It was too late now to alter tactics. He'd chosen Adam, and Adam had always done his job. This morning the relentless, seasonal verdict would be in; that was how fashion was, that was the way he wanted it. They would know by noon.

"They're ready, Marc," Heidler said. "If they'll ever be ready, they're ready now."

"Yeah." He hesitated, not wanting the drama of the moment to splinter against reality. He remembered old Norell, the greatest designer America ever had, so high-strung the day of a collection that he got down on hands and knees with a pail and a brush, scrubbed the entire showroom floor just to work off the tension, and then donned his dinner jacket to go out to greet the editors.

"Marc!" Heidler cried impatiently, pantomiming the movement of his watch.

Street looked around once more, seeing Adam glancing this way and that, shouting orders, chivvying a model, as Heidler threw an arm around a girl who had just lost a contact lens and was on the verge of tears.

"Okay!" Marc shouted. "Let's do it!" and the music began to pound.

In a corner of the showroom Carl Lazer perched uncomfortably on a little gold chair and wondered why the hell he was there. Young Street, French Jake's boy, had wanted him to come. He sat watching the collection, enjoying the young women, not understanding what they wore, wondering why the music had to be so loud, and cringing at the breathy gasps of the audience. He recognized none of them. Fashion editors were not Lazer's territory. He found the clothes bizarre and concentrated on the girls. He had never been a man who chased, to his wife he was a faithful husband, but such girls . . .

When it was over, previously sensible people leaped from their chairs, knocking them over, applauding and crying for the designer. The mannequins, twenty of them, returned to the runway and stood there clapping their hands and smiling at men they recognized in the crowd.

"Adam! Adam! Adam!"

A slim, quietly dressed young man appeared at the back of

the runway, and the room exploded into passionate shouts. He grinned shyly, slipped his arms around two of the girls' waists, and walked halfway down the runway, looking this way and that, proud and placid, smiling more broadly now.

"Adam! Adam!"

Lazer, who had heard about such men, stared, trying to discern if the boy's hips swayed as he walked. He could not. In fact, Lazer had to admit, Adam moved regally, as men do who know just who they are, and how good. Despite himself, Lazer was impressed.

It was the first fashion show Lazer had ever attended. But, like Marc and Adam, like Coco Chanel, he was in the fashion business. It had begun during the Second World War. Lazer started by dealing in stolen clothing-ration stamps, then in counterfeits. He bribed procurement agents, and contracts for uniforms were let to firms controlled by Lazer, firms paying him protection money. When material ran short, his men hijacked shipments of cloth, buttons, lining material, dyes, thread, and zippers, which all found their way to garment makers with whom he did business. Certain of his closest associates—men like French Jake—were put in charge of individual garment firms, small companies like Majesty Fashions. After the war such men became owners; they still worked for Lazer, still did his bidding, but they now had their own little profit centers as incentive.

It took Marc Street nearly an hour to disengage himself from the buyers and the chaos of showroom selling. Lazer's limo was at the curb, and the two men got in and drove uptown to Steak Row, an anonymous West Side restaurant. When the waiter asked Lazer if he wanted his steak rare or medium, he said, "Yes." When Lazer refused a drink, Marc shook his head as well.

"This Adam, he's good?"

"Yes, very good. Going to be better."

"That's fine, Marc, I'm pleased for you. Your father would be proud."

"Thank you, Mr. Lazer." His father had told him about this man, his voice full of respect.

"Our arrangements, they go well?"

"Yes, Mr. Lazer. No problem from our point of view. Are you satisfied?"

Lazer nodded. "I see the figures. My accountants are pleased."

Marc had the feeling he was being cross-examined in silence.

"I'm glad you came to the show. I wanted you to see the work we're doing."

"I don't understand it, of course. But the people received it very well."

"Yes."

"Who were they?"

"Oh, retail buyers, fashion editors, some of the suppliers, the fabric people."

Lazer nodded. "And the ones who spend the money are the buyers?"

"Yes."

"Then the others are not necessary."

Marc tried to explain the role of the editors, the need for publicity, the significance of good reviews, the desirability of good relations with the suppliers, their need to see the work the designer was doing so as to work with him more smoothly the next season. Then Lazer said, with a small smile, "It is odd to be in a business where publicity is desirable, where you invite the reporters to come and write about you." He paused. "I spent a lifetime avoiding stories in the newspapers."

Successfully, Marc thought but did not say. When his father had been crucified by the press, Lazer's name had never even come up. Marc knew he should have resented this, but he did not. He respected competence.

"This Adam, he's a homosexual?"

"Yes."

"And this is not a problem for you?"

"You mean personally? Not at all."

"No, I didn't mean that, Marc. I knew your father, I know what kind of fellow you are. I meant in business."

Marc permitted himself a small laugh. "Mr. Lazer, most fashion designers are gay. Most of the big-name designers, certainly."

"It is very strange, working with such beautiful women and not to be able to enjoy it."

"They enjoy it in their own way."

"And your Adam, does he feel sorry for himself?"

"No, I don't think so. He seems to have come to terms with it. We don't talk about it very much."

"And you made him a partner in the business."

"Yes, he deserved it. He's worked very hard." Then, defensively, "It's a minor partnership. I retain clear control."

"I know. My accountant showed me the papers." The voice was flat, cold, annoying Marc.

"And you've said yourself the arrangement we have is working well for you. Your accountants say so." He could not resist the line.

"Yes," Lazer said, mildly this time.

Marc was also mild. "Then we have no problem. I run the company and you get your money laundered."

Lazer said nothing at all this time. It was not prudent to discuss such things in public. Who knew who was listening, who might be wired? He was angry that Street had used the words. Young people, he thought, young people have no sense. French Jake would never have said such a thing aloud. Employing homosexuals in important positions, giving away a piece of the business, speaking such things in public places. As powerful as Lazer was, there were always more powerful men, somewhere in the shadows.

They finished lunch with small talk. When the bill came, Marc took it. When they went out into the autumn afternoon, Lazer shook his hand and then got into his limousine, the chauffeur holding the door, hesitating, wondering if Marc would be joining them.

There was no invitation, and the man swung the door shut and trotted around to the other side of the car. Marc suddenly became concerned that he'd said far too much over lunch. Then, abruptly, Lazer pushed a button and his window slid open.

"Marc, this is family business, first with your father, now with you. I want you to think of me that way, as family. As your

'Uncle Carl.' You remember I told you that once before, long ago. Remember?"

"Yes."

"I'm 'Uncle Carl.' "

He was only nineteen when he first met Lazer, and he had a broken nose and a broken hand and ribs that were starting to purple.

"Well," Carl Lazer said, "it must have been quite a war."

"I want to know why you sent those bastards."

From behind the large, uncluttered desk, Lazer looked up at this tall young man, continuing to smile. "You're so sure I sent them?"

"They told me they worked for you."

Lazer nodded. "That's true, though they are not supposed to tell people for who they work, you know."

"We made them tell," Marc said.

And they had, he and Bobby Swaggerty of the Westies. It was the week after his father's death, and Bobby was with Marc in the office of Majesty Fashions when the three men came in. Swaggerty had come downtown to console him; it was pure accident that he was there. When they pushed in past the terrified receptionist the three men knew only that French Jake was dead, that some teenaged kid was taking over the company, and that not to take profitable advantage of the situation would be sinful. They did not carry guns. In the protection racket it is the threat of violence that is effective. Few Seventh Avenue manufacturers are heroes.

"You the new owner, sonny?"

"I'm the owner. What can I do for you?" To his right he could see Swaggerty, still in a chair, drinking a beer. It was past five, and the office was nearly empty. The three men were professionals. They had chosen the time.

"Well, sonny, we just came by to wish you luck and to remind you about the collections."

"What collections?"

"Every month, one of our people drops by, you know, just to

be sure everything's okay, that no one's hassling you. You pay the fee; you get the service."

Marc had seen enough gangster movies. He was also French Jake's son. "You mean pay protection."

"Sure, you want to call it that. We call it a service. Everyone on the Avenue pays it, the cost of doing business."

Only the one man, the small one, talked. The two bulky men just stood there, looking bored.

"Suppose I don't pay it?" Marc asked, glancing at Swaggerty.

"Sonny, don't be stupid. *Everyone* pays. It's just good sense. Otherwise you got troubles. Like your goods don't get delivered and your sewing machines fall off the tables and there's maybe a little fire and maybe your production man falls down and breaks his leg. You know, sonny. And maybe one of your models has to go away for a while and not come back and like maybe you get sick. Understand?"

"No," Marc said, his voice very steady. He could sense that Swaggerty was tensed now, ready to move.

The small man too seemed to be getting bored. He turned to the others. "Look, all this talk makes me thirsty. I'm going to go downstairs to the corner for an egg cream. You guys explain to sonny."

As he started for the door, Bobby Swaggerty exploded from the chair and smashed him in the head with his beer bottle. The man screamed and stumbled against the wall. Before the other two could move in, Marc dove at them, putting a shoulder into one's midriff and driving him against and then over a desk. When the man was down he began to punch him in the face, sprawled atop his body. The third man was still free, until Swaggerty got to him.

After that it was two on two, feet and bare fists. In a few minutes it was over. He and Bobby propped up the small man, who was holding a bloody handkerchief to his head and sobbing. The other men lay on the floor, one motionless, the second moaning and swaying, holding a smashed kneecap. It was then that the small man told them they worked for Carl Lazer.

"Sit down," Lazer said now, "I'll explain you a few things."

Marc sat. He was cooler now.

"Young man, you know who I am? Your father told you?"

"Yes."

"Good. You must understand, this is a large organization. Not everyone knows what everyone else is doing. These three men who came to see you, they thought they were just doing their job. They don't know everything that is happening, better they don't. All they know is that there is a new owner of a company in the garment industry and they should go see him, sell him the usual service. They know that French Jake is dead. They don't know you. They could care less. You're a customer is all."

"Then you didn't send them?"

Lazer didn't bother to answer. He waved a small, delicate hand.

"Your father was a good man. I mourned when I heard about it. I have already asked for information about the people who killed him. If I find out, the right thing will be done."

"I want to know."

"It is better that it is handled within the organization. Do not destroy yourself in anger. You're a young man. Run your company if that is what you wish. Do not become caught up in vengeance. Is that what you wish, to run the company?"

"Yes, I think so. My mother thinks I should."

"Good. If you need help, come to me. I only ask that if you wish to sell, you let me know. Your father and I had certain financial arrangements, we were of service to each other. I would want to continue such arrangements with the new owners, you understand?"

"What arrangements?"

Lazer made a little gesture. "Don't be so suspicious. They are profitable to your company. Your father could have told you. Ask your mother about Carl Lazer. Then come see me again. You're a good boy."

Marc got up. "Okay, Mr. Lazer. And there won't be any more guys coming to sell me anything?"

Lazer shook his head. "No one will bother you." He waited a moment, and then he said, "That boy who was with you, in the fight."

"Yes?"

"Stay away from those Irishers. They're crazy, you know."

"Bobby's my friend. He helped me."

"I know, I know. But remember what I say, they're crazy." Lazer took him by the arm. "One more thing. I'm not 'Mr. Lazer.' Not to French Jake's boy, you understand? This is family business. I'm 'Uncle Carl.' You understand?"

Street nodded.

"Yes, 'Uncle Carl.' "

"I'll always be your 'Uncle Carl.' "

That was fifteen years ago. Majesty had continued ever since to launder money for Carl Lazer, the burden weighing on Street. He resented having to defend Adam, to explain away what Adam was, and what he had to be. To Marc, long orphaned, Adam was family now. He resented Lazer's wariness of Majesty's explosive success. Perhaps it was time for the arrangement with "Uncle Carl" to come to an end. He owed Lazer, but there were things he owed to Adam, to Majesty, to himself.

It was a terrible thing to have to weigh one debt against another.

9

Spirit and shape! Spirit and shape! Everything else in fashion is detail.

Mode, July 25, 1978

All that winter they worked hard, long hours, long
days, long weeks, Marc and Adam both. Some nights there were
buyers in the place writing orders until after ten.

"I'm not sure I want to be rich," Adam groaned, back aching
from hours at the drawing board.

"Come on," Marc said, "let's get a drink."

They wandered east in the soft dusk of early spring to a joint
on Second Avenue. Marc was thirsty. "A Heineken."

Adam asked for something mixed.

A tall Irishman, Brooks-Brothered and marginally oiled, was
at Adam's elbow. Some other people were with him. "I know
you," he told Adam. 'You're . . . "

"Yeah," Adam said, "my name's Adam."

The man snapped his fingers. "I *know* your name, dammit.
You're in the fashion business. Wait a minute . . . "

"Adam," Adam repeated.

"Don't tell me. I know it as well as I know my own."

This went on for another minute or two.

Then the Irishman put his hand on Adam's shoulder.
"Look," he said, "I and my friends—"

Marc reached over and knocked his hand away. "His name

is Adam. He told you that twice. You asked and he answered. You talk and you don't listen."

"Hey, wait just a minute, friend," the Irishman said, turning from Adam to Street.

Marc looked at him. "We came in for a drink," he said, "not to talk."

"Yeah?"

Marc looked at him. "You're either dumb or you're drunk," he said.

The Irishman, both drunk and dumb, bristled. "What are you, a couple of queers?"

People stepped back. And when the Irishman started for them, Marc hit him. Twice.

"Come on, Adam," Marc said.

The Irishman's friends were trying to get him up.

"Jesus," Adam said, impressed, "where'd you learn that?"

Marc shrugged. "Swaggerty."

In the heady first years of Majesty it was always like that, us against them. Adam designed the clothes and Marc sold them.

"I've got a shrink of my own, Marc," Adam exulted one morning over coffee.

Street screwed up his face.

"Well, why shouldn't I? Most people have one if they can afford it."

"Sure," Marc said sourly, "a status symbol, like cocaine or a Mercedes."

"Hey, it can't hurt. I talk and he listens."

"Designers. You're all nuts."

"Sure we are," Adam agreed, "that's what makes us designers."

Marc put down his cup. "But aren't you afraid that if this shrink cures you of whatever ails you, then you won't be nuts anymore and you'll lose whatever it is that makes you a designer?"

Adam thought for a moment. "I don't think so," he said, "all we ever talk about is sex."

Marc laughed. He had never been able to talk to anyone else like this; he felt needed and happy at the same time. At work, he and Adam made something that endured. How many people could say that?

When Marc flew off to Paris that spring to buy models from the couture, models that Majesty would reproduce by the thousands, Adam went with him, buying other models from which he could take inspiration, from which his own fertile imagination would create other beautiful things, things that had their roots in Europe but would ripen here at home, on Seventh Avenue, into something at once elegant and American.

"Boys, we're building bridges, right across the Atlantic," Heidler said. "With Marc running the business and Adam stealing the designs, why, there's nothing we can't do."

"Stealing? Sydney, I don't steal."

Marc laughed. "Adam, a designer who doesn't steal is a lousy designer. And you know it."

Adam looked hurt. "Marc, I may breathe the air. But steal? Never!"

Marc stayed where he always stayed, at the San Regis on rue Jean-Goujon. It wasn't a matter of money. He was at home in the place. Adam went to the Plaza Athenée and held court at a table in the Relais. Brugère had driven out to the airport the night before to meet them, his car no longer a Mercedes but a Rolls Corniche. Marc saw Adam's eyes widen. Brugère took them to their hotels to drop their bags, and then they drove across the Seine to the boulevard Montparnasse and a big table in the back at La Coupole.

Adam made a face. "I thought we'd go someplace chic." Then he saw Jean-Paul Belmondo in a group of people, and he relaxed. "Well, maybe it's not so bad."

"Thank you, dear boy," Brugère said sarcastically.

Marc laughed. Adam could be, as Heidler had once put it, "piss elegant."

Jimmy de Bertrand did not join them for dinner.

"He's fatigued," Brugère said, "he's worked very hard. I think you will like this collection very much."

It was better without Jimmy. Two designers together was like two entrées in the same meal: either of them was fine, two were too much. Besides, Brugère was funnier, bitchier without Jimmy to flatter and to fuss over. Now he was telling the latest story about Castillo, who had been sacked by the House of Lanvin.

"His little assistant took it even worse than Castillo. He was a nice, gentle boy who never drank except for a little wine, and now he was so upset over the dismissal of his master that he went in and out of bars half the night, drinking Scotch and weeping. Finally, about dawn, the boy found himself in front of the Maison Lanvin on the Faubourg St.-Honoré, drunk and desolate. He stared at the display windows and the showcases for a time, at the scarves and jewels and blouses and accessories carrying the label of Lanvin but each of them designed by his hero, all of it the work and sweat and the inspiration of poor Castillo."

Adam leaned forward, listening attentively, caught up in Brugère's tale.

"Finally he picked up a stone or a brick from the gutter and hurled it through the window of the shop, smashing the glass, smashing the display. And then he just stood there, weeping, until the police came, waiting for them to come, knowing he would be arrested, wanting to make that last, gracious gesture toward his *patron*."

"Poor sap," Marc said.

Adam wheeled on him. "But, Marc, don't you understand. That's what he *had* to do!"

After dinner Brugère's car took Adam back to the Plaza. "I've got to work tomorrow," Adam said, disciplined, intent.

But when the car turned toward the rue Jean-Goujon, Marc stopped Brugère's driver. "Listen, I'm not sleepy. Do you want to go to Castel's?"

Brugère declined. "Jimmy will be still awake. During the week of collections he sleeps badly, he gets paranoid. I'd better not."

"Sure, I understand."

Brugère dropped him at the head of the rue Princesse, and Marc walked down the narrow street toward Castel's. Just outside the place the mandolin lady was playing. Marc gave her ten francs, and she tried to kiss him. He could smell her breath, and he dodged. Inside the door there was a window like a movie theater's ticket booth. The girl inside looked at him and waved him past. Whether she remembered him or he simply looked as if he belonged didn't matter. Castel's was a club, and by this time, Marc figured, he was a member without portfolio.

It was two o'clock in the morning and the place was warming up. Marc said hello to Jean Castel at the *table de concierge* and then went downstairs to the bar. Behind him people were dancing. A small blond girl came to stand by him. They talked French for a time; then she led him onto the dance floor, holding him close to impertinent breasts. Then a buyer from Boston called to him from a table and he sat down with him, watching the blond drift back to the bar. It was not that he was saving himself for anyone. There *was* no one. But this was the season of work, a monastic time; even Adam knew it and had gone home to his sketch pad and an empty bed. After one drink Marc got up and walked toward the stairs, as the blond eyed him from the bar.

That next afternoon at three he and Adam attended the Chanel collection. The designer had been an assistant at Dior for years. He tried, but it just wasn't the same. They had paid their eight-thousand-dollar caution, the entry fee that entitled them to buy two dresses to copy and reproduce.

"I can't *find* two we should buy," Adam whispered in his ear, a nearly unmarked notebook open on his lap.

Marc nodded. "I know." It was sad. He sat there on the little gold chair as the mannequins paraded by, watching the mirrored staircase where Coco used to sit on the third-floor landing during the show, poking him in the shoulder and hissing her comments on her own work, cadging cigarettes from him, taking a few puffs and then dropping the lipsticked butts into a gold ashtray on the step. He could see her now, hear her rasp.

"Don't bother with that one, *mon pauvre,* nothing. It is nothing. Wait for the navy evening dress. It is important. Try to tell me why it is important. I keep telling you what to look for and you are still blind. *Zut,* regard that woman's legs in the front row. How can a fashion editor be so dowdy? I should give her the door but she would lose her job. I don't want to be accused of that. They speak enough piggishness about me already. Ah, yes, this suit is rather nice. The armhole is everything. If the armhole is not cut high enough you might as well wear sacking. No one understands that but English tailors. That's where I learned it, from rich men who had tailors in Savile Row. Give me another cigarette, *mon petit,* I know they're bad for me but what is one to do?"

Chanel would cross the rue Cambon from the Ritz at one in the afternoon and enter the salon, mounting to the second floor, where the tailors and the assistants would be waiting in their white smocks, nervous, frightened, wondering what mood she would be in. When Marc was there, she turned on the charm; with a man she was always flirtatious. The assistants loved to see Street arrive, his presence softening her nasty tongue. The mannequins, half-naked Swedish or English or German blonds, virtually interchangeable, regarded him with cool curiosity. They all had their own arrangements, of course, but to have a man there during the fittings added a certain spice. The male tailors they ignored. Capons. Marc they had difficulty figuring out. Was he sleeping with Mademoiselle? No one knew. Coco enjoyed the intrigue, the speculation.

"All this beastliness, it is despicable," she complained, grinning as she said it, poking at a tuft of wig straying from under her flat straw hat.

In those early days when he first came to Paris, his mother's letters sent fluttering before him like diplomatic envoys, Marc was confused, dismayed by the intricacies of the couture, and vaguely aware that at his mother's urging and through his own pride, he had taken on a complicated task for which he was totally unsuited.

"What the hell am I doing here?" he demanded of Sydney Heidler. "What am I trying to prove?"

Patiently, old Heidler led him by the hand.

"As professional buyers we pay the French what is called a 'caution' to see the collection. Depending on the size of the cau-

tion, we can buy and take home one or two or more dresses or
coats. Back in New York, the seams are opened up and the garment is taken apart and laid out flat. We cut a paper pattern precisely to its shape. From the paper pattern we cut a toile, a canvas
pattern. And on the basis of that, hundreds of layers of cloth are
cut to match. They are sewn together, linings and buttons are
added, and we show it to the retail buyers. Is that too complicated
for you, Marc? You're a smart boy, is that too much?"

Of course, there was more to it than that, much more.
Heidler was describing only the line-for-line business, the precise
duplication of a design. Adaptations were something else again.
Heidler knew where to buy good European fabric that was not
quite the original cloth, so the copies could be made for a price.
He knew which subcontractors in New Jersey gave honest work.
He knew the union people, the ILGWU. He knew the truckers,
the showroom saleswomen, the models, the accountants, the sewing machine repairman, the store buyers, which of them had to be
paid off with theater tickets, which with a girl. And when Marc
threw up his hands in confusion, Heidler shook his head. "I am
fifty-eight years old, Marc. I was fourteen when I came into the
trade. You're barely twenty! Are you so eager to declare yourself a
failure?"

Coco gave him the same counseling. "I was an ignorant girl
from the Auvergne. Not a great lady from the *seizième* with a
parasol. In the Auvergne they were so shrewd they sold water to
the Parisians during the Revolution. An Auvergnat wouldn't give
you the hour without a small fee. I cannot sketch, never could.
But I learned cloth and I learned shape. You too can learn."

And her knobbed, arthritic hands would drive another
straight pin through the tweed as the mannequin braced, trying
not to flinch.

Marc Street thought of her now as he sat on the little gold
chair watching her successor try unsuccessfully to recapture the
magic. Next to him Adam was doing sketches of lovely clothes
that resembled nothing they were seeing in the salon of the great
Chanel.

The next two mornings were taken up with Givenchy and
Saint Laurent, where the collections were good and it was easier

to buy, with no problem filling out the caution. Here Adam sketched what he saw, not what he was imagining. His slender hand moved swiftly over the paper, the felt-tipped pen slashing and darting, brilliantly capturing the spirit of the clothes. And then the shape. Those were the essential elements; all else was incidental. Marc had learned this from Heidler, from Chanel. Adam knew it instinctively: spirit and shape.

Adam had met a boy in Paris, a male model who sold scarves at Hermès to support himself between assignments. He had a nice smile and a little English. He was working that night on a photo spread for one of the fashion magazines and was going to meet Adam late at Régine's. Marc and Adam dined together at Lipp. Adam was still raving about Saint Laurent.

"It isn't fair. All that talent and still in his thirties."

"He's good."

"Good? He's great. I always loved his dresses. But those gabardine coats. And the pants . . . "

"Remind you of anything?"

"Chanel? Marc, you're obsessed. Give Yves some credit, for God's sake. You'd think old Coco was your damned mother."

"Well, in a way she was. And I give Saint Laurent plenty of credit. Dior screwed him, you know."

Adam's face lit up. "I knew we'd end up talking sex."

"Funny. No, seriously, when old man Dior died, Yves got the job. He was maybe nineteen or twenty. Just a kid. And he saved the house. M. Boussac, the owner, was ecstatic. He got Yves a deferment from the army on grounds he was essential to the balance of trade or something. The Algerian War was on. Then Yves came up with one lousy collection and Boussac threw him to the wolves. 'The boy must serve the nation like everyone else. France expects every man to do his duty. *Vive la France!*' Of course, Yves had a nervous breakdown and was out of the army in six weeks, but without a job. He sued the Dior house for what the French call 'abusive rupture of contract,' and he and Bergé raised a little cash and they opened their own house. Dior never quite recovered."

"And Saint Laurent got rich."

"Uh-huh. Boutiques, perfumes, men's wear, the lot."

Adam had finished his meal, and he pushed the plate aside.

"Marc, why couldn't we do those things? Perfume, for example. We could make a fortune too."

"Because you don't know how to create a perfume, and I don't know how to sell it."

"We could learn."

"Pretty expensive on-the-job training."

The waiter came to clear the table, and Adam looked at his watch. He was excited about meeting his friend at Régine's. With only one more day of collections, Adam felt some indulgence was permissible. Marc stayed behind for coffee and a *fin*. When he left he saw Lincoln Radford's pudgy, pouty face and mop of gray hair, centerpiece of a table that included Bernard Lanvin and his new designer, the Belgian Crahay. Radford did not bother to look up as Marc passed.

The last day of the collections was Jimmy de Bertrand's. It was a flop.

Out in the street in front of the house, there was a rush of cabs. Very few buyers had stayed behind to salute Jimmy. Later they would go back to buy their caution. They had to. But no one enjoyed congratulating a man on his failures.

"Not so great," Marc said, genuinely regretful.

"Great? It stunk!"

"Okay, but when you talk to him, put it more gently, Adam."

"Hey, I can do better stuff than that. And I'm just another one of *those* Americans." De Bertrand had been quoted earlier that year in *WWD* as saying just that. Adam had not forgotten.

"Adam, give him a break. You of all people know a designer doesn't hit one every time out. You've got two or maybe four collections a year. Four first nights, and the critics are just as tough as Broadway."

"Well, sure, but it was disappointing."

He didn't look disappointed. It didn't surprise Street. He never knew a goddamned designer yet who wanted anyone else to have a big success.

But there was more than bitchery in Adam's reaction. Lincoln Radford, in Paris for the couture collections, would sum it up more articulately in *Mode* magazine's next issue than either Marc or Adam could have done, and with considerably more objectivity:

> Something fundamental is happening in world fashion. Paris is no longer the dominant force it has been for most of this century. Oh, there are still enormous talents among the French: Saint Laurent, Ungaro, Cardin, de Bertrand when the mood suits him, Givenchy, even the erratic Courrèges. But the giants have vanished: Balenciaga, Dior, Fath, Chanel. For the first time in memory an impressive and almost implausibly young array of American designers is challenging French suzerainty: Calvin Klein, Lauren, Halston, the still raw Perry Ellis and Adam Greenberg, several young women, all of them talented, ambitious, and hungry. Perhaps "hunger" is the operative word, the passion that fuels their *defi Americaine*.
>
> These young Americans really believe they are as good as the French.
>
> That is the extraordinary thing. Even in the time of Norell, Seventh Avenue was deferential toward Paris, insecure, lacking confidence. And as good as they were in their time, such as Geoffrey Beene, Weitz, Donald Brooks, Blass never really thought deep in their guts that they belonged on the same level as the French. This brash new generation of Americans does. They think nothing is impossible. They hurl defiance.
>
> Where Americans once genuflected to Paris, today's Seventh Avenue thumbs its nose. These young Americans may not yet be as good as the French. But they *think* they are.

Adam Greenberg certainly thought so.

10

The Coty Award is a political arrangement, beneath contempt.

Mode, November 8, 1978

After the warming glow of the *Mode* magazine
editorial listing him among the more promising young American designers, Adam was genuinely slighted by the failure
of Lincoln Radford to attend his latest show. Street was more
pragmatic. He knew designers traveled with paranoia as a companion.

"It's a slap in the face," Adam complained.

"Look," Marc said, "he makes a point of this sort of thing.
At heart he's a snob. He went to Yale and we didn't. He's an in-
tellectual and you and I are a couple of Jewboys grubbing out a
living in the garment trade. He brags about not going to the
American collections, only the European. And it isn't even true.
He and Norell were thick. He gets along with Galanos. Blass and
Calvin show him their stuff privately."

Adam made a face. "Maybe I should too."

Marc laughed. "Forget it. Start sucking up to him and he'll
know he has you bullied. He's a son of a bitch. Just smile when
you see him, and read his damned magazine."

"Why should I? He doesn't come to my collection."

Street shrugged. "Do you read *anything*, Adam?"

"Of course I do," he said indignantly, *"Vogue* every month,
and I have a subscription to *People*."

Marc urged him not to let Lincoln Radford bother him, get

under his skin. And of course the headstrong designer ignored the advice.

Adam called Radford, and after an insulting delay was given an audience, over lunch at La Côte Basque. Adam was nervous. He had made the reservation, he was paying for the meal, but it was Radford to whom the waiters and captains deferred. A "Jew-boy," that was all he was, just as Marc said, playing in the big leagues with a minor-league bat. Except he truly believed he was as good as any of them. Radford didn't, yet.

"Your work is very . . . promising."

"Thank you."

"For what? Promise isn't achievement." Radford giggled.

"No." Adam realized he was being teased. "You go to the French collections. I've seen you. Why don't you come to . . . "

"Yours?" Radford's pouty face changed to a simpering smile.

"No, not just mine, the American collections generally."

Radford raised an eyebrow. "Come now, Adam, you don't mean that at all. You didn't ask me to lunch to plead the cause of American fashion. That sort of selfless idealism belongs to another age. You're here for yourself, pleading your own cause. And why not?"

Adam realized he was being baited. "You said you liked my work. How can you know?"

"I said it was promising. I see the pictures, I have sources."

Adam toyed with his wine in silence.

Radford reached out to pat his hand. "Dear boy, there's nothing shameful in promoting yourself. It's a natural thing. We all do it," he said, giggling.

Lunch arrived. Adam had recently begun eating in places like this. He was still uneasy. The banker Herbie Allen was at the next table. Richard Burton and his agent, Lantz, were across the room. Brooklyn was very far off. Radford, with that chess player's mind, understood this. He waved enthusiastically at Beverly Sills and dove into the *paillard*. Adam, nervous, drank too much wine, and Radford kept pushing it on him, beckoning the captain to re-fill their glasses.

"How's your boss, Street? I know him, you know."

"My boss? He's not my boss. We're partners."

"Oh, of course," Radford said smoothly, "he must have told me that and it slipped my mind."

"Well, it's so," Adam said, suspecting he was feeling the wine and not making all that much sense.

"I'm sure it is. A talented boy like you ought to make a percentage. Only way to keep you from going across the street to work for someone else."

"Yes," Adam said, not really responding to Radford's point but saying, for no reason, "you know I won the Coty Award."

Radford giggled again, disdainful. "The Coty Award is a political arrangement, organized by a press agent called Madame Lambert, and voted by a jury of superannuated fashion editors who pass it around each year among their favorites. I refuse to vote on the Coty. It is beneath me, and it is beneath you to boast of it."

Adam had enough sense to refuse the brandy.

Back at Majesty, Marc shook his head. Adam slumped on a couch in his office, head down.

"You're stewed. What the hell did he do, slip you a Mickey?"

"We drank some wine. What an awful man he is. He kept giggling at me."

"Didn't I tell you to stay away from him?"

"Don't beat up on me, Marc. I'm sorry. I just thought I could get him interested in me, in us, in what we're trying to do."

"Leave the heavy thinking to me, Adam. You design the clothes. I'll sell them. And sell you to people like Radford when it's necessary. Which it unfortunately is sometimes."

Adam stared at the floor, looking glum and embarrassed. "I made an ass of myself."

Marc laughed. "Look, go home and take a shower and sleep it off. I won't get a damn thing out of you today. Don't worry, we all do dumb things. And stop brooding about Radford. You're worth a dozen of that guy."

Adam got up. "I love you, Marc."

"Me too, Adam."

Loving Adam and relying on his judgment were not the same thing. Marc was not as complacent as he tried to make himself sound to the troubled boy. He took Heidler to dinner at Pietro's to talk about it.

"I worry about him, Sydney."

"He's a boy, Marc, give him time."

"I know. He's got the talent, but sometimes the ambition is bigger than the talent."

"He'll grow into it," Heidler said.

"I just don't want him to screw himself up. Or to screw up Majesty. He wants desperately to be a star. Making money and being successful isn't enough."

"A lot of people want to be stars, Marc. You should know that."

Street laughed. "The funny thing is, I don't. I just want the money. And for the damned thing to work. I don't want headlines."

Now it was Heidler who laughed. "Marc, on Seventh Avenue such humility is against the law. Don't you know?"

Street shook his head. "It's not humility. I'm as fond of myself as anyone. It's just that if I know I'm good, really know it, that's enough. I don't need anyone else telling me."

Heidler's face darkened. "Marc, remember that Adam isn't you. He needs things you don't need. He has to be told, over and over, how wonderful he is. He needs that."

Marc nodded. "He needs love."

Heidler looked at him and bit off the words. It was not his place to tell his employer that they *all* needed love, maybe even Marc Street.

Adam never knew of this dinner, or of how they worried about him.

His November collection was very good, in some ways the most subtle, the most complicated he had ever done. Majesty was still doing some line-for-line work, accurately copying the clothes

Marc and Adam had seen and bought that summer in Paris. It was a big part of the business. During Chanel's time, it had been the whole business. Now Adam was becoming a true designer, not just a copyist and adapter. Even Lincoln Radford, who once again had not attended the collection but had sent emissaries, remarked on it in his magazine:

"Young Adam Greenberg (he hates the surname and prefers that it not be used; vanity declaring his given name to be sufficiently famous already) has for several years been one of the most tasteful copyists on *Septième* Avenue. With his new line for spring Mr. Greenberg displays for the first time the primitive creative spark. His coats are outstanding, the dresses less so. And his sportive clothes, especially the pants and those loose, blousy tops, are very fresh indeed."

Except for the ritual bitchery about his name, this very nearly constituted a rave review. Adam recognized it as such. Old Sydney Heidler was ecstatic. Marc urged caution. "Let's see if he follows it up with pictures. They're what sells clothes."

Adam made a face. "Always the salesman."

"You bet, Adam. That's where the money is, and don't you forget it."

There were others who read Radford's critique and drew conclusions. One of them was Stanley Baltimore, who invited Adam to call.

"I'm glad you could come," Baltimore said, "a busy time for a man as successful as you."

He was not subtle. If flattery was called for, he ladled it on. Adam recognized this, but still found it pleasant.

They were in Baltimore's office on an upper floor of the General Motors Building, on Fifth Avenue. Lauder and Revlon and several other lesser cosmetic and perfume companies had offices in the same building, causing it, inevitably, to be known as the "General Odors" building. Baltimore's office was more like a living room, with big, comfortable chairs, a couch, small tables, lovely pictures on the wall, a marble sink, a wood fire burning.

"Have you ever thought of putting your name on a perfume, on a cosmetic line?" Baltimore now asked, getting to the point without small talk.

"Yes, I have. But that's as far as it went."

Baltimore was a large, sleek man with a sharp-pointed nose. Adam wondered if sniffing perfumes made it that way. There was a deep scar at the corner of his mouth. Adam wondered about that as well.

"Well," said Baltimore, "perhaps it should go further. I think it could, you know. I think the Adam name could sell."

Adam thought so too. But he was cautious. There was no one in fashion who didn't know Stanley Baltimore, who wasn't wary of "the pimple man." Confronted by silence, Baltimore shifted in his chair and then got up and went to a bar wagon. "Drink?"

"No, thanks." Adam had been burned by Lincoln Radford. Baltimore poured himself a Perrier. Adam wished he had thought of that.

"Sure, it's a good name. Simple. Recognizable. In a couple of years it could be a very big name. 'Adam.' Nice sound to it. You could spin off a complementary line. Call it 'Eve.' I'm only talking off the cuff, of course. But in this business you never underestimate the value of a good name."

"Of course not."

Adam hadn't told Marc of Baltimore's invitation. He wasn't quite sure why not. Marc might tell him not to go. It could reignite their argument over Radford. Besides, he didn't like the idea of having to run to Marc about everything. He was the designer, not Marc, *he* was what made Majesty Fashions go. That wasn't what he said to Baltimore, however.

"It's not my decision to make," Adam said. "Marc Street runs the company."

Stanley Baltimore was a seasoned negotiator. Shrewdly he said, "And what does Mr. Street think of our getting together like this?"

"Well, he thought it was fine."

Baltimore knew the boy was lying. So Street didn't know. Good. A possible split between them. He did not say this.

"A successful line of cosmetics and perfumes could make you both a good deal of money. Nice to have your name on a couple of million bottles as well. And in all those ads and commercials."

Adam said, this time with total honesty, "I've thought of that."

"I'm sure you have. You're a smart fella. Some people don't understand how the fashion magazines work. The big advertisers get the big editorial play. And it's the cosmetic companies that buy the ads."

"I know."

It was true. Marc often complained about it, saying it was unfair to a designer like Adam.

They talked some more and then, virtually in mid-sentence, Baltimore got up, walked to the far corner of the room, where there was a pink marble washbasin and mirror and a small shelf with comb and brush and toiletries, unzipped his fly, and, while continuing to talk, urinated into the sink.

Adam left, shaken. There were those lovely, delicate paintings on the office walls, pictures about which Baltimore spoke movingly, intelligently, with knowledge and taste. There were the flattering, tantalizing hints of promised wealth and fame, the deferential suggestion that Adam was *needed*. And there was the crude evidence of the man's vulgarity.

Baltimore was satisfied. He had not expected to do a deal during this first meeting. He had probed for weakness and thought he had found some. The money and the fame had been dangled; now he would explore other avenues, something in Adam's past, some flaw in Street or in Majesty itself. Who knew who evaded taxes on Seventh Avenue? There were ways to find out if you had connections. And Stanley Baltimore had connections. He stroked the scar at the corner of his mouth, remembering the man who had put it there, remembering what had happened to him.

Adam did not tell his partner, Marc Street, about any of it, which was a mistake. Mr. Baltimore believed it was always simpler dealing with one partner than with two. And that was how Lincoln Radford came to know of Adam's "secret" visit to the "General Odors" building and how a report of that visit found its way into the trade gossip column of the following week's *Mode* magazine.

BOOK THREE
CHELSEA

Like young Lochinvar, she came out of the west.

Mode, January 21, 1979

In the first week of January, Chelsea West packed her bags and flew to New York. Will West objected, but she was past twenty and there were limits to his power. She was the last of the Wests, and he had no intention of breaking with her over what even he had to admit was the natural restlessness of a young woman living on an isolated ranch in the winter mountains. His chauffeur drove them both into Denver to the airport. When he said good-bye he held her. She was happy to be going. But she nearly cried. She did not understand this, but the old man did.

"I'll be back before you know it," she said, hugging him again.

"Of course you will," he said, not believing it, fearing he was losing her.

He stood for a long time watching through the window of the VIP lounge as the plane rose and started to climb toward the mountains and the bright blue sky that led to the east.

Marc was lunching with Bill Blass. They were at the front, right table of La Grenouille, owing more to Blass's fame than to Marc's. He understood that fashion's pecking order was crisply delineated in establishments like La Grenouille. Marc had met

Blass in Paris, where Jimmy de Bertrand introduced them. He liked Blass, and their luncheon was fun, not the commonplace shoptalk of such meals.

They were chatting now when a very tall, astonishingly beautiful young woman entered the room. People stopped talking and started looking.

"And who the hell is *that?*" Street asked aloud.

Blass shook his head. He knew everyone. But not this time.

Her golden hair was long and loose, framing a face that shone with a skier's tan in a season when sickly pale was the norm. Her eyes were a blue off an artist's palette. She wore a long coyote coat, knee-high Eskimo boots, a suede skirt, and a turtleneck sweater, not precisely Manhattan going-to-lunch clothes. But on her they looked right, better than right. Her luncheon hostess was Eileen Ford. Mrs. Ford just sat there watching the rest of them watching her, and smiled. Complacently.

"Well?" Street said, not so much to Blass as to himself.

Blass just shook his head, his cigarette bobbing, an eyebrow raised. "You can't say she's dull."

Chelsea West moved like a large cat, a cougar or a jaguar; she was an open, outdoorsy girl with a firm handshake and a steady gaze, a quotable, conversational candor, and the confident sense of who she was, that she was a West. Within a week *WWD* had done a profile of this new girl in town. When the reporter asked how tall she was, she said, straight-faced: "About five-twelve," a line immediately picked up and quoted all around town. The Ford model agency knew its business. And they knew that in Chelsea West they had pure platinum.

She had an instinctive gift for self-promotion. The *WWD* profile inspired Enid Nemy of the *Times* to interview her; *Vogue* hired her to pose for fashion photos by Dick Avedon; Andy Warhol threw a party for her at a new restaurant someone wanted plugged. Press agent Harvey Mann was retained, but found himself having to do very little. The media apparatus that revolves around fashion cranked out stories. Her nickname, for example, inspired by the fact she was conceived in London, where her parents were attending Wimbledon and had leased a home just off the Kings Road, Chelsea. The *Today* show made inquiries. A publicity-conscious filmmaker offered her a role. Liz Smith put her in the column. Lesser columnists began to get releases from press agents of remarks she never made in restaurants where she never ate. The marketing of Chelsea West had begun.

"That's the girl!"

Adam had been hanging around Richard Avedon's studio in Manhattan, there to have lunch with Dick, patiently waiting as the photographer worked on an advertising spread for Estée Lauder. He lounged in a director's chair, drinking Tab and half watching, as Avedon moved this way and that, urging the model to dance, to shake her head, the blond hair spraying out this way and that, clicking off the shots, the whir of the motor-driven camera like the buzz of worker bees. Behind and around them the rock music pulsed and pounded, inevitable accompaniment to a fashion shoot. Avedon talked constantly, his voice low and polite, wheedling, praising, urging, stroking.

"Yes, yes, that's it. Oh, lovely. Like that. More of that. Just so, just like that. That hair, shake it out. Lovely. Super. Do it, do it!"

The girl moved, anticipating his commands. She *knew.*

Most models don't. Only a handful, only the best have the instinct. Adam leaned forward, no longer bored, caught up in the ritual dance of camera and image. Behind her a vast, endless stretch of dead-white background paper hung from the wall like an oversized roll of toilet paper. In the foreground were the camera tripod, the ranks of lights, the silvered umbrellas reflecting softly. Onstage, the focus of it all was a girl, tall, blond, vital, a large and beautiful animal. Adam was following her every movement now, every gesture, every pose, as precisely as Avedon's lens. Where had Dick found her? What agency had discovered her? Who *was* she?

When the shoot was finished Adam bounded from his chair, applauding and shouting. Avedon, soaked with sweat, laughed.

"Adam, control yourself."

"But, Dick, that girl was *born* to wear my clothes. I can see her now in the next collection."

"That girl" had already left the studio, as drained as Avedon.

Avedon shrugged. "Come on, you're buying lunch. Or have you forgotten?"

They went to Lafayette, just east of Third, opposite the Random House building. A chilly day, and in the small dining room the fireplace blazed. Drinks were ordered, and then Adam demanded again, "Who is she?"

Avedon screwed up his face. "Adam, we're going to have to hose you down."

Over lunch Avedon told him who she was, who represented her. That afternoon Adam called Eileen Ford. She was away, and he talked to Jerry.

"Look, I want Chelsea West. I won't be coy. I want to work with her on the collection, and then I want her to show it. I probably want her to do the ads, and if we do any commercials, those too."

Ford agreed only that she would see Adam. "Up to her, you know," he said. And the following Monday morning Chelsea West was on Thirty-eighth Street in jeans and boots and a ski jacket, drinking coffee with Adam Green and talking about his clothes.

"Sure," she said, "sure. I'm for sale if the price is right."

"I don't mean that. It's not just a business deal. You're made for my clothes!"

She grinned. "Hey, I like your stuff. I even wear it when I'm a civilian."

Implausibly delighted, Adam bundled her off to lunch, confident of his charm.

"It's like making love," he babbled, "the designer and the right model. The instant I saw you there with Dick I knew you were the spirit of what I'm trying to create."

"Well, hooray," she said skeptically, still unsure just how genuine such New York enthusiasm might be, "so long as you're happy."

"I am," he said eagerly, "and we're going to work together."

But they would have to wait awhile. She had already signed

with both Calvin Klein and Adolfo for that season, and then there was a GM commercial to be shot in Baja.

"I'm sorry, Adam," she told him, "but I promise you next season if I'm still in the business and you still want me."

"I will, dammit."

"How can you be sure, how can you know about tomorrow?"

"I know," he said, smiling and absolutely certain. "I know. Tomorrow is always going to be better."

The last week in January Adam and Marc flew to Paris. Heidler again stayed home. "What's the need of me?" he asked. "You two geniuses know everything."

It wasn't true yet, but they were getting there. Forgotten was Marc's anger over Stanley Baltimore and Adam's secretiveness. They'd had it out, a slanging match, complete with threats of firing by Street, of resignation by Adam. The fight was healthy, an explosion between brothers, clearing the air. Business was good. For the first time Majesty's annual sales had exceeded ten million dollars. There were no inquiries by Carl Lazer's accountants. Why should anyone complain when things were going well? Soon, Marc thought, the company would be big enough, there would be enough money, that he could afford to break with Lazer, get out of the laundering business. He hoped it would not be too long. Lincoln Radford's *Mode* magazine was doing a series on garment industry racketeering. Because of the libel laws, few company or individual names were mentioned, but the stories seemed to be describing companies that sounded very much like Majesty Fashions, uncomfortably like men who resembled the shadowy Carl Lazer and even Marc himself.

In Paris he could put such things behind him for a few days. But there were other reminders of New York.

"It's going to be the party of the year!" Adam cried.

They were in his suite at the Plaza Athenée, going over the sketches from the collections and comparing notes. Adam had a new friend, a photographer named Francel, a young Austrian.

Marc sensed that Francel was using Adam, that he wanted very much to get to America, to make it in fashion photography, and that Adam was going to be his passport. But when he suggested this, Adam blustered. "Hey, Marc, do I check out your women? Give me a break. Francel's fun, that's all. This isn't hearts-and-flowers time."

Francel paled in comparison to Adam's excitement about the big party. The *Chambre Syndicale de la Haute Couture,* the trade association of French high fashion, was taking over the palace at Versailles for an evening. It was not the sort of thing the French did very often. "We're too cheap," Brugère admitted. But there were a thousand buyers and designers and manufacturers and press in town for fashion week, and the Chambre considered, soberly, that it was worth doing. And when the French brought themselves to the painful decision that money should be spent, they giddily tossed away restraint: Nureyev would dance, Maxim's would cater, Anne-Aymone Giscard d'Estaing would play hostess, Taittinger would pop the corks, the Garde Républicaine would flank the graveled paths during the *son et lumière,* and fleets of limos would transport the gentry from their hotels into the country.

He and Adam drove out together. The Austrian, Francel, was somehow to make his own way. The country was snow-skimmed and glistening under a cold moon. Lighted houses, far off, seemed warm and beckoning.

Versailles was so vast that even the enormous throng was swallowed up by its great public rooms and long, marbled halls, its winding staircases and parlors, its culs-de-sac and galleries. In the hall of mirrors at midnight, Nureyev danced, the huge, muscled thighs as powerful as ever, the vaguely Asiatic face the same, only the lean midriff having softened with the years. Francel had arrived, and the two men watched, excited into rapt silence, with Marc watching them. Adam was wearing tails, slimly elegant, a man made for this night and this place.

"Happy?" Marc asked after Nureyev had finished and the applause was fading into echoes.

"Yes," Adam said, "oh, yes."

And it was not just the blond boy with him, Marc knew.

Brugère and Jimmy de Bertrand caught sight of Marc.

"*Alors,* not quite Seventh Avenue, then?" Brugère asked, sarcastic as always, but chewing at a fingernail in his nervous delight.

"It sure isn't," Marc conceded. He loved France and took no offense.

Jimmy was happy. This time his collection had been very good and Saint Laurent's slightly off.

"Yves isn't here," he said, competitively smug.

"Perhaps he's ill," Brugère remarked, with undisguised malice.

Marc admired Saint Laurent, so he said nothing. These were the designers, this was how they were. He hoped Adam would always be the way he was, nice, open, generous. He was capable of stupidities, of being victimized by more clever men like Radford or Stanley Baltimore, vulnerable to climbers like this Francel. But how much could he ask of an unlettered boy whose primers were the fashion magazines and *People*?

A tall, graying, but still beautiful man loomed before them.

"Hubert, you go well? You know my American friend, Marc Street."

Marc shook Givenchy's hand. The Frenchman had a soft, pleasant voice. He and Brugère chatted for a moment, and then Givenchy went on, a head taller than most of those in the hall, bowing this way and that, an aristocrat among the peasants, with whom a lovely Frenchwoman with a great name had fallen in love; and in her despair at being ignored, had driven her Alfa Romeo convertible into the Seine one afternoon in an unsuccessful suicide attempt.

Only in Paris . . . only in fashion.

At two in the morning, beginning to feel the champagne, Marc found himself dancing with an attractive woman with a title. He had only roughly caught her name and title when Jimmy de Bertrand introduced them. Adam and Francel had disappeared. The woman was pleasant, delighted at last to be with an American who could speak civilized French. She jabbered away. Marc, taller than she, only half listened as he looked over her head at the spinning kaleidoscope of the magnificent hall, the gowned women and the evening-suited men, designers and models and businessmen and their women, the chandeliers and the mirrors and the liveried footmen standing stiffly at bored attention against the walls. It must have been like this two hundred years before. Only then it was courtiers who watched, a king who danced, a revolution still unimagined.

Then he saw her.

In just a few weeks, she had changed. Her blond hair was no longer bouncing free but braided into a French knot, her skiing tan had paled, the furs and leathers and boots were gone. Now she wore a simple satin sheath of deep blue, not quite navy, that seemed to darken the blue of her eyes. At her neck was a simple gold chain. In a room full of jewels, it glittered; in a room full of exquisite women, she shone, taller and younger and, he thought without any of the reluctance he expected, more beautiful.

When the music had ended he absent-mindedly thanked the Frenchwoman and continued to stare. Then, suddenly, Jimmy de Bertrand and Marc Bohan were at his side. Bohan, the Dior designer, pinch-faced, keen-eyed, followed Street's gaze. "That," Bohan said, "is the most fascinating woman in the room."

Jimmy nodded. "Yes, Marc, but who is she?"

Not knowing which Marc was being addressed, Bohan just shrugged.

Marc Street answered. "She's from America. Her name is Chelsea West."

Jimmy sensed something in his voice. "Do you know her?"

Street shook his head. "No."

Nor did he really want to. Just another gossip-column phony, spoiled and ego-oriented.

At least that was what he told himself as he continued to look at her.

12

Everyone wears a label somewhere, even Jacqueline
Onassis.

Mode, June 6, 1979

Y ou're getting too big, Marc," Carl Lazer grumbled.
"Too big and too noisy."

"I've never seen anything like it," Street confessed.

Lazer frowned. "I don't like surprises, I worry about the unexpected."

They were at a table in the back of a small Jewish deli on
Second Avenue, the kind of place Lazer frequented. Two men sat
at the next table, not eating, but sipping tea from glasses and
watching. Lazer seemed warier now. One of his associates had
been killed the month before. The men were bodyguards.

Marc knew what was bothering Lazer; he was even sympathetic. Majesty Fashions that spring had simply exploded.

The little Seventh Avenue house that had lived modestly for
so long off its faithful line-for-line copies of Chanel suits was
suddenly a fashion powerhouse. Adam had done it. His latest
collection had the editors squealing their delight and, more
substantially, the retail buyers sharpening their pencils and writing orders. Stanley Baltimore, with a candor that made him uneasy, had now come directly to Street with his proposal for a
perfume deal. For two years Majesty had been turning out a line
of unlabeled jeans for women designed by Adam and manufactured by sweat labor in Haiti. Even Adam would admit that they

were just jeans, nothing original. Well cut, sturdily constructed, with denim faded in the style of that season. For the past six months the jeans had an added attraction, a small leather label stitched to the back pocket that read, "Adam."

Now Lazer was complaining about those jeans, and Marc was trying to reassure him.

"A sop, Uncle Carl, that's all it was. Adam was feeling antsy and I told him it was okay to put his damned name on the jeans, if it made him feel better. Well, he did. And now this happens . . ."

"This" was a full-page, front-page photo in *Women's Wear Daily* showing Jackie Onassis emerging from Orsini's on West Fifty-sixth Street in a pair of Adam jeans. The picture had been taken from the rear, with Mrs. Onassis's familiar face frowning in half profile. The "Adam" label was in perfect focus. *People* magazine had picked it up, as had the television networks, and in New York alone Bloomingdale's had ordered ten thousand pairs of Adams for its jeans department.

"Publicity makes me nervous," Lazer said now, absentmindedly stirring his tea and looking bleak.

"I know," Street said, "but it was a fluke. We didn't set out to get it."

Lazer snarled: "Mistakes you don't mean to make are still mistakes."

He wanted a nice, quiet, reasonably profitable garment industry firm to launder his money. He didn't want fame. During the years French Jake ran the company, nothing like this had ever happened.

"And I worry about this homo. It's not as if he were a real man like you or your father."

"Adam's okay."

Lazer shook his head. "Such people are animals," he insisted, "screwing one another in the ass, taking drugs. God knows what. How can you rely on such a person? On his discretion?"

"I can trust Adam," Marc said, trying to restrain anger.

"Maybe. I don't." Left unsaid, the thought: "And I'm not sure I trust you."

Adam was unaware of the arrangements with Carl Lazer. Now that he was a partner in Majesty, he was entitled to know, but Marc didn't want to burden him. It was more important that Adam just keep doing what he was doing, turning their company into something bigger, more important than his father would ever have dreamed. Chanel would have been proud of them. He shrugged off his worries about Lazer, his fleeting guilt over not having leveled with Adam. To hell with it, he thought, these were just the normal growing pains of a booming business.

Certainly Adam wasn't worrying about it. For the first time in his life he was making real money. His salary had soared from fifty thousand dollars to five times that much. And as a minority partner he was sharing for the first time in the profits, profits that dwarfed his salary. The money was important, but so was the celebrity. He felt embarrassed about having met behind Marc's back with Stanley Baltimore, ashamed of having gone begging to Lincoln Radford.

"They're going to need *me* pretty soon," he boasted, "and not the other way around."

He had a new lover, a handsome young Broadway actor who, as his press agent put it, "reeks of Hollywood."

Marc had never interfered in such matters. "Look, it's his business," he told himself. Perhaps this one would be good for Adam. Marc tried to think so.

Even aside from the actor, for Adam life was good. There was an old house in Sandy Lane in Barbados, a nice house with gingerbread facings and a modest backyard, overgrown with lush greens, alive with lizards and great bugs, aswarm with ants, the damp paving stones steaming as the hot sun rose over the palm trees and into the high blue sky. The actor had leased it.

In the mornings they lazed in the yard, enjoying the early cool that would soon enough burn into heat, drinking the sweet, creamed coffee and munching the rolls a young native woman fetched, reading the papers and smoking cheroots, enjoying their suntans and remembering their bodies together in the night.

The actor smiled across at him, a hand dangling. "I never want to go back, you know."

"I do."

"Why, Adam? Isn't this heaven, just as it is? No pressure, no traffic, no goddamned cocktail parties and Manhattan poseurs."

A lizard bounded past, startling Adam, who felt he could live without lizards very nicely.

"Adam? You didn't say why."

"I didn't? Oh, because New York is where tomorrow is."

It sounded corny, he knew, though he meant it. But when he started talking about it, telling the actor of his hopes and dreams, the actor said, sure, he felt the same way, and then carelessly suggested that they have a quick swim in the pool and make love before lunch.

In late May Baltimore had firmed up his proposal for a perfume bearing Adam's name. It was going to make both Adam and Marc very wealthy men if it worked. The deal seemed a good one; Marc's lawyers, who labored over the paperwork, said so. But for Majesty Fashions there was another, higher authority to be consulted. Carl Lazer.

Adam, still suntanned and sleek from Barbados, cocky with celebrity, demanded to know why. "Why the hell do you have to clear things with this guy, Marc? You like the deal, I like the deal, the lawyers say it's okay. Who's this *schmuck* Lazer?"

Street fobbed him off. Lazer was a friend of his father's, a longtime adviser, a man whose counsel he could trust. Adam should get cracking on the new collection and leave the sordid details of business to him. Adam shrugged; well, okay then . . .

It was not that easy. Lazer kept offices on lower Seventh Avenue. The receptionist was a plain, businesslike woman in her middle years. But beyond her there were two men in the anteroom who frisked Marc before he went in. "Sorry," they said, "but you know how it is." Lazer was becoming more cautious in his age, less avuncular.

"I don't like the deal," he said flatly, after Marc explained it and showed him the papers.

"It's a good deal, Uncle Carl. Good for the company, good for me."

Chelsea

"And for that queer partner of yours? I notice his name is on the bottle. Not yours."

"No one gives a damn about me. It's the designer's name that sells. Don't worry, Adam's earning his money."

Lazer grunted.

"Besides," Marc said, "I'm like you. I don't want the publicity. Let him get the press clippings. The company gets the dough."

Lazer pushed his chair back from the desk.

"Marc, you're a good boy. I like you. For that reason let me explain myself. Usually I don't bother to explain. I tell someone go, and he goes. I tell him yes, he does something. No, and he doesn't. With you I take the time and the trouble to explain. Because I like you. Because French Jake was a good man. Understand?"

"Yes."

"Majesty Fashions exists for one purpose and one only: to launder money. Everything else is bullshit. All those years you made a nice living knocking off that French dame, Chanel." He pronounced it "Channel." "People like your coats and suits. You made a dollar, no one bothers you, my money passes through and comes out the other end like it was drycleaned. Everyone's happy. No one gets nosy. Then you hire this fairy of yours and he starts making dresses, jeans, every other damn thing. He gets his name in the paper. Jackie Kennedy gets his name in the paper. Now you want millions of bottles of fifty-dollar-an-ounce perfume in the stores with his name on it. This is smart? Next thing you know, *Fortune* magazine will be doing an article. They'll be around asking questions. They'll want to see your balance sheet. The IRS will come around. What happens then? Your little fancy boy is going to tell them about Uncle Carl Lazer? They'll slap him across his goddamned nelly face once or twice and he'll tell them whatever they want to hear. To listen to this kid squeal we kidnapped the Lindberg baby already."

"Uncle Carl, Adam doesn't know anything. He can't tell them what he doesn't know."

"So you say."

"Uncle Carl, I appreciate everything you've done for me. For my family. But this company has a chance to grow. Legitimately. Why don't we just forget our arrangement? Surely there must be other companies that would love to improve their cash flow and to work with you. Then you wouldn't have to worry about Majesty's getting too big. You wouldn't have to worry about publicity."

Lazer leaned forward. "You think you just walk away in this business, boy? Is that what you think? I'll tell you what I think. I think French Jake would turn in his grave."

Marc said nothing.

"You think about what I said, Mr. Marc Street. Just think hard. And remember, walking away ain't so easy as it sounds."

"I'd walk friendly, Uncle Carl, you wouldn't have to worry about that. And I don't talk. My father didn't down in Washington that time, and I won't now."

Lazer smiled. "That's a good boy. I like to hear that. Of course, some of my associates maybe don't have the feelings I have for you after all these years. Maybe they don't trust you so much."

"I don't care about them, Uncle Carl. I *do* care about you. What you think."

"Good. Then I'll tell you what I think. You walk away from this organization and even if I stood at the window waving good-bye and wishing you happiness, without me you wouldn't be the same. Everyone on Seventh Avenue owes something to somebody. You remember that. And if you walk, it isn't going to be good old Carl Lazer you share a glass tea with. It's somebody you never even heard of, someone who wants a piece of what you got, a bigger piece than I ever took. You get me?"

"Yes."

Lazer made a motion of dismissal with one manicured hand. "Good, then you think about what I said."

"I will," said Street, "but we're going ahead with the perfume deal."

Lazer smiled. "You're like your father."

Marc mistook the smile and the words for something they were not.

"And remember what happened to your father," Lazer said.

Early in June Marc flew to Hong Kong to negotiate a deal for additional jeans capacity with one of the big sweatshop operators. It took three days, long, boozy dinners with his Chinese associates, the usual bribes to be paid, the requisite tour of Kowloon and the New Territories. On the first morning he woke in his posh hotel on The Peak, and pulled open the vertical blinds, only to be confronted with a huge billboard photo of Chelsea West, a champagne glass in her hand, the copy in English and Chinese. Self-consciously, he looked down at his nakedness and drew the blinds, leaving them closed for the rest of his stay, surprised that he could be aroused by a mere photograph.

Back in New York there were other shocks. Old Heidler took him aside when he walked into the office, still jet-lagged.

"Marc, I've been keeping this quiet. But there's trouble."

"Oh?"

"Yes," Heidler said, looking older than Marc ever remembered him, "two of our trucks were hijacked coming in from the Pennsylvania plant with goods. The plant manager in Haiti says there's a strike . . . "

"Sydney, goddammit, there's *never* a strike in Haiti. No one ever—"

"Marc, this time they did. They walked."

"Well."

"And there's more. A break-in here the other night. The watchman got sandbagged and someone tossed a stink bomb into the cutting room. I had to have the place fumigated. A lot of goods was lost."

Suddenly Marc thought of their most precious asset. "Adam? Is he okay?"

Sydney Heidler smiled for the first time. "That boy? Of course he's okay. He's always okay, that poopsie."

"Good. And you were right, Sydney. Let's keep all this as

close to the vest as we can. You didn't call the cops, did you?"

Heidler opened his hands. "Marc, how long have I been on Seventh Avenue?"

"Good old Sydney."

That night Marc called someone who thought he knew where Bobby Swaggerty could be located. If there was going to be a war, he wanted Bobby in uniform.

13

Sports Illustrated claims to be a magazine about sports.
Nonsense. It's a fashion magazine.

Lincoln Radford in *Mode*, July 5, 1979

Chelsea West was back in New York, sharing an apartment with another model, a bouncy brunette from Finland by way of Paris. Her name was Toy. Just Toy.

Chelsea's grandfather had flown east to see her. They had dinner in the bar room of the "21" Club. He hadn't seen her for nearly half a year. Time had not mellowed the old man.

"When are you coming home?" he demanded. And then, before she could answer, "Why not a place of your own? Who's this woman you're living with?"

The questions rained down on her, rattling sensibility. She was relieved when Sheldon Tannen came to the table, solicitously bending toward them, suggesting specialties and taking orders. Will West said he wanted a "damned hamburger, well done." Chelsea ordered grilled sole and a salad.

"What the hell's the matter with you? You on a diet?"

"Grandpa, you can't eat steak and eggs for breakfast and get your picture in *Vogue*. They like those skinny girls."

"Well, I don't. I like you the way you were, all kind of round and blossoming."

A huge smile went along with this. When her grandfather chose sarcasm there was no doubt as to the target. She knew this was love. "Well, I'm still blossoming but I'm not so round. At least, I hope."

Her grandfather grumbled. She was glad he wasn't following through on his questions so much as tossing them out and then moving on to the next point of irritation. This was Will West, the way he was. It terrified some people. She understood; not terrified, but wary. As the waiter prepared their table, she looked around. At a table to the left sat Kissinger and his wife and some people she didn't recognize. The Sinatras had a table. Betty Bacall was there with her latest leading man, the Bacall table diplomatically sited as far as possible from Sinatra's, a man with whom she had once enjoyed a passage at arms. Will West groused and ate and complained about the service and the food and chewed out his granddaughter. He was, she suspected, as famous as any of them. Bette Davis came in, smiling her crooked, knowing smile, huge eyes popping and blinking. And Will West dove into his shrimp cocktail and talked a blue streak about the ranch and the local gossip.

"Had to sack a couple of men. Caught 'em smoking pot. Much of that back here?"

"Oh, no, Grandpa. Not that I've seen." She hoped her face was staying straight.

"Good."

"Though they do drink a little."

"Oh, hell, people are always gonna drink. I hope you don't, Catherine."

"A beer or two, once in a while."

"A couple of beers never hurt anyone, long as you don't drive."

He seemed to have forgotten her mysterious roommate. Toy would hardly have passed the West catechism.

She had met Toy on St. Bart's when the two were working for *Sports Illustrated,* doing the annual swimsuit issue. Toy got drunk that first night. It didn't take much. The barman filled the water glass with vodka and ice and she then banged it twice on the bar and drank it off in a single draft.

"Ha!" she shouted, slamming the empty glass again against the bartop.

After five of them she was carried off to bed. In the morning, over grapefruit and mango on the hotel verandah, she appeared in a bikini bottom and a T-shirt. The T-shirt bore a simple, unmistakable legend: "Let's fuck."

The fashion editor quietly took her aside. "Toy, I don't think you can wear that here in the hotel."

Toy looked puzzled. Then, brightly, she asked: "No T-shirt? Just bare?"

"No, I don't need money," Chelsea told her grandfather. "I'm doing pretty well."

"It's all tied up in trusts," her grandfather said, "but if you need a little more on your allowance . . ."

"No, really, I don't."

"No?" he asked suspiciously. "Then how are you making it?"

"Grandpa," she said patiently, "you know what they pay me a day to pose for pictures?"

"No, what?"

"Twenty-five hundred bucks."

He inhaled. "For one day?"

"Yeah."

"Jesus. It's better than the depreciation allowance."

She grinned. Then his face masked again in doubt.

"You posing naked or something?"

"Grandpa. It's for *Vogue*."

And it wasn't only for *Vogue*. She worked for other magazines, wearing the new clothes, the new cosmetics, the new toothpaste. And for one magazine, *Town & Country,* she wrote about fashion, her own view of it, what was right and what was wrong about the clothes she saw, the clothes she modeled, the clothes she bought.

Her writing style was naïve, unpolished, but not her thinking. There was nothing naïve about how her mind worked.

It was this article that Marc Street saw. And read.

The day he read it, Adam had disappeared.

"Where the hell is he?"

Heidler shook his head. "Marc, you know Adam. He's here, he's there. Like the Scarlet Pimpernel, he's . . . *everywhere*."

The truth was somewhat simpler. Summer had come and the beach had beckoned. Adam was in Provincetown. There was no reason why he shouldn't be, Marc told himself. The boy worked with a savage intensity, sixty, seventy hours a week when a collection was in the balance. Why shouldn't he take some time off to relax, to recharge? Still, Marc felt an irrational resentment. He'd had to fly to Haiti on a Saturday morning to help settle the labor dispute. That in itself was simple enough: he bribed a couple of labor union officials. Five thousand apiece and the plant resumed merrily producing Adam jeans. Marc was reasonably confident that none of the money would ever find its way into the pockets of the workers. The money wasn't important to him, and the stoppage had been brief, if inconvenient. The puzzle remained. Had Carl Lazer's tentacles reached out to put pressure on a recalcitrant protégé?

Swaggerty thought so. Marc had found him.

Bobby was living in the Algonquin in a good-sized suite, with a tall brunette with a cigarette dangling from her lips, and a cocky grin on Bobby's hard, still boyish face suggested affluence.

"Yeah, Marc, I'm doing great. You too, what I hear."

The girl was sent, sulking, into the night on a transparent errand so they could talk.

"Nice, huh? Met her in Vegas. A dancer. She went mad for me and I decided to give her a break, bring her to the big city."

"You're all heart, Swaggerty."

"You know it."

They sprawled in easy chairs and drank Scotch. Swaggerty talked about himself.

"I got steady work. There's certain jobs these Mafia goombahs won't do for themselves. They're all going legit. They don't wanna ruin their manicures. The old days, they did the head-breaking theirselves. No more. They hire out the work. Me and some of the other Westies rent them the muscle. It's a shame. The wops used to be tough, but the drug business spoiled them. They got so much money now they're afraid of messing up and getting busted. So guys like me get the work."

Marc wondered about a red-haired girl, Bobby's cousin.

"Penny? She married a cop. Lives in Huntington. Got a bunch of kids." Bobby refilled their glasses.

"Look, I've got a problem."

"Business or personal?" Bobby asked, suddenly the professional, listening and taking mental notes.

Marc told him about their troubles, the hijackings, the strike in Haiti, the stink bombs, all of it.

"Who's doing it?" Bobby asked.

"I dunno. But it might be Carl Lazer."

Swaggerty whistled. "Hey, that's heavy stuff. How'd you get tangled up with Carl Lazer?"

Marc laughed. "Uncle Carl. That's what I call him. Uncle Carl."

Bobby looked bleak. "Uncle Carl, like you call him, kills people."

Street sobered and told him about the laundered money, about Lazer's fear that they were getting too big, too important, too well known. And about how he told Lazer he wanted to break away and to free-lance.

"But you didn't go to the cops."

"No," Marc said, "I came to you."

"Good," Bobby said. The half-empty glass had been put aside and he was all efficiency and economy now, nothing wasted. "Lemme see what I can find out. The guineas and the Jews hate one another. They're forever fighting over turf. That's where the Westies come in. We hit one of Lazer's guys a couple of months ago."

Marc nodded. That was what had Lazer so jumpy.

Bobby got up. "The chick'll be back. Lemme look around and I'll call you. You done right, Marc, not bringing the cops in. Lazer's probably got his sources at Headquarters. He'd know as soon as the cops did."

Marc gave him his office number and the unlisted number at the apartment. "I appreciate this, Bobby."

"What the hell, Marc, what the hell."

Then, as Marc started for the door, Bobby grabbed his arm. "Just a minute." He went into the bedroom and then re-emerged with a cloth bundle. It was a gun and an old leather holster.

"Take this with you, Marc. It's got no numbers on it. A .38 Smith & Wesson, military and police special, four-inch barrel. You probably couldn't hit the room from inside with it, but if anyone tries to rough you up, whack him with the barrel and he'll pay attention."

Street considered saying no. Instead, he took the bundle and, feeling self-conscious, stuffed it into the waistband of his trousers. He could feel it there, cold and heavy, as he drove across town in the back of a cab. He shouldn't have taken it. But he had. Well, he could always throw the damned thing away and Bobby would never know the difference.

It did not occur to Marc that in a small, tentative way, French Jake's son was going home.

14

Some people believe the business of fashion is clothes.
Others insist it is giving parties.

Mode, November 20, 1979

On the last Sunday of July Percy Savage, the public relations man for the house of Nina Ricci, gave his annual garden party for the buyers attending the Paris couture collections. Percy was a tall, ginger-haired Australian who invested a good deal of imagination in these parties, which Robert Ricci paid for. When Street arrived, a nude black boy, his skin oiled, bowed and ushered him toward the rear of the ground-floor apartment, which led out into a pleasant, flowered garden.

There were already perhaps a hundred people there, drinking and chatting in the sun, turning occasionally to observe and remark on Percy's latest novelty, a tiny donkey saddled with two large wicker baskets, one on each flank, filled with fresh fruits and sweets and raw vegetables. The donkey was supposed to wander about the garden so that Percy's guests could pluck an apricot or a stalk of celery or a bunch of grapes from the baskets as it ambled past.

This was not the way it worked out. For reasons unknown to anyone but the animal itself, the donkey became sexually aroused and tried, braying and snorting, to mount several women, who backed away shrieking while cucumbers and oranges tumbled from the baskets.

"Oh my God!" Savage said, running to corral the donkey, which promptly attempted to kick him.

Both men and women were moving quickly toward the French doors that led indoors and to safety.

"*Ce n'est pas drôle*," an indignant woman in a straw hat murmured as she pushed past Marc to get away, her skirt smeared with the donkey's saliva.

"Hell, it's only a damn donkey, for God's sake," a clear American voice rang out, and coming across the lawn was Chelsea West, followed by a pale young man.

"Here, hold this," Chelsea ordered, shoving a champagne glass at her companion, "while I get hold of the damned bridle."

Marc watched as, with a strong tug and then another, she wrapped the rope around the donkey's neck, yanked the animal into a corner, and forced it under control.

"Chelsea," Savage shouted, "I love you."

There was a smatter of applause from those still in the garden, and when the naked boy led the donkey away in disgrace, Marc started toward her, wanting to say something, but she had already turned back to her escort, laughing together in an intimacy that shut him out.

She was in Paris to model the collections for *Vogue*. He saw her at the shows and around town. Her hair was shorter now, but it still shone. One night at La Coupole, where he and Brugère were dining, she was a couple of tables away, with four or five Frenchmen, all of them talking rapidly and with gestures, trying to make an impression. He could hear her laugh, clear and young as school bells. For an instant, he thought she was gazing at him thoughtfully.

The year progressed gloriously. Adam's newest collection was again a smash, and Majesty and Marc groaned under the weight of fresh orders.

On Monday of Thanksgiving week Pauline Trigère asked Marc to dinner at her apartment on Park Avenue. Lincoln Radford's *Mode* had just named him one of the year's leading "fashion executives," and Trigère, a gracious woman, put competitive rivalry aside. Chelsea West was there.

It was raining, a chill November rain, and she was wearing a classic old camel hair polo coat, a preppy scarf, knee socks, a Fair Isle sweater, and a kilt skirt.

"My God," Trigère said from behind dark glasses, "you look like a schoolgirl."

"No," Chelsea said solemnly, "I was thrown out."

They had drinks in the library, and then dinner was at four or five tables set up in the dining room and the living room, six people at each. Marc was at Chelsea's table, directly across from her, flanked by a woman who ran the American Theatre Wing and by Moss Hart's widow, Kitty Carlisle. The conversation was intelligent, informed, but he found himself looking at Chelsea, watching her eyes, trying to hear what it was she was saying to a gray-haired man that had him smiling. After dinner a plump ad agency executive sat at the piano and played old show tunes. Outside the rain slashed against the windows. It was nice being inside, feeling the wine and listening to the music. Marc found himself sitting on the floor next to a chair in which Chelsea sat.

"I liked what you said in *Town & Country*," he said.

"Oh yeah? Thanks. I was afraid it was going to come out sort of pretentious. I mean, who the hell am I to be defining fashion?"

"Why not? You wear clothes beautifully."

"Ha, you mean *this?*" She looked down at her knee socks and rain-dulled loafers.

"You could wear overalls and look fine," he said. "And I've seen you doing the collections. In Paris."

She looked thoughtful. "Yeah, I remember you. Weren't you at La Coupole one night? Sure, I remember."

He felt an irrational pleasure.

When the evening ended, a butler stood in the foyer handing out the coats. By some mix-up he held out a sable coat to Chelsea and, laughing, she shrugged into it. Behind her Simone and Bill Levitt waited, amused. Mrs. Levitt took Chelsea's polo coat and preppy scarf.

"I must say, Simone," said her husband, "it's very youthful."

The four of them went down in the elevator together.

Chelsea looked down at the coat, hugging it to herself. "You better get this back before we hit the street," she said, "or you're going to have a hell of a time getting it back at all."

Laughing, they exchanged coats in the lobby, and the Levitts went out into the rain to cross the avenue to their flat.

"Drink?" Marc asked when they were alone.

She turned to look at him. "Thanks, but I've got a late date."

"I wanted to ask you where you learned to lasso donkeys."

"Were *you* there that day?" she asked.

"Yes." He was disappointed that she didn't remember that as well, and she heard it in his voice.

"Hey, this isn't a brush-off. I really *do* have a date. Give me a raincheck."

"I'll call." A cab splashed up to the curb, and when some people got out he held the door for her.

"Good night," she said, looking up at him in the rain, drops running down her face.

Damp and shining in the cold rain, she looked more beautiful now than she ever had on the cover of *Vogue*. But when he phoned the Ford model agency the next day and left a message, it went unanswered. He tried twice more, and then it was Thanksgiving weekend and he saw her name in Eugenia Sheppard's column as being a houseguest at some rich man's party on Lyford Cay.

He threw himself into work. The deal with Baltimore was going well, with a line of cosmetics bearing Adam's name rushed into the stores in time for the big Christmas shopping season. The perfume itself would take longer. Marc understood this. Chanel used to talk about perfume, about how long it took to blend the flowers and the essential oils and the fixatives and to get one of the highly paid noses to sniff all the permutations and to pronounce one of them *right*. The bottle had to be right, too. The perfume business was replete with stores of great scents badly bottled that had died on the retail shelves.

"How did you get a line of cosmetics out so soon?" he asked Stanley Baltimore during one of their meetings.

Baltimore laughed. "You think I created a whole new cosmetics line in three months? Don't be naïve. I just put Adam's name on the same shit I've been peddling for years."

"You're kidding."

"The hell I am. You think women know one face powder from another? You think there's a big difference in nail polish, except for the color? My factories put out maybe three hundred shades of polish. I just took two dozen shades Adam liked the look of, and off we went." He paused. "The packaging took a little while. That's why we're late on deliveries to the West Coast. I. Magnin and J. W. Robinson are sore, but listen, we did a hell of a job in most markets. You and your boy Adam are going to have quite a Christmas."

When he told Adam, the designer just shrugged. "I guess that's how it's done," he said. Then: "While you were there, did he piss in the sink?"

Baltimore was right about Christmas. The orders and money poured in. It had been too late to mount any sort of a serious ad campaign in the fashion magazines, but television was full of commercials, sleek, slick, compelling. Adam's name, Adam's face—almost nothing said about the products. No one complained. *Women's Wear Daily* reported the week before Christmas that the Adam cosmetic line had been one of the most successful new launches in seasons.

Adam preened and opened negotiations to buy a co-op apartment in the building on Fifth Avenue where Jackie Onassis lived.

"Why not?" he told friends. "She wears my jeans. Why shouldn't we be neighbors?"

His latest boyfriend grinned. "Adam, you're a genius."

"Yes," he said thoughtfully, "you may be right."

Manchester Industries came calling. Marc flew to Greenville for a daylong meeting. The recognition value of Adam's name had impressed them. Market research indicated that after Calvin Klein, Ralph Lauren, and Bill Blass, his was now the best-known and most favorably viewed identity in American fashion. Manchester had excess capacity in its domestic plants. What would Mr. Street think about their putting out a collection of sheets and pillowcases next fall with an Adam label?

"I dunno. Adam's pretty damned busy already. We're not really a very big company, you know. This isn't a team effort. It's one guy who's working sixty hours a week right now. It's very flattering to be asked, but I don't want to run Adam into the ground."

One of the Manchester executives laughed. The others turned toward him, annoyed.

The senior executive of the group waited until the stir had subsided. "I don't think you understand, Mr. Street. We appreciate how busy your designer is, the demands on his time. That's the beauty part of a license deal such as we'd like you to consider. Adam wouldn't have to do very much. We would work up some designs, fly them to New York for his approval, and we'd go on-stream with those he selects. Manchester would do the work. He would supply his name and, of course, cooperate with our promotional efforts in advertising and marketing the line."

"You mean he wouldn't actually have to design anything," Marc said, wanting to be sure.

The executive shook his head, and in a quiet, courteous southern voice, he said: "Adam won't have to do a goddamned thing except spend the money."

Marc went down the hall to Adam's studio. As usual, a couple of good-looking young men were hanging around, drinking Tab and gossiping with Adam's secretary, a Bryn Mawr girl someone had talked him into hiring, who never, to Marc, seemed to do anything.

"Let's talk," Marc said. Pointedly, he closed the door behind them.

"Sure."

He outlined the Manchester proposal. Adam was beaming before he was halfway through.

"Well?" Marc asked.

"What do you mean, 'well'? Of course I want to do it," Adam said.

"It's a lot of money," Marc admitted.

"Of course it's a lot of money. You think I'd do it for nothing?"

"No, Adam," Marc said slowly, "I don't think you'd do it for nothing."

There were other license deals, none particularly demanding, all profitable. Lingerie, pantyhose, a line of wool-and-polyester-blend sweaters, scarves. When a new Adam bra was announced, Lincoln Radford noted maliciously in *Mode* that Adam had once been quoted as remarking that he had no interest in designing for any woman who needed a bra.

"The hell with him, Adam," Marc advised when an infuriated Adam stormed into his office with the offending copy of *Mode*.

"The *hell* with him? Easy for you to say. You're not the one he's making sound like a hypocrite."

"Hey, Adam, a year or two ago he couldn't spell your name. Now you're in every issue he puts out."

"The bastard."

There was more of this. And the deals continued to come in, the money came in. None of *that* seemed to bother Adam. And Marc found himself wondering if Adam wasn't the one who was right. Why not take the money and run? Wasn't that the essence of the business? Why should Marc agonize if Manchester and Stanley Baltimore and the XYZ bra company did all the work and sent them checks that didn't bounce?

One night, just before Christmas, with Adam in California, Marc stood in the living room of his apartment on Madison Avenue, staring out of the darkened room into the lighted street, at the buses and cabs rolling past, the shoppers hurrying in the cold night, the partygoers hurrying to wherever it was happiness would be found, and thinking about a life that for all its rewards seemed more and more lonely. Of course, there were women he could have. He had money, a certain amount of power, the necessary connections. In this business he gave employment to some of the most beautiful women in the world. He could, to put it on a practical basis, ask something in return. But he held back. All very well for garment manufacturers to use their power to get laid. It was not Street's way. He glanced at the telephone, white and mocking. All he need do was pick it up and inside of an hour a woman would be here, a beautiful, eager, teenaged mannequin with legs and a soft mouth and a magnificent, responsive body, ready to respond, ready to do whatever he wished. It was all so easy, all so impossible.

There was a John Wayne shoot-'em-up on television, and he poured himself a Scotch and turned it on. He half watched, wondering where Chelsea West was spending Christmas. The phone sat there, untouched.

15

A "walker" is a wonderful convenience. Who else takes a
woman to lunch, tells her the gossip, and is satisfied with a
kiss on the cheek?

Mode, December 19, 1979

Everyone has a million dollars," Adam exulted, "and if
you don't, it's in the mail."

He reveled in their success, in the sheer torrent of money,
spendable, tangible, wonderful; a child for whom Christmas
morning had brought every toy on the list. Street did not share his
joy.

"Sometimes," he confessed to Sydney Heidler, "the money
frightens me."

Heidler shook his head. "Marc, money is why we work. The
reward."

"This much, Sydney?"

The old man smiled. "The way Adam spends, can there be
too much?"

It simply poured in, stunning Street, delighting Adam,
eventually causing even Heidler to shake his head in amazement
and mutter cautionary wisdom about salting some away against
bleak futures. Five years ago Majesty's sales had been under five
million dollars. Then, suddenly, they hit thirty. This year, fifty.
Next year they had a shot at a hundred million dollars.

"God knows, Marc," Heidler said, almost in awe as he pored
over computer printouts. "It's a money machine."

Adam's trouble began innocently enough.

"I'm too skinny," Adam announced one morning as the two men sat in his studio drinking black coffee.

"Who the hell says?"

"Everyone."

That meant some new lover, Marc was sure.

"I'm going to build myself up, really work out. An hour every day. I'll feel better, look better, work better."

"You'll be a goddamned wonder."

"Well, I *will*."

A Nautilus machine, rings, parallel bars, and gym mats were installed the following week in what had been a sample room off his studio. Adam used them faithfully.

"Won't he hurt himself, Marc," Heidler asked, his face creased in concern, "such a skinny fellow doing all that jumping and lifting and sweating?" Heidler who never exercised in his life.

Street laughed. "Let him go. He'll get bored soon enough and find another toy."

When they went to Paris Adam wondered aloud if he should take the Nautilus machine along.

"It's really helping. I hate like hell to lose my edge now."

Marc stared at him. The machine weighed half a ton and was bolted down. "Muscles, for a week in Paris you can do push-ups."

His next toy was a racehorse. "They have these claiming races, see, and you know in advance how much a horse is going to cost, and if it wins, you can buy it for that. And it's not that expensive. Maybe five thousand bucks."

"Adam, you don't know anything about horses."

"I'm learning. I read the *Racing Form* now every morning."

The horse he bought, for seven thousand dollars, went lame in its first race.

Then there was politics. "You never voted in your life," Marc exploded, "and now you're backing candidates for President?"

"Just because I don't vote doesn't mean I'm not interested. It's just that until now no candidate ever got me involved. Bunch of old farts."

The candidate was an ambitious young senator from Arizona with a firm jaw, a mop of carefully arranged unkempt hair, a wealthy, slightly older wife, and a store of inspirational lines. Adam gave a fund-raiser for him at his apartment one evening. Perhaps forty people were there, New York fat cats gathered out of curiosity, a few party regulars, the rest of them, like Marc, bludgeoned by Adam into coming.

"Here's my check for a hundred bucks, Adam, and that's it."

"Marc, don't be so cheap. America's future depends on new leadership, new directions."

When the senator had finished, Marc grabbed Adam's arm. "He keeps talking new and I keep hearing old. Every idea he has comes out of Jack Kennedy and 1960."

Adam looked hurt. The senator had made a fuss over him, and he was flattered, grateful.

Something else that was new to both of them were private clients, wealthy women who bought their clothes wholesale, who insisted on private fittings, patronizing the handful of American designers *WWD* or *Vogue* or Lincoln Radford had canonized that season. Seventh Avenue had long since become hardened to women who insisted that clothes weren't worth wearing unless they could be gotten wholesale. Majesty Fashions went along with the pack, insisting only that the clothes be taken out in unmarked shopping bags so that retail stores couldn't complain about unfair competition. What was new was the sort of women who had now discovered Majesty. And Adam. These women were *important.*

"It's incredible," Adam enthused one afternoon as Nan Kempner left the studio. "She knows more than I do."

If this was ingenuous, it was also inaccurate. Mrs. Kempner didn't know as much as he did about fashion; but she knew with a chill certainty the clothes that were right for her. She knew her own body, her chiseled, Aztec face, her pale blondness. Adam was hardly stupid. He learned from women like her, and not only about clothes. Chanel always said it. You design the clothes for the women who live the life; no one designs for hermits.

Adam started going to lunch with such women, dining at the corner banquettes of pearl-gray restaurants where the wine cards were bound in leather and it was considered bad form to speak

English to the waiters. His own wardrobe, until now casual, easy, American—jeans, sweaters, loafers, and tennis shirts—came under the influence of these women. His suits now came from Poole's in London, his shoes from Lobb, his shirts from Turnbull & Asser, his ties from Hermès and from narrow shops in Jermyn Street. He was developing a style that had no links to his hard, mysterious early life in Brooklyn; he was becoming a different sort of person. He was no longer a boy.

No longer, Street sometimes and uncharitably thought, so simple, or so nice. The actress Marcy Tone came in for a fitting. They all gushed over her classic blond beauty, Adam most enthusiastically of all. A few months later, over the dinner table at a party given by Mary Lasker, her name came up, and Adam remarked that, yes, he did some of her clothes.

"She's so lovely," a woman remarked, "she must be just dreamy to design for."

Adam laughed. "Dreamy? Well, if you think a flat chest and heavy thighs are dreamy, maybe so."

"That was pretty nasty," Street told him later over the brandy. "Marcy's a good girl and a loyal customer. Why trash her like that?"

And Adam snarled back: "It's a designer's job to make aesthetic judgments. Nobody's perfect. It's because I *know* her flaws that I can do something about them. She looks good in my clothes, doesn't she?"

Other women came to stand in his studio in their bras and panties, smoking cigarettes and sipping coffee or wine, chatting with Adam about the affairs of the day, the latest scandal, the brilliant new play previewing on Broadway, the next big film, whatever tattle was being retailed about town. All this while Adam literally knelt at their feet with a mouthful of pins, adjusting hemlines and trying to sound as clever as he believed them to be.

Not all these women were vapid or silly or vicious. And he did learn. He was a quick study. He'd not had Paris, Chanel, or a good prep school and a year at Cornell.

"I'm learning on the job," Adam told himself defensively. And it was not far from the truth. For the first time he was buying books. Not that he read many of them, but he tried to read the book reviews in the *Times*. People talked about books over dinner and during cocktails, and he felt left out. He had always gone to galleries. He liked pictures, and as a designer he had a sense of color, of form, of composition. Now he snapped up the art magazines, cramming himself full of wisdom about pictures he already knew empirically. He got on the first-night list of Broadway producers and became something of a figure on the aisle. Publicists invited him to private screenings of the new movies, to the latest disco's unveiling, to wine tastings and new bistros and galas at the Plaza and the Waldorf and the Pierre. Wealthy women asked him for country weekends and small, intimate Park Avenue dinners, begged him to lend his name to their committees, insisted that he sit next to them, share his thoughts, listen to their confidences, hover and attend and amuse. Adam appeared to enjoy it, but sometimes, late in the day in his studio, Marc saw his eyes give way to something that looked like desperation. Adam no longer belonged only to Majesty: he belonged to the world.

A shallow tutelage, but as Adam began gradually drawing away from Marc, it was all the tutelage he had. And with it came the money, always more money, the sense of professional triumph, and the fame. He wasn't perfect, he knew, he wasn't really happy, but he was famous. Out of that he tried to extract a facsimile of contentment.

16

Never ask who owns what on Seventh Avenue. One day
you might find out.

Mode, January 2, 1980

Paramount asked Adam to do the costumes for a big new
film starring Robert Redford, both the women's clothes and the
men's. He broke the news to Street over dinner. Marc nodded,
unenthusiastic, realizing that this would be time stolen from Majesty.

"How much are they paying you?" he asked after a moment.

"Does it matter?" Adam bubbled. "Think of the publicity."

"I am," Marc said. And he assumed that so too was Carl
Lazer.

Forbes magazine had discovered Majesty Fashions. The reporter had called Street and asked him to sit still for an interview.
At first, Marc refused.

"Okay," the reporter warned, "then we'll do the story without you. Your competitors will give us most of what we need. But
you really ought to cooperate. You can get your own point of view
across, and it'll be a better story."

Street recognized the ploy as standard, but in the end he
went along. At least this way he could exercise some degree of
control over what they would write about Adam, about him,
about their no-longer-little company. But there was no control
over Adam.

"Jesus, Adam, you gave them everything but the combination to the safe."

The designer looked hurt. "I thought the story was very favorable. It said we were the hottest house on Seventh Avenue. What's so wrong with that?"

Marc exploded. "For chrissakes, you told them our sales volume, you told them how much you made, you gave them the profits, you told them what percentage you own. You're not stupid, Adam—don't you recognize the need for discretion?"

Adam turned sulky. "I told them because I'm *proud* of what we've done. Aren't *you?*" Marc stared, hot and angry. "Calvin Klein made sixteen million bucks last year. Calvin himself, not the company. Lauren makes nearly as much. Saint Laurent is rich. You tell me Cardin's a lousy businessman, but he's making millions on license deals. Valentino has a palace in Rome and a villa on Capri and an apartment here. For God's sake, Marc, these days fashion is better than owning a seat on the Exchange, and all you do is bitch. I'm making us both rich, and you go around wringing your hands like a cheated wife on the soaps."

Marc struggled for control. "I'm proud of what we've done, most of it. But not these new license deals. We do nothing but cash the checks. That's bullshit, that's stealing. I want the money, but I want to work for it. I suppose that's primitive, but it's how I feel."

Adam smirked. "Your old pal Swaggerty, your boyhood chum, the gangster? You think he's just swell, but you gripe about perfectly legitimate business arrangements with great corporations, with Baltimore, with the Manchester people."

Street resisted the temptation to slap him. Digging fingernails into his palms, he said, "Adam."

"Yes?" Adam said, sullen, bitter.

"Look, we mean something to each other. Don't ignore what we have."

"You resent me," Adam persisted, "you resent my success."

"Oh, that's stupid," Marc said, shaking his head, wondering how to end this. Now Adam paused as well, both men realizing that it had gone too far, neither wishing to be the first to capitulate. Finally Marc said, "Okay, let's drop it. I guess we can live with the license deals."

"I certainly can," Adam said, still pugnacious but calmer now.

Both knew that they were only papering over their differences, that they would go on earning money for doing nothing, just selling their names. Carl Lazer and French Jake weren't the only gangsters, Marc Street concluded. He and Adam had joined their ranks.

It was Adam's way to forget unpleasantries, putting them rapidly behind him. Worrying about the past didn't solve anything; it only curdled the future. And what was to come was surely going to be even better. Chelsea was working for him now, Eileen Ford having extorted a ransom and cleared some time on Chelsea's schedule, and she was modeling for Adam's new collection.

"My instincts were right," he declared, "I knew you'd be perfect."

"My grandpa might argue that," she said.

"I mean it."

He watched, sketchbook in hand, while a tailor and two fitters basted sleeves to the shell of a suit jacket she wore over nothing but a bodystocking, her long legs firmly planted on the studio floor, never moving, never flinching, while they pushed and prodded and pinned. Like so many young designers, Adam worked from sketches, with technicians cutting, sewing, and fitting. He restricted himself to checking their work, to ordering minuscule changes and making final adjustments. Most models ignored what was being built on their bodies, gossiping and chewing gum and talking about last night. Chelsea was different. "Shouldn't the armhole be higher?" she asked thoughtfully.

"Yes, yes," Adam said, "it's got to be higher. Get it snug!"

"Yes," she said when the pins had been reset, "that's much better. Now it feels right."

After a week of working with her he knew he had more than

a model. He had a new right hand, a new inspiration, a mascot. Street knew that she was in the building and stayed away. He never interfered with Adam's choice of models, and her snub of him after Pauline Trigère's dinner still rankled.

Adam took her to dine at Si Newhouse's home. Hardy Amies was the *plat du jour,* telling wonderful stories about London, the Royal Family, and stuffy old Hartnell, who made the Queen's dowdy dresses, how Princess Margaret was now known, privately, as "Her Drear," and about the young English designers who were standing fashion on its elegant ear. "They roam the Kings Road, Chelsea," Hardy said, "wearing the most extraordinary costumes, hair chopped short and dyed green and purple, safety pins punched through their cheeks and their earlobes, teeter-tottering along on six-inch heels, mini-skirts to the crotch, mesh stockings, sequined blouses by day, tattoos and fringed shawls. They call it . . . they call it 'punk.' "

Newhouse, who owned *Vogue* and tracked trends, seemed to be taking mental notes. Chelsea laughed. "Hey, sounds swell to me."

Amies raised eloquent eyebrows. "If I had the temerity," he said, "I'd tell the Queen Mum to go 'punk.' It's all the rage."

Adam laughed with the rest of them. A few years ago he was reading about men like Hardy Amies in magazines like *Vogue.* Now he was having dinner with Amies in the house of *Vogue*'s proprietor, with the most famous cover girl in America at his side. Such things were important, they were accomplishments, they mattered. Why couldn't Marc understand?

As Marc had expected, it didn't take Lazer long to react to the *Forbes* article with its embarrassment of intimate financial details. Marc was again summoned, again frisked. He wondered what Lazer would have said if he'd brought Swaggerty's gun.

There was no wrangling, as there had been with Adam. Lazer was businesslike, stolid behind his desk.

"We will be sending you no more moneys," he said. "The time has come to terminate our arrangements."

Though there was no menace in his voice, Marc's relief mingled with other emotions. "No, I understand. I wasn't surprised when you sent for me."

"We couldn't continue. Not with these newspapermen living in your pocket and that homo spilling his guts to them. It was an impossible situation."

"Mr. Lazer, I'm not arguing. You're right." Instinctively, he knew it was time to stop calling him "Uncle Carl."

"Yes," Lazer said, "you don't launder money in Macy's window."

"Of course not."

This was all very polite, but Marc felt it was somehow incomplete. Lazer was dismissing him, but he wanted to say something.

"Mr. Lazer, there's something else."

Lazer mistakenly thought there was about to be a final appeal. "No, there's nothing more to say. I've decided."

Marc shook his head and put his hands on the edge of the big desk. "Mr. Lazer, I just want to thank you. That's all."

The old gangster looked surprised.

"You were faithful to my father's memory. You helped me and my mother. You let me run the company and you left us alone."

Lazer sat there for a moment, and then he stood up and extended his hand. "I wish you well, young man. And I don't think I have to say anything to you about the need to be discreet, do I?"

"Of course not. The past is sealed."

When he left, rejoicing quietly and secretly, hugging himself with pleasure, Marc barely noticed the men in Lazer's anteroom, the men with whom he would never again have to deal.

"Free at last, free at last!" he exulted to himself, consciously echoing Martin Luther King, Jr. Majesty was legit, the money laundering was ended, his final links to crime were severed. He had Adam to thank for it, his flamboyance, his homosexuality, his loose mouth. But what did it matter? Lazer was forever behind him. Then, chilled, he recalled what French Jake always knew— that in this business good-byes were not necessarily farewells.

17

Rosalynn Carter is not, one is forced to conclude, a woman terribly interested in fashion. Or good at it.

Mode, January 23, 1980

A White House invitation pointed up the widening chasm between Adam and Marc. Adam had been invited to a formal presidential dinner honoring American artists and American art. Skeptical, Street asked, "And where was the First Lady when you and I were still doing line-for-line, back when we needed her?"

"Don't be so cynical." Adam looked pained. "People didn't know then who I was. Now they do."

It had become "I" and "me" instead of "we" and "us." Sensibly, Marc found it amusing. There never lived a designer to whom egomania was a stranger. Wertheimer owned the Maison Chanel, and no one outside of Switzerland ever heard of him crouching there in Zurich counting his money while Coco posed for the pictures. Bergé did the same thing with Saint Laurent, and Brugère with Jimmy de Bertrand. Marc accepted that as they matured, as the company grew, as people put themselves out to be nice to Adam, it was natural that they grow apart, that simple relationships would grow complex. Still, Marc yearned for what they were losing, for what they once meant to each other, for those evenings when two young men ate pasta and breadsticks and drank cheap red wine in dingy joints in Little Italy, sometimes alone, sometimes with Adam's latest number or Marc's new, transient girl. Still, even with his newfound pride and importance, Adam—forever searching for love, never surrendering to disillusion—would come to Marc, his face freshly alive, as he did now.

"His name's Peter Feeley, he's an Irish kid from Boston, and he's in law school. At Fordham. His old man's a fireman and they don't have a nickel and he's smart and works like a dog and he's just a great kid."

Marc made the usual dubious crack. "If he were Jewish he'd be perfect."

"Well, he is, damned near. Perfect, I mean."

But for once Adam wasn't exaggerating. Feeley *was* a good kid, blond and nice-looking, of course, but solid, intelligent, independent. Adam had met him at the theater, something experimental and Off-Broadway, and had invited him to a party given by the producers. Feeley had gone along out of curiosity. He knew who Adam was, but didn't seem terribly impressed. Law school students whose fathers work for the Boston Fire Department don't have a lot of money to throw around, and a free drink and canapés weren't to be snubbed. Afterward, they went back to Peter's place, a shabby furnished room up near Columbia on Morningside Heights, and sat talking until dawn, surrounded by books and cheap prints and drinking Cokes.

"We just talked," Adam told Marc, "that's all. It was strange, but in a way that's all I wanted, to talk. He's very political about being gay. It's new for him and he gets all excited about civil rights." Adam sounded puzzled. "And he's not sure he's ready for a relationship."

"But you'll try to convince him," Marc said.

Adam grinned. "I just might."

It took longer than either of them, or perhaps all three of them, expected.

Adam started coming to work late. "We were talking," he explained. Marc no longer had to ask with whom, but he began to worry. Was Feeley a tease? Would he use Adam for his money and celebrity and then leave him—or leave him disillusioned? Finally, Marc realized it wasn't that way at all. The boy had a casual confidence, an inner calm, that Adam—and Marc—found extraordinary in one so young.

"I like his frown," Marc admitted, "it's a thoughtful look, as if he's really listening. Maybe even thinking."

"I know," Adam said, not bridling at implied criticism, but taking warmth from Street's approval.

He and Peter were sleeping together now, the long nights of talk carrying them both to something more than the dawn. Adam was no longer simply tired when he arrived at the office; he was smug, pleased, satisfied. He didn't have to tell Marc; his face, his slim, relaxed body communicated joy. Feeley was what he had been waiting for.

Peter was not only carrying a full academic load at law school but working two nights a week as a waiter in a Columbus Avenue pub, a job he refused to quit.

"But you don't *have* to work," Adam argued, "it's silly. You need some time to yourself. I've got the bread."

Feeley shook his head. "That's the point, it's *your* bread. Don't worry, I'm used to it."

"Stubborn," Adam muttered, but liking him all the more for it.

Nor would he move into Adam's place on Fifth Avenue. "This room's fine. It's me. It's all I need."

Adam tried to dress him. "Don't be stupid. Why buy when you can get it free?"

Feeley grinned at him. "Adam, don't you realize that being Irish Catholic is even worse than Jewish guilt? You do enough already that my conscience is bothering me. Give me a break!"

They settled into a placid, domestic arrangement, the boy coming over to Adam's apartment each evening after class, books under his arm, walking through Central Park, a solid-looking, athletic kid with straight, sun-bleached hair, a slightly pug nose, clear blue eyes, and a pleasant mouth. Adam found himself going home early from the office to stand in one of the windows facing the park, straining to see him come, much as a parent might watch a child returning from school. Even an unfashionable law school like Fordham imposes a heavy academic burden, and night after night Feeley pulled himself away to work at his books.

"But you've got to, Adam, there's no way of sliding away from it. You do the work. There's no shortcut. I want to be a good lawyer, and this is how you get there."

Adam resented the time lost but respected Feeley for his dedication. Night after night he sat there, curled up on the couch or propped against bedroom pillows, watching silently as Feeley pored over books and notes, scribbled comments in margins, leaned back to think, and plunged again into the books. Adam sat and watched, listened to his breathing and the starchy sound of the pencil. He was ten years older. But which was the parent, which the child?

"Adam?"

"Yes?"

"In contracts they ask about intent. When you and Mr. Street began working together, what did you expect of him? And him of you? Do you remember? Did you ever talk about it?"

Adam pondered for an instant. "Just that I would design the clothes and he'd sell them. Why?"

Usually Adam had no answers. The boy posed questions Adam had never asked. He had never been analytical; Feeley was all analysis. And when Adam threw up his hands and confessed this, Peter was sympathetic.

"Don't worry about it. You're so rich you don't need this stuff. Or if you ever do, there are a dozen Wall Street firms that will do it for you. I was just bouncing it off you because you were here."

Not since he had first gone to work for Street had there been anyone Adam could talk to, listen to, or simply sit with in silence, without wondering about advantage gained or lost. Everyone except Street and Heidler wanted something from him: money, an endorsement, patronage, a job, the intimacy of his celebrity. Peter called them leeches, and though Adam snapped back in argument, defending them, he knew there was something in the criticism. He was vulnerable to flattery but not stupid.

Feeley did not understand fashion. "I mean, Adam, it's swell that you're so good at it and making all this money, but who needs it? I've got one suit, a down jacket when it's cold, a couple of sweaters, two pairs of shoes, sneakers. I even have a couple of neckties. The Chinese laundry turns the collars of my shirts when they get frayed. I'm happy. No one's going to take my picture. I'm out to pass the bar exam and do a bit of good in the world, not get written up in *Esquire*."

In other, lesser people Adam would have found such disinterest contemptuous, would have bridled, argued, raged, or sulked. He took it from Feeley, sensing genuine conviction and not a calculated pose. In fact, in his current state of mind he was ready to take much more from Feeley than a wry and casual indifference to hem lengths or whether jeans should be flared or cigarette-slim. Even his craft had suddenly become moot.

He showed off Feeley proudly to Marc, to Heidler, to Chelsea, but not to his old set, his gay friends, too fast-track and self-absorbed for Peter. It wasn't their gayness that repelled him, but their superficiality. "They keep staring at my goddamned clothes," he confessed to Adam. "I know it's stupid of me, but I feel uneasy." Peter had his own gay set, classmates and a few slightly older men with law degrees, and a subgroup of the city's Gay Caucus that met weekly on plans to lobby New York for a gay rights bill. Adam did not share their crusading zeal, but their seriousness of purpose made him love Feeley all the more. So instead of Christopher Street, the leather bars, and the gay tea dances, he and Peter went dancing with Chelsea in the discos or dined in Upper West Side restaurants. She was a pal, a kid sister, a pretty girl with whom they could joke and flirt and have fun without complications.

"Peter's terrific, Adam," Chelsea whispered enthusiastically one night at the Ice Palace. "Smart and decent and nice, really nice. I wish I had a guy like Peter."

"We should all have someone like Peter," Adam responded seriously, knowing the boy's value, knowing that the restless, haunted nights of random coupling were now forever behind him. "We should all have someone like Peter. Or Marc." He left the words hanging there, a seed perhaps planted. She said nothing, and he let it drop.

Of course, he and Peter could not always be together. There were still conventions.

No one knows precisely when it happened, but at some point

the fashion designer moved from the category of privileged servant to social equal, and then beyond that to lion. Adam didn't agonize over it; he accepted the convention that as a fashion designer he was expected to attend certain dinners, preside over certain charities, appear at certain parties, and by so doing contribute to the grist of the next day's gossip and society columns.

"Chelsea, Happy Rockefeller called. She's chairing some goddamned committee. Can you go to the Pierre Thursday? Black tie, short dress. I have exactly the one for you. I know it's a bore, but Happy practically begged."

He lied. Mrs. Rockefeller rarely begged, and he didn't think it a bore at all. Nor did Chelsea, still new to New York, the parties and the people. Besides, she got to wear any dress she wanted in Adam's collection.

"Of course I'll go, Adam. Who'll be there?"

Such invitations fell into his life like snowflakes; he kept them all, handsome cardboardy things from Tiffany and Cartier bearing famous names and exquisite penmanship. He was wanted, he was loved, his benediction sought. Two or three nights a week he and Chelsea went out into the elegant Manhattan night in his limo, and the *paparazzi* fell into a frenzy to see them come.

"They are," gushed Suzy Knickerbocker, "the handsomest couple in New York." It was nearly true, Adam slim and tall, born to wear evening clothes, Chelsea with a year of modeling behind her and an entire wardrobe, a woman's fantasy, at her disposal, knowing instinctively what to wear and how to wear it. Hostesses gushed and the lenses clicked and crystal stemware was lifted in admiration. They were perfect together. The uninformed whispered of romance, even of marriage.

They knew nothing of Peter Feeley sitting at home in Adam's den poring over lawbooks and looking again at a clipping of Suzy's column across which he had slashed the word "FRAUD!"

"Peter, you don't understand," Adam argued. "I know half the world is out of the closet. But half the world doesn't do business in Middle America. There are nights I've got to be on display. It's role playing; it's a pain in the ass sometimes, but I do it. I'm a professional. I'm not selling a lifestyle, I'm selling pants."

Peter resented it. Not that he disliked Chelsea West; in fact, he admired her for knowing who and what she was. But when Adam squared his shoulders before a television interview, perceptibly lowered an already deep voice, and carefully skirted any question that suggested homosexuality existed, Peter rankled. With the zealotry of the newly converted, he harassed Adam.

"What do you care what the world thinks of you?" he demanded of his lover. "Why should you hide what you are? What we are?"

Adam, in love, was patient. "Peter, you're going to be a lawyer and change laws and defend gay rights and great things like that. But until you change the whole damned country, I'm not sewing on any gay labels. If people think I'm gay, fine. If they think I'm straight, fine. Keep 'em guessing and don't admit a damned thing."

"It's pretending, Adam, making the whole world your closet."

"It's not pretending, it's business."

"It's bullshit," Peter shot back. And so they waged occasional war and unremitting love.

Bed was part of it, of course. But there was more. Peter came home full of the exultation of new knowledge, complaints about querulous professors, muddled in academic confusion or elated by sudden comprehension, anecdotal, amusing, insightful, self-deprecating. Adam, who knew nothing of the law and little more of schooling, found himself caught up as if he too had been seated in that stuffy amphitheater, taking notes and trying to understand the finer points of disputation. Feeley, just as ignorant of fashion, listened intently as Adam spun tales of Seventh Avenue and its people, of scheming showroom models and giddy saleswomen, of the businesslike Street and the wise and aging Sydney Heidler, of ambitious assistants and dextrous patternmakers, of sleazy retail buyers and jealous, piratical rivals, of traditional graft. They swapped sad tales of lost loves and shared bright dreams. Sometimes Adam's chef prepared dinner, sometimes Adam himself did, or else it was Peter's turn to grill burgers and chill the beer.

Sexually, Adam was by far the more experienced. He knew precisely what he was and had been since his teens. How many lovers had there been? He chose not to count. Too many of them had been, like that Roger who first paid his way to Paris, crass and mechanical. Others had been casual couplings, warmed by the night and by hunger, by quiet talk and convenience. Some had been fierce, pulsing, passionate. Often the other man meant nothing to him beyond an available body, a "Princess Tiny Meat." Sometimes he was the aggressive partner, sometimes the passive, the "pitcher" or the "catcher," as gay parlance had it. In his own mind Adam vacillated between the two. He wanted a lover in whom power and vulnerability were equally found.

Feeley, young and raw, had an innocence about him, a lack of guile and calculation, that only increased his appeal. What he lacked in knowledge or technique he made up in enthusiasm, in a willingness to try new things, to experiment, to adapt himself cheerfully to Adam's needs and wants. One evening they dined at Nicola's and then, in the clear, windless night, walked home to Adam's place.

"I ought to say good night and beat it," Peter said. "There's an eight-o'clock class tomorrow on contracts. And you know me and contracts."

Adam laughed. By now he felt he knew as much law as he did fabric. "Don't worry, we'll go to sleep early."

Often they did, without having made love, two young men holding each other close or sprawled sleeping across the king-sized bed, a hand or a foot touching, or not touching at all. When he woke in the night, Adam felt satisfied simply to lie there watching Peter sleep, looking at his face, his body, his tousled hair in the near darkness, remembering the feel of that body, the taste of his mouth, the incredibly exciting look and feel of Peter's blond head bobbing vigorously between his legs, the dim shine of pale buttocks rising, the feel of the slim, taut arms holding him tight. There had been more-imaginative lovers, cleverly tutored men with more athletic, more creative techniques, but Adam had not loved them.

Marc could see it. So could Heidler.

"He's just, I dunno, Marc, sweeter. Can I use that word?"

"I know what you mean, Sydney. Adam's always been a good boy, full of himself, of course, the way all good designers are, and sometimes, on a bad day, full of shit."

Heidler laughed. "And now?"

"Now," Marc said, "we have ourselves a genius in love. Let's just hope he doesn't decide to elope."

They even resumed the old poker games, with Feeley the house kibitzer.

"I can't throw the bucks around the way you guys can," Peter admitted with that likable candor, "but I'll make the sandwiches and open the beers and get some studying done out in the kitchen."

Adam beamed. "Isn't he great?"

Even Marc had to admit he was okay, and perhaps more than that.

18

Adam Green is one of fashion's coming stars. Trouble is, he knows it.

Mode, April 4, 1980

T here never was such a spring," Adam Green announced, lying on the sunny bank of a grassy dune.

"I know," Peter Feeley said, "Eliot was wrong."

"Eliot who?"

"T. S. Eliot. A poet who insisted April was the cruelest month."

Adam, impressed by Feeley's range of knowledge, laughed. "Well, whoever he was, he never spent April on the Vineyard with someone he loved."

Feeley had a weeklong spring break from law school, and Adam had wanted to take him south, to the islands somewhere. "I can't afford that," Peter said. "Why don't we go to the Vineyard? You've never seen anything like it."

In the end, after the usual haggle over his refusal to spend Adam's money, Adam caved in and they drove north, taking the ferry out of Woods Hole and a suite in an old inn in Edgartown. The tourist season hadn't yet begun, the college kids had gone south to Lauderdale and Bermuda, and they took long walks along the rocky beaches and through the narrow streets of the town, pricing antiques, lunching in fussy tea shops, and sitting long over buttery lobster and cold ale in nearly empty restaurants. They didn't care that they were alone.

"You were right, Peter. This is wonderful."

Adam was content, more than content. The May collection, largely built around and on Chelsea West, was nearly ready. He had filled Peter in on every detail, the boy's puzzlement and reticence only urging him on, making him elevate his own celebrity. Lincoln Radford of *Mode* had put him on the cover of one of his issues. The new royalty deals were grinding out the money. Martha's Vineyard was a pleasant surprise. And he had Peter.

Street was glad that he did. Adam was more than an employee, a partner, a friend. He *was* Majesty. In fashion they said of the designer: "On Seventh Avenue the assets go home at five o'clock." Marc knew how true it was, and if having Chelsea in the studio inspired Adam's work and having Feeley in his bed brought happiness and personal stability, Marc would pose no objections. Why should he? Adam would never be a choirboy, of course, but this friendship with the girl, this love for the law student, glossed over imperfections.

On a soft spring Thursday Adam, Peter, and Chelsea dined in a small restaurant halfway up Amsterdam Avenue, the sort of anonymous place Peter liked and had winnowed out. They were doing this a lot, Chelsea and Adam wrung out from work, glad to get away from the Avenue and the pressure, with Feeley walking uptown from the Fordham campus at Lincoln Center. There was nothing particularly memorable about the meal or the evening. Peter was quiet, but Chelsea dismissed that. By nature he was quiet, and law exams loomed. Adam was more than normally talkative, full of excitement about the new collection. Chelsea enjoyed being with them, listening to their talk, bearing witness to what they had. In small ways, it made her jealous. They had each other. In larger ways, she shared in their joy. She liked Adam too much for envy, and Peter seemed so right.

"Come with us to the Studio," Adam begged her, "we won't stay late."

She groaned. "Tomorrow is Paris. That cosmetics job. I can't get off the jet looking like Phyllis Diller. You guys go."

Adam's chauffeured car dropped her at Sutton Place. There was an awkward moment when Feeley held out a hand as if trying to keep her with them, as if he did not want to be left alone with Adam. Chelsea kissed them both and scampered inside the lobby, suspecting it was just her imagination.

As they walked down Sutton Place toward the car, Peter tried to take Adam's hand. Adam gently shook him off.

"Why can't we walk in public holding hands, Adam, like real people?"

Adam tried to be light. "*Paparazzi* behind every Pontiac, Peter. Hey, that almost rhymes!"

Peter was silent.

"Peter? The Studio?"

"No, Adam, not tonight. Let's just go home."

Adam undressed in the bathroom, glad that Chelsea had refused their invitation, glad that Peter had made him come home. The discos were fun. But to be alone with Peter? There was no comparison. He pulled the silk robe tight against his lean body, knotting the belt, and went barefoot to the bedroom, excited and eager. Feeley was sitting on the side of Adam's huge bed, still dressed, smoking a cigarette and looking up at him with troubled eyes.

"Not ready, or do you just want to talk?" Adam said.

"Adam," Peter said, continuing to look up at his handsome face in the muted glow of a single lamp, "I have to tell you something."

"Yes?" Fear began to steal over him, chilling and damp.

"Adam, I'm sorry. I tried, God knows I tried, but I don't feel I can love you the way you love me. You're a wonderful man, but somehow I can't be my own man with you." Peter seemed on the edge of tears.

Adam fell into a chair near the bed, sick to his stomach, feeling the ground slipping away from beneath his feet, even the soft, deep fur carpet abrasive to the touch.

"For months now I've followed you around, dancing in your discos, watching you dress up for parties, watching you on TV— watching you kiss Chelsea for the newspapers. I don't like that life. You love the glitter. You love it so much that you won't let the world see you're gay. I'm in the Gay Caucus, Adam; I'll probably get arrested at a protest one of these days. I want to be a lawyer involved in gay rights. I want to be *out*. Sure, I love being with you. But you overwhelm me. I need someone I can hold hands with on the street—somebody my equal."

Adam stared at him, looking into his eyes, trying to discern a lie. He found only openness. Confusion, commitment, regret. But no deception.

There seemed no way for Adam to respond. He could not give up fashion, risk his celebrity, and tell the world he loved Peter. If he did that, he wouldn't be the Adam he was. And Peter did not love that Adam.

"Adam, I know it hurts. But I had to tell you. The way I am now, if I tried to stay with you, I'd just make you unhappy. I'd destroy everything we had. I might even destroy you. What if I accidentally let the world find out about us? And you've been too damned good, you're too decent for that. If I stayed I'd make you miserable. You'd end up hating me, I know it. Our worlds are too different."

Adam listened, every word searing, punishing. He recognized, in the brutal honesty of Peter's agonized apologia, another, selfless love—a responsibility for something larger and more important than fashion, celebrity, the transient social games that passed for love or success. Peter, tormented by regret, waited for a response.

"Yes," Adam said quietly and with a dignity summoned from resources he did not know he had, "you'd better go."

Marc expected him to fall to pieces. That would have been the normal thing. A man loses his lover and starts to drink, to take drugs, to search desperately for another; his work is neglected, his friends are avoided out of embarrassment, his familiar haunts shunned because they might remind him of the sweet days of love. This was what Street anticipated, and it puzzled him that it didn't happen.

It was not that Adam had simply shrugged off loss. He had not. Peter had been more than a fling, more than a flirtation, more than a hot night of passion. He had loved Feeley and had lost him. That night, the next morning, all that day, the next two or three days were an empty, cold, tormented hell. He flayed himself with the notion that Feeley was making a mistake, that somehow he could change so utterly that Peter would love him, that with Adam Feeley would have found enduring happiness, fulfillment, a richer, better life. Why? Why?

But he would not crack up. Whether Peter liked it or not, he was Adam Green, a great designer, perhaps even a great man. On the third day he went back to work, serious and dedicated, ready to take on the challenge of the new collection. Heidler saw him coming and scurried away, not knowing what to say, how to behave. The studio personnel, the showroom girls, the workers in the sample room fell silent when he appeared, fearing his anger, knowing, as Seventh Avenue always seemed to know, what had happened, and fearing the reaction.

Chelsea was in Paris, and only Marc Street dared talk to him.

"So he walked out."

"Yes. He said he couldn't love me."

"A damned shame, Adam, I liked him."

"Yes," Adam said flatly, "and I loved him."

Marc said nothing, wanting to say the right thing, the comforting thing, and not knowing how, wanting to pull Adam to him and hold him, to soothe and comfort. And not knowing how to do it.

Adam threw himself into work. Marc looked over his shoulder at the new sketches. There was maturity here, a fully developed creative mind at work, sensitive and yet pragmatic, comprehending a woman's body and a man's desire at the same time. The basted samples were even better, melding the design with the cloth. Marc never demeaned their craft: clothing, shelter, food, these were the necessities, and on the basis of what Adam was creating now, no one in America was doing clothes any better, any lovelier, any more wearable and flattering.

But Street knew something bad was looming when Charlie Winston reappeared.

The old man—who, Marc knew dimly, had once been

Adam's patron when he was at FIT—lived a weirdly reclusive existence with a caged bird as his only companion and dog-eared fashion magazines as his only surround in the Chelsea Hotel on Twenty-third Street, eking out a living by selling fashion sketches to less talented but more commercially successful Seventh Avenue designers. Winston had once been big, as big as Norell or Mainbocher or any of them. The talent was eroding and the judgment, the control was gone. Street tried to avoid him, but Winston camped in his outer office, persistent and abusive, and finally Marc had let him in, a sketch portfolio under his arm. Before Marc could ask his business, the portfolio was slammed down on his desk and opened, sketches tumbling out by the dozens.

"Look at this, Mr. Street, and this. Recognize them? Of course you do. Right out of Adam's last collection for Majesty. And did I get my money? Did I get a scintilla of credit, even a word of thanks? That's gratitude for you. The designers rape me, bugger me, steal my children. It's criminal, and I'm not having any more of it. Look at these models, just look!"

Street looked at them, pen-and-ink sketches, brilliantly rendered, with tiny swatches of fabric attached with straight pins to indicate fabric and color. The clothes were contemporary, beautifully proportioned, and, he had to admit, several of the designs closely resembled some of Adam's current work.

"They're lovely," he said, "but what have they to do with us?"

"Everything!" Charlie Winston shouted. "They've been stolen by your designer. He came like a thief in the night, like some mugger in the alleyway. Get him in here. Let me confront him. See if he dares deny the evidence of his own eyes."

Marc closed the portfolio and sat down behind the desk. He didn't want Charlie going berserk right here in the office. Neither was he going to be bullied.

"Mr. Winston, there *are* similarities. But Adam showed his collection a month ago. It was prominently reported in *WWD* and in the *Times*. Wouldn't he be justified in claiming that *you* stole *his* ideas and not the other way around? Couldn't you have done these sketches since Adam's show?"

Charlie crouched down and shook his fist at the floor. "No, by God, I *don't* steal! These sketches are all dated. Look at them, man, just look."

"Who dated them?"

"I did, Mr. Street, dated them myself. I've always been punctilious about such things. Doesn't pay to be careless."

Winston's fury subsided, and he smiled almost beatifically. There was an innocence about him, as if the possibility he had postdated the sketches simply didn't exist.

"Please sit down, Mr. Winston," Marc said gently. This was one of the giants, mad now, perhaps, but that didn't deny what he had been.

"Well, yes, I will, Mr. Street. Gracious of you to hear my plaint."

As they talked, Marc could not help noticing the threadbare cuffs and elbows of what had once been an expensive tweed suit, the fraying collar of a blue denim workman's shirt, the greasy silk tie. But the shoes were polished.

In the end Marc promised, without conceding a thing, to ask Adam about the sketches. Charlie seemed satisfied. It was as if, having vented his rage, he had won a small victory.

Marc decided against questioning Adam. It was tough enough after Feeley to handle Adam, and there was no need to offend his sensibilities on what might be after all nothing but the ravings of a crazy old man. Instead, he sent a messenger down to Twenty-third Street with an envelope containing five hundred dollars in cash. He included no note, requested no receipt. He was canny enough to know that on such things a zealot like Winston could build lawsuits. He also knew that the old man, down at the heels, could use the money. And he remembered Adam's account of how Charlie used to trot him around Manhattan to museums and galleries, how he had opened his mind to beauty.

So he sent the cash and hoped that Winston would be mollified, that he wouldn't see in this small surrender the goad to further demands. If Winston began making accusations or if Lincoln Radford got hold of him and decided there was a juicy, muckraking story in it, Adam would have to respond publicly. Winston might be nuts, but there were always those ready to believe anything. Some mud would stick. Marc made a mental note to send Charlie some money every month. He knew that reputations in the fashion business rose and crashed like meteors. Winston could be any of them. Stolen sketches or not, all of them in fashion owed the old crazy a few bucks.

And there was another reason he did not ask Adam about the sketches. He was afraid of the answer.

19

Dior dead, Chanel, Balenciaga, Fath, Norell. Yet elegance
survives, a small miracle.

Mode, April 11, 1980

Chelsea West flew into New York, back into their
lives, not knowing about Adam's traumatic loss, not knowing
about wild, irrational schemes that had begun to seize at Marc
Street. Her roommate, Toy, left a note for her. "Adam phones.
Pleese call him tonights if your abel. Love."

She shook off jet lag and pulled on a pair of Adam jeans and
joined him at a small table against the wall in the bar of Elaine's,
where he told her about Feeley.

"Oh, Adam, how rotten for you. What a goddamned shame.
Wasn't there anything you could do?"

"No. He wouldn't let me try. I couldn't be what he wanted
and still be Adam. It was so good, *we* were so good. And now it's
over."

He drank a lot, they both did, and then Elaine sent over the
waiter with some Williams pear brandy, icy and clean until it hit
the stomach. At midnight Chelsea was falling asleep, feeling the
loss of hours, feeling the booze.

"You go home, Chelsea, I'll be okay."

"I don't want to leave you alone."

"Don't worry," he said, trying to smile. "I'm never going to
be alone anymore. That's one thing I've learned. Never count on
anyone, never get hurt, never be alone."

"Holy God, Adam, what happened?"

His nose was broken, his lower lip swollen, one eye blackened and closing to a slit.

Adam had phoned from his apartment, mumbling into the phone, telling Marc that he had to see him, he was sick. Marc grabbed a cab and went up to Fifth Avenue. Adam was slumped on a couch in the sitting room, his Filipino houseboy wringing his hands and looking distressed. Marc threw himself into a chair. Adam tried to grin, but it was painful even to look at.

"I'm thinking of giving up sex," he said, attempting humor.

It was the old story, a smile, a pretty face, a whispered invitation to delight. Only in Adam's case the seductor was a boy, a stranger, and larcenous.

"When Chelsea went home I went and picked him up at the Studio," Adam said. "He knew who I was, of course, and we had a drink. Maybe we had a couple. We went downstairs to smoke some grass and then it was, you know, time to go home. We went to his place."

"Adam, how dumb can you get? You didn't know this guy and you went home with him?"

Adam started to move forward, but felt the pain and sank back. "Hey, you've never gone home with some girl you just met? Don't you understand that's part of the excitement? The unknown? Why strangers are more erotic?" He hesitated, and then he said, "Anyway, just as we were getting ready, he slugged me. Took my cash and my watch. I tried to fight, but he was just too damned strong. Afterward I washed myself up as best as I could in the bathroom and got out of there. He just lay there on the bed, watching me. Wearing my watch and watching me. Not saying anything. Just watching and smiling."

It was then that his bravado broke and he began to cry. Marc went to him and held him, feeling his body shudder through the sobs.

"It's okay, Adam, it's okay. It's over now, I'm here, you'll be okay."

"Sure," he said, continuing to cry.

Marc held him tight, one arm around him, pulling him close.

"No one ever held me when I was a kid," Adam whispered. "My mother was working, my father wasn't there."

"I'm here, Adam, I'm here." Marc lifted his free hand and patted his head gently, smoothing his soft, damp hair. "It's okay," he said, "it'll be fine."

"No one ever held me." What racking emptiness there was in that admission.

Marc felt near tears himself. He pulled his arm free and stood up, looking down into Adam's bruised face. "God, you look awful. *GQ* would disown you."

Adam, sniffling, tried to laugh. "Kleenex," he said.

Marc went into the bathroom and came back with a box. Adam blew his nose, tenderly. "Ouch, it hurts."

"You should have my nose," Marc said, still trying to cheer him. "A punch would be an improvement."

Adam did laugh then, painfully, but it was a real laugh. Marc went into the kitchen, where the Filipino lurked, apprehensive, and told him to make coffee.

"Has a doctor seen you?" he asked when he got back.

"No."

"Well?"

"I'm too damned embarrassed to have anyone see me."

The flatness in his voice suggested that this was not something Marc could argue about.

"What about the cops? I assume you didn't call them."

"Of course not. Can't you just see this on Page Six of the *Post?*"

"Okay, what's the guy's name? What's his address?"

"Paul, his name is Paul. But I don't want you going down there. It won't do any good."

"You want your watch back? You want this guy to be told if he ever pulls anything like this again he's in trouble?"

In the end Adam gave him the address. That night Bobby Swaggerty sent two of the Westies calling. The money had been spent, but Adam got his watch back.

"Did they hurt him?" he asked Marc.

"Of course not," Marc lied.

Adam borrowed a friend's house in the islands for a week, and when he came back, suntanned and fit, only a bump in his nose remained. Marc made arrangements with Tom Rees to straighten it out, quietly.

Then Marlon Crist was murdered.

Crist was a friend of Adam's, a decorator in his fifties, the heir, some said, to Billy Baldwin and Sister Parrish. He'd done Adam's new apartment in Jackie Onassis's building, which was how even Adam still referred to it. Marc had met him at one of Adam's parties: a lean, wasted man with soft hands and a vicious tongue. Crist lived over near Bloomingdale's, in a walkup. Adam said that Crist wrote his telephone number on men's room walls and left his apartment door unlocked at night, hoping someone would drop by. Someone did. And three days after his death, Crist's body was found by a cleaning woman, his head crushed by repeated blows of a heavy ashtray, his money and jewelry gone.

"I hope you get the message," Marc told Adam.

Adam looked pained. "I *never* leave my door unlocked. Never!"

They never found out who did it. But Marc felt better about having sent Swaggerty's boys to call on Paul. Adam's carelessness frightened him. So did other things.

"While we're talking about it, I may as well get out something else that's bugging me. Cocaine. Just how much of a habit do you have?"

Adam erupted. "You're so goddamned stupid, Marc. You sound like some old Victorian. You don't know a damned thing about coke. First off, it isn't addictive. Everyone knows that. And I don't do a hell of a lot of it. But I will if I feel like it. Jesus, you'd think I was strung out in the office. Have I ever missed a collection? Do I ever not show up for work? Damned rarely, pal. And you bloody well know it!"

"Okay, okay. So I don't know anything about drugs. But I've got the right to worry. The designer is the only thing we've got."

"Stop worrying, for God's sake."

"I'll worry if I want to. It's my company."

Adam stared at him, and in a low voice said, "It's my life."

In the late sixties a fat old Seventh Avenue tycoon named Abe Goode, with more imagination than capital, declared in an interview with *Women's Wear Daily* that it was time American fashion stop functioning as a cottage industry and grow up—streamline itself, introduce modern business practices, and begin making some real money. Even then, in the populist hysteria of antiwar protests, money was duly respected.

Abe Goode knew how to manufacture clothes, how to deal with unions, who the best (most crooked) bookkeepers were, how to make deals for cloth, buttons, belts. He knew Lincoln Radford and John Fairchild and the editor of *Vogue*. He knew the shop stewards and the gangsters and the political fixers and the retail buyers and the fabric salesmen and the people who supplied the trucks. He knew which showroom models gave head and which went home to their husbands. He knew how to get theater tickets and tables at La Côte Basque and hotel suites and box seats for the Knicks and the Rangers. And he knew a handful of talented, financially strapped young designers. In the end, he brought people and knowledge together.

Marc Street knew about Goode. So did everyone else in fashion. And they knew why his idea, logical and sensible and modern as it was, didn't work.

"The trouble with Abe was," Lincoln Radford declared in an editorial, "that he was a burnt-out case. His brain was fine. It was his giblets that failed him."

So did his brilliant young stable of designers. Abe centralized their billing and their fabric buys and their trucking and their tax accounts, charmed the buyers, wooed the press, cut costs, and even made a little profit. In the end the designers took their gains and walked smiling away from the old man, each to set up in business for himself. For years after people would see Abe Goode pass and make respectful obeisance. It was the others who made the money.

Marc remembered. And now, ten years later, he decided it was time to try the same thing again.

In March 1980 Lincoln Radford had run an interview with Chelsea West in *Mode*. In it she analyzed the Paris couture collections. Again, she made sense. She isolated the significant new directions, concentrating on the spirit and the shape of the clothes, ignoring the little details that so fascinate provincial fashion-page editors. Marc remembered the way Coco used to talk about clothes, with that same ability to pinpoint the essentials and slough off the unimportant. He remembered his flight from Paris that January so long ago, after her funeral, when he had dreamt of finding another Chanel.

It was crazy, he knew. But, distrusting phone messages left with Eileen Ford, he sent Chelsea a short, businesslike letter, asking her to lunch with him.

20

Chelsea West is the best model fashion's had since Suzy Parker.

Mode, April 18, 1980

H ey, don't you know anything?" she demanded when he told her how he'd tried to get her by phone after Trigère's dinner. "There are always nut cases calling up trying to get hold of models. The Fords never give out numbers, and most of the messages never even get passed on. For all they know, you're the jolly neighborhood rapist."

Feeling defensive, he said, "I thought they'd recognize my name."

"Well, la de dah, they didn't."

"You should have given me your home number that night at Pauline's."

"Well," she said, "I blew it, didn't I?" She waited for him to say something and then, seeing that he wasn't in the mood for this sort of fencing, she said, quite seriously, "I was working for Majesty, there every week or so. Adam knew how to get hold of me, had my number. Don't you guys talk?"

"Yeah," he said, "I should have thought of that."

She recognized the reticence in his voice and she shut up, waiting.

They had one of the front tables at Le Cirque. Sirio himself came over and took their drink orders. Marc enjoyed the fuss.

Five years before he wouldn't have been able to get a table here. He owed all that to Adam, he supposed.

Purposely, he delayed getting to the reason for their meeting. "Tell me about yourself," he said.

The drinks arrived, and she raised her glass. "Uh-uh," she said, "everyone knows about me. I'm a goddamned publicity hound. You're the mystery man. I want to hear about you. Is it true you're a gangster?"

He realized she was just playing wiseass, but that one cut close to the bone. "No more than anyone else on Seventh Avenue."

"Adam told me you got into a fistfight one night when you were with him. Knocked some guy out with one punch."

"The man was drunk. He fell down."

"Not what I hear," she said.

He didn't argue. Let her play her little game and get it out of the way.

"I think you're sinister," she said. "Do you carry a gun?"

"Adam tell you that, too?" he asked, startled despite himself.

She laughed. "Hey, I'm only kidding."

"Only sometimes. Sometimes I carry a gun."

It threw her. "Who's that?" she asked, glancing at a corner table, wanting to distract him and catch her breath.

He looked.

"Zipkin. He collects cufflinks. Real estate money. Talks to Nancy Reagan long distance to California every day, they say, peddling the gossip. I suppose if Reagan beats Carter, Jerry Zipkin will be Secretary of State or something." He lighted a cigarette and began. "Look, I want to talk to you about business. About Seventh Avenue itself. How it works. How we work. The stuff you don't see when you just drop by."

She sobered. "Okay, go ahead."

Not for nothing had she dined at Will West's table since childhood. She knew there was always something to learn if she listened.

"Most people think Seventh Avenue's ugly," he said, "filthy, rotten, vulgar, greedy, grasping. A horrible place. That's the image. And often the reality. Even the mayor realized it. A couple of years ago the city tried to improve the image. They put up street signs that said 'Fashion Avenue,' and they sent platoons of streetsweepers through. Everyone laughed. No one ever called it 'Fashion Avenue,' and the streets are dirtier than ever. The buildings stink and they're full of roaches and the showroom models are hooking on the side and the mob owns half the business and runs most of the trucks. The cops are on the take, the sanitation department has to be bribed to pick up, the elevator men let the thieves in at night, the designers all steal from one another. There isn't a decent restaurant on the Avenue, and the kids who push the racks are dealing pot. The buyers want kickbacks and the fashion editors want free clothes. The blacks complain they get all the lousy jobs, and they do. The old Jews who own the companies are cheating on their taxes and screwing the showroom girls and robbing their partners and underpaying the seamstresses."

"Sounds delightful," she said.

"Sure," he said, "just like the rest of America."

"That's pretty cynical."

He didn't deny it. He just went on, his voice steady and serious. "It's all those things. And it's also where we make the best damned ready-made clothes in the world. Paris can't touch it. We're smart and tough and resourceful and we work hard as hell. We're survivors. You think we'd still be in business with the Japs and the Chinese and the Mexicans and every other fifty-cents-an-hour country competing against us if we weren't? We're the best and we know it. Look, Chelsea, in some ways it's the pits, but if you're in fashion it's the most exciting damned street in the world."

Chelsea could hear the excitement in his voice. She sipped at her drink, unaccountably put off by his intensity, uneasy with a man who talked not about himself or about her, but about his work. "Well, look, I know most of that stuff. I've been around you guys long enough now. And I like it. Don't worry, I think Adam's great. I love what he's doing. And I'm going to go right on modeling his clothes whenever he wants me. I'm not deserting him for Calvin or anything. Adam's too much my friend for that. I'd even pay retail to wear his clothes."

Marc laughed. "Well, that's a first."

They relaxed a little then, and when the maître d'hotel arrived to give the specialties, she ordered grilled turbot and salad and another Perrier instead of a drink. She was very beautiful.

"I really do want to know about you," he said. "I don't believe half of what I read."

"You didn't say if you wanted me to model exclusively for you."

"I don't," he said.

He left it at that, and she seemed puzzled. She had become accustomed to being wooed and he was being cool, marginally distant. "Well, then, what is it you want?"

"I don't know," he said, "I have an idea, a business idea, not modeling. It's more complicated than that. But before I start to talk about it and maybe make a fool of myself, I want to know more about you. I've seen you work, I met you that night at Pauline's, I've read the magazine stuff, especially that article you wrote for *Town & Country*. Adam dotes on you. But I have the feeling there's a Chelsea West behind the label."

"Isn't there someone real behind every label?" she asked, her lovely face serious now. "Isn't there a real Marc Street somewhere behind what people say about you, that gangster stuff?"

"You're turning the tables again."

She laughed. "Okay," she said, "I'll tell you about me. Am I under oath?"

"Absolutely."

"Well, I'm Will West's granddaughter. I know it sounds phony to start off with that, sort of like I'm bragging, but if you don't know about my grandpa, there's no way you can understand me."

He sipped at a vodka and said nothing. He wanted her to tell this her way, without prompting.

"My father's dead. Killed himself in a car crash. They think he was drunk. None of that got into the papers, because Grandpa owned the papers. My mom ran off, left him the year before he died. I was just a little kid. It wasn't a great success as a marriage, and my grandpa hated my mother. She was very beautiful. I've seen pictures. But she wasn't what you might call a model wife and mother."

The waiter brought the food. When he had gone, she continued. Marc noticed that people at nearby tables were watching her. There was a sort of electricity. She dove into the fish and the salad and then, between bites, resumed.

"Grandpa brought me up. Mostly on the ranch where he lives outside Denver, up in the hills near Aspen. I went to local schools. One year I came east to some fancy girls' school, and I wasn't exactly your average deb. I grew up around cowboys and ski instructors, and I guess I was pretty free and easy, too damned free and easy. It wasn't as if I were dumb or illiterate. My grandpa's one of the smartest men in the world, and the house was always full of experts. Financial people from Wall Street and foreign bankers and oil experts and diplomats and stuff. They talked over lunch and dinner. I was always included, expected to listen. And if I said something, Grandpa insisted that it make sense. So I learned a lot. And I read. He's got a big library, and I was expected to read. The classics mostly, Tolstoi and Dickens and Proust and Hardy and Shakespeare. I did it first as a chore and then because I wanted to."

She finished off her turbot and then said, "So I may be a hick, but I can read and write and count to a hundred."

He laughed. "What about your name? Is that true, that you were conceived in London?"

"Yeah. My mom and dad did their wedding trip in Europe and he was a tennis nut and they took a house off the Kings Road in Chelsea for the fortnight of Wimbledon. That's where it happened. I was born in Colorado. My straight name's Catherine. Nobody calls me that but my grandpa. He can't stand 'Chelsea.' Reminds him of my mom, and he still blames her for my dad."

"You were with an Englishman one night in Paris at a party. I saw you."

"Oh yeah, that night at Versailles. I met him in London doing a modeling job. A chinless wonder, but fun."

"Where do you live now?"

"I've got a flat here. With another girl. I know I'm supposed to say 'with another *woman*.' But if you know her, you've gotta say 'girl.' She's a character. Named Toy. A model."

"What about modeling?" he asked. "Are you serious about it?"

She shrugged. "It's easy. I mean, you work long hours and it can be boring as anything, but the money's good and I don't have to hustle. Eileen Ford gets me all the work I can use."

"But it's not a career."

"Hey, I'm twenty-two years old and no college. What skills do I have?"

"But you like fashion. I mean, you seem to know something about clothes."

"Yeah, I guess I do. When I was growing up on the ranch I had subs to all the fashion magazines. I mean, you need a break from Thomas Hardy once in a while. Nobody got dressed up out there except the dudes who came west to ski. I made some of my own clothes. We had a Mexican housekeeper, and she was great with a sewing machine. She taught me a lot. I used to copy stuff from the magazines, got pretty good at it. Even Grandpa said so."

"He's pretty much of a perfectionist?"

She raised her eyebrows. "Oh, man . . ."

Their waiter rolled up the dessert trolley, and she looked at it longingly.

"Nope," she said finally, sending him away. Then, looking down at herself, "I'd be two hundred pounds if I ate everything I want."

He liked how candidly she talked. But this lunch was business, and over coffee he made the beginnings.

"Adam's very good."

"Oh yeah," she said, "*I* think so."

"But I have this idea. Adam does four collections a year and designs the jeans. The company has some license deals besides. We get paid royalties and Adam's name goes on the label, but there really isn't a hell of a lot of work to it. I'm thinking of using some of that royalty money to expand."

"Can Adam handle much more work than that?" she asked. It was an intelligent question.

"No, frankly, he can't. He's got other things on his plate as well. Designing a Hollywood movie, and he wants to do a Broadway play. No, my idea is to bring in another designer . . ."

"You mean, to help him? An assistant?"

"No. He's got a mob of assistants now. That isn't it. I mean an entirely different designer who'd do an entirely different collection under the Majesty Fashions umbrella. Maybe even two or three other designers. They and Adam would work separately, entirely on their own. They wouldn't exchange ideas, wouldn't even let the other guy know what they were doing, so we'd have two or three different collections each season, each one under the designer's name but all of them manufactured by Majesty. We'd have a couple of different looks but centralized billing, shipping, fabric buying, marketing, and so on. It was tried once before in fashion, and it would have worked if a man called Abe Goode had been younger and if the designers had played fair with him."

She asked a few questions, and he tried to answer them.

Then she said, "Why tell me all this? I think it's a great idea, but so what? I don't know of any designers you should hire."

Street was a man who played hunches. He'd taken a chance years before with Adam. He was about to take another chance now. He liked the girl's attitude. Of course, she might simply laugh it off. She probably had all the money she needed. She might object to exploiting her family's name, her connections. To hell with it, he told himself.

"Chelsea, I think you could design clothes. I'd like you to try it."

"Me?" Her shock was genuine.

"Yes, you."

She shook her head. "You're nuts, you know."

He looked into her beautiful face. "The hell I am," he said, remembering a young girl from the Auvergne who had never even learned to draw and who had changed forever the look of women.

21

Anyone can make clothes. All you need is a small factory
and a large tent.

Mode, April 25, 1980

It was a stunning, intimidating, even frightening proposal,
but she promised to think about it. Diane von Furstenberg had
done it, with those sexy little wrap dresses, and she knew nothing
about technique. They were trying to launch a line of clothes with
Gloria Vanderbilt's name on the label. Russ Togs was talking to
Christie Brinkley about a sportswear collection. Street reminded
her that there *were* precedents. What frightened her was that instinctively she knew he wasn't looking for another Diane or another Gloria Vanderbilt; he was in search of another Chanel.

It was with a certain relief that Chelsea left New York. She
needed breathing room, time to think. She and Toy and two male
models had been flown to Kauai to film a television commercial.
An automobile was airlifted to the lip of a volcano crater by a
heavy-duty helicopter, and the four models struck poses for an ap-
oplectic director who'd obviously seen too many Saturday-after-
noon serials as a kid. The 30-second commercial took four days to
shoot.

They were lodged in the Kauai Hilton Hotel, the best Hilton
in the world, just off the black sands of the beach.

On the third night of the shoot she'd stayed late in the
hotel's lounge, rapping with members of the crew, the serious,
sober technicians for whom this wasn't the glamor of Madison

Avenue or of television but simply another job of work. Toy, popping 'ludes, had gone upstairs to her room with a male model. The director, making it a point of pride not to socialize with crew or cast, was seen only during working hours. Breaking one of her rules, Chelsea had some wine. The crew were all drinking liquor, and it seemed priggish not to have something. Toward midnight she said good night, exchanged the usual insults and brotherly kisses, and went to her room. There was a balcony, and after she undressed she walked out on it in a cotton nightdress, feeling the ceramic tiles cool under her bare feet, watching the moonlight reach toward her across the metronomic roll of the waves and the beach, even blacker than the sea. It would be wonderful to be here with someone she loved. The soft breeze pressed against her.

She turned from the balcony, leaving the lovely night behind her, and slid into bed, pulling up a flowered sheet against the sea breeze. She lay there awake for a long time. Remembering. And thinking. She'd promised Street an answer when she got back. Should she simply tell him the thing was absurd and to forget about her? Or should she blow modeling a kiss good-bye and give his idea a try, for better or for worse? Or, being Will West's only grandchild, should she bargain?

She lay there, listening to the sea, thinking about Toy and her lover a few rooms away, feeling the imperceptible weight of the bedclothes against a body aching with need, puzzled and confused by what this Street offered, as a businessman. And as a man.

Roughly, she pushed down the bedclothes and stripped the cotton gown off over her head in a single, angry motion to look down at herself, at her body, just visible in the muted Pacific night. Her breasts rose and fell like the sea, her belly stirred more gently, her legs, slightly parted, mocked her, long and shapely and unused. She had all this, she *was* all this—and it was all being wasted. Again a child, again a schoolgirl, her hands reached for her breasts, felt her nipples spring to erect life, and she began to move, squirming in the bed, breathing faster now, moving faster, her hands everywhere and nowhere, damp now with sweat, damp with her.

In the morning, over breakfast, still alone and certain there was more for her in life than this, she knew that she would meet again with Marc Street. And, being a West, she would bargain.

They met in Street's office. It was to be a business negotiation, and he wanted the mood to be businesslike. She was tanned from Hawaii, long and even lovelier than he remembered. She took a chair opposite his desk and refused coffee. The hovering secretary was dismissed. Chelsea glanced across the room. She liked the brisk, economic feel of it, with none of the froufrou she associated with the men she met in fashion.

"Look, Mr. Street, this business you—"

"The name's 'Marc,' you know that."

"It *was* 'Marc.' Now we're talking business. You're 'Mr. Street.' "

"Okay, *Miss* West," he said.

"Good. Now I'd like to start with the negatives."

And she did. She asked Street all the questions he'd asked himself. And more. And just as when he had asked himself the questions, some answers came crisply, cogently, while to others his replies seemed now as fuzzy and ill-thought-out as when he'd been talking only to himself. She seemed to recognize this. Once or twice she snapped, "That doesn't make much sense." Or "Do you really *believe* that?" When she was finished he talked to her about Chanel. She made a face.

"Look, I'm a girl from the hills," she objected, "not Coco goddamned Chanel."

"I know that," he said, "and what the hell do you think Chanel was, Pablo Picasso? She learned to sew at home, maybe for a time she did a little hooking to keep body and soul together. She never did know how to draw, never went to FIT, never apprenticed at anyone's knee. She had no education and no family, and the only connections she had she made for herself. Compared to Coco, you're a Harvard Ph.D. But for all the things she didn't have, there was one thing she did. And I think you have it. I'm gambling that you do."

"And what's that?" she demanded, angry at his anger.

"A sense of style," he said, pointing his forefinger at his head.

"Something up here, something instinctive and rational at the same time that tells you what's tasteful and what's vulgar, what works and what doesn't, who looks good and why and who doesn't. You may not be able to articulate it. I know Coco couldn't always. But you know when it's there. And you sure as hell know when it isn't."

He sat back in his chair. She stared at him. "Hey, you really believe this shit."

He nodded. "Yes, I do."

"I guess *so*." She was impressed despite herself. "What sort of backup would I have? I mean, would there be an assistant who knew what he was doing, who understood the craft?"

"I wouldn't let you start on day one without a really good right hand. I'd insist on it."

"Would my name go on the stuff?"

"Absolutely," he said bluntly, "that's a big part of it, trading on your name, exploiting hell out of it."

"My grandpa's going to *love* that," she said.

He shrugged. "This modeling you've been doing, hasn't it worked that way?"

"Yeah, I guess so. Okay, when would I start? When would you show the first line?"

He wanted to start working with her now, in the spring, and launch a line in November, with next spring's ready-to-wear collections.

"What does Adam think about all this? Does he like the idea?"

"I don't know," Marc said, risking honesty.

She jerked back, erect and alarmed. "You mean he doesn't know? Jesus, I thought you guys were friends!"

"We are," he said coolly. "In the long run this'll be good for him, too. He probably won't think that way at the start. But it will, I'm sure of it."

"Oh, boy," she said, "were you right about Seventh Avenue. You people are something else again. He's your partner, your pal, and you're negotiating with me behind his back!"

"Don't be so goddamned virtuous," he snapped. "This is business. I'm making a business proposition."

She saw the chill in his eyes, the anger. She was Will West's granddaughter, and she said, just as coldly, "Okay, then, the hell with friends. We ought to talk money. How much will you pay me? And do I get a piece of the action?"

They haggled for a time over money. It surprised him. He assumed that with her family's resources this wouldn't be a sticking point. It was. At one point he threw up his hands.

"Is this conscience money? Because you feel guilty about Adam?"

"No, this is *Chelsea* money. Because I feel good about me!"

"Look, I'm hardly Will West."

"And I'm not Miss Rich Bitch, doing this for a lark. Sure there's a lot of money. But it's tied up in trust funds and my grandpa's will. Someday I'm going to be a very rich woman. But that's not now. And even he says he's too mean to die young. He might live to a hundred. Meantime, I've got an allowance—"

"How much?"

"None of your damned business. Now, how much are you going to pay me?"

In the end they settled. On a three-year deal, starting at a quarter of a million a year in salary, rising to three fifty the second year and half a million the third. He refused to give her a piece of the business. It was his company, Adam had a small percentage, and Marc was not going to dilute ownership. They compromised with an in-house royalty arrangement, one percent of the profits on merchandise bearing her name.

"You mean one percent of the profits, *if any*," she said, laughing, relaxing at last.

"If any," he agreed. He stood up and extended a hand. "I'll have my lawyer put this into a letter of agreement, and if your lawyers approve it, we're in business."

She grabbed his hand and shook it. He could feel her strength.

"Thanks, Marc, I'll do my best for you."

"I know you will, Chelsea."

"Miss West" and "Mr. Street" were behind them. If only Adam were.

22

Adam Greenberg and Marc Street, Marc Street and Adam
Greenberg. Once as inseparable as Butch and Sundance.
And now ... ?

Mode, October 28, 1980

I loved you," Adam said, his voice shaking, his face shattered and close to tears.

"I know that," Marc said in a choked whisper.

The two men had not seen each other in a month. Adam had spent March in California working on designs for the Redford film and then hanging around watching the production. Marc had his own concerns nailing him to the desk.

With Lazer's departure from the scene, Majesty had to put up with the usual garment industry harassment. Shipments were hijacked; union shop stewards demanded, and got, their bribes; petty thieves created nuisances. All these things were expected and tolerated. "The cost of doing business," Street had said, shrugging them off. It was more than that, of course, and he took steps to do something about it. When Swaggerty and the Westies provided certain services, payment was made in cash, with no entries in ledgers, no withholding taxes, no Social Security deductions. Lazer had withdrawn his patronage, and the Westies, with a particular savagery, kept the peace. A small-time garment industry thug, realizing that Lazer's hand was no longer in the game, attempted a little free-lance extortion. Street informed

Swaggerty, and the man was given a lecture and had his kneecaps smashed with a baseball bat.

The Avenue had always been like that. When he was new in the business he had asked Heidler one night, over dinner, "Who really runs it? Who runs Seventh Avenue?" and the old man, lifting cautionary eyebrows, had said nothing but only held up three fingers. Even then Marc understood. Three fingers was Tommy Lucchesi, doing business as "Three Fingers Brown," the organized crime boss, and Marc never asked again.

Sometimes Street agonized over the nature of this "business." He was *not* French Jake, not a gangster. The laundering of money for Lazer, as he matured and began to understand its source and its uses, had bothered him; Swaggerty's strong-arm tactics rankled. He was paying criminals to protect him from other criminals. If only the police were more efficient, more energetic. But they weren't. And along Seventh Avenue men like Marc Street continued to retain men like the Westies as routinely as they hired night watchmen and installed burglar alarms.

Out in Los Angeles, Adam knew nothing about it. He had won another Coty Award; one more Coty and he would ascend, as Blass and Norell and Klein had done before him, into fashion's Valhalla, into what was called, with typical hyperbole, "the hall of fame." He had that and he had Hollywood. Feeley was hardly forgotten, but in success there was balm for his pain.

People made a fuss over him. He had a bungalow at the Beverly Hills Hotel, and there was a new lover, a young stuntman who'd progressed to small, walk-on roles and in whose career Adam was taking a less than objective interest. He lounged now at poolside, in a chaise the pool boy kept moving every half hour to stay with the sun, watching the stuntman swim laps, working on his suntan, and gradually retreating from last night's cocaine high. He liked Hollywood, liked the people, liked learning about the technical side of filmmaking. Everything was clean out here, clean and hot. New York would be cold and grubby, with snow caked along the curbs; after the St. Patrick's Day parade drunken high-school boys would urinate against the park wall across from his house, and drunken girls would vomit on his doorstep.

"Who needs it?" he asked himself. Maybe after another couple of years he'd get out of fashion entirely, do movies, put up some money, maybe even direct. It was a technique that could be learned. And certainly he had the artistry, the sense of color and composition. The first Hollywood producers had been Russian Jews from New York's fur industry. What they had done, he could do. He was sure of it!

And it didn't hurt that there was a functioning gay network. Gay producers got the first crack at hot scripts by gay writers. They naturally tended to employ gay directors, who, in turn, offered the best roles to gay actors and staffed their productions, as much as possible, with gay editors, cinematographers, assistant directors, and technicians. A young director glowing with promise told Adam how it worked.

"Obviously, you don't cast no-talent mutants in important roles simply because they're gay," he said. "But when it comes down to the choice between two actors who can both do the job, well, you go with your pals. You can do just about anything you want in the movie business, from drugs to S & M, just so long as you don't talk about it. Like in the old days with producers handing out roles to the girls they screwed. It's just that the casting couch is no longer exclusively heterosexual."

Adam had laughed.

The young director, very much the local boy, the Californian, said, "Isn't it that way in fashion? You promote your friends?"

Adam laughed again. "Josh, in fashion there's no choice. I don't *know* any straight designers."

So he lazed in the hot winter sun, sleek and comfortable, and fantasized about making witty, sophisticated movies and helping boys like the stuntman become rich and famous.

Just then a beautiful young girl undulated by wearing a pair of Adam jeans, drawing eyes, and he knew instant gratification. He stopped thinking about movies and remembered who he was and why he was famous. He picked up the pad and soft pencil from the table at his elbow and started to sketch.

"Who needs it?" he had asked rhetorically of fashion. And the answer was, he realized with a silent laugh, "I do." No matter how seductive Hollywood was, no matter what Peter Feeley had thought.

Two days later, California shaken from him like sand from his shoes, he was back in Manhattan and working on the May collection. That weekend, over a dinner Marc had cooked badly in his own apartment, drawing elegantly unspoken criticism from his partner, Marc told him about Chelsea.

"You did this to me. Without warning, without reason, just stabbing me in the back."

"There *were* reasons," Marc muttered. This was going badly. He couldn't seem to find the words that would make it better.

Adam got up from his chair at the dinner table and went to stand at one of the windows, not looking out, just standing there with his back to Marc.

"We were always different, you and me. Everyone else on Seventh Avenue screwed his partner and cheated on the books and stole and lied and cut deals. Not us. We only needed a handshake those first few years. I believed in you, believed in what we were doing. We were a team."

"We can still be a team, Adam. We still *are* a team."

The designer whirled, his handsome face tear-streaked and angry. "You call it a team after you've just broken it up? Do you think I'm some sort of moron?"

"Of course not. It's still a team. We've just added a player."

"Oh, sure," Adam said, bitter and sarcastic, "the fifth wheel we've always needed."

Marc pushed his chair back from the table. "Look, listen to me, let me walk you through this, give you my reasons."

"Yes, you do that, Marc, I really want to hear them." He turned again so that Street was talking to his back. Anger was rising in Marc, too. Adam was acting as if he'd been slapped across the face. This was business, dammit, and it made sense. The difficulty was in trying to get Adam to recognize that. He struggled for control and resumed, his voice quiet and measured.

"Adam, Majesty is going to come out of this reorganization even bigger and better. Better for you, better for me, better for the company. We amortize our costs over a broader base. You continue to do your thing, no change. But we add a second line. We get a better deal buying fabric, paying rent, trucking, subcontracting costs, accounting, front office, even a break on what we pay for an ad in *Vogue* or *Women's Wear*. You own a piece of the business. It's got to be good for you if it works out as I think it will."

"You're right, I *am* a part owner. You make decisions like this without even consulting me?"

"Maybe I was wrong on that, maybe I should have talked to you about it. I didn't. But it's done. We can't go back and do things over differently now."

"Why not? Just tell her you've changed your mind."

"I haven't," Marc said, hardening.

Adam threw himself onto the old leather couch. "Everything was going so well," he said, less angry than remorseful now, "great business, that second Coty up on the mantelpiece, the royalty deals, the perfume deal with Baltimore. Why fix it if it ain't broke? That's what gets me. And the fact that you sneaked around and did it without telling me."

"Think of General Motors, Adam—they've got a Cadillac division, they've got the Chevy. We appeal to a broader market, we sell more goods, we make more money. You do your line and she does hers."

"And which am I, the Chevy or the Caddy?" he asked sourly.

"Look, for this new deal to work we had to be making money. You did that for us. You brought in the bucks, made expansion possible. No one denies you every bit of credit for Majesty's success. Without you, there couldn't be a Chelsea West."

"And why the hell does there have to *be* a Chelsea West?"

Marc exploded. "You said yourself she has an instinct for fashion, that she was the best model you ever had, that she inspired your collection. You said all that, I didn't. You were the one who got me thinking about her."

"Being a good model and being a professional designer are not precisely the same thing, and you know it. Does she know a damn thing about buying fabric, about sketching, about cutting and sewing, about editing a collection?"

"She'll learn. The way I learned, the way you learned."

"Marc," Adam said, his eyes hot and darting, "if you want to bang her, fine. But on company time?"

Street stopped arguing then. Struggling to keep from hitting him, he said, "That's all, Adam. This company needs more than one designer and we're going to have more than one. Let's have no more bullshit about it."

"It's my company too!" Adam shouted.

Marc resisted the urge to shout back. He did not trust himself to retain control. Instead, his voice just above a whisper, he said, slowly and with finality: "One person controls Majesty Fashions. And that's me."

Adam left then, running from the apartment, eyes blinded by tears. Marc made no attempt to stop him. Both of them had said enough, had said too much.

He could still hear Adam's voice, snarling that crap about Chelsea and him. And he could still hear that same voice, wounded and pitiable: "I loved you."

Adam stayed away from the office that week, alternately sulking and raging, considering resigning and talking to his lawyer. He'd lost Peter Feeley, now he'd lost Marc Street, one to a world he couldn't share, the other to Chelsea, his own protégée, his friend. Bitter and hurt, he cursed them both. It was all so damned unfair. No one could have loved Peter more passionately than he had, no one loved Marc longer or more faithfully. And they both had abandoned him.

Anger and pain can be sustained for only so long. In Adam's case, they gave way to sulky resentment. His attorney analyzed his contract with Majesty and concluded that he had no escape clause. There was nothing in there that said Street couldn't hire another designer, a dozen others. In the end Marc made a concession, financing Chelsea's operation solely out of his own share of the profits, not out of Adam's. Of course, if Chelsea were successful, Adam wouldn't share in the proceeds.

"Fine with me," Adam told the attorney, his handsome face screwed into permanent resentment.

That ended the battle. It hardly ended the war, a psychologically murderous struggle that alternated between open combat and secretive, nasty guerrilla sniping. Increasingly, Adam turned from Marc and even from Heidler, seeking out the consolation of other, newer friends. Marc agonized over whether he should have leveled with Adam, told him he was vulnerable, the company's weak link, that he no longer trusted Adam's discretion, his common sense. Adam was reckless, and it was Majesty that was put at risk, a hundred-million-dollar fashion empire with but a single tangible asset, a troubled, vulnerable, cocaine-snorting core.

He said none of this. He couldn't. He and Adam had been brothers. Now . . .

Chelsea came to work in May. Majesty had gradually expanded from one floor to four in its Seventh Avenue loft building. They needed the space, and now Marc leased yet another floor, just for the new Chelsea West operation. He could have squeezed her in somewhere, but he wanted Chelsea and Adam to operate independently, to be kept physically apart. Adam had a crew of assistants by now, his own patternmakers, his gofers, and his office and secretary. In miniature, Marc set Chelsea up the same way. As an assistant he hired a Frenchman, Jacques Dufour.

"He okay with you?" he asked her one night after she and Dufour had spent hours together, talking and getting to know each other.

"He's fine," she said. "Hey, he's forgotten more about this stuff than I *know.*"

Dufour was wicked, egotistic, talented, and difficult to handle, full of himself, arrogant, and exactly what Marc wanted. The prudent course might have been to recruit a born number two, a malleable, capable sort without a personality. Instead, he went for Dufour, a former chief designer whose last two companies had gone into Chapter Eleven. Street knew he was good, that the companies involved had been undercapitalized. He was hedging his bets. If Chelsea faltered, Dufour would do the collection himself. If she had the guts and the brains he thought he saw in her, she would learn from Dufour and keep him in his place.

All that spring and into summer Marc worked with them. Dufour argued, raged, pushed his own ideas, and bullied her. In the beginning, she let him shove her around. After all, he'd been trained in Paris at the house of Jean Desses. He'd been a Seventh Avenue designer for ten years. She was a kid with a year of modeling and a primitive sense of what she liked and didn't like about women's clothes. Marc enjoyed watching the relationship develop.

"You're an idiot, Chelsea, a *cretin!*" Dufour would shout as they worked over sketch pad and toile.

"I know it, Jacques. You don't have to tell me."

"Then you're not completely stupid if you know that much," he sneered.

In July Marc and Adam flew to Paris for the couture collections. Pointedly, Chelsea was left behind. Adam, still sulking, drew consolation from that. But in Paris he and Marc had their different hotels, and the two men saw each other only at the collections, spoke only to discuss which models they should buy. The rift was real. Jimmy de Bertrand and Brugère saw it and tittered in malicious glee.

Adam went on to see the fabrics in Zurich and in Italy, and Marc flew home alone. On Thirty-eighth Street, something had changed. It was Dufour's turn to whine.

"That bitch! Impossible! She thinks she can tell me something? Me, who created the chemise before Givenchy ever thought of it?"

Marc strolled into Chelsea's studio. She was wearing a denim shirt, Adam jeans, and Adidas sneakers, her hair tied up in a colorful bit of rag. Her face was shiny, there were Band-Aids on several fingers, and she was chain-smoking unfiltered cigarettes.

"Well?" he said.

"Just keep that little fairy away from me," she said, her jaw set and the words hissed between clenched teeth.

"What happened?" Marc asked, rather enjoying the scene, leaning against a worktable.

"He doesn't understand a damned thing about American women, doesn't know diddly about what we want or how we look. He wants to turn us into some pale imitation of something he remembers from Paris a century ago."

Marc led her on. "But you said he was 'wonderful,' that you could really learn from him."

"Bullshit!" she said, the cigarette bouncing up and down between her lips. Her tan was gone, she looked as if she'd lost weight, her shirttail was hanging out. Marc had never seen her look so beautiful.

This was what he wanted, what he'd hoped for. That she'd absorb Dufour's professionalism, pick his brains, and then, when she had both feet planted flat on the ground, she would discard him and go to work driven by her own ideas, her own sense of style, her own instincts. And she was doing it. He looked over the sketches, saw the first canvas toiles. She'd calmed down now and sat there at his elbow, looking over his shoulder, making occasional comments, and dropping ashes on his sleeve.

"See, this is what I'm trying to do. Look at the skirt, the movement, the flow. And the fabric. It's in the same easy, flowing spirit. You do see it, don't you, Marc?"

He did. And he also saw things that *didn't* work. But he had expected that. They still had time. November was more than three months away.

They went back to work, Dufour muttering but subdued, the girl more confident, more certain every day. Heidler worked with them; so did Marc. Only Adam, returned from Europe, remained studiedly aloof.

His resentment focused not on her but on Street. He assumed that they were sleeping together. That was how women were, using their sexuality to get what they wanted. Chelsea was beautiful, intelligent, likable; he conceded her all that. He missed working with her, not only the actual modeling but having her there in the studio, smoking cigarettes and drinking Tab and telling him what she thought about the clothes, over quiet, amusing dinners with her after they left the studio, taking her to the discos and talking together until dawn, gossiping, cutting up his rivals. All that was finished now, and he treated her with casual carelessness, as if she weren't there. It was Marc's fault, Marc who had betrayed him, Marc who had fallen for a pretty face.

Chelsea made an effort to break through. When Adam repulsed her, she shrugged and went back to work. That was what drove her now, work and learning and her first collection. All the length of Seventh Avenue the talk was of Marc Street's new girlfriend and whether she could do it.

Lincoln Radford came around, sniffing and rooting. Street gave him just enough to whet his appetite, nothing more. Stanley Baltimore came to call. Adam cosmetics were booming. His perfume would make its debut for Christmas. Did Marc think there was a potential cosmetics line in Chelsea West?

Street laughed, and lied. "Mr. Baltimore, don't be ridiculous. We won't even know if the ready-to-wear line will be ready. Far too soon to think that big. But we'll keep you informed."

Baltimore, shrewd and suspicious, said that would be fine with him. And he promptly made arrangements to bribe one of the showroom girls to keep him apprised of just what was happening inside Majesty Fashions. It occurred to him to ask Adam, who would surely know. He sensed the rift between Adam and Chelsea and decided that if Adam told him anything, it would be biased and probably inaccurate.

Finally, it was November. The country chose up sides, Jimmy Carter versus Ronald Reagan, while on Seventh Avenue the designers buried themselves in their own egos, their own concern, their own self-interest, Chelsea among them. When her grandfather phoned from the ranch, warning her against voting for "those goddamned Democrats," she laughed. "I don't even know who's playing, Grandpa."

Marc had rented the Hall of Mammals at the Museum of Natural History for the show. Chelsea goggled when he told her.

"Hey, we're really going to tiptoe into town, aren't we?"

"Well, there was no way of doing it quietly, so why not raise a little hell?"

She thought for a moment. "Well, if I flop, I'm in the right place. The curator can stuff me right there and then."

On election night he took her to dinner. It was too late now to change anything. They took a cab into Brooklyn, where he had reserved a corner table at the River Café. It was a cold night and clear, and beyond the windows tugboats plugged up and down the river and the Wall Street skyline rose glittering through the darkness. They stared at it, over cocktails, and silently.

"A great city," Marc said finally.

"Yeah, you know, when I first came here I didn't really like it that much. I mean, most folks were nice to me, tried to make me feel at home. But I was this kid from out west and a bit lost, out of my depth. I settled down in the end, but it hasn't been until these last few months that I ever really felt I belonged."

"And now you do?"

"Oh yeah. With old Sydney and the folks at Majesty and even with that son of a bitch Dufour." She hesitated. "And you."

He sat silently for a moment, savoring her words, trying not to read too much into them. Then he reached under the table to pull out a large manila envelope he had carried under his arm. He undid the metal closure and pulled out a framed picture wrapped in tissue.

"Here," he said, "she gave me this a long time ago. I thought you might like to have it. A good-luck charm of sorts, a kind of talisman."

She slipped the picture out of the tissue and turned it right side up to look at it. A woman in a white jacket looked out at her through dark eyes, a cigarette held in one hand. "Chanel?"

He nodded. "Around 1930 or so. She had a lot of pictures of herself and I wanted one and she picked out this."

Chelsea looked at it intently. "Fifty years ago and it could be today. That look, the jacket, her hair. Even the cigarette."

"Yes," he said.

She rewrapped the photograph carefully and slid it back inside the envelope. "I went to her funeral, too, you know."

"No! You did? Why, you must have been just a child. Why would you—"

"My grandpa knew her, Chanel. He took me."

"A tall, lean man in a cowboy hat?" Marc was stunned.

She stared at him. "You saw us. You remember after all this time."

He nodded. If he believed in omens . . .

"Come on," he said, "I'm taking you home. And we're going to hang this damned picture on your living-room wall."

"To bring us luck?" she asked.

"I'm not missing a bet. We need all the luck we can get."

As they went out, sending for a cab, he said, "Whatever happens tomorrow, win or lose, it's been worth doing. I'm glad we tried."

"Me too," she said, and meant it.

23

Her clothes say as much about what America wants in its wardrobe as the voters last week said they wanted in their politics.

Mode, November 10, 1980

O n the day after Ronald Reagan was elected President, Chelsea West showed her first collection.

The rest of the country was still arguing whether Carter should have conceded so early and wondering whether Reagan could get the hostages home from Tehran. But fashion is a country to itself, with its own provincial concerns, its frontiers and rivalries, and at eleven o'clock that Wednesday morning every little gold chair was filled, with store buyers, fashion editors, *paparazzi*, elegant women with nothing more important to do. Also there, feeling defensive about it, were reporters and photographers from the news magazines, the wire services, and the great daily papers. Chelsea was more than fashion; she had become news.

It was an enormous but calculated gamble on Street's part.

Marc realized there was simply no way of slipping her under the flap of the circus tent. There was too much curiosity, too intense an interest. She had to be unveiled in the center ring. Before she ever spoke her opening line she was a star. The footlights blinked on, the drums rolled, and Chelsea would rise or fall in a brilliantly lighted fishbowl.

Adam already had his opinion. As a professional, he despised amateurism; as an unrequited lover, he wanted her to fail, wanted Marc to regret his folly. His growing entourage played its role, telling Adam that he was the creative genius of Majesty Fashions and that this crass *businessman* Street and his whore were headed for disaster. It was what they deserved after the sleazy way they'd treated a truly great designer. Failure, which Adam and his friends all confidently expected, was too good for Chelsea and Marc. Humiliation was what they wanted.

Marc and Chelsea were at the museum before dawn. She was the calmest of them all. In that she was like Adam.

"You're a cool one," he said.

"You ever stood at the top of a downhill run scared as hell and staring down at glare ice?"

He could hear an echo of Adam's voice, different people, but with the same sort of gutty resource. If only Adam were here, he thought, it would all be perfect. Marc's anger had cooled, and he felt now only as if he had lost something.

Chelsea frowned as a model passed, adjusting her necklace. "That's a mistake, that dress," she said flatly. "I ought to pull it."

Street shook his head. "Too late for that now. Besides, it's a damned pretty dress."

"No," she said, "there ought to be a sleeve, just a quarter sleeve. Older women are going to love that dress, and no one over twenty should ever go sleeveless."

Marc stared. "Where the hell did you hear that?" he demanded.

"I didn't *hear* it anywhere. I know! The upper arm softens and you flatter it with a sleeve. It's just nature and good sense."

"Yes," Marc said quietly. He remembered Chanel's telling him precisely the same thing, in almost the very same words. He had forgotten, but Chelsea instinctively knew. He regarded her with something approaching awe.

He wanted to tell her that, to say something, but this wasn't the time for blurted-out compliments. For months he had held his tongue, things he had wanted to say and had not said. It was business, commerce, a straightforward deal. Let Adam think otherwise. Chelsea was his designer, nothing else. Only he knew this was a lie and she had become much more. Still, he said nothing.

Interrupting reverie, a gofer dashed up, breathlessly announcing that a "Mr. and Mrs. Swaggerty" had arrived, without tickets and noisily demanding seats. Street knew there was no "Mrs. Swaggerty," but in all probability a curvy showgirl.

"Okay," he said, "put out a couple of folding chairs. Up close."

The gofer blinked. Marc made no explanations. He understood loyalty.

He turned again to Chelsea. She was shaking her head, glancing this way and that, pushing her golden hair back, muttering suggestions to Dufour, to the models, to the hairdresser, even to Heidler.

He went to her. "You look like hell."

"I feel like hell," she said, smiling grimly. "I've been back here as a model. I always thought it was easy, that everyone else was behaving hysterically. I knew what I had to wear, knew what I had to do, that long walk down the runway, a couple of turns, letting the skirt flare out, wiggling my hips, smiling, using my shoulders, prancing and strutting and selling the dress. I never realized that for a designer back here could be so . . . lonely."

He hesitated. "Lonely now?" he asked.

She looked up into his face, the brown eyes deep under heavy brows, the look of concern, of support, perhaps of something more. "No," she said, "not now."

He did not know how much to read into her words or her look, and so, feeling inadequate, he said simply: "Okay, it's your party. *Merde.*"

She looked at him, grinning now, the tension washed away, her face sweat-slicked but unaccountably happy. "Do you know why the French always say '*merde*'?"

"No, they just do. Like theater people saying 'Break a leg.' A reverse 'Good luck.' "

"Well, you ought to know, being French and all."

"Well, I don't, for God's sake," he snapped impatiently, "and why does it matter?" They were about to start the show and she was putting him through a catechism.

"It's from World War I," she said. "When they went off to war everyone cheered and sang and the French wore bright blue uniforms with red stripes. Then, after a year in the trenches, when all those guys were killed, no one was wearing bright uniforms anymore, no one was cheering or singing. And when they went over the top, guys just said, 'Shit.' "

He stared at her. "How do you know these things?"

"I read a lot. I *told* you."

There was a momentary silence, and Heidler bustled up, waving his hands. "*Are* we going to have a show?" he demanded.

Marc leaned over and kissed Chelsea on the cheek. It was the first time he had kissed her. "*Merde,* Chelsea."

She stood there for an instant, looking at him. Then she wheeled and shouted, "Okay, Dufour, send 'em out."

Later, fashionable people who had been miles or continents away would claim to have been there the morning Chelsea West first showed. They'd claimed that after Marc Bohan's first collection for Dior, when Gittler of Ohrbach's came out raving, "He's saved the house!"; when Saint Laurent showed his first independent collection in that charming *hôtel particulière* on the rue Spontini; when André Courrèges led the buyers up the winding staircase to his loft and Andrew Arkin came down trumpeting about the revolutionary shape of trousers and mispronouncing the new hero as "Courageous."

They began applauding when the first six models came out all at once, in their oversized crisp white cotton blouses and those big, swirling patchwork skirts, and they never stopped. Oh, it wasn't perfect. As *WWD* sniffed, "Miss West's evening looks suggest she has never been let out after dark." But the day clothes—this free expression of a sportive America that Chelsea understood because it came from within her—the day clothes were a spectacular success. Perhaps Lincoln Radford of *Mode* put it best:

"Miss West is a young American making clothes for young America. Contemporary, yet borrowing from the past; easy without ever being sloppy; exuberant and tolerant and wise. Her clothes say as much about what America wants in its wardrobe as the voters last week said they wanted in their politics."

Even *Newsweek* was caught up in the excitement: "An American heiress gives fashion a bequest."

Street threw the requisite party that night, taking over the upper deck of the Water Club. Bobby Short played piano and sang Cole Porter and Gershwin, the foggy, throaty voice quavering and lovely, hushing the cocktail chat and the tinkle-tinkle of glass. The models got drunk and danced in stockinged feet, the *paparazzi* snarled at one another and flailed about with their Nikons, buyers and fashion editors talked shop, with Chelsea the hub of a whirling, never-ending kaleidoscopic rush of adulation. Andy Warhol came in, pale and faunlike. Marc remembered someone's line about Andy, that he'd go to the opening of an envelope.

"She's so pretty," he whispered to Marc, "you're so lucky."

Street thanked him, not trying to explain the inexplicable, that they were in business together and that was all.

"She's a genius," Andy said, "and so young."

Well, she wasn't a genius. Marc knew that. But he knew she had that indefinable "something" that people like Diana Vreeland were always raving about. She had worked hard, and so had he; they'd pulled it off. Maybe it was a freak, maybe she was a one-shot, maybe she'd never be able to do it again. But she'd done it this once. And he could ask nothing more of her or of himself or Heidler or Dufour.

Stanley Baltimore lurched toward him through the crowd, a champagne glass filled with Perrier in one hand, his arm around the tiny waist of a teenager in a black evening dress.

"Street, that Chelsea is a winner! My congratulations. I should own a talent like that."

"Thanks, Stanley. She worked very hard."

Baltimore shook his head. "Hard work? Any *schmuck* can work hard. She's a big talent, baby." He paused. "And what a piece of ass, besides."

The child looked up at him from under his arm and giggled.

Marc got himself a stiff Scotch on the rocks and went outside, onto the restaurant's deck. The night was cold and the river flowed past, black and silent, toward the sea. Across on the far shore he could read the lighted sign on the *Daily News* printing plant and see the headlights moving along the expressway toward

Brooklyn. He felt good about things. He just didn't want to be inside there anymore.

Tomorrow was a working day. Chelsea had done her part. Now it was up to him to exploit her success, to choreograph what she had done into something far bigger than the reality of her achievement. It was how fashion worked. Tomorrow, cold as ice, he would go to work magnifying an image. He had turned a pretty girl with a great name into a designer. Now he would try to turn her into something bigger: an American Chanel, coldly and with calculation trading on her name, honing and polishing a naïve, unpracticed talent.

He stared back through the cold-steamed windows to where she stood, surrounded by people telling her how wonderful she was. Well, it was her night. He'd never tried to share Adam's triumphs, nor would he share hers. He would leave her to it. He walked back through the room to the hatcheck and got his topcoat and went out to hail a cab and go home without ever having talked to her.

24

Who will dress the new First Lady? Blass, Adolfo, and Galanos certainly. The Inaugural gown? Don't ask. Not yet, at
least.

Mode, December 3, 1980

Seventh Avenue isn't an address," Chelsea remarked,
"it's a state of mind."

She'd stolen that line from Sydney Heidler to use on television shows. Sometimes she varied her remarks, instinctively sensing the moment, even startling the imperturbable David
Hartman on *Good Morning America.*

"Isn't fashion a sort of fantasy world?" he asked, his large,
slightly bulging eyes fixed on her.

"Yeah, I guess. Maybe like the cave myth."

"What's that?"

"You know, Plato. There were these people who lived in
caves and never saw the sun. They thought the shadows on the
wall of the cave were reality. Then one day one of the cave people
wandered outside. And when he came back he said, 'Listen, guys,
I've seen the outside. *We're* the reality, not the shadows.' "

"Yes?" Hartman said, waiting.

"So they stoned him to death."

"Oh."

"Yeah, fashion's like that, not knowing where clothes start
and people leave off. Of course, Plato wasn't talking fashion. The
cave myth was really about the death of Socrates."

Hartman hurried to a commercial.

Johnny Carson smirked at her, raising an eyebrow for the television camera. "I've got to say this, Chelsea, you look better in dresses than Bill Blass."

It wasn't very funny, it was unfair to Blass, but it was how people seemed to feel about her success. She was new, she was beautiful, she seemed to have talent. She had a famous American name. As *Time* magazine put it, "Chelsea West HAS IT ALL!"

Street knew she had also been lucky. Adam had shown his own spring collection three days later, as subtle and mature a look as he had ever done, and while it sold well, the line went almost unnoticed in the press. There were other good collections that second week of November, from Lauren, Klein, Perry Ellis, Donna Karan, and Trigère. But as it was Ronald Reagan's week, it was also Chelsea's.

Heidler, busily writing up orders and dickering by phone for additional plant capacity and fabric to supply the demand, seemed to have shed years. "Get her right back at it, Marc," he urged, "we could get a resort collection out of her this winter. Strike while she's hot."

"We're not in this for the quick kill, Sydney. She's a kid, she's just learning. I want her to go to Paris with you and me in January, see the couture collections, think about what she'll do in May, watch how you buy fabric. There's no rush."

Heidler noticed he hadn't mentioned Adam. Well, that was between Marc and Adam. He'd been in the business too long to insert himself between warring partners.

Adam left town right after the show. "I need a break, Marc."

"Sure."

Usually he would bore Marc with delicious details of his vacations, drawing colorful word pictures of rented beachfront houses, of chartered jets, of palm trees and sandy beaches and turquoise seas, and of the rich and famous friends who would be accompanying him. This time Adam said nothing, just that he would be back the first of December.

"Fine, Adam," Marc said, and the two men turned away from each other, coldly and without even a handshake.

"I never thought I'd see that," Heidler told Marc sadly. Marc shrugged.

Chelsea was not there to see it. After doing the *Tonight* show in Los Angeles she flew to Denver. One of the West limos was waiting at the airport.

"Your grandpa's excited as hell, Chelsea," the driver told her, "all this stuff about you in the papers."

"Excited or furious?"

"Oh, he's excited. Asked me this morning before I headed down here if I seen you talking with Johnny Carson and I said, sure I had. Hell, I think he would of fired me on the spot if I didn't, would of fired all of us."

The great hills were already snow-covered, and as the road climbed out of the city she slumped in the back of the big car, watching the country. She had belonged here for so long. Still, she found herself wondering what they were doing now in New York, what mischief Toy was up to, what might be worrying old Sydney, whether Adam was still sulking, what Marc Street was doing and saying and thinking.

"Well," Will West said from the porch as she got out of the limo. That was all he said, but there was a grin on his leathered face.

"Yep, it's me."

He opened his arms then and she ran to him, taking the steps two at a time.

Her birthday was November 15. "Twenty-three," West grumbled, "all grown up."

"Still a kid in lots of ways."

"I know," he said, "and damned glad of it."

He liked birthdays, even his own, and on the evening of hers he had done his best to fill the house, with some of the neighboring ranchers and their wives, girls from town with whom she had gone to school, the local doctor, the judge, some local businessmen, the foreman and his wife and daughters, some of the more respectable cowboys who worked for him, the people who ran the ski resort, the ski lodge operators, a couple of his executives who happened to be among Chelsea's favorites and who had been flown in for the occasion. There were no outsiders.

"Don't need outsiders," he grumbled in response to a question she hadn't asked. "New York is full of strangers. Thought you'd like to see some friendly faces for a change."

He gave her a sapphire necklace, blue as her eyes, but not until their guests had left and the two of them sat in his study, the mountains beyond the windows gleaming in the moonlight.

"It's lovely, Grandpa, really beautiful. I love it."

He watched as she hooked it around her neck. "Not as lovely as you are."

She got up then and went to him to kiss his forehead. "I love you," she said.

"I believe you do, Catherine. Not many do love me, though there are some who claim to."

She stood by the window, looking at the mountains in the glorious Colorado night.

"Miss it?" he asked.

"Yes. No. I dunno. I miss you. And this place. But New York hasn't turned out bad. I've been lucky, I have a good job, there are some nice people."

"This fellow you work for, Street?"

"He's nice too, I guess."

"You don't sound so sure. He a Jew?"

"Yes. Half Jewish, anyway."

"Then he's a Jew," West said flatly.

She didn't argue the nicety. If she argued all her grandfather's prejudices, they'd never talk about anything else.

"I don't trust Jews much," he said, "never have."

"Well, Street's okay. He tells the truth, tells you what he wants, he treats people fair. I like him."

"But?" he said, sensing she was holding back.

"Well, you know, in the modeling business I got kind of used to having guys making passes at me. I mean, there's all this supposed glamor and the money and your picture on magazine covers, and men seem to think that's like a 'for sale or rent' sign on the front lawn."

"And *are* you?" he asked.

She laughed. "Hey, Grandpa, you think I'm gonna tell you that?"

He didn't laugh. "But Street's different?" he said.

"Yeah. I can't figure it. He's a good-looking-enough guy. He's got money, brains, he's interesting to talk to. But he doesn't seem to have a steady. I dunno."

"He queer?"

She laughed again. "Grandpa, by this time I *know* the gay ones. Believe me."

"Don't like queers," he muttered.

"You don't mean to tell me."

It was his turn to laugh. "By God, Catherine, you're missed around here. No one else ever makes me laugh."

The Thanksgiving crowd had begun to arrive in Aspen. Every night there was a party. Committees met, planning the big events of the Aspen "season": the Historical Society's "Sweetheart Ball"; the Music Associates of Aspen; the art auction of the Community School; the Art Museum's Patron's Dinner; a benefit for Ballet/Aspen. Steel people came from Chicago and bankers from Denver and filmmakers from Los Angeles; a woman who owned a fried chicken franchise company from Kentucky; and the Leonard Lauders from New York.

Will West was asked to everything and went nowhere. This was not considered a snub. Will West had his own set of rules. No one really expected him to come. His granddaughter now, that was different. Her name was hastily added to lists, chauffeurs hand-delivered invitations, the phones at the West ranch rang constantly. Most nights she stayed home with her grandfather. She went to two or three of the parties, those hosted by people she really knew, not to those drawn by her name, her new celebrity. The people she knew made her welcome, their homes were attractive, the food and the drink plentiful and the best, the conversation witty, informed. A year ago on such evenings she would have found delight. Now it was all brittle and empty.

Marc Street was two thousand miles away.

She skied, her face tanning, and enjoyed feeling the pull of muscles unused in New York. This was what she missed, the sun and the cold and the mountains. When her plane landed at La-

Guardia it was warm, raining, and the cab driver was complaining about Koch and the Taxi and Limousine Commission.

"Welcome back," she said, half to herself.

"Huh?" the driver asked.

"Nothing."

They came in over the Triborough Bridge, the city's lights dim in the rain, but as they came down the FDR Drive there was a big tanker riding high in the water, steaming south parallel to them, as big as an apartment building, slick and dark and mysterious. New York!

Toy wasn't home. There was nothing strange about that. It was night, and Toy was a creature of the night.

In the hallway of their apartment there were flowers in the vase, browning and curling now at the edges, with a card propped against the vase. She picked it up. Toy had scrawled a message on the envelope: "These came a week ago. I reed the card, nice?"

The flowers were from Marc Street: "I know your birthday's around now but can't find the date. Hope I'm not off by too much." It was signed "Marc."

New York! It felt like home.

25

In Washington they await the new administration. What will
Mr. Reagan do? In Paris they await the new *haute couture*
collections. What will M. Saint Laurent do?

Mode, January 6, 1981

Adam came back to work from somewhere vague in
the islands, suntanned, slim, perhaps more handsome than ever.
Stanley Baltimore reported gleefully that his perfume, finally in
the shops, just in time for the Christmas retail season, was selling
out. The price was right, the bottle sleek and distinctive, the name
recognizable, easy to pronounce. Men whose tongues twisted over
"L'Air du Temps" or "Je Reviens" could say "Adam." At fifty
dollars an ounce, it moved. Even Baltimore, hard and cynical,
admitted, "It doesn't smell like piss, either." Annual production
of Adam jeans had passed the five-million mark. Majesty Fashions got a dollar royalty for every pair. Adam himself already
made more than a million dollars a year just on jean sales and
talked of buying his own jet, of getting a house in the South of
France, establishing a chair in his name at FIT or Parsons School
of Design. He had, it was whispered, a new lover, a famous young
television actor. He should have been happy and was not. Chelsea
was still eating at him—Chelsea and his betrayal by Marc Street,
his partner and oldest friend. Had Peter Feeley still been around,
it might have been different.

Chelsea could shrug off his resentment. She and Adam had
once been pals, collaborators, star model and brilliant creator. He

had babbled about her beauty and her fashion instinct while she gloried in wearing clothes by "the best designer in the country." Mutual admiration had given way to a chill courtesy. Once they were friends; now they worked on separate floors.

During office hours, as best anyone could discern, Street treated them as equal partners, which puzzled Chelsea. They had been together for eight or nine months now, and Marc was still keeping his distance, measured, professional, dispassionate. She was not accustomed to being ignored. His disinterest was mystifying, aggravating.

The third week in January they flew off to Paris for the collections. Adam left a day early. Marc and Chelsea left together. Sydney Heidler had come down with flu, and Street ordered him to stay home and go to bed.

"But, Marc, you wanted me to be there, to work with Chelsea."

"I'll work with her."

"And carry messages between you and Adam," Heidler said, unable to resist the jibe.

"Sydney, you let me worry about that. Adam and I will communicate. We always have."

He meant it. If Adam could afford to sulk, *he* couldn't.

Chelsea was staying at the Ritz. Adam had a suite in the exotic new L'Hôtel on the Left Bank, presumably with his new friend. It was an establishment with an exterior garden under glass, complete with tropical birds and chained sambur monkeys. Marc continued loyal to the San Regis on the rue Jean-Goujon. When Chelsea got to her room, it was filled with flowers, including an arrangement from *Vogue,* one from Bohan at Dior, another from a French boy with whom she'd once dined, and three dozen roses from her English milord, accompanied by a note threatening to fly over from London for the week.

There are those days in winter when Paris is captured, like the fly in amber, in the mid-flight of perfection. They sing of April in Paris, but in April there is rain. The tourists flock in summer. November is foggy and rainy, the rains seeping down from the North Sea, chilling and depressing. Winter is neither as dank as London nor as cold as New York, but with alternating periods of gloom and delight. This, fortunately, was one of those weeks of sun and warmth and unseasonable skies, deep blue by day and star-spattered by night. The sunsets were early and long; dawn broke rosy and calm, as peaceful and lovely as mornings in Eden.

"I love Paris," Street announced, "I love it."

He and Chelsea had taken a cab from the rue Cambon door of the Ritz and crossed the Seine on one of the short bridges to the Île, where he had a table at L'Orangerie, not one of the great restaurants in the city, but picturesque. Saint Laurent was there, bored, entertaining a couple of buyers from New York. Gerard Depardieu sat across the room with a plump, influential critic and the critic's teenaged girlfriend, who was watching Depardieu and not the critic. Marc and Chelsea talked of the people at the other tables, and of nothing, during dinner, and then afterward they went across the street to the *sorbet* shop and bought ices. It was a soft night, perhaps sixty degrees Fahrenheit, pleasant for walking through the narrow streets of the Île and along the river, the Seine rushing black and mysterious. They stood for a time in mid-river on one of the stone bridges, watching a *bateau mouche* pass below like a brightly lighted child's toy.

"Walk?" he asked.

"Yes."

They crossed back to the Left Bank and ended at St.-Germain, where they found a table at the Deux Magots, as filled now on a January night as it might be in July.

"Coffee?" he asked.

"No," she said, "I think I'd like a brandy."

She was not much of a drinker, and he was surprised. But he gave the order.

"Your French is a lot better than mine," she said.

"Ought to be," he said, "my mother taught me."

They sat there at one of the metal tables, watching the late-evening crowd passing along the sidewalks, watching the spotlights illuminating the old church opposite, sipping Calvados and thinking their own thoughts.

Chelsea broke the silence. "You've been wonderful to

me, you know that. And I appreciate it, I don't have to tell you."

Street looked down at his drink. "You've done the job. That's all. Everyone knows it."

"Look, I'm a kid. You taught me, you gave me direction, support. You and Sydney and even that bastard Dufour."

Marc laughed. "He is pretty awful, isn't he?"

She laughed too. Then she sobered. "It isn't Dufour that grabs me. It's you."

The young men in their long university scarves and their tweed jackets went by, and the chic young women, heels clicking sharply on the pavement. Marc watched them pass.

Then he said, "Why me? You said I'd helped."

"Yes," she said, her voice somber. And he knew this was not the moment for a wisecrack. Or for debate. Let her talk.

"I dunno," she began, with the typical inarticulateness of her age, "there are things I don't understand. Things I want to ask about. Things you don't tell me. Never say."

Marc looked into her eyes but said nothing.

Chelsea hesitated for a moment. She knew what she wanted to say but she wondered *if* she should say it. Well, this was the time. She could taste the Calvados in her mouth.

"Look, you and I have been working together for nearly a year. I've been working for you, to be precise. It's been fun, we've done okay; Adam's pissed off but you expected that. But everything else went good. By some lucky fluke I gave you a good collection."

"Not lucky," he said, "it was good. *You* were good."

"Okay," she said impatiently, "so it worked. But that isn't what I wanted to talk about."

"No?"

She shook her head. "Oh, Marc, don't you *know?*" She did not want to be this blunt. But the words just tumbled out.

"No," he said, "I don't know."

Chelsea pushed the half-empty glass away from her, sliding it across the metal table. The waiter hovered, his white jacket shimmering in the lights, until Marc waved him off with a big hand. The waiter raised his shoulders and left.

A swift cloud marked the moon, and Street imagined the night had grown suddenly cold. "Do you want to go inside?" he asked.

"No, I like it out here. I like the night."

"Yes," he said, not understanding.

She let a moment pass, and then she took up again what she had, self-consciously, begun. "You leave me alone," she said.

"Of course I do. I'm not a designer. You're the one with the ideas. I just pay the bills, do the paperwork."

This was going badly. She knew it.

"Look, Marc, I don't know how to say this. But I'm not used to being ignored. That's not vanity talking, I promise you. It's just that . . ." She stopped again, and then, before he could say anything, the words poured out of her.

"I don't understand you. We spend eight hours a day together. We share everything. We take these enormous risks. We lose a few, we win a few. And . . . when it's over, it's . . . over."

He decided he should say something, feeling stupid but not wanting to jump to conclusions. "Well, isn't it? Isn't it over when it's over?"

She slammed her fist down on the table, setting the two glasses to tingling. "No, dammit. It isn't. It hasn't even . . . dammit . . . *begun!*"

He paid after that and together, slowly, with arms around waists, they walked down again toward the river and the bridges that led to the other bank, leaning against each other and talking all the way, the barriers between them broken at last.

26

It has long been an accepted belief that it is against the law not to fall in love in Paris at least once in your life.

Mode, January 27, 1981

They slept together that night. And for the first time since Raker, the first time since the abortion, she had an orgasm. It came suddenly, fierce and pulsing, forcing her to cry out and to flail arms and legs against and around him, her nails raking his buttocks without meaning to, her teeth clamping down painfully on his lower lip. His reactions were just as powerful, instinctive, unprogrammed, uncontrolled.

It was as if both of them had been waiting for a long, long time.

"I wondered," she said, sleepily and content, "when you would finally ask."

He grunted. "Easy for you to wonder, harder for me to say."

"Why?" she murmured.

"Because," he said seriously, "I wanted to ask the first time I ever saw you. In La Grenouille. It was lunchtime, and you came in all in furs and boots, snow melting off your hat."

"You were with Bill Blass."

"You *know.* You *did* see me!"

"How could I not?"

He laughed that one off. "Everyone in the joint was looking at *you,* that's how."

"Just because I was new. And tall. And—"

"Sure, five foot twelve."

"You remember?"

"Yes, I remember."

She asked him, then, why he had been so distant and for so long.

"I had my job. I thought that was enough. I started when I was nineteen, and those first years it felt like cheating if I let anything or anyone distract me. Later on, well, there were the usual girls you meet in bars or at parties, stews on the prowl and an actress and a couple of twenty-year-old airhead models and that was it."

"And now a twenty-three-year-old airhead."

"The hell you are. That was part of it too. I liked you, admired your head, and when you went to work for me I wanted it to be strictly business. There are too damned many phony relationships on the Avenue, deals built on sex. I didn't want that. It wouldn't be fair to you, wouldn't be fair to the company."

She listened, saying nothing, curled close to his body.

"Then there was Adam," he said. "He's sure we were lovers all the while."

"Dear Adam."

"Look, Chelsea, it's a lot more complicated than it seems. Adam and I have been together a long time. I knew he was going to resent the hell out of anyone else I brought in as a designer. Man, woman, whatever. It had nothing to do with you. If Dufour were the designer, Adam would have hated *him.*"

"Easy man to hate."

"Not the point. Adam and I are close. *Were* close, for a long while. I hope we're going to be close again. I dunno, it's as if he were my kid brother. Adam's got his faults. He's susceptible to flattery. Ever since he lost Peter Feeley, he's gotten this entourage that lives off him like parasites. He listens to them because they tell him what he wants to hear. He pays too much attention to people like Stanley Baltimore and that bastard Radford. He sleeps around too much. He can't resist a pretty face."

"And you can."

"Well, yes, I can, I try to do my thinking with my pants on."

"My grandfather would love that line."

"Anyway, if I'd started a hot romance with you right after bringing you into Majesty as a designer, Adam would have interpreted it as couch casting. Which it wasn't. I thought then, think now, that you can be a major force at Majesty, and sex had nothing to do with it. But Adam wouldn't have believed that."

"So sex has nothing to do with us?" she asked, teasing.

He rolled over onto an elbow and looked down at her face. "Oh, yes," he said, his voice serious, "not with business. But with us."

She pulled him down toward her, long legs moving, slender body raising to meet his, her blue eyes open and reacting to his every move, widening and unblinking, readying herself for the wonder of total abandon that she knew would come again.

In the night while he slept she rose and went to the window, opening it and stepping out onto the minimal balcony, shivering in the night air, the sweat drying on her body, staring out over the rooftops to where the Arc de Triomphe glowed against the western sky.

She had not told Street about Raker or the abortion. Too early for that. There had been men since Raker and she had slept with them. But always there had been a part of her, the very core, that held back, curling inward, resisting. She threw her legs apart, opened her mouth, gave them her breasts. But not herself. Tonight, with Street, this was different. It had been building with him for a long time, longer, perhaps, than either of them knew. Still, one night did not make a life. Sex was not love. She remembered first loves, her first beau, her first time. She had told Street none of this. He had been more open, telling her about the party girls, the models. Why did she assume candor on his part? She had heard enough lines by this time. When you looked the way that she did, there were always lines, always men, persuasive and convincing, to deliver them.

She half turned to peer back into the bedroom. She could see his big body under the sheet, indistinct but undeniably there. All she had to do was to go back inside, wake him, press her mouth on his, and it would begin again.

Maybe she was wrong about Street. Maybe he was just another Raker, out for a quick lay, not after a few hundred bucks but after something more. A lot more. She was Will West's heir. Seventh Avenue bred few heroes; even Marc admitted it was a hard school; she knew it herself. What was it he'd said? "I had a lousy love life. I was working too hard." Could she believe that? Why should she?

Then she remembered his touch, his feel, the intensity of his passion. And she suspended doubt. No, she told herself, this wasn't Raker.

High across the rooftops lights flicked on in an apartment. She remembered that she was naked, and she took a deep breath and stepped back into the room. She went to the bed, looking down at him, watching him breathe.

"Marc," she said, her lips brushing his cheek.

"Yes," he grunted, lost in sleep.

"Marc," she said again. "Marc."

At dawn he took her again. Or they took each other, rolling together in the half sleep of morning, gentle and spent, and yet quickly roused and waking.

"I've wanted to do this for so long," he murmured.

"Me too," she said, "oh, how I've wanted this."

"Yeah," he said, "yes."

Her mouth was on his. How good she tastes, he thought, even in the morning. He remembered other girls, cocaine-excited. This was a girl fueled only on herself. How much time they'd wasted, how many empty nights had passed. For her, after so long, the cowboy Raker was forgotten, the dingy Denver clinic, the draining emptiness and the sorrow, vulgar and terrible.

Marc started to roll Chelsea onto her back.

"No," she said, her voice strangled with desire, "let me."

He tensed, not knowing what she meant, and then as her strong arms guided him, he relaxed and rolled back, lying prone as she moved on top of him, her face kissing him, her hair hanging over him like a silken curtain. When he was flat, she straddled his big body, her long legs outside his, her knees bent back, her feet tucked. He looked up at her, into that lovely face, seeing her blue eyes, widened by desire, her face shining, slick with sweat, her mouth half open and panting, the long hair damply swaying and heavy. Ferocious and tender, she leaned on his shoulders with her strong young hands, pinning him down, her long body leveraged against his, her weight against his, gravity helping, his willingness helping.

"Yes," he said, guttural and waiting, "oh, yeah."

Her head dipped toward him, shrouded by the blond hair, and then pulled away quickly as her pelvis slid atop him, letting him enter, pinioning herself on him, just as swiftly pulling away and then again bending to him so that her breasts hung and swayed over his groin, low and barely touching, nipples teasing and swinging, only to pull away and be replaced, just as swiftly, by her opened mouth. He was inside her and then outside and then inside again, always, it seemed, a different orifice, a different sensation, each of them exciting, each new and electric.

When he came she withdrew immediately so that he splashed against her belly and, as she slid down the length of his body, against and between her breasts. When the pulsing had ended, she lay there, wet and spent, and then, rolling away from him, her hands came up to knead and rub the wetness into her torso, deft and soothing, the way women apply suntan lotion.

After a few moments he got up and went toward the bathroom. "I'll get you a towel," he said.

"No," she said, her voice choked and low, "I want to dry like this, to have you on me."

He paused and looked back at her, long and sleek and wet.

Night after night it went like this, and sometimes at lunchtime or in the afternoon. They had appointments and they kept them. But when they were not working, they mated, desperate and wanting, as if neither of them had ever made love.

"It's different, isn't it?" she said once. And he agreed, not knowing why or how, but simply that it was so, "Yes, yes, it is different."

And it was. Even the faded floral wallpaper of this room in the San Regis became important, the long, old-fashioned bathtub where they played, the closet in which she hung her clothes, the ashtray where she stubbed out a cigarette. He thought of La Grenouille in New York, where he had first seen her, so long ago, a restaurant once and now a shrine. He knew these things were silly, and he reveled in them.

They kept their separate hotels. Some nights they went back to the San Regis, some nights to the Ritz. The evening after the Givenchy collection they had dinner at the Brasserie Lipp.

"Some businessman you are," she said.

"Why?"

"We could be saving all this money for Majesty Fashions by getting a double room somewhere."

He laughed. "Next time. We're still getting to know each other."

And they were. At the collections they sat together, with Adam, in the front row, all three of them taking notes. Afterward they would have lunch or, if it was an afternoon showing, go back to one of the hotels and sit in the bar over cocktails, comparing notes and deciding how to spend their caution. She was deferential toward Adam, intelligent about not pushing theories. He was, after all, far more experienced. Sometimes, if there were no agreement, Marc would decide. She noted he was careful usually to decide in Adam's favor. Adam was still pouting, but not as sourly as he had in New York. It was impossible to work together in such proximity and not be cordial. Adam's new hotel had turned out well, and so had his young actor. At night they disappeared, leaving Chelsea and Marc alone. She took him to bistros she had found while working in Paris as a model; he took her to restaurants and bars he had known for years. They found smoky little joints neither of them knew, where they sat late over brandy, smoking cigarettes and talking, knees or thighs touching lightly under the table, her hair falling softly across her lovely face, her eyes lively and huge in the dim light. An intimacy was growing that had something, but not everything, to do with bed.

"You're pretty shrewd, you know," he said one night, spent in her double bed at the Ritz with the curtains drawn back to let moonlight filter in from the garden.

"Oh?"

"Sure, it's your grandfather coming out in you. If I let you work on the business side for a year, you'd probably be running Majesty and firing *both* Adam and me."

"But never Sydney."

"No one can fire Sydney," he said, "he knows where the bodies are buried."

"And *are* there bodies?" she said.

"Everyone has bodies somewhere," he said, staring at the molded ceiling, knowing this time would come and dreading it. They barely knew each other, and he was not yet sure enough of her, or of himself, to tell her everything. How could a wealthy young woman from a famous American family understand about Carl Lazer and laundered money and about how his father lived and how he died?

"Hey, I was only kidding," she said, "don't get so. uptight."

He turned to look into her face, looking even younger now than usual, scrubbed and unmade, her hair damply straying across the pillow and his bare shoulder.

"No," he said, "it's just my old man once had some trouble in Washington. There was an investigation of graft and racketeering on Seventh Avenue, and he was a witness. It happened when I was in my teens. I don't like to think about it too much."

"I understand," she said gently, reaching out a hand to find him and to draw him again toward the slickness of her body, once again ready for love.

"You don't understand a damned thing," he thought, but said nothing, moving toward her, his big arms pulling her close as she told him about her nipples and how she wanted now to use them.

Jimmy de Bertrand threw the traditional closing party Friday evening in his Left Bank house, a lush overdecorated *hôtel particulière* in the *septième*, with elephant ivory and leather screens and Moroccan rugs so deep your feet disappeared in them. The buyers were all there, and the fashion editors and the fabric suppliers and the elegant women who were his private clients. Lincoln Radford was there. So was Stanley Baltimore. Everyone was there but Jimmy, who made a brief appearance, languidly shook a few hands, and dove into secret recesses of the house, not to be seen again that night. It was left for Brugère to make the running. The collection had not been a success. But parties, once arranged, are impossible to cancel, and so they all went, out of courtesy rather than enthusiasm.

"Come on, Jean-Pierre," Marc told Brugère, "no one can be sensational every season. You know that. So does Jimmy. What the hell's he sulking about?"

Brugère shrugged and ignored the remark. "So this is the new genius of Seventh Avenue."

"Some genius." Chelsea laughed, trying to keep it light. "Just a girl from the country who got lucky. Marc and Adam are the geniuses."

"Well, I agree with that!" Brugère said briskly. "And it must be so, because they have been telling me such things for years."

They were speaking English because her French could not keep up. Brugère had a thick accent. But he knew the words, knew what he was saying.

A buyer from Magnin's and Lincoln Radford joined them. Radford sensed tension. The buyer gushed, "M. Brugère, I wish I could speak French. Your English is so good."

Brugère smiled wickedly. And in slowly measured words, he replied, "I . . . can . . . *count.*"

Radford ignored the buyer. "So, Jean-Pierre, you've finally met fashion's new girl wonder?"

Brugère smiled, but there was no joy in it.

"Oh, yes, Lincoln, we are so honored to have Mees West among us. The next Chanel, I have heard it said."

"Oh, I see," said Lincoln Radford. "So many young girls . . . presume . . . to be Chanel."

Marc took Chelsea's arm firmly. "We've got to be going, J.-P. Please tell Jimmy thanks."

"I will not fail to do so," the Frenchman said coldly.

When they had left, Baltimore sidled over to join Radford and Brugère. "Do you think Street's screwing her?" he asked.

Radford inquired, wickedly, "Wouldn't you?"

Stanley Baltimore just licked his lips.

Brugère left them then, but not before uttering one more word. "Whore!"

Lincoln Radford wondered just when and how he might put the evening's tensions to use. Perhaps if he were to tell Adam that Marc and Chelsea were lovers . . .

27

Ludwig Amtorg, the great Swiss fabric designer, will freely confess over lunch that as a boy he wept to touch fine silk. You may find this strange. But then you are not the great Amtorg.

Mode, February 3, 1981

After Paris they flew to Zurich to see Amtorg, the fabric man, who took them to dinner at the Kronenhalle.

"Over there, at that table, James Joyce wrote *Finnegans Wake*. I had difficulty reading it myself, but truly, this is where it was written."

Chelsea had read it, Marc hadn't. Amtorg, who must have been a child at the time, told them stories of Joyce's drinking, his writing, his gradually going blind. And he talked about silk.

"When I was a boy I would pick up a bit of silk, touch one of my mother's dresses, and cry."

When they left Zurich on the night train back to Paris, he came down to the station to see them off.

"Here," he said to Chelsea, "here is something for you to remember Zurich by," both shy and proud at the same time. It was a cardboard tube, and when she opened it in their compartment on the train it was a signed print by Braque. It was very lovely.

"What a nice, strange man."

"Fashion," Marc said thoughtfully, "is full of strange people. But not all of them as nice as Amtorg."

They went straight to the dining car and had one of those

wonderful European railroad meals with good wine and a French waiter. The car was only half full, with smug businessmen, travelers who looked like international couriers, one beautiful, lonely woman with sad eyes, men with the pursed lips and dark suits of diplomats. No tourists. Europe in winter has its consolations. They skipped coffee and went back to their compartment and undressed and made love in the narrow lower bed, feeling the clicking of the track beneath them. At Dijon she woke and raised the shade a few inches to look out at the garishly lighted station, at travelers, sleepy-eyed and muffled against the cold, at the busy workmen and railway officials, and beyond them the station hotel and narrow streets winding away into the sleeping town. She turned to look at Marc in the narrow ray of light. How hard he can look sometimes, she thought, and now in sleep, how gentle. Her hand reached down to touch her belly, no longer rippling with the reactive spasms of love.

She pulled the shade and lay there, listening to the slow panting of the idling engine, smiling in the dark, alone with her thoughts and her love, satisfied and complete.

Paris was a two-day stopover to clean up business Street had left hanging. When they got back to New York he changed clothes and left immediately for Hong Kong. More jeans capacity had become available, and he wanted to see the quality of work at first hand. Adam jeans were booming, and he had begun to think of a jeans line for Chelsea. It was not an idea that would meet with universal enthusiasm.

When he got back from the Orient a week later, jet-lagged and frazzled by hours of haggling with more than usually secretive Chinese businessmen with air-conditioned offices on The Peak and sweatshops in Kowloon, he called Dugan at Marine Midland and they lunched at a bankers' club. Dugan was bullish about Majesty Fashions but bearish on jeans.

"Marc, the jeans boom has gone on for ten years now. It can't last forever. And you're going in there against some real heavies. Levi Strauss, Blue Bell, and H. D. Lee are the Big Three and they don't play games. Levis alone spent thirty-six million dollars last year on jeans advertising. You wanna go up against that? You could get steamrolled."

"Dan, we've been in business nearly twenty years, I think I know what I'm doing."

"I'm sure you do, and the bank thinks so too. I'm just raising a point."

"I know, Dan. And I don't need any money right now. I just want to know about a line of credit when the time comes."

"You'd have it, I'm reasonably sure. But we'd all be happier if the money went for something other than jeans."

Marc nodded. "Look, if we were talking basic, five-pocket jeans, I'd agree with you. The baby boomers are growing up and there's bound to be a fallout. But I'm talking fashion. Jeans with a different look. With a designer name. I don't want to sell fifty million pairs. Just a couple million or so. Fashion can make the difference."

"Like those button-fly things?" Dugan said sourly.

Marc laughed. "I agree with you. A cheap, vulgar gimmick. But it worked. For about six months they were hot as hell, and then it died. I'm not talking gimmicks; I'm talking real fashion. Shape, spirit, new colors, maybe stretch fiber, I dunno. That's Adam's department."

Dugan snapped his fingers at a waiter. "You're right about that! There's a very bright guy I know named Jay Meltzer, at Goldman Sachs. He follows the rag trade. Says that for ten years the jeans companies never knew they were in the apparel business. Says they thought they were selling canned goods."

"Well, I don't want to sell canned goods. Innovation. Style. Fashion. If we get it right, the stuff'll sell."

Dugan shrugged as the waiter cleared the table and took their coffee order.

"Another thing," Marc said, "I'm not buying factories and hiring thousands of people, you know. No big cash outlays, no heavy debt servicing, no major capital projects. We lease factory capacity by the year. I know jeans aren't forever, but if we get a couple more good years, fine. Once it starts to fade, we get out."

The banker smiled. "That's one of the reasons we like you, Marc. Unlike most people in the business, you're marginally rational."

"Only marginally?"

Dugan laughed. "How's this new designer of yours, Chelsea West? Every time I pick up a magazine or turn on television, there she is. Great publicity."

"Suppose we put out a Chelsea line of jeans, Dan?"

"*Another* line? You've got Adam jeans already. Wouldn't you just be competing with yourself in a market that one of these days is going to start shrinking? What would Adam say?"

They talked about it for a while, and then Marc let it drop, as if it were nothing important. Even with Dugan, who was a friend despite being a banker, he held back some things.

He went to bed alone that night, still feeling the flight and having talked with her briefly in the office and then by phone to her apartment in the evening.

"I understand," she said.

The tiredness had melted by the next day, and they had an early dinner at Orsini's, wonderful creamy pasta with truffles sliced thin and a white Antinori that ached with cold.

"You feed me pretty well," she said. "I think I'm falling for you."

"Good. I'm going to keep feeding you well."

They had a late drink in one of the new places in Soho. It was a fresh, starry evening, rare for early February, between snowstorms; they could cross at the corners without sinking up to the ankles in slush.

"Now," he said, "my dark secret."

"You're gay."

"No," he said, "you've never seen my apartment."

When he'd opened the door and switched on the light he stood back, not saying anything, just watching her.

"Well," she said, looking around, "it's not precisely *House Beautiful.*"

Marc grinned. "Adam hates it."

"Is that supposed to make me like it?"

He walked around the living room, still wearing his overcoat. "Look, I like old buildings. Buildings with air conditioners sticking out of the windows. That means they're pre-war, with high ceilings, and those corny moldings in the plaster. Big rooms. What the hell, there's plenty of space."

He walked through a hallway past one darkened room that might have been a bedroom, past a big kitchen, to the main bedroom. "I hate to turn on the light."

"Why, roaches? God, I hate roaches." She shivered, visibly.

He flipped the switch. "No, I don't have roaches," he said fiercely. "At least not very often. But all those woolly things under the bed. It's embarrassing."

She leaned down. "My God, when did you last dust under there?"

"I dunno. Last time I gave a cocktail party. I had a woman come in. She got all the woollies out, but she stole a bottle of gin. Hate people who steal. I would have given her the bottle."

"Marc," she said, as a schoolteacher might, "there *are* honest maids, you know."

"I know. It's just so much trouble finding one and telling her what to do and buying brooms and polish and rags and all the stuff she'll need. Can't face it."

They walked back into the living room. There were piles of magazines, an efficient-looking stereo, a working fireplace, good, overstuffed furniture, lots of lamps and ashtrays, and some decent small tables. She casually ran a finger over a tabletop.

"I can't believe you," she said, regarding her fingertip. "You run an organized business, you've got taste, you have money and brains."

"But no maid," he said, slightly defensive.

"No *books!*" she said. "Don't you ever read?"

He took off his overcoat and tossed it over the back of an easy chair, relieved to have changed the subject.

"I've got some. In the closet. If I had some bookcases you'd see them."

"Boy," she said, taking off her own coat. He took it and disappeared into the hallway. He didn't want her to start looking into closets.

They had a chilled pear brandy in the living room. He'd fiddled rather competently with the stereo.

"Hall and Oates," he announced, as the music flowed out into the room.

"Hey," she said, "from your generation I was expecting 'American Pie.' "

"Brat."

She undressed in the bathroom, and when she came out he was lying on the bed, smoking, watching her silhouetted against the light.

"Will you buy me a toothbrush?" she said. "I had to use yours."

"Sorry. I'll get one tomorrow."

She came over to the bed and he moved, making room for her. She stood there.

"Have you got a T-shirt?"

"Sure." He got up and got one out of a dresser drawer. When she put it on it stopped at the top of her legs.

"Nice," he said. "Never looks that good on me."

"I think it's sexy," she said, dropping down onto the bed, baring her belly as she did.

"So do I," he said huskily. They had not been together for more than two weeks.

"Good," she said. "Let's screw."

In the morning she was gone before he woke. The kitchen and the bathroom had been scrubbed. Things actually shone. She had left a note:

"You need Mr. Clean, Fantastik, some steel wool, Ajax, and paper towels. A vacuum cleaner wouldn't hurt. Or some Endust. I charge five dollars an hour and don't do windows. Love, C."

The old rented apartment had never seemed so much like a real home.

"I'm surprised," Chelsea said, "that he's so gentle."

She and Toy were watching television, eating dinner on trays in their laps. It was, for the roommates, a rare encounter. Toy, mentally vague but physically hyperactive, seemed to spend every night at discos and in someone else's bedroom. New York had swallowed her in these last months. Chelsea could see the changes in the girl. She put it down to drugs.

"You know," she said, "you look like hell."

Toy laughed. "I fuck too much."

"Come on, be serious. I mean it."

"Me too."

"Oh, yeah," Chelsea said sarcastically.

They were watching *Brideshead Revisited.*

"Why is Sebastian always drunk?" Chelsea said. "He has so much going for him."

Toy thought for a moment. "Maybe that's why."

In all their months of sharing an apartment, it was the most insightful remark she had heard Toy make. For a long time, Chelsea had been on the edge of telling the girl that living together just wasn't working, that each of them needed a place of her own and could afford it. But then Toy would make some sweet gesture, or get off a remark like that one, and Chelsea pulled back, biting her tongue. After all, when she first came to New York, got her first modeling job, Toy had been open and friendly and loving. Perhaps, Chelsea realized, she owed the girl something. And so she did nothing. And now, wrapped in robes and with their hair washed and damp and swathed in towels, they talked as young women have always done in dormitory rooms and apartments, about themselves, their loves, their men.

So she told Toy about Marc. "You've heard the stories about him. He's supposed to be this big, strong tough guy, this Seventh Avenue gangster."

"Sure, I heard. I heard all that stuff. He shoots people."

"No, Toy, he doesn't shoot people."

"No?"

"No!"

Toy was enjoying their evening together. She liked sex, of course, but even for Toy, her sexual passages were not entirely satisfying. Men told her to do this, or say that, or move this way, or move that. Chelsea was different. She talked to Toy without asking her to open her legs, open her mouth, roll over on her stomach and shove her ass into the air, or use her tongue to do unusual things. Toy liked talk.

She grinned, putting her half-eaten dinner aside, ignoring the tube. "Tell me about him, Chelsea. He sounds so . . . sexy."

"He's *very* . . . well, he's a nice guy. He . . . uh . . . has lots of magnificent ideas about fashion. Chanel was his mentor. I don't know if that's the right way to say it, but it's what she was. She taught him . . ."

"Chanel? The couturier? In Paris?"

"Yes. *That* Chanel."

Toy smiled a self-congratulatory smile. "A dyke. She had black lovers. Famous black boxers from America! A very fascinating woman . . ."

Chelsea laughed. "Well, what was she? A lesbian or a woman who slept with black prizefighters?"

Toy thought for a moment. "Both," she said, "that's why she was so interesting."

"You know this?" Chelsea said skeptically.

Toy laughed. "I don't know *nothing*, Chelsea," Toy said, smiling like a caught child.

How could you be annoyed with her? Chelsea asked herself. She wondered what Marc would think about their conversation. Probably he'd object, both to being discussed with Toy, someone he didn't even know, and to having his idol Chanel slandered. But Chelsea wanted to talk about Marc to somebody. It was all happening dizzyingly fast.

"Anyway," she said, "he's a good guy. I like him."

Toy nodded. Then, solemnly, "Chelsea?"

"Yes?"

"Does he fuck good?"

The answer to that, which went unspoken, was yes, he did. Or rather, yes, they did.

Love had begun in Paris, where it was required by statute. But it matured and deepened in New York. In bed. And in other places.

"This," he would say, "is my favorite place. I've never brought anyone here before." And they would both laugh at the lie. He seemed to know everyone—bartenders and headwaiters and the women who checked coats, people who rented cars. It wasn't the way people knew Adam, or the way she was recognized from her pictures. Sometimes they were corny people, in corny places.

"I just like to see you come into a room," he told her one night in the cocktail lounge of the World Trade Center. "I'm sitting there, nursing that first drink and feeling pretty good about the world, listening to the talk, to women laughing, to the sound of ice in the glasses, watching cigarettes being lit, and staring out through the windows at the night. Just enjoying being alone. And knowing that in a couple of minutes you're going to be sitting there in that empty chair, or next to me on a banquette. Maybe people are wondering about me or feeling sorry for me, that I'm alone. And then I hear something, or I sense it, and I look up, and there you are, with the captain hurrying over to you with the menus and his list of reservations, and you sort of half talk to him, but only half, because you're looking for me. And then you see me. I don't stand up or wave or anything. I just wait until you see me. And then something changes in your face and you brush past the captain and you weave in and out through the tables or past the guys drinking at the bar, heading for me. And I just wait, watching the way everyone turns a little, trying not to be obvious about it. I just sit there, hugging the secret to myself."

"And what's the secret?" she asked, knowing the answer, but crinkling her nose in pleasure.

"That you're here to meet me. My date, my girl, maybe my lover. Only you and I know just what. They all *think* they know. But only we *do*."

At that she leaned over and kissed him, very lightly, on the lips. "For someone who can't read," she said, "you can be very poetic."

"Does it scan?"

"Oh, yes."

There were other places where they met, or went, and fell more in love. East Side bars, the backroom of Clarke's, and small, dark lounges off the lobbies of large, busy hotels, in rented cars he drove up into Connecticut or out to Bucks County for meals at country inns, on the deck of Malcolm Forbes's yacht on a cruise down the harbor, at movie screenings in the Gulf & Western building or at MGM off Sixth Avenue, in Bloomingdale's on Saturday afternoon, in discos when she insisted and he relented, and once in a porno movie theater on Broadway.

"Please, please, please," she said, "I've never been to one and I have to know if men really wear raincoats and do things right there in the balcony under their newspaper."

He took her to the Pussycat Cinema.

"My God," she said, "they really do!"

And afterward they went to her apartment or to his and they made love and slept. And sometimes woke to make love again.

He cooked her meals. Or tried to.

"Look," she said disapprovingly, "I appreciate the gesture. But do you eat steak and frozen French fries *every* night of your life?"

"No, sometimes I bake a potato."

She chased him from the kitchen, went down to the Gristede's on the next block, and came back with the fixings for guacamole and chili and a huge tossed salad for which she made a vinaigrette dressing laced with hot mustard.

"Where did you learn this shit?" he demanded, genuinely impressed.

"We had a good cook when I was growing up. My grandpa believed a woman ought to know how to cook, whatever else she does with her life. I know lots of stuff, even better than this."

"You're amazing," he said, meaning it.

"Sure," she said, "life doesn't start and end with a TV dinner."

He grunted. Until now it had.

On an impulse he rented a car one Saturday morning and picked her up at her apartment.

"Come on, we're going to Vermont. I want to look at the snow."

They drove through Connecticut and Massachusetts and up Route 7 to Manchester, an old white clapboard inn in the town, across from a Protestant church with a steeple out of Norman Rockwell and white hills framing the village just beyond the houses and the church.

"It's lovely," she said, "I've never been to New England."

"Sure," he said, "that's why we came."

As if on cue, snow began falling at dusk, big, fluffy flakes, and after dinner in the inn they walked across the village green chasing each other in little sprints, throwing snowballs, and shouting in the cold night. Their room had a huge four-poster with a down quilt and windows that faced the church. After they'd undressed and turned out the lights, he pulled up the shades so they could watch the snow fall, lying there together in the big bed.

"I suppose you get bored seeing snow fall," he said, "being from Colorado."

"Sometimes," she said, "toward April, when you've got cottage fever and it seems like spring's never going to get there. Not now, though, not with you."

"We had an apartment on Seventy-ninth Street once," he said, "when I was still very small, and my bedroom window looked out onto the street. There was a lamppost, and whenever the radio said there might be snow I'd lie there in bed at night with the shades up like this, looking at the light from the lamppost, waiting to see that first snowflake start to fall. Usually I'd fall asleep first, and then when I'd wake up in the morning it would be all over or there'd be a real snowstorm, but sometimes, just every once in a while, I'd get lucky and see the first flake. And I'd lie there for a long time watching, the snow turning yellow in the lamplight. I loved watching it."

"But you never skied?"

"Nope," he said, "but I had a Flexible Flyer sled and we used to go into Central Park to coast."

"A sled," she said wonderingly.

"Yes," he said, thinking of the old sled and watching the snow fall and then moving closer to her, a big arm pulling her shoulders close so she was tucked in next to him, one body fitting the other the way pieces do in a jigsaw puzzle.

One evening they were at Gino's for a drink, and when they came out onto Lexington Avenue a cold rain was falling. The taxis, as is traditional in Manhattan, had all flicked on their "off duty" signs and raced down the avenue, splashing pedestrians. Chelsea consigned herself to a long wait or a wet walk. But Street stepped out into the gutter, waving and gesturing, and miraculously, a cab skidded to a stop and they got in.

"How the hell did you do that?" she demanded.

He grinned. "Cabalistic signs," he said. "Cabbies and me, we understand one another."

He knew how to get theater tickets for sold-out plays, tables in restaurants when they hadn't made reservations, and a barman's eye at cocktail hour in P. J. Clarke's. He always had postage stamps in his wallet and the right change for coin phones and a penknife that worked; he knew which cross street intersected with house numbers on Park Avenue and Fifth and York. When he was short of cash he always had a gin mill where they'd cash a check. Salesladies at Saks waited on him first, and bums knew him for a touch good for a buck, and he had an all-night florist who would deliver anywhere in town.

"You're amazing," she acknowledged, impressed. "I think if there was still Prohibition, you'd have a reliable bootlegger."

"I know a couple of good after-hours joints."

Without even touching him, she cradled Marc to herself, possessive and loving.

He took her one night to the Garden for a basketball game. The Knicks were playing the Celtics. She had never seen a professional game. Only college games and high-school games at home. But she understood basketball. She'd played in school. They had good seats, just behind and slightly above the home bench. During the warmups she gawked at the players, huge black men in satin sweatsuits, palming basketballs like oranges.

"Gosh, the size of them."

"They're big," he agreed.

She looked around. "All those blonds behind the bench. Who are they, the cheerleaders?"

"The players' wives."

"Really?"

"Hell, I dunno. Let's watch the game."

During the second half a beefy, red-faced drunk seated behind them, a loud man with a filthy mouth, spilled beer on the back of Chelsea's seat.

"Hey, watch out there," Marc said.

"It's okay," she said, "missed me."

The man started to bluster. "It was an accident, man. The broad says she's okay. So forget it."

"Sure," Chelsea said, turning back to the game and a Celtics rally.

Marc said nothing. Chelsea sensed anger, and she reached out to hold his arm. "Hey, it's okay. Forget it."

"Yeah," he said. But she could feel the tension in his arm.

When the game ended, with the Knicks falling just short by a basket and the Garden roaring, the drunk resumed screaming obscenities. Marc turned around slowly. "Will you knock it off, pal?"

"Hell with you! I bought my ticket," the drunk shouted, reaching out an open hand as if to shove Street from his slightly higher vantage point.

It was then that Marc hit him, twice, very fast, once with the left hooking in toward him, short and hard, then with a brisk right uppercut that slammed the man back into his seat, nose bloody and eyes glazed.

"Come on, Chelsea," Street said calmly, "the game's over."

"My God," she said.

She'd seen cowboys fight in Aspen bars, once saw two men fight in a Paris discotheque. She'd never seen anything as quick as this. As surgically clean. As they left, and Marc made it a point to leave slowly, mingling with the crowd, the drunk was still sitting in his seat, upright now, holding a handkerchief to his nose and looking dazed, confused. No one seemed to be paying any attention to him.

"Where'd you learn to do that?" she asked.

Fury had oozed out of him. "Growing up with the West Side Irish," he said. He sounded almost regretful. If he had boasted she would have hated it. But he didn't.

And she remembered what she had said to Toy. "He's so damned gentle." Not with everyone.

BOOK FOUR

ADAM

28

For the fashionables, Key West is fast becoming Fire Island South.

Mode, February 10, 1981

dam?"

Sleepily, drugged by the midday sun, Adam answered, sprawled lazily in a canvas chaise with a sketch pad and a couple of number two yellow pencils lying on his flat stomach.

"There's an article about you in the Miami paper. It says you're 'movie star handsome,' that you look a little like Richard Gere."

Adam didn't move. Eyes still closed, he said: "Richard Gere looks a little like *me.*"

There was an appreciative laugh all around the small pool. The king was in his court and the courtiers knew their place.

It was one of those perfect Key West winter days, with a dry, gentle north wind barely rustling the palm trees and a hot sun boring down out of the blue sky, tanning bare flesh and baking the ceramic tiles of the poolside. It was Stanley Baltimore's famous million-dollar house on Duval Street, a house lent to Adam for a midwinter break. Adam had jumped at Baltimore's offer. He wanted to show off his new Learjet, and he and his entourage had flown out of LaGuardia in a cold rain, the three-hour flight one long cocktail party, a party that had continued for nearly a week now in the Florida sun.

Adam rolled over on his stomach. When the pad and pencils spilled onto the tile, a young man hurried to retrieve them. He had done some work, sketches for the fall–winter collection, to be shown in May; they were only doodles at this stage, but the germ of ideas showed through. Adam was taking the rivalry with Chelsea as a personal challenge. He did not intend to let her sweep the board for a second time.

Key West was a good place, with galleries, restaurants, studios, boutiques, bars, the docks, the green water, and always the bronzing sun. Oh, there were negatives. One morning he went into his private bathroom to wash and shave and when he picked up the tube of Colgate toothpaste, its cap and rim were covered by tiny, swarming ants. In a panic, he'd thrown the toothpaste away, and had wondered about flying back north. In the end he had sealed his toothpaste in a plastic bag.

Key West was people as well as pests, a good group on this trip. His latest friend, of course, the actor, physically as appealing as Peter Feeley, and less equivocal. There was the hairdresser, an imaginative young man whose name had once been Sal Galvani and who now called himself "Genghis Khan." It was Khan who supplied the cocaine, and sometimes other things.

Included in the entourage were one of Adam's assistants and three famous models: the gray-haired and still glamorous Meg Niland; Toy, the spacey *Sports Illustrated* girl who was living with Chelsea West; and the new sensation, Bunny Lamb. Bunny's mother had also come along, a red-faced, boozy woman with Bacall's husky laugh and a dancer's legs. There was no way Bunny could have gone with them without Mother. She was beautiful, six feet tall, and fifteen. Adam liked having models around. They were fun, especially when they got stoned; he could visualize them in his new designs and he liked looking at their bodies. Besides, they gave the party a heterosexual imprimatur. Even though it rankled him when he thought of Peter Feeley, even though he felt vaguely guilty about it, image was still important. It didn't matter what you did so long as you didn't seem to be doing it; for also with them were a photographer and reporter from *Celebrity* magazine, doing a cover story on Adam. The proposed cover line: "His name is on Jackie's bottom."

"I'm not sure the editors will go for it," the reporter confessed, "but I just love that headline."

So did Adam. He saw Mrs. Onassis in the building from time to time. They were on the same elevator bank and sometimes he ran into her in the mornings, as she was going to work at Doubleday. They spoke, nothing substantive, just time-of-day conversation. But she was always genial. And he was pleased to see that when they reached the lobby and went out to stand together under the canopy on Fifth Avenue, the doorman was sent to fetch her a cab and it was *his* chauffeur who hopped out of the Rolls to open the door. New York and fame; how sweetly they went together. Not even Chelsea West or estrangement from Street could spoil everything.

Genghis Khan got up now from the towel where he was sunning his small, swarthy body. He wore the same Munich *braukeller* student's cap that he wore in Manhattan, peak pulled low over his heavy, arching brows. Adam could just see him from where he lay, the small, tight buttocks barely sheathed in a yellow bikini bottom, and remembered seeing those buttocks bared and spread just a week before in the murk of a West Street leather club where Khan diverted the clientele with the leg of a barstool.

A mutual friend had Genghis down pat. "He has absolutely no redeeming virtues, Adam. But he supplies great coke."

"Anyone for a snort?" Khan asked now, ambling toward the canvas pavilion that shaded the pool's cabanas.

Adam shivered. After all, there was a reporter with them. But how could you control Genghis?

"I'll have some," the reporter said, and Adam relaxed.

Meg and Toy were in the pool, not so much swimming as shedding the noon heat, while the photographer idly snapped pictures of them. Bunny Lamb lay on her belly with her bra top off, sunning her back and those incredibly long legs. Her mother was drinking daiquiris, summoning the houseboy from the kitchen with refills. The actor read aloud from the Miami paper's story about Adam, tactfully omitting a mention of Chelsea that appeared in the piece. Adam rarely read anything, even about himself. But he listened attentively. The story said such nice things.

He felt a spasm of regret. Street used to say things like that about him.

"Eek!"

Adam twisted abruptly and sat up. Bunny was on her feet, running toward the house, tiny breasts bouncing white against her brown torso.

"It's just a lizard, Bunny," Adam's assistant said. "They're good. They eat bugs."

"Yuck," the girl said. "I'd rather have bugs."

She stood there now, fists on slender hips, looking back to where she'd been lying, to where the lizard had scampered into the roots of a dwarf palm.

The photographer turned his camera to focus on her.

"Don't you publish any of those, you naughty boy," her mother said over the rim of the daiquiri glass.

"Of course not," he promised, not meaning it. Bunny Lamb's bare tits? What Bob Guccione wouldn't pay!

Finally calmed, the girl ambled back to her towel, her body moving as easily as if it had just had a lube job. So what if she was still flat-chested, the cameraman thought, continuing to snap pictures off the Nikon's motor drive, focusing now on the curving, child's belly and the legs; she'd be a juicy lay. And with the mother stewed, who knew?

That night they dined in a Cuban restaurant in one of the small alleyways near the Pier House. Adam was slightly high, pleasantly so. Most of them were. But not Meg or the young girl. Her mother was drunk and on the verge of falling asleep right there at the table. Meg was playing mother, and she and the kid were talking about school. Genghis had picked up a young couple somewhere, a tough boy in a motorcycle jacket and jeans and heavy boots and his girlfriend, a little chippie with an easy laugh and a foul mouth.

"Do we need *them?*" the actor asked Adam out of the corner of his mouth.

Adam shrugged. "Genghis collects freaks. It amuses him."

They went on afterward to a couple of the tourist bars and then returned to Baltimore's house after midnight, a half moon bathing the old white house in a soft light. Mother Lamb was out of it by now, and Meg and Bunny helped her upstairs and went off to their own rooms. The photographer, a fatalist, accepted his loss and turned his attention to Toy, lush in a linen mini-skirt and a cotton tank top. The stereo was playing rock, and the marijuana smoke rose slowly into the warm night sky. Adam had thrown himself into the chaise by the pool and slouched there, listening to the music and watching the others by the light of hurricane lamps. Khan was into heavy conversation with the biker, while the boy's girlfriend and Toy danced dreamily alongside the pool, each isolated in her own thoughts, to the beat of the music.

"Hey, everybody, let's have a little entertainment."

Genghis Khan stood on a cocktail table under the canopy of the cabana, cupping his hands, his bright eyes gleaming out from under the peak of the cap, playing sideshow barker. Adam suddenly grew more alert.

"Toy and what's-her-name here are going to do a little dance."

The biker's girl grinned stupidly, and her boyfriend went to her and took her by the arm, talking to her animatedly.

"There's a hundred bucks in it," the biker said.

"Oh, sure. Okay."

"Hey, I dancing already, Genghis," Toy said, amiable but confused.

"Sure, sure, sure," he said, "but just relax a little. The party's just warming up."

"Okay, Genghis," Toy responded cheerfully, "you tell me what to do."

"C'mere."

Toy and the biker's girl, whose name nobody seemed to have caught, both came to him at the table, and he held out his hands, placing one on top of Toy's head, the other on the girl's. Toy might have been half a foot taller, but the girl, short and tough, was bulkier in leather jacket and jeans.

"Okay, the show's about to begin. Now you, honey, I want you to bare from the waist down. Just keep your jacket on. Love that jacket, don't you, Adam? And you, Toy, keep your skirt on and get rid of the tank top. Like it, Adam? Nice contrast?"

Adam waved a joint at him, bored and sleepy. "Whatever you say, Genghis."

As the girls undressed, Khan pulled out a glassine envelope and two straws.

"Now let's give you each a big hit first. Toy, let's do it, babe. And Ronnie, shove another cassette in there, the Blondie."

Toy had tossed the tank top aside, and she stood there, snorting the coke, watching the shorter girl struggle out of her jeans and panties. Then, while the new girl took the straw and began to inhale, her body jerking spasmodically as the stuff hit, the biker threw her boots back to her.

"Put your damned boots back on, Drina." Then, to Khan, "That okay, mister? I like to watch 'em in boots."

"Okay? It's brilliant, great fashion touch."

The girl Drina sat down on the tile, bare-assed now, and tugged on the boots. She had a stupid smile on her face, and her nose was running. Toy just looked at her.

They didn't dance together very well, but that wasn't the point. As stoned as he was, the photographer retrieved one of his cameras and fired by flash, Toy's breasts bouncing, her long legs jiving beneath the mini-skirt; the smaller girl grinding, leather jacket unzipped, heavy breasts swaying, her bare bottom and chunky legs and swelling little belly gleaming in the light. Adam's assistant had taken the coke from Genghis and was passing it around now. They all took a hit, as Khan went on stage-managing, prancing this way and that around the two girls.

"Do it!" he shouted. "Do it!"

The biker stared, not at his own girl, but at Toy. Adam, too, watched, disoriented, as if he were outside his own body, as if he were not really there but a distant witness. His actor friend came and sat next to him.

"All right, Adam? You okay?"

"Just fine," Adam said, slurred and disembodied. The actor put his hand on Adam and turned to watch the girls.

They were flagging now, tiring fast, their bodies slick with sweat, legs shining. Drina, in her leather jacket, felt the heat worse.

"Hey," she shouted to no one and everyone, "can't I take this damn thing off?"

"*No!*" Genghis yelled. "Keep it on, bitch!"

He went to them then and shoved another straw at Toy. Panting, she inhaled again, choking and sneezing, but getting it into her. Drina took hers more easily, slack-mouthed and bovine.

"Now, *dance!*" Khan shouted.

And they did. Until they could dance no more and the two girls fell into each other's arms, exhausted. Locked together, they slumped to the poolside tile, soaked with sweat. There was a moment of stillness, only their panting audible over the tape. Khan went to them.

"Okay, girls, that was Act One."

Toy's eyes rolled up at him. "Hey, Genghis, forget it. I don't dance no more, too hot."

He shook his head, his flat mouth widening. "No more dancing, Toy. Now you two make it."

Toy didn't stir, and then the biker moved behind Drina and gave her a savage kick in the rump with his boot. "Screw her, stupid, that's what we're getting the bread for."

Toy's beautiful eyes, glazed and hurt, turned desperately to Adam's.

Suddenly, with a fury that surprised even him, Adam sprang from the chaise.

"*No!*"

The others froze, as if caught by a fast lens.

"That's enough of this shit!" Adam shouted, still feeling the coke but feeling something else, Toy's helpless eyes on his. "Get them the hell out of here, Genghis. Just get them out!"

Khan stared at him, started to say something, thought better of it. "Sure, Adam, if that's what you want—"

"What I want is no more! No more!"

He was searching for other words, more effective, lacerating words. But, strangled by anger and cocaine, he cried out again, "No more! No more!", a cry of violence against violence.

Toy stared at him, no longer focusing, in no way recognizable to readers of *Sports Illustrated,* but vaguely aware that someone had come to her rescue, that someone cared. Adam wheeled this way and that, furious, defiant, looking for an argument. He got none.

After another moment they began to drift away from the pool, seeking out the shelter of darkness. Adam picked up a beach towel and went to Toy, draping it carelessly around her shoulders.

"You go to bed, Toy," he said.

"Yes, Adam. I go." She kissed his cheek, lightly, briefly.

In the shadows, the biker grabbed at Khan's arm. "Hey, man, you promised me, remember! A hundred bucks and we put on a show. And then I got my turn."

Genghis stared into the angry face.

"You told me *I* could have Toy," the biker persisted.

Khan shrugged. "Listen, sometimes things don't work out." He turned and walked away.

When they had all gone, Adam stood alone by the pool. The things we do, he thought, the people we hurt.

Then his actor friend called from a window. "Adam, you coming in?"

Adam nodded, saying nothing. Then, slowly, he walked across the slick tiles of the poolside toward the lovely house. Behind him Deborah Harry sang to the empty tropical night.

29

In fashion, you always invite your enemies to the party. It's as LBJ once said of Hoover, that he'd rather have him inside the tent pissing out. . . .

Mode, March 9, 1981

If you can't come up with a collection that's every bit as good or even better," Street warned Chelsea, "they'll be all over you. They'll call you a one-shot, someone who got lucky once and can't pull it off again."

"I know. Don't make me any more scared than I am."

"It's normal to be scared. I'm not trying to worry you, just get your attention."

She laughed. "You got it, man."

"Good girl." He meant it, too. She *was* a good girl, she worked hard, she listened, and even Dufour was beginning to give her a grudging respect.

"You know, Marc, she is not so bad as I t'ought."

"Dufour, you're all heart."

"Comment?"

At Marc's urging she was reading about fashion, cramming into just a few months what students at FIT or Parsons took four years to learn. Quite naturally she gravitated to the female designers, Chanel, of course, Schiaparelli, Grès, and Mme. Vionnet.

"Don't forget," Marc prodded, "we've had some damned good Americans. Claire McCardell and Anne Klein and Bonnie Cashin. And it was Mary Quant who put London back on the fashion map before anyone ever heard of Carnaby Street or punk."

"Funny that you mention it," she said mischievously, "I'm *thinking* punk."

"You go punk on me, West, and I'll ship you back to Colorado."

"Not take me for a ride? Get one of your gangster pals to bump me off?"

"Don't kid," he said.

She sobered. Marc had told her nothing of "Uncle Carl" or of anything beyond his father's testimony before a congressional committee; secrets still held close. But Marc sensed something in her manner, and worried.

Not all fashion's work is done in studios and on runways. Marc had made a minor career out of avoiding the socializing that had men like Adam and Blass and Calvin Klein out on the town three or four nights a week. Now, with Chelsea's sudden prominence, the invitations were more frequent, more pressing. Most nights they declined and just stayed home. Sometimes it was impossible, when there came up an important retail customer, a valued private client, an irresistible publicity opportunity, and so, grudgingly, he agreed to go. It was unfair to Chelsea always to say no. She was young, she was beautiful, people wanted to meet her, it was selfish to keep her to himself. To Street these evenings were a chore; to Chelsea, still finding herself and enjoying fame, they were fun. Sometimes they were ridiculous, like that night at the Mudd Club.

Chelsea showed him the invitation. "Hey, can't we go to this? It sounds pretty good."

He handed the invitation back. "Isn't there enough Eurotrash in New York already without importing a couple of more phony titles?" He made a face. "The Erbprinz und Erbprinzessen. Come on, 'prince and princess' isn't good enough for them?"

Chelsea laughed. "I've never met an 'Erbprinz.' "

The limousines were double-parked halfway down the block, with a couple of bored cops ignoring them to watch the arriving guests.

"A freak show," Marc sneered as he and Chelsea left their

taxi at the corner and pushed through the crowd to the disco's doors.

"Maybe they think *we're* the freaks," she said. It had never occurred to him, not amid the rock stars, hairdressers, models, transvestites, crashers, and glitterati of such occasions, but it was typical of her, sensible and unexpected.

When they finally eased their way past the bouncers, Marc waving the engraved invitations and pushing Chelsea ahead of him, the heat and the smoke and the crashing music beat against them.

"Jesus," he groaned.

"Oh, give me a break," she said, "we don't have to stay all night. Let's get a drink and watch."

Marc shoved a twenty-dollar bill at a beautiful boy in satin basketball shorts, who cleared a few inches for them at the bar and poured the drinks. The whole place, smelly, crowded, hot, would have fit into a supermarket aisle. For the visiting royalty a band had been imported, lean black men in dreadlocks and leather, pounding out reggae and rock.

At midnight the Erbprinz and the Erbprincessen arrived. He was balding, weak-eyed, and fifty; his wife, the Erbprincessen, was perhaps twenty, a curvy little girl in a blouse open to the waist, with her blond hair standing on end in a punk cut. They danced together, just once, gyrating wildly. Sweat shone on his face, on her chest. Strobes flashed above and the lights of the *paparazzi* on the floor. When they broke, the young princess danced with a pretty red-haired woman while her husband chatted up one of the bartenders. Having made their appearance, having diverted the mob, they soon left, the Erbprinz with a slim boy, the Erbprincessen with another girl.

"And I used to think Seventh Avenue was wacky," Marc said in the cab home.

Chelesa laughed. "The least you could do is buy me an Erbprinz of my own."

He grinned at her. "Or an Erbprincessen."

The next morning the New York papers were full of photos of European "nobility." A few nights later it was Halston's turn, a black-tie buffet dinner and dancing in his vast apartment overlooking St. Patrick's Cathedral, a *plat du jour* of movie people: Scorsese and Bobby De Niro and Liza Minnelli and Pacino. Marc found himself chatting with a plump, pleasant man and his wife, people from Chicago, people whose names he didn't quite get.

Chelsea laughed: "But, Marc, don't you know anything? That's John Belushi!"

He might not know everyone, but he recognized the exquisite irony that a year before it had been Adam who escorted her to such affairs, and Adam, who had lost Feeley, had now lost Chelsea as well.

Then it was time for the true aristocracy to visit Manhattan and a chance for Marc to offer olive branches. Jimmy de Bertrand and J.-P. Brugère had come to town. The Metropolitan Museum was staging a retrospective of Jimmy's work. Mme. Vreeland, who had been editor of *Vogue* and now ran the museum's costume wing, organized it. Street saw no reason to be soreheaded about what had happened in Paris in January, no reason to let momentary annoyance become a feud. He understood Jimmy, knew how badly it hurt to lose one. He'd been through it with Adam in the early days; he'd been through it *before* Adam, when all Majesty did was line-for-line copies of other people's designs. He'd seen it happen even to Coco, remembered how she treated defeat, shrugging it off with waspish bitchery about the incompetence of fashion editors, the cretinous banality of retail buyers.

"I want to give them a dinner party, Sydney," Marc told Heidler. "They've done it for us every time we went to Paris."

Heidler nodded. Then, thoughtfully, "Does Chelsea agree?"

"Hell, yes. Why wouldn't she?"

"You said Jimmy snubbed her in Paris."

"Come on, she doesn't hold grudges."

Heidler thought for a moment. "And Adam?"

"Of course he's invited. How could I not?"

"Ah, yes, but will he come?"

Marc was right about Chelsea. "I think it's a great idea. As long as you take them to a restaurant and not that grungy apartment."

"My apartment is not *grungy*. There may be a little dust here and there. But grungy? No!"

They decided on La Côte Basque; Mme. Henriette was gone and the new management had put the place back on the rails. Brugère, brisk and businesslike as if the scene in Paris had never occurred, made the arrangements with Marc by transatlantic phone, choosing the guest list, deciding who should sit next to whom. Protocol mattered.

"Is it that important?" Chelsea asked. "When my grandpa has people for dinner, even important people, senators and bankers and the governor, he just says, 'Let's eat.' And we do."

"Your grandpa, Chelsea, is *not* in the fashion business."

Everyone came. As Lincoln Radford remarked, "The only thing worse than being insulted by the French is being ignored by them."

Capote and Warhol came, favorites of Jimmy or perhaps of Brugère; Diana Vreeland, of course; Nan Kempner, Betsy Bloomingdale, Annette Reed, women who bought clothes; several of the Americans (a French *geste*), Ralph Lauren, Calvin Klein, Perry Ellis; Radford, John Fairchild, Grace Mirabella of *Vogue;* Stanley Baltimore, Leonard Lauder, Paul Woolard of Revlon (for who knew *when* a perfume deal might beckon?); several retailers; Cheryl Tiegs, the De Loreans, Iman, Christie Brinkley, and other "beautiful people."

Adam came.

Chelsea was seated next to Ralph Lauren, a small, neat man with a soft voice and a slight speech impediment. She had met him once, when she posed in one of his ads. He didn't seem to remember that. The man who ran Bergdorf's was on her other side. Conversation did not precisely lilt. With reluctant enthusiasm Marc worked the tables, six tables of six people each, set up in the rear of the restaurant. She was pleased to see that Jimmy de Bertrand was smiling, with no hint of his Paris sulk. Brugère was deep in frenzied dialogue with Miss Tiegs and Lauder. Adam sat between Mrs. Kempner and another woman. They were making a fuss over him, and he was smiling. At one point Marc stopped by his place, and the two men exchanged a few words. It was odd, she thought: in their dinner jackets Marc and Adam, both dark, tall, and with just a few years between them, could almost be brothers.

When the dinner plates had been cleared Marc got up and
said a few words about transatlantic amity, about the links between the French and the Americans. She wished she'd known he
was going to talk. She would have given him a good quote about
the French from Thomas Jefferson. Then Jimmy got up and ram-
bled on pleasantly, ending with a toast to Diana Vreeland, who
perched there birdlike, with her lacquered last-Empress-of-China
hair and her sculptured face, her myopic eyes staring in the wrong
direction.

"Well, it went okay," Marc said as he and Chelsea left.
Jimmy and Brugère and some of the others were going downtown
to dance at that new place, the Pyramid Club, way off in the al-
phabet land of Avenue A. Adam found himself standing behind
them at the coat check, and on a whim, Marc asked if he wanted
to join them for a drink at Clarke's or someplace.

"Sure," he said, "why not?"

Frankie got them a table in Clarke's back room, and the
three of them had a drink, Irish coffee for Chelsea and brandies
for the two men. They talked about nothing, really, but it was
pleasant. This was the first time since she had come to work for
Majesty that the ice had thawed, even slightly. Marc was obviously pleased. As for Adam, he was still shaken by what had
happened in Key West, and it was nice to be with Marc again, to
share a table and to talk.

"You know what I felt so good about there tonight, Adam?
It was seeing you and Perry and Calvin and Lauren there at the
same table with Jimmy and realizing just how good you guys are,
how good American fashion really is. That even up against
Jimmy and Yves and Ungaro we don't have a damned thing to
apologize for, that we've really come of age here in this country.
Twenty years ago that wouldn't have happened."

Adam looked thoughtful. "No, I guess you're right," he said,
"we're not so bad."

There was a nice, unexpected diffidence in the way he said it
that she liked. And she liked, too, that Marc had not mentioned
her. That he had not included her name among those of the other
young Americans. She knew she didn't belong there, not yet at

least. And she realized that in omitting her Marc was making a small, gracious gesture toward Adam.

Adam left soon after that, saying he had to meet someone.

Chelsea reached out to touch Marc's hand. "You're a good guy," she said, "asking him to join us."

He shrugged. "What the hell. He's not so bad either when you get him away from those bastards he runs with."

Two nights later Mme. Vreeland staged her show at the Met, and Chelsea, who had been particularly asked for by Jimmy de Bertrand, was one of the models. So were Miss Tiegs and Mrs. De Lorean. And when they came up one celebrity model short, Chelsea got Toy the assignment. She was lightly tanned and very beautiful, and she wore clothes as superbly as she always had. But there were dark smudges under her eyes, and up close she looked tired.

"You okay?" Chelsea asked in the dressing room.

"I swell, Chelsea."

But her eyes were blank, and Chelsea wondered what she was on now.

30

You don't have to be a partner in Lazard Frères down on Wall Street to know where the real money resides in fashion: perfumes and cosmetics!

Mode, March 16, 1981

Stanley Baltimore had not lent his house in Key West to Adam out of sheer philanthropy.

"That boy's a goldmine and Marc Street's going to ruin him," Baltimore grumbled to his vice-presidents as they held their weekly sales meeting in Stanley's office.

He had the figures in front of him: the Adam line of toiletries, the Christmas launch of Adam perfume, both indicating steep, dramatic climbs on the graph of week-by-week retail sales.

"Looks good to me, Stanley, where's the gripe?"

"Asshole, I know it looks good. Looks *great*. But it ain't gonna stay that way if Street keeps pushing that West dame. It's bound to cut into Adam's appeal. Street's in over his head. He'll promote one or the other of them to the hilt. Can't do both. And he's sleeping with the chick. That leaves our Adam sucking hind tit."

One of the other men continued to object. "Stanley, the money Street spends advertising Adam is peanuts. We're spending the real tonnage. What does it matter if Street cuts back a bit?"

Baltimore's sharp nose quivered. "I'll tell you how it matters, jerko. We're in the name game, right? Name designers. The bigger the name, the better the perfume sales, the toiletries, the cosmetics. And there's only one way to get a big name in fashion. You turn out great clothes. You get on the cover of *Vogue* and *Bazaar* and *Mode* and *WWD*. It doesn't matter worth a damn if you make money on the clothes or lose money on the damned rags. You get the publicity, the editorial, the whooping and the shouting and the ink. It's the clothes that have the fashion editors wetting their pants and having hot flashes. The perfumes live off the excitement. They live off the goddamned clothes. If Street plays down Adam's collection, sure as hell his perfume will curl up and die in the stores. I've seen it happen. Norell's still a great scent. But since Norman died, where is it? Saint Laurent gets rich with Opium and Y and Rive Gauche because he makes great dresses. He doesn't make a nickel on the clothes. He makes millions on the name!"

They all knew this. They also knew that Baltimore enjoyed telling them how dumb they were. It made Stanley feel good, and they were all well paid for their tolerance. But only Baltimore was sufficiently Machiavellian to read into the coming of Chelsea West a threat to sales of Adam perfume.

"Okay, Stanley, what do we do?"

Baltimore rubbed his hands together. "We take young Adam off by himself and assure him there are still people out there who think he's the fairest of them all."

One of the vice-presidents laughed. "You mean 'the fairy-est.' "

Baltimore chortled. He liked corny jokes.

When they left he stood for a long time staring north from the huge picture windows of his office, not seeing the spring buds and the greening of the great park, not even seeing the early April sky, but seeing somewhere out there a dark vision of his own. His houseboy in Key West had given him a reasonably colorful account of how Adam and his friends had cavorted. There was leverage there, somewhere. Perhaps through this dealer-hairdresser of his, Genghis Khan. Perhaps through the model, Toy, the one who shared an apartment with Chelsea West.

Thought of Chelsea aroused him. He wished the positions were reversed, that it was Chelsea he was going to take away from Street and put to work for him. Well, dammit, that wasn't how it was. Adam was the vulnerable target, Adam the one he would steal away from Majesty Fashions and absorb into Baltimore Inc.

He turned briskly from the window and went to the Louis Quinze table, jabbing a thick, powerful finger at one of the telephone's array of buttons.

"Yes, chief?" Lester, the vice-president of corporate communications, more actively employed and better known through the executive suites of the company as Stanley's procurer, was very good at what he did, well paid for his talents. It was said of Lester that he could provide a blond at high noon in Nigeria on fifteen minutes' notice.

"Lester, you got that new copywriter of yours handy? What's her name, Kitty?"

"Yessir, bright girl, chief, glad you like her stuff."

"Yeah, well, send her up."

It took only a few minutes for the girl to get there, letting herself in through the leather-padded double doors. The room was darkened now, the blinds drawn. Baltimore lounged in shadows on one of the sofas.

"Yes, Mr. Baltimore?"

She wore a pretty, flowered Ralph Lauren country skirt, long, to midcalf, and a crisply tailored white shirt. A very pretty girl, small-boned, young, pert, with long auburn hair. She had been employed by Baltimore Inc. for a month now and she had done very well. Her salary was a thousand dollars a week. Of course, she wrote no copy. This is not to say she could not have done so. She was quite intelligent, quite imaginative. She told everyone she was nineteen.

Only Lester and Mr. Baltimore knew the truth. She was a sixteen-year-old from Alabama, and a virgin. Lester, who had personally recruited her, had taken pains to have her examined by competent medical authority. She was the sort of curiosity Lester knew appealed to the boss.

"Come over here, Kitty."

"Yes, Mr. Baltimore."

She had been here twice before and she knew what was expected.

Baltimore lay back on the couch, pillows crammed behind

his broad back, and she slid in next to him, cuddling against his body. He reached a big hand inside her shirt, cupping a small but promising breast, tweaking the nipple. Then, with his other hand, he hit a switch, and a movie screen dropped on the opposite wall.

"You'll like these, Kitty. They're very lovely."

The darkened room blazed into light as the slide show came on: beautiful and famous paintings, one after another, marvelously reproduced on color slides.

They watched for several moments, and then Baltimore said, "You have a lovely mouth, Kitty."

"Yessir." She was bored with looking at the pictures and was relieved that they had gotten to the point of her visit.

"I want you to please me with your mouth."

"Of course."

She knelt over him on all fours, still fully and chastely dressed, her auburn head moving slowly up and down, up and down. Baltimore focused on the movie screen, where a Monet and then a Degas and then a Matisse hesitated, briefly and beautifully, as in the darkened room, Kitty's head moved faster.

Key West had been Baltimore's opening gambit. His second ploy was uncharacteristically direct.

He had lunch with Street at the grill room of the Four Seasons. It was one of their ordinary days. In one corner sat David Rockefeller and Henry Kissinger, in another the architect Philip Johnson mixed Cinzano and soda. Michael Korda huddled with an author, Korda's intelligent, narrow face masking boredom. Si Newhouse, the owner of *Vogue,* and Alex Liberman shared a banquette. Baltimore took note of none of them except Newhouse. So far as Baltimore was concerned, he was the real power.

"Marc, this boy of yours, Adam. We've done very well with his name."

"Good, Stanley, I'll tell him how pleased you are."

Baltimore sensed the dislike in Street's voice. How dare he? Baltimore could swallow Majesty Fashions before breakfast and never burp. But he controlled himself. Better to do it this way, if it could be done.

They had drinks. Marc had a Stolichnaya on the rocks with olives. Stanley took Perrier. He neither smoked nor drank, having been informed years before by physicians who knew his appetites that abstemiousness enhanced a man's sexual vigor.

"Here's how I look at it, Street. You've got two designers. Adam has a track record, Chelsea has a big future. We're all making good money on Adam's line of perfumes and cosmetics. Not a fortune, but a decent payday. You're happy, I'm happy. Right?"

"Right, Stanley."

"Maybe one day you and me will do a little deal with Chelsea. Why not? Pretty girl, good name, a lot of talent, nice cosmetic prospects there."

"Sure, one day."

"But that's not what I wanna talk about today. She's maybe tomorrow. Or a year from next Tuesday. Adam's right now. I've got an investment; you've got an investment. And the boy ain't happy."

"No?" Marc said opaquely, not knowing how much Baltimore knew and not wanting to hand him any gifts.

"You know he's not. How could he be, with another designer brought into the house? I had him down to my place in Key West last month, Marc, and believe me, the boy's not happy."

Marc knew Adam had been in Florida. He hadn't known where. Or with whom. But he tried to mask his ignorance. "There are always tensions," he said vaguely. "Creative people. You know."

"Of course I know," Baltimore said expansively, sensing he'd touched a nerve.

He made the move then. Why didn't Street sell Adam to Baltimore Inc? They could work out an equitable figure. An ongoing royalties deal could be explored so that Majesty would continue to profit from the perfume line for a time. Marc would be freed to concentrate his limited resources (Baltimore stressed the adjective) on his new designer, Miss West. Adam would probably be happier. Chelsea herself would in all likelihood be relieved not to have to compete with such an imposing rival in-house.

Marc listened. Over the *paillard* he said, "No."

Baltimore shrugged it off. He'd tried diplomacy, God knows he'd tried.

That afternoon he spent several hours on the phone, talking to department store presidents, boutique chain owners, bankers, labor union leaders, fashion magazine publishers, fabric manufacturers, newspaper columnists, and even a tame senator. These people all owed Stanley something. In some cases, their debts were honorable and all business. In others, they were murkier. Money had been passed around, friends had been given jobs, old scores had been settled. In a few instances, Lester, the PR man, had been helpful. Young women had made themselves, well, complaisant. Baltimore had held paper on all these debts, some of them for a very long time. But he had a long memory. And now he was calling these debts, with one aim:

"This guy Street, the one who runs Majesty Fashions . . ."

"Yes, Stanley?" (Or "Mr. Baltimore," according to the degree of intimacy.)

"I want him to have . . . difficulties."

Baltimore's debtors promised to do what they could.

"That's all I ask," he said equably.

Baltimore had never demanded the impossible. He understood that in life there are always limits. In 1943, when he was still in his twenties and driving a black-market truck for a textile company with mills in North Carolina and sales offices and showrooms in New York, he had come up against the hard reality of such limits. A hijacking, on Route 1, south of Trenton. Baltimore had sassed the hijackers. One of them, a dark, polished man with a heavy accent, had listened to his protests for a few moments and then, without saying another word, slashed him across the mouth with the barrel of a revolver, the sighting blade at the muzzle cutting into his cheek and slicing the flesh at the corner of his mouth.

The police were never informed, and no complaint was registered. If black-market goods were hijacked, well, it was tough luck. Baltimore had carried the scar ever since, and never for a single day was he unaware of what it had done to his ruggedly handsome face. He never forgot the scar, or the man who put it there.

By seven o'clock his last calls had been made, those to the Coast. Pleased with himself, he fell back against the pillows of his couch, reaching for the remote-control device of the slide projector that showed his paintings. But before he punched up the first slide, he unzipped the fly of his trousers and buzzed Lester.

"That little Kitty still in the office?"

"Yes, Mr. Baltimore, I told her to hang around in case."

"Send her up."

He punched the buttons, and the movie screen descended. For several minutes he looked at a Mondrian, hard-edged, brilliant, inspiring, then at a subtler Gris. There was a noise at the leather-padded double doors, and he said, without taking his eyes from the painting, "Come right in, Kitty."

It was a fortunate man who could combine his passions.

31

No one ever confused Seventh Avenue with a covered-dish
supper at the M.E. church in Ames, Iowa.

Mode, April 13, 1981

Heidler felt the pinch first. Marc, trying to keep Adam
at least reasonably content, and himself obsessed with Chelsea's
crucial second collection, was uncharacteristically insensitive to
what was happening.

Old Sydney came to him one night, when the two men were
alone in the office, Seventh Avenue's spring ignored outside in the
gloom and the smog and the noise of taxicabs in the filthy streets.

"Marc, we've got problems."

Street laughed, short and bitter. "Sydney, you taught me
years ago, in this business there are always problems. Sometimes I
think you should have said, 'Marc, there are *only* problems.'"

"Well . . ." Sydney said, shrugging and easing himself creak-
ily into a chair. Then, quickly, "It is all right if I sit? You're not
occupied?"

"Sydney . . . for you? Don't be ridiculous." Marc lighted a
cigarette and sat back.

"Someone's putting pressure on us, Marc. Suddenly orders
are being canceled in stores we did business with for donkey's
years. Textile suppliers are asking for their money upfront and
not the usual ten days with discount. The *Wall Street Journal* and
WWD both had reporters call me asking if we were experiencing
money troubles, if our cash flow was okay."

He went on. Street just sat there, listening. Of course Majesty, like everyone else in the business, occasionally ran short of cash. Outlays were irregularly spaced; so were incoming payments. But the company was more than sound. Dugan of Marine Midland had assured him that a substantial line of credit was there, waiting. Sure they were spending a lot. You couldn't expand without its costing. What was more disturbing were the cancellations of retail orders. In this business, if you didn't sell, you died.

"Which stores are canceling?" he asked.

Sydney told him. Several of their biggest West Coast customers, a big Dallas store, a small but rich specialty chain in the Carolinas and Virginia. Two New York stores, one of them with a dozen important suburban branches. A big Chicago outfit. A Toledo department store. And they weren't just cutting back. That always happened if a line wasn't moving. There were across-the-board cancellations of both Adam's and Chelsea's lines.

"This is crazy, Sydney," Marc said. "These lines are good lines."

"I know, Marc. That's why I say we're being pushed by someone."

Marc nodded. "Baltimore?" he asked.

Heidler shrugged, looking older and more waxen than Marc had ever seen him. "Could be. He wants to buy Adam so he puts financial pressure on you to force the price down. Such a thing happens."

Marc got up and began to pace the floor. "Okay, Sydney, tomorrow call your sources and find out if Stanley Baltimore does a lot of business with the stores that canceled. Maybe there's a pattern. If he's a big supplier, he could bring leverage on them to cancel us. Meanwhile, I'll ask the bank if that line of credit is still there. I don't think Marine Midland can be pressured, but I'd better find out. And, Sydney . . ."

"Yes?"

"Don't say anything to Adam. I don't want him worrying about money when he ought to be concentrating on the collection."

Heidler nodded. He understood what Marc meant without having said it: that perhaps Adam knew all this already.

On the way home Street passed a newsstand at Seventh Avenue and Fortieth Street. The papers were all laid out, neat as tombs. He ignored them. But the one headline, in the late *Post*, caught his eye: WESTIE MOB KILLING!

Street pushed some change at the newsie and grabbed the *Post*. In the second graf he found Swaggerty: "Police sources said a white male named Robert Swaggerty was being sought for questioning in the shooting."

He *knew* it was Swaggerty! Jesus! That tore it. Running a protection racket on Ninth Avenue and *killing* people, two different things entirely. He could see Bobby's face, small and fierce. Could see the boy Swaggerty. And Swaggerty the man. He remembered his cousin Penny, red-haired and panting, remembered the day Carl Lazer's boys tried to muscle them and how he and Bobby had thrown them out, remembered how Bobby and his girl, "Mrs. Swaggerty," had taken seats up front at the fashion show.

That was the Bobby he knew. But there was another Bobby. He knew that as well. A Bobby whose heroes cut off heads and toted them up and down Ninth Avenue in shopping bags, who killed for hire, who remarked, as Bobby once did when Marc asked why the Westies hired out as killers to the mob, to the Italians or the Jews, or whoever could pay the price: "We're like Park Avenue apartments, Marc, everyone wants to rent us for a reasonable price."

He flagged a cab and fell into the back seat, barely able to tell the driver where they were headed.

Chelsea was waiting for him, wearing one of his shirts. She had a key now. And it was easier to meet here than to run into Toy, and her occasional friends, at Chelsea's flat.

She regarded him solemnly. "You need a haircut," she said, as serious as if she were measuring him for a shroud.

"Sure," he said coldly, "I need a lot of things."

"What's the matter? I talk about a haircut and you jump down my throat."

"Sorry." He handed her the paper.

"What?" she asked. "So what?" Then she saw the headline. And the story. "Oh, Marc, your friend."

He nodded. "He's done it now. This tears it."

She came to him and slung an arm around his neck. He could feel her body tucked close to his.

"Maybe it's wrong," she said, "maybe they got the wrong man. Maybe it was self-defense. That's always possible." She ran a hand through his hair.

"I dunno," he said, "I'd like to think so."

Chelsea cooked dinner while he sat in the living room, idly paging through the paper and listening to the radio news. The killing was reported twice an hour. It was odd, hearing the name of a man you knew so well on the news. "Robert Swaggerty." When had anyone last called him "Robert"? Perhaps a nun in parochial school. And now some thirty thousand New York cops were looking for him, a red-headed boy with whom he used to have fistfights, who stole his baseball mitt, who had come up to Riverdale to see him play football, who had helped him rout Carl Lazer's goons, who had once promised that if Marc ever needed anything, he, Bobby, would always be there.

After dinner they lay together on the couch, watching the late news.

"You still need a haircut," she said.

"I know."

She leaped up. "Come on," she said, wanting to distract him, "get undressed and get a big towel and I'll cut your hair."

"Sure," he said, but without enthusiasm. He didn't care. He was in his shorts, wrapped in a towel and sitting on a stool while Chelsea, brow furrowed in concentration, circled him with a comb and scissors, snipping and cutting, when the buzzer sounded.

"I'll get it," she said, "don't move. You'll have hair all over the damned house."

"I remembered you didn't have a doorman," Swaggerty said, "so I walked right in and came up the stairs. Didn't want to have no conversations in the elevator."

Marc shook loose hair onto the kitchen floor and got into a

robe, and the two of them went into the living room while Chelsea cleaned up.

"What happened?" Street asked.

"I suppose it would be a waste of time to tell you it was three guys named Irving."

"Well, was it?"

Swaggerty grinned crookedly. "Nope, it was me, all right."

Chelsea came in then and stood, watching them and listening. Bobby looked up at her.

"Look, honey, maybe it would be better if you don't hear. Then if anyone asks you any questions, you can say you don't know."

"If Marc knows, I want to know."

"Okay." Bobby shrugged. He looked older, more tired than Street had ever seen him, and when he started to talk his voice was flat, defeated, little of the old Swaggerty cockiness coming through.

"It was a mob thing. Us versus them, the good guys against the bad guys. Though it'd be hell trying to say which guys wore the white hats." He inhaled. "Could I have a drink, Marc? Whatever you got."

Chelsea went into the kitchen to pour them both a stiff Scotch.

"... so Lazer put us on retainer. This other bunch, wops, were muscling in on one of his loan-sharking operations. Some guys had been beaten up, some money taken. Quite a lot of money. No one got killed but it wasn't friendly. I and my people were told to put the heat on the other guys. That's what I was doing this morning over on the docks near the *Intrepid,* trying to scare off one of their hoods. Trouble was, he had a gun. I got in the shot first."

"So it *was* self-defense," Chelsea blurted out.

"Sure." Swaggerty laughed, a dry, brief laugh. "Except I'm toting a rod without a license, I've got a record, the other guy never got a shot off. The cops might have a little problem with buying my case."

They talked for more than an hour. Street wanted him to give himself up. Bobby was stubborn.

"I don't want to go up, Marc. I don't wanna do time."

"Well, a good lawyer . . ."

"They got good lawyers too. Besides, the wops have a lot of muscle inside. Maybe I get three years with time off. Probably I don't live three months up there. They got ways . . ."

Chelsea made them another drink and fixed Bobby a couple of sandwiches, which he wolfed down. "Didn't stop off for dinner," he said, smiling at her.

"Do you have a place you can stay? Someplace they won't know about?" Marc asked.

"Nope. Not in town. Best I go somewheres else, maybe Florida, maybe the Coast."

"Got any money?"

He shook his head. "Not enough. You could help me there. If you can."

"Sure." Marc got up and went into the bedroom. His wallet was in the back pocket of his pants, but when he took it out there wasn't much. He went back into the living room.

"Only eighty bucks, Bobby. I can get as much as you want in the morning, when the bank opens."

"Oh, hell, don't worry," Bobby said, seeing the gloom and regret in Marc's face. "Eighty is fine. I'll get by. Just seeing you guys and getting a little food and a jar makes me feel better already."

"I've got some money," Chelsea said, "maybe three hundred dollars."

Bobby held up a hand. "Hey, babe, that's sweet of you. But don't you get involved. Me and Marc is one thing. You ain't even a honorary Westie."

She shook her head and went into the bedroom. When she came out she had the money, and she pushed it into his hand.

"Three hundred and fifteen dollars," she said. "Take it."

He hesitated. "I'm no lawyer, kid, but doesn't this make you an accessory?"

"No, just a sucker for Marc's dubious acquaintances."

They all laughed then, not uproariously. Swaggerty slept on the couch, and when they woke in the morning he was gone. Left behind was a note:

"Thanks, guys. If they ask, say I came in with a gun and took your dough and said I'd kill you if you called the cops. I'll try to keep in touch. If you get a message from '9th Avenue,' that's me. Love, Bobby."

Chelsea knew now about Bobby Swaggerty. She'd heard Carl Lazer's name mentioned. Marc still hesitated to tell her the rest of it.

32

Klein, Lauren, Blass, Perry Ellis, Donna Karan. Add two more
to their ranks this season: Adam Greenberg and Chelsea
West. Add them, but do not invite them to the same dinner
party.

Mode, May 19, 1981

In early May, Adam and Chelsea both showed their collections. Again, his was good, but once again, hers was a sensation.

Lincoln Radford wrote: "The mark of a good designer is
continuity. Miss West avoids the cheap trick, the easy path, and
builds upon the promising foundation she laid down in November, paying tribute to the same old American fashion values. For
fall, her polished taffetas become chunky tweeds, her linens rough
wools. Even as it evolves, the spirit remains, sportive, young, pure.
And salable."

Radford was not alone in "regretting" the collection's final
note, a pair of jeans worn by Chelsea herself, with the words "Go
West!" on the seat. "Unfortunately," Radford tut-tutted, "but
perhaps forgivable in one so young."

If the critics raised eyebrows, the buyers did not.

"A sellout, Marc," Heidler crooned. "Some of them are even
buying the jeans."

"The jeans? That was a joke. Chelsea's idea of a humorous
sign-off."

"They weren't laughing. They were buying."

It was something for Heidler to sound impressed. Some of

the big stores hadn't sent their buyers. Whoever was pressuring them, whether it was Stanley Baltimore or someone else, they had gotten the message. But the buyers who showed up had plenty of "open to buy" money. And they spent it.

They also spent at Adam's collection. Xenon was that season's big "new disco," and it was there that Adam threw his post-collection party. Chelsea had shown three days before. Adam had read the reviews. So had Genghis Khan, by now very much his chief sycophant.

"It's sickening, the way they drool over her."

Adam just looked gloomy. He was not accustomed to sharing fame. Khan stared at him from under his student's cap, the dark-ringed eyes fierce and angry. "You ought to do something about her, Adam. I mean it!"

Khan had the true capacity for hate, Adam only the capacity to suffer. Adam was passive, a quality Genghis did not understand and could not accept. He railed now at Adam, pausing only when friends and fans, in and out of the business, came up to their corner banquette to congratulate Adam, to wish him well, to urge him to join them later at their tables, clustering about in cheerful, nervous adulation. To all, Adam was the evening's hero, the giant, the benefactor, the source. A few might even have been sincere in their gushing.

"You're a fool, Adam," Khan hissed when they were alone. "Destroy the bitch before she ruins everything. She's got Street dazzled. This is your time, your company. She's taking it away from you. Stealing what you built. That Street . . ."

Adam shook his head. "I fought that battle, Genghis. Lost it. She's no phony. Her stuff is pretty good. Marc's just doing what he thinks is good for Majesty."

Genghis Khan stared at him. "I can't believe how gutless you're being. How you can let them do this to you. Before Chelsea came along you were the king—"

Adam whirled on him, taunted into anger. "I'm *still* the king, and don't you forget it!"

Beyond them his guests milled about the dance floor and the bar and the tables, gossiping and enjoying a party they were not paying for, while two dancers, a boy and a girl, shuffled to a disco beat in wicker cages hung above the room, their bare young bodies shining in the key lights. Genghis Khan, sullen and vengeful, retreated into the men's room to snort cocaine and wonder which he hated more, Street or Adam.

Stanley Baltimore had come to Adam's party out of duty, not for pleasure. He had an investment in Adam. It paid to make the occasional gesture. Like dogs, designers appreciated attention. Baltimore stroked Adam as thoughtfully as he might a favorite poodle, still intent on splitting Adam and Marc Street. Street had made a brief appearance at the party, shaken a few hands, exchanged a few words with Adam, and disappeared. Baltimore noted the coolness. Then too, glancing around the room, he noticed other things. He had been given one of the *banquettes d'honneur,* near Adam's, near the dancing, where he could watch. Lester and two other men were with him. There were no women.

He had a Perrier in his big hand when Adam came over to him. "Everything okay, Stanley?"

"Wonderful, Adam. Great collection, great party."

"Well, there's a lot of noise." Adam looked around.

Baltimore laughed. "You're right about that. Can't talk here. Why don't we lunch tomorrow? Caravelle? At one? There are so many things I want to talk about."

Adam shook his head. "I'll be a basket case tomorrow. How about Friday?"

They made the date. Adam beckoned, and a waiter brought him some more champagne. He sat there next to Baltimore for a few moments.

"Your pal Street was in a hurry," Baltimore remarked.

"Yeah, well, you know Marc."

Baltimore recognized the evasion. "Sure," he said, "work, work, work."

Two girls came over to the table, models who had shown the collection. "Adam, this is super, come dance." Baltimore made him nervous, and he was glad of an excuse to get away. The other girl flopped onto the banquette next to Baltimore.

Baltimore looked at her, a tall brunette in a mini-skirt and a cotton T-shirt plastered to her body in the heat.

"I'll be back, Stanley," Adam said. Then, seeing Baltimore's eyes on the girl, he said, "Stanley, this is Jana. Jana, this is Mr. Baltimore, the man who makes perfume."

The girl sat up straight. She was seventeen and impressed. "Gosh, *the* Baltimore?"

"Yes, the one and only."

"Hey, how about that."

When Adam and his partner were on the floor, Baltimore waved to a passing waiter. "Waiter, whatever this young lady wants, just bring it. Understand?" He handed the man some money. The drinks were free; he was making a gesture.

"Yessir."

"Hey," the girl said again, "Stanley Baltimore . . ."

He looked down at her. "You've got nice tits, Jana."

"Gee," she said, "that's nice of you to notice, Mr. Baltimore."

By Friday Adam was still feeling the party. They'd closed Xenon and then a bunch of them had gone down to West Street. Adam had wakened late the next afternoon in Khan's apartment, in bed with two boys. He and Genghis had made peace, but he couldn't remember ever having seen either of the boys before.

"Sure you do, Adam," one of them said, "Genghis introduced us."

He remembered only the cocaine. Now, somber in a double-breasted gray flannel suit by Cardin and a Hermès tie, he walked into La Caravelle. Robert greeted him with a half bow and led him to Baltimore's table, halfway down the right side, against the wall. It was one of the tables where you could see who came in, where men could talk and not be overheard.

Adam ordered a bloody mary. "I'm still a bit rocky. Wednesday night went on and on."

It had for Baltimore and Jana as well. But Stanley was feeling just fine. Let these kids do their booze and their drugs, all the better to remain sober and enjoy.

When the bloody mary came, along with another Perrier for Baltimore, he got right to the point. "Look, Adam, I'll level with you. A couple of weeks ago I met with Street. Told him I thought he was screwing up. There's no way two designers in one house can work. He's going to hurt you, playing up to that girl. Told him so, flat out."

"And?"

"He said he knew what he was doing, what was best for you. I argued the point. Finally, stubborn as he was, I said I'd like to buy out your contract."

"What do you mean?"

"Just what I said. Buy him out and set up an Adam division within Baltimore Inc."

Adam was trying to think very clearly now. This was important. He didn't want to flub it. He pushed his drink away.

"And what did Marc say to that?"

"Refused. Turned me down flat. No bargaining, no discussion. Told me to go to hell." Baltimore paused, shrewdly. "Didn't he even tell you?"

Adam chewed his lower lip and tried to think. Baltimore sensed his confusion.

"He should at least have told you, Adam, given you a chance to express an opinion. You're his star, the talent that made Majesty what it is, after all."

"Yes, that's true enough."

Baltimore leaned forward. "Look, Adam, I won't try to kid you. You're a smart guy. I need you more than you need Baltimore Inc. You make a lot of money. I know that. So I can't buy you. You're too proud to be bought, anyway, or I'd try."

Adam knew he was being played. Which didn't make Baltimore any less effective. Adam admired professionalism. "Go ahead."

Baltimore beamed. "I want you to come over to my side, Adam. Ours is a huge organization. Makes Majesty look like the five-and-dime. We don't *have* a designer. Not one. We work with a half dozen, but just on their perfumes and cosmetics. If you come aboard you'd be the only fashion designer in the house. I'd promise that, put it down on paper. We'd back you to the hilt. Advertising, sales promotion, publicity, PR. I'd have you and your name on every magazine cover in the country, every talk show. You want to design a Hollywood movie? Great! I'd pay you a bonus. Not like Street, always pissing and moaning that you're taking time away from the office. You want a couple more assistants to help out with the load? Name 'em, you got 'em. You want a house somewhere? Pick it out. You want that jet of yours paid for by the company? Just say so. You want a yearly income guarantee, a pension investment trust, sheltered by the best tax men in the business? My tax man used to be the Undersecretary of the Treasury. Reagan has him to dinner."

Baltimore had done all the talking, but it was Adam who had to catch his breath. "Wait a minute, Stanley. You're going too fast."

"There's more."

By the time the plates had been cleared and they were sipping strong, bitter *café filtre*, Adam was sold. He hadn't said so, not yet, but they both knew it.

Sure, Adam thought, it would solve so many things. Leave Marc and Chelsea to each other, eliminate the awkwardness, the resentment they all felt, give him the freedom to create an identity of his own separate from Majesty and from Marc. It was an ideal situation; it would be a front-page sensation. He thought of the publicity, the fringe benefits Baltimore promised, the freedom to do films. He thought, too, of the money. Millions and millions of dollars. His head swam.

Baltimore, relaxed, confident, talked about an upcoming auction of paintings, knowledgeably and with the flattering assumption Adam knew as much about them as he did. Adam remembered afternoons with his first mentor, Charlie Winston, strolling through the galleries and the museums, learning about pictures, listening to Winston the once-great designer tell him what they were looking at, and why. Marc Street never talked about art; Marc wouldn't know a Rembrandt from a Wyeth. Stanley *knew*. Small things meant something.

When they left La Caravelle for their respective limousines, two rich men sharing interests, Baltimore said with a studied casualness, "Maybe my attorneys ought to look at your contract. I don't want to give Street an excuse to litigate."

Adam grunted. Then he extended his hand to Stanley Baltimore.

"Sure, Stanley. But you know, until recently Marc and I never *had* a contract?"

It was Baltimore's turn to be confused. "No contract? How the hell did you guys work together?"

Adam replied, his voice bitter: "Simple. We trusted each other."

33

Ten years ago the experts were writing off the designer
label as passé. The label is still selling clothes today
whether it's Pierre Cardin or Brooks Brothers or Levi's.

Mode, June 2, 1981

Swaggerty dropped from sight. New atrocities monopolized the front pages.

Marc assumed he had gotten some money somewhere. He
couldn't have gotten far on what they gave him. For days Street
tensed whenever the phone rang, when there was a knock at the
apartment door. How could they not trace Bobby to him? Didn't
anyone remember their West Side origins?

No one did. May melted into premature summer, and in the
humidity of a baking Memorial Day he and Chelsea flew west to
Denver.

"Look," she said, "I'm falling for you, which is probably the
dumbest thing I've done since Tuesday afternoon. But it's happening. And I damn well want to see you on my own turf, back
home, and let my grandpa get a look at you before I do something
I might regret."

He knew how serious she was beneath the wisecracks. He felt
the same way about her, had the same doubts. But he had no
"turf," nothing she didn't already know, whether it was New
York or Paris. Nor had he someone against whom to compare her,
someone to whom he could show her off and get reactions. He
could hardly discuss her with Adam or with Sydney Heidler or

with Swaggerty, even if he weren't a gunman on the run. He wished his mother were alive.

"If she were still around I'd pass you under Chanel's nose," he warned. "She'd tell me if you were the real goods."

"Oh, no," Chelsea said, "that's a competition I wouldn't want any part of. Whether you know it or not, you're still in love with her."

There were just the three of them for dinner in Will West's dining room, large enough to seat forty. They'd gotten in just before dusk, with the sun still bouncing off the peaks, but the ranch and the high pasture were already in gloom. Will West had them into his library for cocktails before they sat down.

"I always mix the drinks," Chelsea said. "He taught me."

"She could mix a decent drink by the time she was nine or ten," West said.

They were given separate rooms. Marc had expected that.

"I suppose I did too," she said, "but it's sort of naïve, isn't it?"

"No," he said, "it's his house. We play by his rules."

Chelsea really hadn't known how her grandfather would behave. Not since she'd had a high-school beau to dinner and seen the boy humiliated by the old man's catechism had she invited a male guest home. Cowboys like Raker were obviously unsuitable, and for the last two years she'd been living in New York. Marc was a first. It was fascinating to watch her grandfather circle around him, probing and testing, not so much out of hostility as curiosity.

"I know nothing of your business, Mr. Street. Of course I read, I hear things. Lots of small companies, generally undercapitalized, family owned, high rate of bankruptcy."

"That's the fashion business," Marc conceded, "plus a handful of giants like Jonathan Logan and Manhattan Industries and Levi's."

"And don't the big boys squeeze you out?"

"Marc is a pretty tough guy to squeeze, Grandpa," Chelsea said.

"Oh, I'm sure of that, sure of that," West said quickly, more graciousness than conviction in his voice.

The meal was fresh shrimps flown in from the Gulf, steaks broiled over mesquite wood, and a huge tossed salad spiced with Mexican peppers.

"Careful of those," Chelsea warned, "they'll peel the soles right off your shoes."

Will West cackled. "You don't *have* to eat 'em," he said. The peppers were obviously a test of manhood.

"Okay," Street said, "I won't," and carefully picked through them.

"See, Grandpa, he's smart, too."

West's thin mouth tightened. She was supposed to be on his side. This Jew was the outsider, Catherine was kin. But he went on. "A lot of weird characters in your business, I suppose."

"Well, they're not all choirboys. Some fine people, some animals. But, good or bad, they're rarely dull. Fashion is part fantasy, part sleight of hand, part necessity. You need clothes, you need food, you need shelter, or you die."

"Clothes are clothes," West interjected sourly.

"You're right, Mr. West. A billion Chinese wear identical blue denim boiler suits. They're content, I suppose. Fashion is something more than body covering. It cheers people up. Makes them more attractive. Gives them self-confidence. Variety. Sex appeal. People express themselves through what they wear." He paused and then plunged in. "Like you. That western shirt. You could wear a Brooks Brothers label or a sweater. But it wouldn't be you," he said innocently.

West cleared his throat.

Chelsea stifled a laugh. "But we were talking about people."

Will West got back into it. "Yes, all these queers and fakirs your business seems to attract."

Street knew he was being called upon for a performance. He gave it. He told them about Pierre Balmain and his Franciscan monk. About the Madrid designer who reputedly hired Spanish gypsy boys to come to the cellar of his castle to be whipped. About Helena Rubenstein, who ate chicken in bed and wiped her greasy fingers on the satin sheets. About Brooke Shields, a good kid who happened to be beautiful. About Sydney Heidler, who had taught him his trade. About Chanel, who had taught him about life.

"Yes," West said, distracted, his eyes unfocused.

Marc glanced toward Chelsea, seeing a warning in her face: old man West had traveled to Paris for her funeral. He bit off something he was going to add about Chanel, but then West, with an effort, came back to them.

"I knew her, you know," West said, "years ago. Perhaps Catherine told you that."

"Yes."

"And later on, when you knew her, was she still the same?"

Street did not know how to answer, since he obviously hadn't known the young Chanel, but he understood West wasn't after data but memories.

"Oh, I'm sure Coco was always the same," Marc said, "wonderful and impossible and wise. My mother had worked for her as a mannequin, and when I got into fashion, knowing nothing about it, my mother wrote Coco. She received me, welcomed me, tutored me. I guess most of what I know about fashion and a hell of a lot else comes from her."

"How did she look?" West asked.

"Still the same, lean, erect, full of energy, full of the devil. One night when we left her shop after dinner it was snowing and she was wearing pumps and they would have been soaked crossing the rue Cambon to the Ritz, so I just picked her up and carried her across the street. She didn't weigh very much. I can still hear her laughter now: 'Ah, what a scandal we'll create entering the Ritz comme ça!' " Marc paused. "She was over eighty then and still wicked, still fun."

Will West stared straight ahead, seeing something neither Marc nor Chelsea saw. Then, breaking the mood, he said, "But that was Chanel. She was different from the others . . ."

Marc went on. "Look, Mr. West, there are characters and there are solid people. Like everything else, every other business. Maybe we're a bit more flamboyant, less structured, more impulsive and instinctive. We work with beautiful things, with critical sensibilities. The press grades us on every thing we do. And after they grade us, it's the buyers' turn. And finally, the consumer has her shot. The press doesn't review the new premium from Exxon, and the guy who drives doesn't try it on first before he buys his gas. In fashion, they do. No wonder we're different."

West looked at him. This was not a stupid man. He didn't buy the whole peroration, but there was something to it. Street sat there, relaxed and easy, just waiting. Will West was accustomed to making young men nervous.

"I suppose the unions give you difficulty."

Marc shrugged. "Some. But the ILGWU is pretty stable. And we manufacture a lot of stuff offshore, Taiwan, Haiti, Hong Kong."

"Smart," West snapped, "damned unions will throttle a business if you don't fight 'em."

"And you fought them," Street remarked.

"Fought 'em and busted 'em."

After dinner one of the maids brought around fresh glasses and a bottle.

"Hope you like old port," West said, "this is 1921. Smooth as a baby's rump."

"That *is* a wine," Street admitted, impressed.

Old man West told stories of his early days as they sat there at the table, of how he built his empire, of the difficulties he had with Washington. "They were always calling me down there on one pretext or another. I testified before more useless committees. Pack of ambitious ward heelers trying to make a reputation off me, throwing mud and hoping some of it'd stick. Some did, most didn't." He paused and then looked at Street over the rim of his wineglass. "They ever get after you down there in Congress, Street?"

"Not yet," he said, trying not to tense or react.

"Good. They scent a little blood in the water and they'll never let up on you, just keep biting and snapping and chewing pieces off of you."

The old man went upstairs after that, and Chelsea took Marc out onto the verandah to look at the mountains in the starlight.

"I think he knows about my father," Marc said. "That bit about congressional hearings."

"He knows about everything, darling. It would be a surprise if he didn't."

They spent four days there, most of it pleasant, driving into Aspen twice for dinner. Chelsea went riding, and Marc bounced along in a pickup truck.

"The livery stable on West Eighty-ninth Street was one place I avoided in my youth," he said.

"Sure, you were too busy shooting pool and chasing girls."

Will West left them on the third day. "Stay as long as you like," he said, "but I've got to go."

There was the threat of a strike at one of his mines up in Utah, and the old man wanted to be there. That night they were alone in the big house, and they could have slept together but they didn't. It was Will West's house. Before he got into the helicopter, West had taken Chelsea aside.

"You serious about this man?"

"Yes, I think I am."

He grunted. "Just be sure, that's all."

"I will. What do you think of him, Grandpa?"

West thought for a moment. "Not a bad fellow, for a Jew."

When they got back to New York Sydney Heidler was waiting for them at LaGuardia, brandishing a copy of that week's issue of *Mode* magazine, with a by-lined story by Lincoln Radford to the effect that Adam was quitting Majesty Fashions to join Baltimore Inc.

34

Not since Charles Revson bought Balmain has there been
as significant a deal between perfume empire and designer.

Mode, June 9, 1981

S o they bought you. You named a price and they paid
it."

"It's not that simple, Marc. You know it isn't."

Adam was cleaning out drawers and tearing up files. Street
half sat on a desk, watching Adam.

"I hope you got everything down on paper," he said, "got a
good lawyer to go over it."

"With Stanley? You kidding? Half the partners at Sullivan
and Cromwell worked on the contract." He kept pulling papers
from drawers, but didn't really seem to be looking at them;
seemed instead to be staring into some middle distance.

Marc lighted a cigarette. Heidler had tried to cool him, and
he was trying to cool himself. But it was hard. Despite Chelsea's
success, Adam was still Majesty's creative spine; he accounted for
the bulk of the company's sales and profit. His departure wasn't
only a personal betrayal but a devastating commercial and financial loss.

"Why did you pull something like this?" Marc asked. "How
could you do it to me, to yourself, to Majesty?"

"You didn't want me anymore. Baltimore did. Simple as
that."

"Bullshit."

"Okay, bullshit. Have it your way."

"I worked for damn near twenty years to build what we have and you're pulling the legs right out from under it."

"Maybe you should have thought of that before you brought her in."

"You know why I—"

"Oh, Christ, Marc, not that same old tired story about Abe Goode and amortizing the investment and efficiency studies. I haven't been on the Avenue this long without learning something about business myself. You wanted her; you got her. I just don't happen to go along with the deal."

Marc suddenly burst into anger. "It's those creeps you hang out with like Genghis Khan," Marc shouted, "guys not worth a tenth of you and you listen to their crap and let them fill your head up with stupid notions about—"

"I'm not stupid. You always think that about me, but I'm not just another dumb designer with a sketch pad. Listen to me, Marc, this deal with Baltimore's going to make me rich. Maybe he's a shit, maybe he's just using me, but wait till you see how I use him and all that wonderful Baltimore money. He's going to promote hell out of me. In a couple of years I'll be bigger than Calvin, bigger than Ralph, bigger than anyone!" He grew quieter. "You were good to me, Marc. You did a lot for me. But there's only so much you and Majesty can manage."

Marc bit his tongue.

Adam went on. "And that stuff about my friends. What the hell business is it of yours? Did I ever get on you about some of the chippies you were screwing? The hell I did. That was your life, this is mine. And if it includes a guy like Khan, that's my problem."

"Adam, Adam . . ."

The designer threw himself into a chair, his face flushed, his eyes seeming on the brink of tears. "Oh, Marc, it was all so good. So damned good."

"Yes, it was."

"And then Peter ran and I was alone and you brought Chelsea in. We used to have each other, you and I."

He didn't say so, he might not even have been aware of it on a conscious level, but jealousy of Chelsea ate at his soul.

Both men were calm now, preternaturally so. Adam remembered that night he'd been beaten up, how Marc had thrown an arm around him, had held him the way one holds a child, the way he had never been held. Marc thought of other things they'd shared, other moments that they'd had, Butch and Sundance, flights to Paris, Coty Awards and triumphs, a boy in the rain the day they buried Coco.

"I know these things happen on Seventh Avenue," Marc said, "people screw one another. They walk out on deals. They sell out. I just never thought it would happen with us."

Adam's face tightened. "Well, it did. Nothing's carved in stone."

"I guess not," Marc said. There was the Adam who sent the jeep to East Hampton and the Adam who had taken Stanley Baltimore's pieces of silver. "It didn't have to end this way, you know."

Adam shook his head and then slowly looked up, his eyes for the first time meeting Marc's. "You're wrong there," he said. "From the day you brought her in, it was inevitable."

"You really think I favored her over you?"

Adam looked at him. "I was your boy, Marc. The only real designer Majesty ever had. I was the one who got you out of the line-for-line business. We were a good team, we got rich together. It could have gone on forever." He stopped; then, his head down again, he added in a hushed voice, "We could have gone on forever."

"Yeah, maybe."

Adam got up and tossed the last batch of papers onto a worktable. "Maybe I could just send for this stuff. Would that be okay?"

"Sure, Adam. Just send somebody over."

"Well."

"Yeah. Well, you take care of yourself. Watch out for that son of a bitch."

Adam smiled for the first time. "He is a bastard, isn't he."

He stuck out a hand, and Marc took it.

Chelsea was in Dallas to make a personal appearance at Neiman-Marcus and to do the local television show. That night Marc sat propped up in bed with a yellow legal pad on his knee, chain-smoking and jotting notes. He worked until well after midnight, writing and crossing out and writing again. Adam's defection meant having to recast Majesty from top to bottom, with no half measures, no pausing for regrets or recrimination. The Seventh Avenue jungle sensed weakness and pounced on it. Majesty had never before been as vulnerable. Everything he'd built for twenty years, all his success, all his hopes for the future, were at hazard now. Adam was a gentleman—Marc was willing to concede that even now—but Baltimore was an animal. It was Baltimore who had forced the crisis on him, and he knew Baltimore too well to expect leniency. Having lured away his designer, Baltimore would step up the bidding, increase the pressure, drive him to the wall, destroy Majesty if he could. He'd defied the man, and Baltimore would never forget, never forgive, never relent.

"Okay," Marc said aloud at one-thirty that morning to his empty apartment, "let's rumble."

When Chelsea came back he summoned her and Heidler to his office. It was a June day, with an early-morning thunderstorm darkening the city and lashing rain across the office windows high above murky Seventh Avenue.

"Here's the plan," he said. "For the moment, it's confidential. Just the three of us. Nobody else, and by that I mean nobody. I don't know how many people in this shop are already on Baltimore's payroll. It's natural that some of our people may feel loyalty to Adam. Baltimore will buy them if he can."

"Marc," Heidler said gently, "they're our people. You're so sure they can be bought?"

Street looked at him. "He bought Adam, didn't he?"

There was no response, and Marc continued. "Okay, first of all I'm suing Baltimore. Try to get a preliminary injunction to keep Adam from working for him. I haven't got a legal leg to stand on, but it'll slow things up over there and distract Adam. I'm meeting the lawyers this afternoon. Never mind if we get thrown out of court, I'll appeal. It'll take weeks. The lawyers will love it."

"The lawyers will get rich," Heidler said dryly.

"Next, we're stepping up jeans production. Every factory."

"Adam jeans, Marc? Making more Adam jeans?" Heidler demanded, incredulous.

"Sydney, we're making more Chelsea West jeans."

"Marc, except for that joke pair of jeans at the end of the show, I haven't done any jeans. It'll take weeks to—"

"Chelsea, relax. We're going to continue making Adam jeans, but your name's going on the ass instead of his. We're changing labels is all. Something Baltimore taught me a long time ago."

"Can we do that legally?"

Marc laughed. "We're sure as hell going to find out." Then, seriously, "If there were copyright protection on blue jeans, Levi Strauss would have put us all in jail years ago.

"Next, we're doubling the promotion budget. I want Chelsea's name and face and, if necessary, her rear end in every woman's magazine in the country, on every female-oriented TV show. Chelsea, I want you to get on the Donahue show again. Try to get yourself back on *Good Morning America.* And no more on Plato's cave! Call Merv Griffin. Didn't he want you last season but you didn't have an open date?"

"Yeah, but—"

"Just do it. And another thing, I want you to romance our top fifty retail accounts. Sydney will make up a list. I want you to agree to do trunk shows at their stores, have lunch with their top people when they come to New York. Store presidents are as susceptible to flattery and a beautiful woman as the rest of us. Sydney, you work with her on it.

"Oh, yeah, two more things. One, I talked to Didier this morning in Paris before I left the house. He's agreed to do a small production of Chelsea jeans in France. They're going to be your own jeans but with a different label, like the jeans in the collection. It'll say 'Go West.' But it'll say it in French."

" 'Allez Ouest'? Will Americans understand that?" she asked.

He shook his head.

"What it's going to say is"—he paused and drew a hand slowly through the air—"is 'Geaux West!' G-E-A-U-X. Get it?"

Chelsea groaned. "Marc, that is the corniest thing I've ever heard."

He shot her a manic grin. "I know," he said, "and if my instincts are right, they'll walk out of the stores. We'll advertise them as Chelsea West's French jeans, maybe Paris jeans."

Heidler looked dubious. "Marc, you always said fashion was more than gimmicks."

"Yeah," he said seriously, "but that was before Stanley Baltimore bombed Pearl Harbor. And the last thing, at least until I think of something else to drive him nuts, we declare war on Baltimore where he lives. We go into the perfume business."

Heidler was too flustered even to object. He just sat there, breathing deeply and looking stricken.

"I'm going to see Lauder and Revlon and Lancôme and every other major factor in the business and see just which of them will work with us to develop a Chelsea perfume and a cosmetic line. That's where the money is, that's where we'll drive Stanley out of his goddamned mind."

"Marc?"

"Yes, Sydney."

"You mentioned money. Do we have enough?"

"Don't worry, Sydney. I'm plowing back my profits and I'll cut back my salary. I'll take out only a thousand a week for the time being. And I'm seeing the bankers. We still have a line of credit."

Sydney did not look impressed.

"Come on, Sydney, cheer up. We have a hole card."

"What's that?"

"We don't have to pay Adam's restaurant tabs anymore."

The fashion war of the eighties began.

35

Fashion wars are just as hard and cruel as real wars except that nobody gets killed; only bankrupted.

Mode, July 17, 1981

Toy had vanished.

Chelsea came home from her meeting with Marc and Sydney to find her closets empty and a note in the refrigerator, taped to the salad crisper, where she knew Chelsea would see it.

"I got this new guy, Chelsea. He very rich. I write you a postcard. Love, Toy."

Marc was philosophical about it. "Your Toy, my Bobby Swaggerty. A couple of lost strays, out there wandering somewhere."

"Well, I worry about her. She's still just a kid."

"Hell," Marc objected, "you're not her mother. There's a limit to what you could have done."

Chelsea shook her head. She felt as if she had abandoned an infant.

"I didn't do anything, not a damned thing."

Nor did her model agency. They phoned a few times and sent a registered letter and then gave it up. Very young models were forever dropping out. They got hooked or they got pregnant or they got fat, and the agencies had no time to waste on salvage projects. As beautiful as Toy was, there were always a dozen more coming along like her. A door had closed, and who cared under what mat the key might be hidden?

In normal times Chelsea would have tried to track Toy down, would have brooded. But there was no time, no leisure for such indulgences. Marc was working her too hard; she was working herself too hard. She and Dufour flew to Haiti to supervise the design and stitching of the new label going onto the seat of the pants of one hundred thousand pairs of what had been, until then, Adam jeans. She gave a dinner party for the executive vice-president of I. Magnin at "21," hosted a lunch for the Marshall Field buying team at La Grenouille, gave a cocktail party for Lord & Taylor, flew to Cleveland to close a sale at Higbee's, and spent a day in Boston signing autographs at Filene's and dining at the Ritz Carlton with the ready-to-wear vice-president of Jordan Marsh. She and Marc talked every night by phone, usually long-distance. They rarely met.

He spent a day in Mexico and returned to New York to change clothes and fly to Taiwan. He went around the world the other way and stopped in Paris to meet with Didier and dined with Brugère and Jimmy de Bertrand and made minor changes in the typography of "Geaux West!" Once more back in New York, he consulted his lawyers (as he had anticipated, the lawsuit against Stanley Baltimore had already been thrown out of court), nailed down a long-term loan from Marine Midland, hired a second assistant for Chelsea, failed to make a deal with either Estée Lauder or Revlon, and ended up negotiating a promising perfume arrangement with the number-four company in the field, one nearly as large and every bit as aggressive as Baltimore Inc.

Begging, threatening, cajoling, negotiating deals and making promises he was not sure he could keep, spending money he was not sure he had, Marc Street fought to right a badly listing ship. He lost weight, smoked too much, slept like the dead, and forgot what it was to lie close to a beautiful woman in the night. The energies he had spent in making love were now dissipated in commerce. But Chelsea did not forget and longed for a time when they would again be alone and together.

Heidler attempted to keep track of both of them and to keep Majesty functioning. He was only marginally successful in the first, more so in the second, the one of them not caught up emotionally in the struggle.

"I'm too old, Marc," he told Street, "I should have retired two, three years ago. I'm not a crusader, like you and Chelsea. I'm old and tired. Better to give me the gold watch and send me to Miami. I'm dragging you down."

"You're holding us together, you old swindler. I need you, Sydney, don't desert me now."

So Heidler went on dickering with the union, bribing the precinct cops not to ticket delivery trucks, sobering up the showroom models, getting theater tickets for out-of-town buyers, maintaining inventory, chivying the seamstresses in the sample room, and consoling the Italian patternmaker for once again not winning the lottery. If Adam had been Majesty's spine, Marc its brain, and Chelsea its vigorous young heart, then Sydney Heidler was its soul.

In July they went to Paris, a week early this time. Heidler stayed behind. There was no one else Street could trust to keep the firm running. There was a long, businesslike luncheon with Brugère. De Bertrand sent "regrets."

"I want to nail down some exclusive models in advance this time, J.-P.," Marc said.

"Oh? That's a change."

"Well, things have changed."

"You mean Adam?"

"You know I do."

Brugère was a bully. Around them, in the banquettes along the velvet walls, Maxim's went about its customary midday commerce, dining and dealing and drinking and negotiating and flirting.

"I love it, I love it, I love it." Chelsea laughed as they crossed the Place de la Concorde under the July sky, tipsy from the summer sun and Maxim's wine, heading for the river and the bridge and the Left Bank.

"Why so jolly?" he demanded. "Brugère held me up as if he had a gun on us."

"Because . . ." She laughed again.

"Because why?"

"You sound like a little boy. Because you got what you wanted. And if it costs more than it's worth to him, it's not nearly what it's worth to you."

He grabbed her hand and pulled her to a stop, spinning her toward him.

"By God, you're your grandfather's girl, aren't you?"

"Yes," she said, "oh yes."

Over the cobbles and beyond low walls flowed the Seine, and they turned now and crossed the bridge, watching the barges and the *cadettes* aswarm with tourists, and so found themselves on the far shore, like so many visitors to Paris, hopeful and in love.

"You're right, of course. Brugère had me where he wanted me. He knew it, I knew it. Without Adam I have to get back to what we once did so well, the line-for-line business. Your collection can carry us in another year or two. Right now, we need help. Every other manufacturer on Seventh Avenue will pay a caution of fifteen thousand dollars to see Jimmy's collection. I'll pay sixty."

"And you feel cheated?" she asked, already knowing the answer.

He laughed. "I'd have paid a hundred!"

"And you'll make millions on it."

"If old Heidler still has the magic, yes!"

They lazed away the afternoon at a table under the awning's shade at the Deux Magots, sitting there drinking *citron pressé* and Coke and watching the tourists and the hikers with their rucksacks and the business people of the quarter passing by until the sun fell and the floodlights illuminated the small stone church across the square. She yawned.

"This is the first time we've had to ourselves since . . ."

"Since I can't remember."

"Do you forget everything about me?"

"No, I could never do that."

She whispered something in his ear then.

"Yes," he said, "I think we should do precisely that."

"So do I."

He called the waiter and paid what, by now, was a considerable bill. And when they got up, she said, teasing, "Shall we walk back? It won't take more than an hour or so."

He grabbed her hand and waved for a taxi.

"No," he said, "we don't have an hour."

There was a side trip to Zurich. He wanted to see Amtorg before the collections.

"But to sell to you and to refuse Adam, well," Amtorg said, "I've worked with you and Adam for years. How am I now to turn my back on him simply because he's on his own now and no longer with you? Is that a fair thing to ask?"

"But you know Baltimore's a shit. And Adam is Baltimore now."

Amtorg gazed at him, took a very deep breath, and agreed.

On the Swissair plane back to Paris and Chelsea, he rejoiced. It was stupid, he knew. Adam could buy silk from a dozen different houses. But he would not have Amtorg's. Only he and Chelsea would.

They had a small suite on the top floor in the back at the San Regis. It was Marc's way of economizing. "I don't care," Chelsea said, throwing the French doors open to the summer night, "I like it."

He hung up his jacket in the armoire and began stripping off his shirt.

"It's not the Plaza Athenée," he admitted. She turned with her back to the window to watch him undress. He had been away from her in Zurich for barely a day, but being alone with him now in the small, moonlit bedroom of a Paris hotel excited her. When he went into the bathroom she took off her summer dress and, without bothering with a nightgown, slipped into bed with the sheet pulled up to her breasts to wait for him. When he came back she curled into his body, and one of his hands began to fondle her breast.

"You know," she said quietly, "I've been holding back with you."

"What do you mean?"

She told him then about Raker and the abortion.

"I know it's fashionable these days to have one. I know women who seem to think you should have one every year, like having a birthday. But to be young and alone and not to be able to tell anyone, and to realize just what it is you're having done to your body, to think about the baby that might have been, it's not a game. It's not like having your hair done. It's traumatic as hell. How could I talk about it with my grandfather? And Raker? He would have lit a cigarette and asked me if I could loan him a few bucks."

"Bastard!"

"No, I was the sucker. He was just being . . . Raker."

She leaned over and kissed him lightly.

"But that's only part of it. I didn't really trust you all that much at first. I mean, you were good-looking and successful, but you were . . . different. I heard all sorts of things about Seventh Avenue, some stuff about you, and I didn't like everything I heard. I was sure when you asked me to work for you that it was an elaborate seduction scheme. I was so used to guys coming on to me that I assumed you were the same. Except more devious. Even our backgrounds got in the way. I was a West, you were a New York guy some people said was a gangster. You were older than me. I was still scared by what happened in Denver when I had the abortion, and I was scared that my money was the attraction, not just with you, but with other men."

"Hell, you don't have any money," he said, trying to lighten her somber tone.

"But I will have. Lots of it. That's always been in the back of my mind that I'm Will West's heir, and it made me cagey as hell. I was always ready to see the worst in people, to suspect motives. It was one of the reasons Toy and I were such pals, despite everything. She didn't know who the hell I was and didn't care. She just liked me."

In some ways, they were both holding back, except that, every so often, the reality of what each of them was broke through the pose, the image. But they didn't talk about it. None of this reticence inhibited their lovemaking. They had grown easy with each other, sufficiently relaxed to experiment, willing to whisper of forbidden needs and desires in the large bed in their small bedroom at the rear of the Hôtel San Regis, high above the First Arrondissement's rooftops and chimney pots and television aerials late on a sultry summer's night in Paris. "Tell me what you want," she told him hoarsely, "and I'll do it."

36

Designers find inspiration where they can: at sea or in great hotels or at the movies. All it takes is imagination.

Mode, July 24, 1981

Adam knew how fashion worked, and the businessman in him knew that now was the moment to nail down the perquisites. His salary alone was now five million dollars a year. And there were fringe benefits.

Fresh from his contractual signing by Stanley Baltimore, early in July he and an entourage of three flew out of JFK on the midday Concorde for Paris. If Marc Street was pinching pennies, there was no reason he should. He had his assistant, a new boyfriend, and Genghis Khan, carried on the manifest as "private hairdresser to Mr. Adam." There were suites at the Ritz, a chauffeured Rolls, and, on Adam's instructions, compartments on the Blue Train to Nice. Baltimore's yacht was moored at Monaco, and Adam had convinced his new employer of the need to rest and relax before taking up the weighty task of attending the fashion collections.

"Have you ever seen anything like it?" he demanded enthusiastically of Genghis Khan as they were given a tour of the ship by its captain on a sparkling blue morning under a baking Mediterranean sun.

Khan shrugged. "I guess it's all right," he said, "if it has stabilizers. If it doesn't have stabilizers we'll be puking all night."

He knew nothing of ships, but then, neither did Adam. The

difference was that Adam's enthusiasm was as genuine as a boy's and Khan's cynicism that of a man tired of life. They sailed on the tide late that afternoon. "You'd think someone could have arranged lunch at the palace," Genghis complained as Grace and Rainier's royal residence, nearly as impressive as the Loew's casino dominating the port, dipped from sight below the horizon.

"I would have thought so," echoed Adam's latest friend, a dumb, beautiful boy who did soft drink commercials.

"You would," Adam snapped, already tiring of this one.

He was also tiring of Khan. Still, Adam had to admit, who but Genghis scored such good coke?

Somehow, he never knew how, Khan had fetched a substantial supply from the States. How he got it through customs, how he dared try, was not something Adam cared to know. And that evening, after a delicious meal served at a table that could easily have seated a dozen, with Baltimore's washes and oils and sketches in their hermetically sealed frames looking down on them, the four young men went up on deck to lounge on the open fantail in overstuffed chairs under a starry southern sky and snort cocaine. In the morning, with a clean breeze coming through his porthole, Adam once again resolved to quit. It was in the long, starry nights that resolution eroded.

The captain and the ten-man crew seemed not to notice. Exposure to Stanley Baltimore and his teenyboppers had left the ship's company immune to astonishment. On the fourth day out they made a landfall at Piraeus, and for the next week they hung about Greece and the islands, sightseeing, tanning, swimming, drinking resinated wine, and making love to the Greek boys Genghis was somehow able to procure, without knowing a word of the language, boys who smelled of olive oil and tasted like sweet grapes.

On the twentieth they were back in Paris, at the Ritz, the soft drink commercial boy having flown back to New York directly from Athens for a screen test, and Adam determined, yet again, to pull himself together for the collections. At Givenchy he and Marc Street sat stonily across from each other, both men busily jotting notes and watching the clothes. Night after night Adam returned directly to the hotel after dinner, leaving Khan to wander, roistering, through the city. In a way, it was Adam's tribute to Street. Had they still been partners, this was how he would have behaved.

"Early to bed and early to rise and, oh, what a good boy am I," Adam crooned to himself as he lay alone, and sober, in his suite at the Ritz, bored and virtuous.

"I don't like his looks," Marc told Chelsea as they strolled up from dinner on the Île on the night after the Givenchy show.

"Who? Adam?"

He nodded. "He looks like hell. He's always done a little coke but under control. This creep Genghis is bad medicine."

"You'd think Baltimore would be keeping an eye on him. After all, he's made a big investment."

"Yeah," Street agreed. "If he were still working with me I'd pull him up short and dry him out. But Baltimore's no dope. He must know what he's doing."

"Letting his designer get wrecked? How smart is that?"

Street thought for a moment. "I don't know, unless he wants Adam just totally zonked and dependent on him so that whatever Stanley asks him to do, he'll have to."

"By that time Adam may be so far gone it won't matter."

"Yeah," Marc said, "and it's a damned shame."

Jimmy de Bertrand, Ungaro, and Saint Laurent were the big winners that season, and Majesty Fashions bought heavily at all three houses. He and Dufour and Chelsea worked together to select the models they bought. Only with Jimmy had they been able to negotiate exclusivity, but there were numbers at Ungaro and Saint Laurent that Marc was reasonably sure no one else had picked. He knew how Adam thought; he had that advantage. And there was a small moment of triumph when he heard, through J.-P. Brugère, that Adam and his assistant had thrown a tantrum when the Amtorg silk people refused to sell them the new floral prints.

Brugère, who loved conspiracy, chortled in delight. "I knew you were behind it," he said. "You're as conniving as the French."

Marc took the remark for the compliment it was meant to be.

They lunched with Emanuel Ungaro in a little place on the avenue Montaigne, full of models and young Frenchmen in their tight, double-breasted suits, and at Marc's urging Ungaro told again of how he had financed his first collection by borrowing money on his girlfriend's Porsche. Emanuel was one of the few designers Marc knew who was straight. Anouk Aimée was with him, a tall, dark-haired woman with lovely, tired eyes and wonderful bones in her face. She regaled them with stories of Mastroianni and of visiting New York with Fellini; when they were invited to lunch with someone in Connecticut, Fellini hailed a New York cab.

"My God," Anouk said, "we didn't know Connecticut was so far." She pronounced the middle "c" in Connecticut.

Emanuel talked skiing with Chelsea and invited them to visit him next winter at his place in Klosters.

"You see," Marc said, "we're not all weird."

Their last night in Paris, they went on to Castel's for brandy after dinner. After midnight Adam came in with a party that included Truffaut, the filmmaker, and two very chic young Frenchwomen. Adam was feeling better. His nights alone in bed at the Ritz had helped. He and Truffaut had their heads together, and the women listened.

"Well," said Marc, "up after midnight and sober. That's a change."

Adam heard him from across the bar. He jerked upright as if slapped, his face hardening. He caught Marc with a chill stare before turning once again to one of the women, who had asked him why he had suddenly fallen mute.

He muttered something. The woman, being French, assumed that he and Marc were lovers who had quarreled.

37

There are rumors that still more key staffers at Majesty
Fashions are turning their vests and joining the enemy.

Mode, August 7, 1981

That evening in Paris with Truffaut was not coincidence.
Hollywood had discovered fashion; out of fashion came ideas,
trends, inspiration, the look of commercially successful movies.
Fashion designers themselves had become stars. M-G-M had
called, and Adam was to create the costumes and, even more, the
entire look of a sleek trifle the studio had ordered up. Even Adam
was stunned by the assignment.

"Have you seen my work," he prodded Truffaut, "the
clothes for Redford?"

"No," Truffaut admitted.

"Then you saw last year's ballet costumes at Lincoln Center."

"No."

"Then how do you know what I'd do would satisfy you?"
Adam persisted, genuinely puzzled. Truffaut was one of the people he truly respected, and his modesty before Truffaut was un-
feigned.

The Frenchman responded with a smile. "My dear fellow,
I've seen your television commercials."

It was true. The commercials by Hiro, working from story-
boards Adam himself had sketched, were a sensation, drawing
Madison Avenue creative awards that nearly but not quite si-

lenced the screams of bluenosed outrage over their kinky, amused sexiness. The commercials starred fifteen-year-old Bunny Lamb in skintight Adam jeans and very little else. M-G-M flew Truffaut and Adam and Miss Lamb west, to milk the announcement of the new movie of whatever value such things have. Adam settled into a bungalow in the gardens of the Beverly Hills Hotel.

"No entourage?" Stanley Baltimore asked, the cynic suspecting all this was going to cost him money.

"No," Adam said, "I'm traveling alone these days."

Traveling alone, and straight. The months since he deserted Majesty had frightened him, wasted and distracting months. With the new contract from Baltimore, he had everything but someone to share it with.

Not that he missed Marc himself. Or *her*, as he inevitably referred to Chelsea West. Marc had wished him well, had shaken his hand, and then, traitorously, destructively, had sued to keep him from working, from earning a living at the only work he had ever done. That the lawsuit was frivolous and had been contemptuously dismissed made no difference. It was still betrayal.

No, Marc hadn't frightened him. Nor had she. Adam had frightened himself. For weeks, months, he had spun out of control: Key West, New York, the Greek Isles, Baltimore's yacht. Easy to blame Khan, to lay it all on drugs. Adam might occasionally delude others, but not himself. He was rich, he was talented, he was thirty-five years old, and in Key West, Greece, and Paris he had stared into the mirror of his soul and hated what he'd seen. For years Marc Street had been there at his side, functioning as his conscience, chiding, complaining, urging, supporting. Now there was no one. Baltimore would pat him on the back and tell him there was one set of rules for other people, one more elastic set for such as they. As for Khan, Genghis believed only in pleasure. There was plenty of sybarite in Adam. But there was another dimension, often obscured, frequently forgotten, at whose existence Khan could not even guess.

As they flew west together, Adam shyly put the situation to Truffaut.

"In Paris men like Saint Laurent and Givenchy and Jimmy de Bertrand are considered artists, like film directors. In this country we're grubby, money-hungry little men and women. When someone mentions French fashion, there are all these shimmering images of Paris. When you talk about clothes in the States you think instantly of Seventh Avenue. Racketeers, union grafters, black kids pushing racks through filthy streets, traffic jams, dirty old men, cheap hookers working the loft buildings."

Truffaut smiled. "Sounds rather picturesque," he said.

"Sure, because you don't live there, you don't have to work there."

Truffaut felt that Adam had the sound of a man who was feeling sorry for himself. "But you have so much. You are very successful."

Before he ever made his first film, Truffaut had been a critic. He still thought as a critic, puncturing facile arguments. He was not being sarcastic when he told Adam how fortunate he was. He meant it. The adulation, the bench-made shoes, the soft flannel suit that suggested Savile Row, his youth, his obvious talent.

But Adam responded gloomily, "Some people have everything."

"I don't. And if I had, then perhaps I'd lack the hunger to go on and do new things. If there is no hunger, no challenge, how can one create?"

"I'd find a way," Adam said sourly.

Truffaut changed the subject then, talking to Adam about the look of the proposed film, its mood, its style, and he was relieved when Adam responded eagerly, tossing out ideas, shedding, for the moment, his self-pity. This, Truffaut told himself, is a boy who has no one to love.

Adam passed a week in Hollywood. The M-G-M people lionized both Truffaut and Adam, delighting the designer by treating him as the French director's equal. His bungalow at the hotel was filled with cut flowers, the bar stocked with champagne and twelve-year-old Scotch and chilled Stolichnaya, and the refrigerator with caviar and sliced smoked salmon for snacks. The studio had leased a Silver Ghost Rolls with two chauffeurs, one for day, one for evenings. There was a press reception and cocktail parties, dinner at Chasen's, a side trip for Bunny Lamb to Disneyland, and a beach party at Malibu, where such constellations as Clint Eastwood and Jessica Lange and Bo and John Derek were trotted out.

"Well?" Truffaut asked him as they sipped cold drinks on the deck of an extraordinary house hung on the cliffs overlooking the beach and the Pacific's swells.

Adam shook his head. "Not too shabby," he said.

Truffaut laughed. He had gotten to like Adam. "Better than your Seventh Avenue?"

Adam made a face. "Oh, God, don't remind me. I'll wake up and realize I'm dreaming."

He was there for a week and was never stoned. Then Stanley Baltimore called to ask when he'd be back in New York to begin the new collection. That night, his last in California, he gave someone some money, and when the cocaine was delivered he locked the door of the bungalow and sat there in the dark, snorting through a straw and fantasizing about quitting fashion and moving west to become a movie producer.

"It's not fair," Chelsea said one night in early August as she, Marc, and Heidler worked into exhaustion until nearly midnight. "Ed Koch only has to run every four years for mayor. We've got to do it every six months."

"And do it right," Heidler stated, with a satisfaction that instantly restored her energies.

"She will, you know," Heidler told Marc as the two men ate bialys and drank coffee in the office.

"I know that."

"She was always nice. You could see that from the first. But when she came here I thought, well, a nice *shiksa,* but what does she know? How hard will she work? Is this just another rich girl with a big name, or someone who will really do something? I confess to you, Marc, I was not all that certain."

Marc grinned.

"I was, Sydney."

"And that's why you're the boss," Heidler remarked shrewdly.

Baltimore had not put away his bag of dirty tricks when he'd stolen Adam from Majesty. Now, in the head-to-head competition between the two firms, with Street trying to get a perfume launched to challenge him on yet another level, Stanley ordered his people to step up the rivalry.

"Marc?"

Street looked up. Tony Sasso, his best patternmaker, a man who had been with Majesty since the time of French Jake, stood in the doorway of Chelsea's studio, looking nervous.

"Tony, come in. What's up?"

What was up was Tony's annual income. Baltimore had hired him away to work on Adam's new collection.

"They're payin' me twenty-five grand more, Marc. No way I could turn it down. You understand, don't you?"

Marc looked over at Chelsea. Her shoulders slumped.

It didn't matter whether he understood or not; Tony was leaving. One of the showroom saleswomen had already left, wooed away over a lunch with Adam, who, in all the years he had worked with her, had never as much as shared a cup of coffee with the woman. A subcontractor in Pennsylvania who had been working with Majesty for ten years gave notice that it was terminating its deal because of the pressure "of other work." The other work, Heidler had sniffed out, was for Baltimore Inc. Two Majesty trucks were hijacked, and a thousand dresses just disappeared. A usually compliant union shop steward had demanded a grievance procedure over the firing of a seamstress who everyone knew had stolen another woman's purse. And yesterday, one of the big model agencies informed Marc that its girls would be unable to work the November showing of Chelsea's designs. They'd been spoken for in advance by Baltimore Inc., to show Adam's collection. And more stores around the country, those vulnerable to Adam's charm or Stanley Baltimore's economic muscle, cut back their orders and failed to reserve seats for next season.

After a relieved Tony Sasso had retreated, Chelsea laid her firm hands on Marc's shoulders. "Are they going to beat us? I mean, does he have that kind of power?"

"He's got power," Marc conceded, "give the bastard that.

And he's smart. He knows where to hurt a guy, he knows where we live."

"Can he put us out of business?"

"Not if we're as good as I think we are," Street said. "He can harass the hell out of us, cut our profits, make life difficult, and give me more gray hair. You come up with another good collection, let Dufour do his job on the Paris line-for-line copies, and we'll make it. We're doing fine on those relabeled Adam jeans. They're selling just as well, maybe a little better with your name on the ass."

"What a gallant you are, a regular Sir Walter Raleigh!"

"Listen, show me the mud puddle and I'll toss my coat down anytime."

The French jeans from Didier would hit the stores around Labor Day, the Geaux West jeans. About those she was still dubious. He wasn't.

"Fashion is serious business but you can't take it seriously. There's got to be some fun, a sense of humor. Trust me, those jeans are going to walk out of the stores."

"I think I love you," she said.

"Sure you do," he said, laughing.

"Well, I do."

He frowned. "We've got too damned much work for love," he said. But that night, even after this most punishing day, they found strength in each other's arms, each other's body.

They went home to Chelsea's apartment, empty now of Toy. As Chelsea stripped for bed, Marc contemplated her in the light streaming in from the river. "All those years when I thought work was enough, that I didn't need anyone. How could I have been so stupid?"

"Well, I wasn't around then," she said, turning to face him, naked now, "was I?"

"No," he said, "I guess all the time I was waiting for you and just didn't know it."

"I know what you mean," she said, remembering those sterile months after Denver and the abortion.

"Of course you do," he said. Chelsea ran her fingers through the hair on his chest. They'd both reached the stage of love where things didn't have to be spoken.

"I just have to look at you," he told her as they lay together in her bed, "I don't even have to touch."

She rolled onto an elbow to look up at him. "Oh, yes you do," she said, "touching is very much part of it."

"Yeah," he said, "I guess it is."

They touched and kissed; Marc felt the weight of Adam, Tony Sasso, Baltimore, and every hijacked truck slide from his shoulders. He had never really trusted anyone before Chelsea. Still he told her nothing about what his father had been, who "Uncle Carl" was. He knew she accepted Swaggerty as an anomaly, a childhood mistake. There was no reason to dredge up the rest of it. Someday he would tell her everything, but not now, not while they struggled to survive. She had enough to worry her.

So they tasted each other, and he did things to her nipples that sent shivers through the core of her, and she teased him with her hair and her mouth, and finally, drained and spent, they slept, Seventh Avenue far more than twenty blocks away.

"I just don't know enough," Marc confessed. "Essential oils, fixatives, attar, what the hell do I know about any of them? Easy to say 'make it smell good,' design a bottle, create some sexy ads. There's more to it. Baltimore knows this shit and I don't, that's the frustrating thing!"

"The perfume people came up with a half dozen scents I liked." Chelsea paused over her coffee. "And maybe a hundred I thought stank. Why couldn't we just pick one of the good ones and run with it? They know their business, don't they?"

"Not as well as Stanley Baltimore does, the son of a bitch. Listen, Chelsea, we go with the wrong scent or package it wrong or market it wrong, and it'll not only flop, it'll kill any chance you have to come up with something better. You do a lousy sportswear collection, what the hell. Next season you'll do a great one. With a hundred-dollar-an-ounce perfume you get one shot. You blow it and . . ."

"Okay," she sighed, "I dig."

He was feeling the pressure. More trucks were hijacked, there were union problems even at plants that didn't have unions, "organizing drives" among workers who'd never shown the slightest wish to be organized. The whole thing smelled of coercion.

He wondered where Bobby Swaggerty was now that he needed him, really needed him.

38

There are malicious whispers that such fortunes are being made on fashion licensing, there will soon be a designer label toilet tissue.

Mode, September 10, 1981

Lincoln Radford commissioned a cover story in a September issue of *Mode* on the growing power of the Baltimore Inc. empire and how entire new categories of fashion-oriented goods bearing the Adam label would be launched over the next few years: home furnishings, domestics, men's wear, designer watches and costume jewelry, shoes, automobile interiors, and vertical blinds, all with the Adam touch. The money to fuel the expansion would be generated by the perfumes, the cosmetics, new jeans bearing an Adam label. The publicity to lubricate its operation would come from Adam's spring and fall fashion collections, from his newly announced movie designs for Truffaut, and from the creation of a major Broadway musical extravaganza whose details, Radford's magazine admitted, were "still sketchy." The catalogue of triumph was so impressive that the *Wall Street Journal* assigned a senior reporter to analyze its financial details and to ruminate on soft goods as a stock market growth area to be watched, much as one did the high-tech and computer fields.

Majesty Fashions struck back, desperate and gutty. Heidler shook his head in admiration.

"Marc, you're a genius. You play them like a violin."

"Sure," Street responded, "but don't forget, we've got Chelsea."

And it was true. *Good Morning America* and the *Today* show, which customarily demanded exclusivity of their guests, both booked her for appearances during the same week, David Hartman having forgiven her for "the cave myth."

How rich was she? Well, she told interviewers, she didn't really know. If you knew how much money you had, you really didn't have all that much, did you? According to her, old Will was a marshmallow, a sweet codger raising lambs and singing in the church choir, having widows and orphans in for Sunday dinner. If they asked if he were really, despite his image, a pretty decent old gent, she shuddered and said no, he whipped his servants and devoured foundlings for breakfast.

Would she ever marry? Well, she confessed, it was unlikely. She had dedicated herself to her work and to her aged grandfather. There were suitors, of course, several Arab sheikhs and emirs among them, but she sort of felt a duty to America. Yes, Prince Andrew was sweet, if a bit rakish. She really thought an older man might be more suitable. If only Dr. Kissinger . . .

When the interrogation came full circle and returned to fashion she announced, on a morning show in Denver, that Majesty Fashions was going to save money on fabric next year with its swimsuit collection. "We're doing these new bikinis. But just the bottoms. No one wears the tops, anyway."

A Denver minister was given equal time that Sunday to denounce wickedness and urge people to return to the church.

They asked her about the punk look, and she made faces. They asked about the preppy look, and she pulled her suit jacket open to show a Brooks Brothers boy's shirt, buttoned-down and all. She showed up wearing a man's fedora, the kind of hat no woman had worn since Garbo. She startled interviewers by saying nice things about other designers.

"I modeled the Dior collection in Paris. Dior is still the greatest name in fashion."

"Yves Saint Laurent is a poet. No one in this country, including me, is even vaguely in his league."

"Givenchy is the most elegant man in the world. If I'm reborn as a man, I want to come back as Hubert de Givenchy."

She even strewed palms in front of her archrival, Adam: "He's darn good. He made Majesty Fashions what it is today, made it possible for me to become a designer."

And her other American competitors: "Blass is a gentleman, and there are damned few of those, believe me."

When they asked about Calvin Klein, she laughed. "In civilian life, I love his jeans."

And about Ralph Lauren: "They always talk about my being a WASP. Listen, for a boy from the Bronx, Ralph is the biggest WASP of us all."

America fell in love with her. But the battle was not fought only on television. Having lost a round in *Mode,* Marc played up to John Fairchild at *Women's Wear Daily* and *W*. He leaked a few early sketches of Chelsea's next collection and phoned John to bring him up to date on developments with the perfume people. He lunched with Bernadine Morris of the *Times* and spent a day in Washington charming Nina Hyde of the *Post* and two days in Los Angeles with Mary Lou Luther of the L.A. *Times*. He wooed Grace Mirabella of *Vogue* and ambitious young editors at *Glamour, Seventeen, Mademoiselle, Self,* and *Cosmo*. He had met Helen Gurley Brown at someone's weekend party, and he called on her. She insisted she knew nothing of fashion, and he insisted she was being modest. He ordered his ad agency to buy full-page ads in each of the magazines, with money he suspected he might not have.

And he drove Chelsea to make the new collection the best she had ever done, better, he insisted, than she even knew how to do.

They went across town to Le Veau d'Or for dinner one night after she'd taped the David Letterman show on NBC. There was the usual wait at the bar and the requisite drink, and when they finally had their table against the wall in the back, she stretched, yawning out loud. She caught him looking at her, an eyebrow raised.

284

"Listen, I know I'm not supposed to do that in public but hell, I've been working hard. You've been working me hard."

"I know. You're swell about it."

Their drinks were brought to them from the bar, and over the rim of her glass she looked at him. "Marc, is it really working? I mean, can we lick this creep Baltimore? Or is all that we're doing just for effect?"

"Sure, we can win. We have you, don't we?"

She made a face. "Come on, don't shit me."

His big hands were knotted together around the glass, nearly rendering it invisible. "I wouldn't shit the girl I love."

She laughed. "Cyrano de Bergerac never got off a more romantic line, turkey."

He grinned and then, after a moment, he began to talk seriously. "Baltimore is squeezing the hell out of us. It's tough. I won't kid you on that. Heidler is scared, and you know Sydney has been around since the goddamned flood. He sees the books. The banks are all graciousness and goodwill. That's something that'll last just as long as we seem to be making it and not one second longer. Bankers are pragmatic people. They back winners; losers they foreclose."

Just as somberly, she asked: "And which are we? Winners or losers?"

"Well, we *can* win. Nothing's impossible. A lot depends on those damnfool Geaux West jeans. If a perfume can be developed. If your next collection is as good as the first two. If no more stores cancel out on us. If Adam drops dead. We're not finished, not yet we aren't."

She listened to him carefully. "And suppose those things don't happen?"

"Then we get our ass whipped."

As she toyed with the hors d'oeuvres, she looked into his face. "You always seem so sure, as if doubt never even crossed your mind."

"Well, I'm not sure. But if I start looking scared or worried or insecure, what in hell do you think that's going to do to our people? Heidler is loyal as an old collie dog, but old. I can't put any more pressure on Sydney. He could crack. So I assure him the world is a fine place and he should ignore the books and look forward to a big bonus. Dufour is Dufour, a snake. I wouldn't trust Dufour to get mustard on a hot dog. Just let him sniff the smell of fear or defeat, and he'll be across the street begging Adam for a job and carrying our secrets with him. Our employees are loyal enough; all the rats have already deserted the sinking ship. Anyone left is with us because he or she really believes. But at the same time, they're people who work for a living and have maybe a couple of bucks in the bank. Let them suspect that we're going under and they'll start looking around for the next job. That isn't disloyalty; it's good sense."

"So you bullshit them."

"Yes, Miss West, as you so elegantly put it, I bullshit them. And it isn't only people who work for us. What about the ad agency? They're buying all this air time, all these pages in the magazines. They're not asking me for the money up front, thank God, because they think we're in pretty good shape. And how about the textile mills? How long do you think we'd have credit with Manchester and Springs and Amtorg and Bianchini if anyone smelled panic at Majesty? And the fiber boys? Du Pont and Monsanto and Courtaulds? And those jeans operations in Haiti and Taiwan and Hong Kong?"

Again she said nothing.

"So I bullshit everyone. Because I really think we can just possibly survive. Maybe even win. And I can't afford to look like a loser."

She pushed her plate aside. "You don't bullshit everyone."

"No," he said, "I don't bullshit you, Chelsea."

In September they reopened Studio 54.

Ian Schrager and Steven Rubell had done their time and been released from federal prison, and in their honor a couple of anonymous trustees had tidied up and swept the cobwebs out of the long-shuttered discotheque and launched it again under what was called "new management." A fortune cookie drew Chelsea and Marc to the reopening.

"You will attend a party where strange customs prevail."
That was what the cookie said. She found it at Hunan on Second
Avenue, where she lunched one day with Toy. Toy, back in town
for a few days, suntanned and beautiful and, apparently, straight.

Chelsea had been astonished when Toy called out of the
blue. "California," she'd said simply, "such men!" She said over
lunch that she hated modeling—and when Chelsea asked her
where her money came from, Toy just smiled sweetly. But now
Chelsea knew enough of high-velocity New York to understand
how Toy, so young, so guileless and beautiful, could disappear
like a tired disco and then reappear again, refreshed; Toy was just
like Studio 54.

She went with Chelsea and Marc to the opening. Rubell
warned Marc to get there early and come in the Fifty-third Street
entrance. Before they even turned into the street they could see
the crowd. "I hate discotheques," Marc said morosely. "I knew we
should have stayed home."

"You love them," Chelsea insisted, "you'd live in Castel's
basement if he let you."

"That's Paris. That's different," he grumbled.

They pushed through the crowd and shoved their way inside. It didn't hurt that Chelsea was with him. The *paparazzi*
knocked people down to get to them, opening a wedge through
which Marc could shoulder his way.

"My God, they're nuts!" His jacket had been pulled half off,
and he shrugged back into it.

Toy was smiling radiantly. "I be a movie star soon, Marc.
And it would be like this always for Toy."

By ten o'clock the fire department was there and the doors
had been sealed against any more celebrants. Marc got Rubell
aside. "How many people did you invite?"

"Maybe five or six thousand," he said, grinning impishly.

"The joint only holds two."

"I know."

Outside on Fifty-fourth Street and around the corner at the
back door hundreds of people, most of them waving legitimate
invitations, milled about in a warm late-summer drizzle, pounding at fire doors and demanding entrance. Two fire engines, their

red lights revolving, blocked the street. Cops were everywhere. Inside, the music pounded, the strobes flashed, and thousands of people, all of whom seemed to know one another, pushed and shoved and sweated and tried hopelessly to dance.

Despite the crowd, despite himself, Marc was having a good time. What the hell, he deserved a break. Harvey Mann, the press agent, came over to talk, plump and wise and witty.

A man resplendent in Pirates of Penzance getup minced by. Harvey raised an eyebrow. "I didn't know Fire Island *had* a navy," he remarked.

Toy and Chelsea danced and Marc watched, two tall, beautiful young women with bodies that moved as if on ball bearings. He sipped a Scotch and watched them try to get dancing room, losing sight of them in the crowd and then finding them once again, pleased to see Chelsea having fun and being happy. She had worked so hard. Under the pressure of Baltimore's assault, she had become stronger, reliable, a fierce, resourceful competitor. Street got his back wedged against a piece of the bar and he hung on to it, smoking and drinking and letting the crowd swell and recede and surge past him. Chelsea had vanished again. High above the dance floor, on a spidery catwalk, a score of young dancers pounded out the beat of the music, spotlights catching their faces and their bodies, shimmering in the chiaroscuro. A pretty girl tried to talk to him, but he couldn't hear.

"Sorry," he said, pantomiming with a hand cupped to his ear.

"Sure." She laughed, understanding. But staying there, leaning against him. He could smell the marijuana, and he just grinned at her.

Then Chelsea reappeared, looked at the girl, and pulled his head down to kiss him on the lips. The girl got the message and left.

"You *are* a competitive sort, aren't you?" he said.

"What?"

"I love you."

She couldn't hear that either, but she grinned at him. The dancing and the music pounded, undistinguishable from Marc's own heartbeat.

When they left at two in the morning they left alone. Toy was up on the overhead platform now, dancing in the spotlight, applauded by the mob below. A bouncer opened the door for them a crack, bracing himself against it so no one could slip in as they left. Hundreds of people still waited on the sidewalk and in the street in the rain. They made their way between the wooden horses set up by the cops. Egon von Furstenberg caught up with them, hurried along by the rush of the crowd.

"My God!" he said.

Furstenberg tried to duck under the barricade to make it across the street, and a cop chased him back. Laughing, Egon said, "So this is how your police treat royalty."

At Broadway they got a cab and went home to make love. For once, he wasn't too exhausted.

Geaux West jeans went on sale that week. Marc had gambled by picking a single major store in each city to handle them exclusively for the first few months. In New York, it was Bloomingdale's. On the night before the launch he and Chelsea dined with Marvin Traub and his wife, Lee. Traub had run the store for years, a gracious, hardworking man who'd fought through France with George Patton. He was enthusiastic about Chelsea's French jeans.

"But who knows," he said, "it's all timing. What the public wants at the moment, whether it's correctly priced and intelligently advertised. And, of course, the product has got to be right. You've done your part, we've done ours. Now it's up to the customers. They're the jury."

Full-page ads broke the next morning. The ads said Bloomingdale's, but it was Marc Street's money. "They call it co-op advertising," he said, "but I don't know where the cooperation comes in. I put up the dough, I supply the merch, the customers come to their store. Traub didn't go to Harvard for nothing."

It didn't matter. Geaux West jeans sold out that first day.

By the week's end, Didier in Paris had been told to cut another fifty thousand pairs. By the middle of the next week Street had upped the order to a hundred fifty thousand additional pairs.

Right across the country, from Bloomie's to I. Magnin, from Jordan Marsh in Miami to Nordstrom's in Seattle, they were a sellout. *Women's Wear Daily* headlined the phenomenon: CHELSEA'S JEANS GEAUX-GEAUX!

Street wasted no time in celebration. He flew to Paris to meet with Didier, to subcontract another half million pairs of the new jeans to French factories.

"No, we can't make them anymore in Taiwan or Haiti!" Marc shouted. "I know it's a gimmick, but it's an honest gimmick. They are French and they're going to stay French."

Didier regarded him from under lowered eyelids. "Marc, my dear boy, you're not serious."

He was. Like Great Britain, fashion had no written constitution. It was for men like Street to compose it as they went along, and in his view, French jeans were French jeans, not Haitian or Mexican.

The full-page ads, the television commercials that had sold out the first fifty thousand Geaux West jeans, that would sell out the first half million, had been done by his ad agency in Paris in July, while he and Chelsea occupied the small suite in the back at the Hôtel San Regis.

The model in the ads, bare from the waist up, her cute, curvy bottom twitching with a French accent, was an American: Chelsea West.

39

Our sources report First Lady Nancy Reagan will have the new spring collections shown privately in the White House. She's waiting for next month's results before issuing the royal warrants.

Mode, October 16, 1981

In late October Chelsea flew to Denver. Will West was ailing. In the limo she asked the cowboy-driver how bad he was.

"Oh, shit, Miss Chelsea, you know the old man. He's too mean to die and too old to get well."

She knew. And yet she was shocked to see the changes. Always lean and stringy, weathered and raw, he was now even more wasted.

"Catherine." The voice was a croak, and not the usual command.

"Yes, Grandpa?"

He swallowed before he spoke, sunken and nearly lost in the great leather armchair of his study, from which he now rarely went forth.

"So you're a big success in New York. On television, in the papers, wearing blue jeans with fancy French names. Imagine, blue jeans fifty dollars the pair. Used to buy them for three fifty and they'd last a couple of hard years in the mines or on horseback."

"These last too, Grandpa. They're made in France. Good tough material."

He nodded, swallowing again. She wondered if there was trouble with his throat. He'd always been a smoker.

"Glad to hear it. Don't want the West name on shoddy goods."

"Nor do I. And Marc doesn't. They wanted to make some of them in Taiwan and places like that. He said no. Could have made a lot more money, but he said no."

"Marc?"

"Yes, you met him. He was here."

"Oh, yes, Jewish feller."

"Yes."

"I thought there for a while you were going soft on him. I worried about that, Catherine. Don't want to lose you at all, and not to some New York Jew."

It was no time for cogent argument. So she said, simply, "No, Grandpa."

That night she dined alone, with a Mexican woman, who looked like every other Mexican woman who had ever worked at the ranch, hovering and changing plates and silently regarding her untouched food.

Marc had not wanted her to go. The November collection was two weeks away. Despite the success of Geaux West, this show was crucial. Majesty tottered on the brink. Adam's defection, Stanley Baltimore's guerrilla war, had wounded the company terribly. Marc had been spending money he didn't have to maintain its image. Geaux West jeans were selling. They couldn't keep up with deliveries. But the ad agencies and the airlines and the French mills sent fast bills, while the American stores were slow to pay. There was a severe cash-flow crisis. If Chelsea's next collection worked, Marc could again sweet-talk the banks and the factors. If not . . .

"You have to go?" he demanded.

"Yes. He's sick. Old and sick."

"Chelsea, I don't mean to be callous about this, but your grandfather's been old for a long time. He's got people around him, servants, staff, corporate types. I need you *here* right now."

She stared at him. "Marc, *he* needs me there. I'm going. The collection's finished. Dufour can tidy up. I'll be back as soon as I can. But I'm going."

It had been a cool good-bye. She thought about it now, after a dinner uneaten, standing out on the great verandah of Will West's house, staring up at the mountains, dark against the starry sky. Each of them was sure he was right, she and Marc, both strong people, sure of themselves, certain that the priorities they set were the right ones. Maybe he was right; maybe she was wrong. It was difficult for either of them to admit error. Ego got in the way, that was the trouble.

She woke early in the cold Rocky Mountain morning and climbed into old running shoes and sweats and was out on the road before seven, doing a hard three miles, enjoying the sweat and the pain and the tiredness, realizing how New York had softened her. Marc ought to run. He was too young to let himself go. She would talk to him about it when she got back. Talk to him about that and about other things. This clean, cold air had a way of cleansing the mind of dust.

As men have always done when they've become disgusted with themselves, Adam was again making resolutions. The Nautilus machine was long forgotten, as was the flirtation with horses, and his brief career as a political angel. Those things were a waste of time, they drained his talent; but it was over other things that he agonized. Not homosexuality; that was accepted, that was *him*. It was the random couplings, the drugs, the wasted days and nights since Feeley, since his break with Marc, that generated remorse. He was an adult; he must stiffen his spine, occasionally say "no," stay away from Genghis and the cocaine, bring discipline and order into a life become chaotic. He sought not virtue but tidiness. Adam wanted to reform. A little.

This collection, his first since joining Baltimore, the first he'd ever done without Marc Street there at his side, chiding, prodding, urging, cheering, and embracing, had to be a good one. Adam knew Baltimore didn't care if it actually made a profit. Stanley wanted publicity, excitement, pictures, debate, big headlines and famous names. Such things created the aura that sold perfume and lipsticks and blush and nail polish and lip gloss and cold cream. That was where Baltimore Inc. made its money, off rich women flattered into paying a hundred dollars an ounce for perfumes and off shopgirls seduced into buying eyeliner for a couple of bucks.

"Sell the sizzle, not the steak." That had always been Baltimore's credo. Except for Geaux West jeans, it wasn't Street's. And now Adam had to make adjustments. His two principal assistants, boys who did something more than hold the pins, were given their instructions. Adam understood what Baltimore wanted: big fashion news, not subtlety. From the moment Adam returned from Europe in early August, he had pounded away on his theme. This collection was crucial: Baltimore must be satisfied, Marc Street impressed, Chelsea West beaten.

Night after night Adam went home from his new studio in the GM building to the apartment on Fifth Avenue. On most nights he dined in solitary splendor, his Vietnamese chef bored and querulous over his master's simple, near-primitive demands. No discos, no coke, no slender young boys, no parties: not since he fell in love with his own body and the Nautilus machine had Adam been so clean. But newfound virtue was not a very satisfactory substitute for sex or laughter or the drug highs to which he had become accustomed. He considered such things as he lay abed at night, the draperies drawn back above the park and the tall buildings of the West Side, where he imagined, as he tossed in boredom, other men who were not alone, writhing and twisting and panting in the sort of abandon he had so long enjoyed and had now voluntarily put aside in the spirit of elegant ambition. And he thought of Peter Feeley, with whom there had been a balance between virtue and excitement.

Will West was feeling better. It was as if Chelsea's rushed visit had been the tonic; even his physician said so.

"Miss West, he's just wearing out. But having you here has the old monster feeling as if he were only eighty once more."

Now the old monster was stirring again, grousing and shuffling through the great house, full of complaints and demands and critical commentary. "I've had the goddamned attorneys in again," he said on the first night he'd carefully made his way downstairs for dinner with her. "My will's been made up for a long, long time. Provisions in your favor, of course, no secret about that."

"Oh hell, Grandpa," she said, laughing, "a couple of million'll do me nicely, thanks very much."

"Don't I know that? I read the papers. I know how well you're doing back there in New York beating out all those queer dressmakers. If you couldn't make it on your own I wouldn't be so damned fond of you."

She was delighted to hear him say it. She knew how critical he could be, especially of those closest to him.

"And it isn't a couple of million, Catherine, you know that."

"I know," she said, more somberly.

"It's real money. That's why I insist you inherit the bulk of my holdings. You're the only close relative I have and one of the few people I respect. Oh, I don't mean you're a financial expert. You don't have the education or the training. But you've got the essentials, common sense, instinct, brains. People aren't going to be able to cheat you or fool you or con you. You may get beat once but not twice. My companies are run by competent people who wouldn't be there if they weren't. But they need a goad. That's you, Catherine."

"Well, Grandpa, you know I'll do my best."

He nodded. "That's all a man can ask."

They went into his den after dinner, where one of the Mexican maids served coffee and a tequila for him and he laid out a brief abstract of his holdings and what she would inherit. She had been aware for years that she was his principal heir. She knew there was a lot of money.

She had not known until now that on his death she would effectively be in control of an industrial empire worth more than four billion dollars.

It made Majesty Fashions petty cash indeed. But when Marc

phoned her next morning demanding to know "When the hell do you get back to New York? I need you!" she felt a spasm of joy that had nothing to do with money or power.

He was in Los Angeles, damping down a delivery crisis with J. W. Robinson.

"Don't move," she said, "I can be there tonight."

They stole a day for themselves, a Saturday, on the beach at Malibu, lying on the hot sand, drinking beer, and watching the surfers ride the long combers, baking themselves and listening to a radio on a nearby blanket reporting a big football game back east, where the light was going and snow was falling, while Marc rubbed Sea & Ski into her back and she smeared it on his big nose, reddening in the California sun.

Both her grandfather and her lover needed her, but right now Marc's need was more urgent. On Sunday, sitting together in the jet, she wondered if she should tell him about the enormous legacy that would one day be hers. No, she decided, with all the trouble Marc had right now, she would just be flaunting the money. It wouldn't be fair. Later she would tell him; later would be better.

Both lovers held their secrets.

.

40

A year ago it was Reagan versus Carter. No contest. Last
week Chelsea West and Adam Green gave us a real race.
Ballots are still coming in from outlying precincts.

Mode, November 12, 1981

F ashion feeds off drama. For weeks the trade press had been
building up to this face-to-face confrontation between Adam and
Chelsea with all the hype and hysteria of the Super Bowl. Stories
were leaked, supposedly accurate sketches were passed around,
Baltimore's men beat the drums for Adam while Street and
Heidler chivied the buyers to reserve their seats early. John Weitz,
one of the few designers who knew anything of sport, remarked
skeptically that he hadn't realized they were restaging the Ali-
Frazier fight.

In a *mano-a-mano* competition on consecutive days in the
same Hotel Pierre ballroom, the two former colleagues dazzled
standing-room-only crowds of buyers and press and private clients. Adam's collection, the critics raved, was his sexiest, most
dramatic ever. "He took chances a less secure designer would not
have dared," raved the usually understated John Fairchild. As for
Chelsea, she struck in the opposite direction, with crisply tailored,
classic clothes that were, as Lincoln Radford wrote, "the orgasmic
dream of a preppie suddenly grown up and grown rich." For
once, his purple prose did not seem overbaked.

Street, watching from behind the pearl-gray curtains that
led to the runway, knew that Chelsea had triumphed from the
first opening explosion of a dozen leggy young women in knee

socks and tartan kilts and startlingly contrasting Gibson Girl blouses cool and bleached as snow. They started cheering then and didn't finish until Chelsea herself came out in a histrionically romantic wedding dress, whose corny tackiness was relieved by a patch of blue denim on the seat that read, self-mockingly, "Geaux West!"

Marc was the first to embrace her when she fought her way back into the dressing room through the photographers and the models and the kisses and the traditional hysteria of a successful collection.

"Thanks," he said, "I needed that."

And he did. Majesty had mortgaged itself to stage this one. The models alone, twenty girls at $2,500 each for the day, had cost $50,000 that he didn't have. The room had cost half that, also with money pledged but not possessed. There were other bills, other promises, other favors begged. Now he could pay.

They went back to Chelsea's apartment, promising, without ever meaning it, to attend a half dozen spontaneously organized parties. She called a local Chinese restaurant and they dined in bed, eating ribs and egg rolls off trays, and drinking cold beer from the bottle, licking sticky fingers and laughing and being happy together, exploring each other and sure that this was what people meant when they spoke of being in love.

Adam attended *his* party. After all, it was a Stanley Baltimore production and Baltimore employees, no matter how elevated their status or how healthy their self-esteem, tended to go along with Mr. Baltimore's whims. The party was on board his yacht, sailed back to America from the Med against the possibility its owner might choose to go sailing—as he now did, with a passenger manifest of more than a hundred leading retailers, suppliers, fashion editors, mannequins, and hangers-on. The food was simple: beluga caviar in enormous silver tureens set in tubs of cracked ice. That was all—just caviar!

"Ya want ham sandwiches, get a handful of quarters and visit the Automat," he snarled at an aide who asked if they shouldn't offer a choice.

For hours the yacht cruised a stately, measured course down

the East River, out into the harbor, then back up the Hudson. It was a freakishly warm November evening, and when the Peter Duchin orchestra struck up, the more adventurous and romantic danced on the upper deck as Manhattan's skyline slid past.

Adam, strangely depressed after the long, celibate season of work and discipline, stood at the rail with his back to the festivities, staring out across the black water at the great city. Baltimore found him there.

"Okay?"

"Sure, just taking a breather."

Baltimore stood there next to him, leaning on the rail, not saying anything, uncharacteristically sensitive. Adam appreciated it.

"Well," said Baltimore finally, "let me know if you want anything."

"Sure, thanks."

Baltimore touched his arm. "You did fine. We'll do okay on this collection."

"Thanks."

Adam knew he had done better than "okay." It had been one of the best collections he'd ever put together. That wasn't ego talking; it was cool, dispassionate professional judgment. A designer might never admit out loud that he'd done mediocre work, but within himself he always knew. But it was the first time in ten years that Marc hadn't been there with him, celebrating their wins, consoling him for their losses. With Baltimore, it was a job.

Genghis Khan, again restored to grace, emerged onto the deck. "Adam, you'll get pneumonia out here. Come on, the party's inside."

Adam let himself be drawn into the noisy, smoky, boozy melee, the kisses and handshakes, the hugs and the adulation. Gradually, he warmed to his triumph. Toward midnight they eased slowly back into the Twenty-third Street boat basin to nose against the fenders of the quay while crewmen ran out gangways, limo drivers awoke to restart cold engines, and cheerful drunks staggered ashore, shouting farewells and throwing kisses. By one o'clock in the morning Adam and Khan and a half dozen other celebrants were at the Studio, dancing and snorting cocaine and ordering magnums of Dom Perignon. Adam would pay for it all, of course. He always did.

A boy with the long eyelashes of a beautiful girl hung on to his arm. "You're a genius, Adam, a genius."

Adam started to shake him off. Then, seeing the boy's open, lovely face, seeing the admiration in his eyes, he relaxed. He'd worked hard to get here; he deserved his rewards.

"Yes," he said quietly, "you're right. I am."

Stanley Baltimore had seen them all off at the gangway, resisting efforts to get him to join them in continuing the party ashore. "No, you kids have fun. It's too late. I'm beat." He called the captain to him. "Take her back out. I'm staying aboard. I like to feel her moving while I sleep."

As the yacht slowly slipped back into the river, Baltimore descended to the master bedroom suite, the one area of the boat that had not been thrown open to most of his guests. There, sprawled on the oversized bed, fast asleep, were the exceptions: two pretty fifteen-year-old girls in lacy nightgowns, curled in each other's arms, their blond hair arrayed across pillows. Baltimore had a bottle of Dom Perignon in his hand, and he stood there for a few moments, inhaling the stale stink of pot, listening to their breathing, admiring their slim, rounded legs and arms. Then he went to the side of the bed and leaned over them.

"Wake up," he said softly, "it's time to play."

When they did not wake, he carefully tilted the bottle just slightly so that the champagne poured down onto their faces and shoulders and breasts.

"Hey!" one of them shouted, still half asleep, as the other sat up, blinking and rubbing pudgy fists into drowsy eyes. They saw him then, and one started to pull the wet nightgown over her head.

"No," he said, "leave it on."

They watched him undress, eyes widening, tossing his jacket and then his tie and shirt over the back of a chair. Then, when he was naked, he went to the dresser and took an envelope from the top drawer.

"There's another two thousand dollars here," he said, "and it's yours if you want it."

"We want it," one of them said brightly.

"Good," he told her, "now what I want you to do is make love to your friend while I watch."

The girl shrugged, staring at the angry scar that marred the corner of his mouth. "Okay, if that's what you dig."

He dropped into an upholstered chair while these beautiful children began to kiss each other, entwining and moving on the oversized bed as a Joan Miró looked down blankly from the state-room wall.

At dawn the yacht docked again at Twenty-third Street and Baltimore showered and prepared for a day at the office while the two children, to whom he said nothing, staggered ashore with their money, drunk and drugged, sore and spent, in search of a cab in the grimy Manhattan morning.

BOOK FIVE

MARC STREET

41

The garment industry is always under investigation. If there were no investigations people would be nervous and irritable and you would see empty tables at La Grenouille and Caravelle.

Mode, November 19, 1981

Someone put in the fix," Bobby Swaggerty announced to the astonished Street when he strode one morning into his Seventh Avenue offices.

"You're not on the lam?" Marc asked incredulously.

"No more," Bobby said, grinning broadly. "There's more crooks in courtrooms than you ever heard of over on Ninth Avenue."

"What happened?" Marc said as they sat down and he buzzed his secretary for coffee.

"Some guy confessed who's dead. They found a note he wrote saying he was the guy who shot the guy that they was blaming me for. Just say I got lucky."

"Where the hell were you all these months? How'd you live?"

"I was down south," he said. "I stuck up gas stations and 7-11 stores. It was easy."

"Don't tell me," Marc said, meaning it.

Bobby laughed. "And people sent me Care packages. They wanted to make sure I remembered who my pals were."

He had a hotel room on the West Side and a new girl. "You'd like her, Marc, she's crazy like me."

Swaggerty had not come merely to socialize. "Look, Marc, I don't have all the details. But there's some shit coming down on you."

"What d'you mean?"

"I dunno, exactly. But the feds are supposed to be doing one of their every-so-often investigations of the garment industry. You know, the usual stuff. Hijacking and sweetheart contracts with the unions, payoffs and loan-sharking and head-breaking and stuff like that. The usual."

Marc shrugged. "So what? I'm not into any of that. Majesty's clean."

"I know that and you know that. But I got a friend tells me they're going backwards and forwards this time. They're looking at Uncle Carl Lazer. They got accountants working on it. The figures guys. Trying to find out about rackets money being laundered by legit businesses. Get me?"

Marc nodded. If it were true, it was better that they not talk too much, not here in the office. They had probably said too much already. He grabbed Bobby and they went down the elevator out into the street. A black teenager nearly knocked them over with a rack of dresses.

"Black guys," Bobby said sourly, "they got no place to go and nothing to do when they get there. What's their hurry?"

Jewish men with beards and yarmulkes and long, shiny black coats clogged the sidewalk, talking, gesticulating, munching bagels. When a tall girl, with the look of a model, passed, a rack boy called out to her in Spanish.

"Shit," Bobby said, "how do you stay here? This jungle?"

Marc laughed; a guy who knocked over 7-11 stores was talking about "jungles."

"No point trying to explain it," he said, "it's just where I live."

Bobby nodded. "You really *would* like my new girl. You're crazy too."

He told Marc what he knew and promised to try to find out more. When he left, Marc asked if he needed any money.

Swaggerty looked blissful and pulled a thick roll from his

pocket. *"You* need any, let me know. And tell that chick Chelsea I'll pay her three hundred back anytime she wants it. With interest. And I mean it."

Street wondered what Bobby would say if he knew who Chelsea's grandfather was and how much he had.

"He's sweet," Chelsea said when Marc gave her Swaggerty's message that night.

Marc raised an eyebrow. "I've heard Bobby called many things, but never 'sweet.' Anyway, he thinks you're quite a 'chick.' "

"Well, I *am.*"

In mid-November, Marc and Chelsea flew to Haiti. It was not precisely vacation, not all fun in the sun. There was a big jeans factory to visit, people to see, officials and labor union bosses to be sweet-talked and paid off. Bribery was the normal cost of doing business in Third World countries. Everyone did it. They were staying at a place called L'Hermitage. She had been there before on a modeling assignment, and he knew it from previous business trips. For five days they worked and played and lay in the sun next to the pool, drinking rum drinks and smoking grass. He stayed away from drugs in the city, even pot. He didn't like the sensation of losing control, not in New York, not where a clear head and quick decisions often meant success. A local politician gave a dinner party for them at what seemed to be a governor's palace, and graceful black men speaking French bowed and kissed hands and lined up to dance with Chelsea. Marc wondered what Bobby Swaggerty would say.

That night, in bed, she spoke for the first time of marriage.

"What do you think?" she asked. "We're pretty good together."

"We are."

"It's funny," she said, "for the past couple of years I've been running scared. Guys are always proposing . . ."

"Or propositioning."

"Sure, that too. More of that, I guess. And I'm always saying

no and slamming doors and jumping out of cars. And out of bed
. . . and now . . ."

He knew that if he said something now, almost anything, she
would be his. Forever.

She continued to talk, her voice almost solemn. "Because I
look like this, because of all the money out there that's going to be
mine someday. But you're not like that, not like that at all. You're
different from them. You work hard and make money for all of us,
and you're fair with people and you treat me like a grownup. I
watch you with Sydney. You can't fool old Sydney, and I know
how he feels about you. It's almost awe." She paused. "I feel good
about you, too. You don't hustle me, you don't hassle me. You
just love me. You're . . . different."

She waited then, expecting him to say something.

He didn't. The day before they left the call had come from
Foley Square, from the office of the assistant U.S. attorney. Swaggerty's information had been accurate.

Instead, he lay there in silence, her head cradled against his
shoulder, his arm around her, one hand resting on a still-damp
breast, and said nothing. She waited for several moments. Then
she said:

"Marc?"

"Yes?"

"I'm asking you."

He rolled toward her, looking into her face in the dim light
of the tropic night.

"I know you are. I want you. I love you. But there are a lot of
things. I want to think about doing the right thing, not just what's
the nicest thing."

He hadn't told her what Swaggerty had said, or about the
federal investigation. Perhaps now was the time. She waited, her
silently held breath as articulate as shouted words in the tropic
night.

"Chelsea," he began.

"Yes?"

She would inherit millions, perhaps billions. He knew there
was a West fortune and she was the inheritor. His company, once

booming, was still in trouble. These were perilous times. Now, the law too could be added to his enemies. Lazer was a target. Why not those who slept with him? French Jake had been harried and hunted twenty-five years earlier. Surely his name was still on their books; surely it would pop up when some bright young boy in Justice or at Internal Revenue pushed the right button on the computer. Dossiers were forever; Europeans understood that. Once your name was on the books of the police, you were always theirs. It was like Claude Rains's line in *Casablanca:* "Round up the usual suspects."

How could he tell her about Lazer, about the money laundering that had for so long paid the bills, about his father's criminal career, about his murder? How could he drag the heiress to the West billions into all that and a federal investigation besides?

Agonizing, he remained silent, trying to tell himself this was paranoia, that this summons from Foley Square was some sort of bureaucratic mistake. His father had been dead almost twenty years. Majesty paid its taxes and its bills, when the money was there. Still, there was this uneasy feeling that disaster lurked just outside the door, across the Avenue and down the street. Seventh Avenue was intimate with fear. It was a rare manufacturer who ever counted his blessings. Life was lived in the vestibule of Chapter Eleven, or the IRS audit, of the loan unpaid and in the shadow of hard men who came to burn down your place and break your kneecaps and slice a razor blade across the face of your showroom model.

"Not yet . . . not yet. Maybe not ever." He watched Chelsea's face melt into confusion. She was sitting up in bed on one elbow, staring down at him, her breasts revealed—and now, for Marc, achingly untouchable.

"Why not? After all we've been through this year? Not even now, now that the worst is over?" She was searching his face, he knew, for something that she had never seen before—something that would ally him not with love but with other men, men like Raker.

"Chelsea, we have to leave things as they are. I wish it were different, but I'm . . . ." He thought of French Jake, of Carl Lazer's courtly evil, and he thought of telling her everything. "I'm a black hole, Chelsea. Trust me that you can't trust me. If you come too close, you'll never get away again."

Her eyes were so blue, so clear. They were Will West's eyes. "All right," she said. "All right. All right. All right."

He watched as her eyes brimmed, as she blinked tears back. He had never seen Chelsea cry.

She fell back onto the pillow and turned her head away. "All right, all right," she murmured, wounded now, saying the words again and again until they had no meaning, until they were abstract and hopeless syllables, no longer words but sobs.

They lay there together and far apart in the hot darkness. Marc listened to her cry until she fell asleep, twisting with dreams he couldn't imagine.

And when he woke her in the night she made love to him, not out of love but out of animal hunger. Beyond the shuttered windows she could hear the chirp of tropical insects and far away the dull roar of the sea, and above them both his hoarse panting and the beat of her own heart.

He took her and she cried out in pleasure, her arms, her legs snaking about him, her mouth open, her belly jerking against him, her breasts taut and swollen, her groin wet and pulsing. He took her and she knew she had been rejected.

She was a West and proud, and did not ask again.

42

Friendly witnesses are hoping to be granted immunity.

Mode, December 3, 1981

T he assistant U.S. attorney was named Giordano, a small, hard-faced young man with a city accent.

"Mr. Street, we appreciate your coming here without subpoena. Counsel can tell you that once a subpoena is issued we go on the record. This conversation is informal and off the record."

Marc's lawyer, a partner at Addison, Burns, had already explained the situation, and now neither he nor Street said anything. Giordano went on.

"The government has no direct interest in you, Mr. Street. Carl Lazer is our meat. The Lazer investigation has been going on for many months. Considerable data have already been gathered. It would be quite possible to follow through on Lazer without your cooperation. Obviously, it's much easier if you play ball."

Marc, under instructions, listened and said nothing. His attorney did the running.

"Mr. Giordano, without conceding that my client knows anything, could you give us some notion of what this investigation is all about and why you believe Mr. Street can help you?"

Giordano smiled. Street's lawyer was smooth as glove leather.

"Yes, Counselor. This investigation focuses on certain illegal activities of Mr. Lazer and his associates over a long period of time and involving a wide range of criminal activities. Lazer and his people are into illegal gambling, prostitution, loan-sharking, drugs, labor racketeering. The whole *schmear.* Where we think Mr. Street can help is in regard to the laundering of illegal funds by Lazer through otherwise apparently legitimate businesses."

"Are you suggesting Mr. Street's firm might have been one such?"

"Yes, Counselor. That's what we're suggesting."

"Mr. Street would deny such a thing most vigorously."

"Shit," Giordano said, "of course he'd deny it. I don't want Street's ass. I want Lazer."

There was more talk. Giordano teased but didn't give very much. There was no hint of how much he knew about the laundered money, no offer of immunity if Marc testified. Marc's lawyer had warned him that it might play this way, that Giordano would lift the edge of the scab and poke around a bit, trying to get Marc nervous. In the end, he did.

When Giordano had finished, and Street hadn't budged, the prosecutor stood up. "Well, you had a chance to help. Sorry you didn't take it."

Street nodded, still mute. As he and his lawyer turned, Giordano spoke again.

"One more thing," he said, glancing down at a memo in front of him on the polished desk. "I'll want to talk with several other employees of Majesty Fashions. This time, under subpoena. I have here"—and he picked up the memo—"a Mr. Sydney Heidler, a Mr. Al Frangione, a Miss Chelsea West, a Miss . . ."

He went on listing the names of employees, getting some of them wrong.

". . . and a Mr. Adam Greenberg."

Street spoke for the first time. "Adam's no longer with us. He works for someone else."

Giordano's intelligent, curious face relaxed. He grinned, almost boyish. "Oh? Is that so? My people must have been misinformed."

When they were on the sidewalk of Foley Square, Marc's attorney started to talk, telling him what the next step would probably be and what response Marc should make. But Marc wasn't listening. He was thinking about having Chelsea and old Heidler hauled into court, bullied, chivied, interrogated.

And he attempted, without great success, to fight off the suspicion that Adam's name had been tossed in as a stalking horse, that Giordano knew damned well where Adam worked. Marc tried to remember what Adam knew about "Uncle Carl," how much he'd been told, how much he might have picked up, and just what he might have already told an assistant U.S. attorney who had tried, rather transparently, to seem misinformed as to the facts.

Inside the federal court building Giordano and three of his bright young men reviewed the notes of the session. Giordano shook his head in mild admiration.

"I like that," he said. "Addison, Burns as counsel. A smart Jewboy garment manufacturer gets his balls in the wringer and he retains Addison, Burns. The Jews and the WASPs ganging up, with a nice, hardworking Italian kid like me in the middle."

One of his aides, a Jew, laughed as loudly as the others. Giordano had the smell of a man with a future at Justice, and it did no harm to laugh at his rough wit.

Street and Chelsea had come back from Haiti with a self-conscious restraint suspended between them, leaden as weights. She was silent, withdrawn, elaborately polite. A limo had brought them into Manhattan in late afternoon, the lighted buildings hung against the curtain of a gray November sky. They drove first to her place. As the driver and Marc got her bags from the trunk she thanked them with the same cool graciousness as if both had been hired by the hour.

"I'll call you later," Marc said.

"Yes, do that."

Even in a fur coat her back was eloquently stiff as she went through the doors of the building past the red-faced doorman. Marc watched until she was gone. That night, he didn't phone. He was afraid there would be no answer.

They had not fallen quickly into love, like people who have

nothing better to do, thoughtless and desperate to fill up lives with something meaningful. They had grown together gradually and maturely, at first through work and a developing mutual admiration, then through the intimacies and aching pleasure of sex, finally in camaraderie and a friendship both thought solid and lasting.

And now it had all smashed on the reef of Marc's inexplicable, cold rejection.

At Christmas she flew out to Denver. They had seen each other each day at work, but the awkward chill was still there. He suggested dinner several times, and she pleaded previous engagements that did not exist. One night at an Irish bar on Second Avenue, not drunk but drinking, he talked to a girl. The girl had made the move, turning from the man she was with to chat with Marc. The man, understandably, resented it and threw a punch. Marc knocked him down, and the defeated gladiator, holding a bloody handkerchief to his face, staggered out into the night while the barman wiped a rag across the surface of the bar and pointedly ignored Marc. Other patrons edged quietly but measurably away. The girl meant nothing to him, and he knew the fight was stupid.

He spent Christmas alone, restless and unhappy. When he phoned the ranch one of the Mexican women answered and he was unable to make himself understood. He gathered that she was not there, that she was skiing. But the uncertainty of translation left everything vague and irritating. He gave his name, but with no confidence that the woman had understood.

There was another informal meeting at Foley Square, Giordano pushing harder now.

"He's trying to scare you, Mr. Street," the man from Addison, Burns advised, "trying to get you to bargain."

"And what do *you* think?" Marc asked.

"Maybe you *should* bargain, Mr. Street. It's an option, you know."

Maybe he should. But "bargaining" was a polite word for betrayal. For turning his back on his youth and those early years when Lazer had helped him keep Majesty going, when labor troubles were settled and mobsters frightened away, when the laundered money had gotten a marginal business on its feet. He had broken with Lazer in his own time and in his own way. Perhaps it was stupid not simply to give him up and cooperate with Giordano, but it went against his code. And he was fiercely faithful to that code.

He had stonewalled in Haiti not only to keep Chelsea ignorant of the early trafficking with illegal funds and with Carl Lazer, but to keep her out of it, to insulate her from harm. What frightened him was the possibility that he would be caught up now in a criminal prosecution, and that she, as his collaborator, would be dragged into it as well. It could be even worse if she were his wife. He had met Will West, not a man who would slough off such things as unimportant. Scandal would hurt the West name, Will West's sense of family, his *business*. Marc was carrying the weight of a fear that he might be the mechanism that could strip Chelsea of her rightful inheritance of the West billions.

She knew only that she had been rejected.

No one at Aspen, or even at the ranch, sensed anything. *Women's Wear Daily* sent a reporter and photographer to capture the beautiful people at their snowy revels, and when it was Chelsea's turn she talked airily of her new skis, of Aspen's latest nightspot, of the coming couture collection in Paris. She said nothing of herself, so skillfully that the reporter never noticed. It was a brilliant Aspen season: two kings, Constantine of Greece and Juan Carlos of Spain, Leonard Lauder of the perfume empire, Rupert Murdoch and his family, a cabinet member and his young bride, the usual Houston oil barons and Hollywood stars, and a pride of Kennedys.

Chelsea reigned among them. Even her grandfather marveled. Will West had moved with a small entourage into a suite in the Hotel Jerome to be with her.

"You dance all night and ski all day and I'll be damned if I know how you do it," he said. "You'd kill a coal miner with hours like yours."

"Grandpa, I get it from you. Bloodlines, you know, like you're always nattering on about."

"Catherine, I do not natter."

But he went out to dinner with her one night at André's; a man who knew how close he had been to death only a few months earlier, now enjoying each borrowed day with the gratitude of the resurrected. She was very gay. It was a performance, but she carried it off. That night she danced with Ted Kennedy and drank with Greek royalty and walked out into the snow with a rich boy from Dallas and turned away another at the door of her hotel suite; she was a famous, glamorous young woman to whom they all wanted to be close. No one knew that inside she was dying.

43

As the old year ends there is much for which we can be grateful: the hostages are home from Tehran, the nation is at peace, and retail sales rose 6 percent during December.

Mode, December 31, 1981

Here is how I see '82, Adam," Stanley Baltimore said as the two men dined at a banquette in Le Périgord in that quiet week between Christmas and New Year's.

"I think the time is ripe for a chain of freestanding Adam boutiques, coast to coast. We'll get some of the big stores pissed off at us, especially the ones that already have Adam shops. But what the hell, selling direct we keep it all instead of cutting it down the middle with the retailers. Those bastards will whimper and threaten to stop buying from us. But they'll back down. None of them have any balls."

Adam did not agree. He knew some pretty tough retailers. But he kept his opinion to himself; Baltimore in full flight was not a man to be interrupted.

"I'm hiring Zipser from Federated to set them up. He knows his stuff. We're talking to Manhattan Industries about a new line of domestics. You won't have to do a damn thing. The hosiery deal you know about. Don't ask me how you can tell one pair of pantyhose from another, but women are nuts anyway. A pair with your name on them will bring a buck more. It's all bullshit. But it works."

He went on, contemptuously dismissing the stores, the consumers, the very industry that had made them both rich, callously unmindful of contradictions. When he had finished and was washing down his salmon with a glass of Perrier, Adam spoke up. "I worry about the boutiques," he said. "Despite what you say, they could really cut into our business with the stores."

"Shit, Ralph Lauren's doing it. Why can't we?"

Adam continued to look dubious.

"And you're a lot bigger than Ralph, Adam," he said slyly.

Adam looked thoughtful. "Yes," he said, knowing he was being stroked, "you might be right."

Of course, there were problems. The competition was the toughest in years: Lauren, Calvin Klein, this Perry Ellis with his bulky, man-tailored coats that were making such an impact, Norma Kamali, a suddenly revived Oscar de la Renta, Beene, and the consistently salable Blass.

And there was Chelsea West.

Majesty's production, compared to the other big houses, was relatively limited. Street's cash shortages restricted his ability to subcontract out as much work as he would have liked. Chelsea's November collection had been a winner, and would generate profits. But it could not do so with the enormous volume of some of the others. The production of her perfume was still lagging, still months away from the marketplace. Only her Geaux West jeans were coining money, and her name, her face, her rear end seemed to be everywhere.

"I'd love to strip the jeans right off her myself one night," Baltimore told his flunky, Lester, "and keep her bent over backwards for a couple of hours."

"You'd show her, Mr. Baltimore."

"Damned right I would."

Lester knew that Chelsea was years too old to interest his boss. This wasn't lust; it was competition. Still, Lester mused, it was a nice rear end.

He'd been summoned for a tongue-lashing. Baltimore wanted to know why *Time* magazine was working on a lifestyle piece about Chelsea instead of Adam.

"Well, Mr. Baltimore, you know, pretty girls sell magazines, I guess."

"And a screamer like Adam doesn't."

Lester was uncharacteristically feisty in his reply. "Adam's done a good job for us, Mr. Baltimore."

"He's still a faggot."

There were limits to Lester's courage. "Yessir, you're right about that."

Baltimore gave him clearly implausible orders to get to the editors of *Time* and convince them to scrap the article about Chelsea West.

"That company she works for is going down the tubes, Street's got the shorts, and there's talk about some kind of government investigation. He's got connections in the rackets. Drop a few hints around. They'll get the message. And if *Time* won't play, talk to *Newsweek*. Who's the editor over there? Take him to lunch. Get him laid. Use the yacht, use your damned head."

"Yes, Mr. Baltimore."

As Baltimore continued to rail and Lester to shrivel, the PR man mentally weighed the quarter million he was paid against the abuse he took and wondered, not for the first time, if the money was worth it. Then, as Baltimore paused for breath, Lester exploited the respite. He pulled a batch of glossies from an envelope.

"Talking about magazines, Mr. Baltimore, this is the girl we're thinking of using in *Seventeen* and the other teen books to promote our girls' line of cosmetics, the acne creams and things."

He pushed the photos at Baltimore before he could say anything. Baltimore took them and went to the couch, flopping down and riffling slowly through the stack.

"Pretty kid," he said. "Looks good to me."

It was not quite the reaction Lester wanted. Too casual, too professional. Baltimore was still distracted. Abruptly, he tossed the pictures aside, carelessly strewn across the couch.

"I want extra pressure put on the fashion magazines. Talk to our ad department. Next time their salesmen come to call, give it to 'em straight. They play up Chelsea West and they can live on

Majesty advertising. I'll pull my pages. Hell with 'em. Revlon, Lauder, and us, we're the advertising tonnage. Marc Street buys a dozen pages a year. We buy a dozen pages an issue. I want Adam played up in *Vogue* and *Harper's*. You get me?"

"Mr. Baltimore, all that's absolutely correct. But if I may, I'd just like you to take one more look at this girl. This one they're thinking of using in the teenybopper ads. I don't want any mistakes made, and your eye is the keenest."

Hurriedly, he grabbed three or four of the glossies and pressed them into Baltimore's big hand before he could say anything.

This time Baltimore looked more carefully. The girl wore skintight faded jeans, sneakers, and a tank top. She had long hair and a sweet, fresh face with a slightly turned-up nose. Everyone's idealized version of the girl next door.

"I've met this girl, Mr. Baltimore," Lester said quickly, sensing an alteration in his boss's mood. "Bright kid, ambitious, and with a very ambitious mother. The old lady would do anything to get the girl into the big time."

"Oh?" Baltimore said.

Lester nodded. "I have that impression, Mr. Baltimore. I can check it out for you if you wish."

Baltimore continued to look at the photos. "No tits," he said finally, "nice legs, cute little ass, an okay face. But no tits."

Lester struck. "She's thirteen, Mr. Baltimore."

There was a sale of paintings scheduled for that evening at Sotheby's, and Baltimore was nervously anticipating a bidding war for an original Lautrec cartoon. That and his complicated marketing and promotional plans for Adam monopolized his thoughts. Perhaps he deserved a distraction. He looked again at the girl in the glossies.

"Thirteen, you say, and her mother's willing to play?"

"Yes, Mr. Baltimore, she made that abundantly clear when I asked."

Stanley Baltimore stroked the scar at the corner of his mouth.

Adam had a new love interest, a young actor named Luke with David Bowie hair, a weight lifter's body, hard and muscled, and the moral sense of a barracuda. It was, for Adam, an irresistible combination. They had met on St. Bart's the week after New Year's Day. Adam was there to sun and rest before flying to Paris; Luke was filming an airline commercial. Genghis Khan brought them together.

"A friend of mine is doing the hair on a commercial," he told Adam. "You've got to meet this boy Luke. I've been watching them film down on the beach. He's got better pecs than Schwarzenegger."

Khan had a bungalow on the grounds of the Hotel Manapany on the beach, and that night he brought them together there at a cocktail party. Adam and Genghis and the two models who'd come down from New York with them played host. The commercial crew was delighted to have a break in routine. Luke was excited to meet Adam.

"Gosh," he said with a studied boyishness, "even before I could afford your jeans, I was wearing them." He laughed. "Don't ask me how I got them. I don't want to incriminate myself."

The director and his assistant were both gay, and they made a fuss over Adam. The incredibly lovely girl in the commercial spent the evening examining her pores in a compact mirror.

"God, but she's dull," Luke said. "People hear how much money we make in commercial work. If they knew how hard it is . . ."

Adam commiserated with him. "Fashion is like that too. Everyone sees the finished product, the perfect suit, the beautiful dress. They don't see the sweat, the detail work, the boredom, the rotten side of it."

"Oh, but the beauty you create, Adam."

"If you knew the people I have to work with." Adam laughed harshly. "Overaged fashion editors with bad legs and the taste levels of delicatessen owners. And they're the ones who make these pious judgments about fashion."

Luke nodded. "If only they were all like Lincoln Radford," he remarked.

"Do you know Lincoln?"

"No, but I've always admired what he does in *Mode*. I think he's a genius."

Mode had just done a spread on Adam's dresses. Luke had seen it.

"Luke," Adam said, "I like you. When we're both back in New York, come see me. We ought to get to know each other better."

Behind him the fag hags gossiped and got drunk and Genghis, rather bitchily, told the commercial's leading lady that they were doing her hair all wrong. It didn't matter that it was Khan's friend who was the hairdresser on the shoot. He had discovered the assistant director and he was playing to *him*.

Dinner was on a small verandah under a tropical moon so low and large it looked like a stage prop. At midnight Adam and Luke found themselves walking on the beach, talking about their work, their careers, Luke carefully deferring to the older, more famous man.

When conversation died, the moon falling toward the silvered horizon of the placid sea, Luke pulled off his shirt. "Hey, this is too good to miss. Let's go for a swim."

He was stripped before Adam could respond. Adam stood there watching the boy sprint toward the ocean, his white buttocks dully gleaming in the night.

"Okay!" Adam shouted. "I'm coming."

He tugged off his clothes, forgetting his fear of sharks and the local lore that they were most dangerous at night, when they cruised in close to the beach, hunting baitfish.

"Great, isn't it?" Luke demanded, his big body compressing and then exploding from the water, sheets of water streaming off his shoulders and massive chest.

Adam, whose swimming skill was basic, treaded water and kept imagining something out of *Jaws* cruising silently, invisibly toward him.

"I've had it," he said, and started to wade in toward the sand.

"Chicken!" Luke shouted, bolder now.

Adam kept going. The hell with it. If Luke wanted to play,

he could play on dry land. Just then a searing pain ran through his left foot.

"Jesus," he groaned, looking down at himself. The water was less than a foot deep and there were no fins. He hobbled beachward, his foot burning and starting to throb. When he was out of the water he threw himself down on the sand and tried to examine his foot.

"What's the matter?" Luke asked. He had materialized on the beach, a huge young god with water coursing down his nude body, his chest heaving, his hair sleeked back from the classic face.

"Shit, I dunno. Something stung my foot, maybe a man-of-war."

Luke knelt, took his ankle, and slowly, competently, turned the foot. "Nah, it's a sea urchin. You've got spines in there."

"I don't care what it is. It hurts like hell," Adam whimpered.

Luke looked down at him. When Adam forgot his pain long enough to look up, there was a sober, concerned frown on Luke's face.

"We've got to get you home and wash it out."

"Should I go back in the water?"

"That'll just make it worse," said Luke, the expert.

"Oh shit, I'm not sure I can walk."

Luke smiled, seeing Adam's head bent over his foot, his hands grabbing his calf in pain.

"There is an emergency treatment, Adam. There's something in urine that cools the burning."

"Urine? What the hell do you mean?" Pain had him befuddled, and he was not sure he had heard correctly.

"Sure," Luke said equably, "you can piss on it."

"Piss on it?"

"Yeah, that's what they do down here."

Adam started to object, and then another spasm of searing pain shot through his foot.

"Oh shit, okay. Help me up."

He leaned on Luke's muscular arm and tried to steady himself. Suddenly, he giggled. "This is so goddamned silly. Pissing on my own foot."

Luke looked into his face, their eyes locking. "Relax, Adam. I'll piss on it for you." He reached down to his penis.

For an instant, Adam remembered another beach, another lover, Martha's Vineyard and Peter Feeley. But when he looked down he saw Luke standing there nude and a spasm ran through him that had nothing to do with memory or even pain.

"Yes," he said, "yes, Luke, you do it."

44

Our sources in Foley Square say that some of the biggest names in Seventh Avenue are retaining eminent counsel and swallowing antacid remedies.

Mode, January 6, 1982

G iordano had raised the ante. During the first week of January Marc was summoned once again, his lawyer warning him that this time might be different.

"They'll turn up the screws," he said, "try to scare you, bully you into cooperating."

"Can they do that legally?"

"They can do any damn thing they want. Then, it's up to you. Tell them to go to hell and serve their subpoenas or get off your back."

"And?"

The man from Addison, Burns shrugged. "And we'll soon find out."

"Yeah?" Marc said.

For the first time in perhaps a dozen meetings, the Addison, Burns lawyer smiled. "Mr. Street, this time they're going to fuck you."

Marc jerked back, as if in reflex. The Addison, Burns man blushed. He had obviously gone too far, but Street got the message. The lawyer stammered. "I'm sorry. I didn't mean to say that. It just seemed like a cogent summary of the situation, of my professional advice."

Like Nick Charles and a cocktail, the warning and the event came swiftly together. Giordano lived up to both.

"Look, Jewboy, you lived for years off drug money, rackets money, loan-sharking cash. It flowed into your neat little sewing machine operation and you got your models on the cover of *Vogue*. Terrific. You're a hero. You have dinner at the White House, breakfast at Tiffany's, Street for mayor. Except all you are is a conduit for dirty dollars from a lot of pushers and bookies and pimps who work for Carl Lazer. Right?"

"You've got the floor, Giordano," Marc said, tight-lipped, trying not to let himself be goaded into fury. Next to him his lawyer moved a hand toward Marc, laying it atop his forearm in restraining caution.

Giordano went on. "It's a pattern that didn't begin the day before yesterday. Your old man was in the rackets, in pre-war Germany, in France, here in Manhattan. We know that. We've gone back into the files. It's all there. He was bumped off right here by another hoodlum. He worked for Lazer, and after he was killed Lazer moved right in. Your silent partner, right there at your side. You dropped out of college and went right into the rackets yourself. You had a chance to go straight, to do something with your life, and you walked away from it. It's in the blood, Street. You had an opportunity at Cornell most kids don't have and you threw it away. You associated with known criminals outside the Lazer organization. Does the name Robert Swaggerty mean anything to you?"

Marc remained silent. The Addison, Burns attorney felt the tension in his forearm. He pressed his own hand down harder, cautionary and alert.

Giordano put on glasses and looked down at his notes. "I should think it would. You and Swaggerty have run together for a long time now. Maybe we ought to dig a little into just how Swaggerty supported himself when he was on the run. Were you sending him the occasional envelope, Street? Was that it?"

"Charges against Swaggerty were dropped, Giordano," Marc said, knowing he should remain silent but unable to stop himself.

Giordano laughed. "Hell, you can fix anything in this town. Don't make me laugh."

Marc's lawyer was gripping his arm now, holding him back. Giordano didn't miss it. He knew he was on a roll.

"When Adam Greenberg left your company you sued to enjoin him. Maybe Mr. Greenberg didn't like the stench and he went to a decent, honorable competitor and you went to law to prevent him. You use the law when it suits your own purpose and you flout it when it doesn't. Nice irony there, don't you think?"

Marc said nothing. Baltimore "decent, honorable"? But he remained mute.

"You replaced him with a new chief designer, Miss West. Miss West comes from a famous American family. Was that merely coincidence? She was the only available designer you could hire? Or was it your somewhat Byzantine notion that if you got Will West's money and power and prestige behind you, no one could touch you? Was that it, Street?"

"Fuck you, Giordano."

The federal man smiled. He enjoyed a hostile cross-examination. He liked it when witnesses blew.

Marc got to his feet. His lawyer, alarmed, got up with him, hanging on to one arm. That was all they needed, for Street to throw a punch at an assistant U.S. attorney.

He had not counted on Marc's lineage. Seventh Avenue was a hard school. Street shook off his hand but made no move toward Giordano's desk. He had regained control and now, almost impassively, he said with contempt, "If you ginzos have anything on me, talk to Addison, Burns here. He handles all my indictments."

In the end they walked away from each other, like snarling dogs.

Addison, Burns knew what was coming next. "A subpoena, carefully leaked to the papers, suggesting you know a hell of a lot more than you're saying. Compared to you, Son of Sam is going to look like Mother Teresa."

Marc knew he was right. Sassing Giordano was one thing, coping with a federal indictment was something else again. Visions of French Jake on television before the Kefauver committee flooded his head. Was he to live out again the same fate? It was as if the malignant forces that chased his father out of Germany and across France had caught up with him here. Only this time it was the American government, just as relentless, and patient, as resourceful and as determined. A generation ago they had been in pursuit of his father. Now they were after him. Paranoia is the bedmate of Jews.

Marc felt fear, the instinct to run. He had not felt fear since childhood, when Bobby Swaggerty stalked and harried him on Central Park West at the subway station. Now, anger cooled, he felt it again before they had ever left the federal building in Foley Square.

Not only fear. Hate. Not so much for Giordano, a man doing his job. But for Adam and, behind Adam, Stanley Baltimore. Each time with Giordano he became more convinced that Adam had been testifying against him. That business about Adam's having left Majesty to get away from the "stench." Just crap! Adam bailed out because he resented Chelsea and because he was weak. Baltimore bought Adam away with money and with flattery and with promises. Baltimore! A man who crushed rivals and worked his own executives into ulcers and cardiacs, who muscled retailers into buying his products and no one else's, who used his enormous economic leverage to smash competition, who cheated and bullied and stole and lied. Baltimore! A man who everyone on the Avenue knew destroyed people, despising even those who worked for him, combining blackmail and the dangled carrot of huge salaries and perquisites in the hiring, blackballing and lawsuits in the firing, a man who cowed employees and sabotaged rivals.

Adam, Marc knew, was malleable. Excuses could be made for him, but not for Stanley Baltimore. Without a shred of evidence, Street knew instinctively that behind Giordano and the federal investigators was the hand of Stanley Baltimore. He knew it!

And he was right, though it had not been premeditated. After Giordano interrogated Adam, Baltimore berated the designer for not having, in his words, "nailed the son of a bitch to the cross." "I'll see this Giordano myself. Maybe I can flesh out the case."

Baltimore hated to waste an opportunity to hurt a rival. Street had defied him over Adam, had rashly gone into competition with this new Chelsea perfume, reason enough to assist in his inquisition.

"His real name is Streit? *Not* Street?"

Giordano shrugged. "Yeah," he said flatly, not understanding Baltimore's excitement, "Streit became Street. His old man was a German. Came here during the war. A garment district mobster. He was bumped off in . . ."

Baltimore said quietly, "In 1961."

Giordano looked up at him, curious now. "That's right. Sixty-one. They found his body in an abandoned car over on West Street."

Baltimore knew he should offer nothing more. Sheer surprise had caused him to blurt out the year. He could have given him the day and the hour, the license plate number on the car, could have told him the number of shots that had killed French Jake Streit.

After a moment, Giordano continued: "They never found the killers. The case is open to this day."

Baltimore smiled. "Gangsters, they're always killing one another, aren't they?"

"Fortunately, yes." Giordano nodded.

Baltimore fingered the scar at the corner of his mouth. "Tell me how I can help you get Street," he said. "I'll do anything I can."

45

Record numbers of buyers will be flying to Paris next week
for the spring-summer haute couture collections. Open to
buy is said to be larger than in years. And the French franc
weaker.

Mode, January 13, 1982

They got a banquette at Le Cirque, just inside the entrance, a brief table away from where Richard and Pat Nixon and Eddie and Tricia Cox were having dinner. Marc arrived first. It was his party. He had not permitted Chelsea to slide away from him this time with filmy excuses. "It's important," he'd insisted over the office phone, "there are some things I have to tell you."

"Sure," she'd said, "what time?" The reserve was still there.

Street had not seen the Nixons at first. Sirio led him to his table, and once he'd ordered his Stolichnaya on the rocks with olives, he looked around. There was Nixon, wattles shaking, the familiar voice growling, the intonations and the look unchanged by age. He was the same Nixon, only more so, a man so often caricatured that the caricature and the reality had blurred. Nixon was talking about De Gaulle and the French. Marc looked away, trying not to hear, trying not to notice. Even Nixon deserved privacy.

When Chelsea came in, heads turned. It was cold and she was wearing a coyote coat and boots, carrying a shopping bag. She shrugged the coat from her shoulders and slipped onto the banquette, the coat tossed against the back of the bench, the bag shoved underneath. She leaned over and gave him a light kiss on the cheek, a cold kiss when held against what they had shared, a professional kiss such as fashion editors exchange, a kiss that meant less than a handshake. She sat next to him, seeing the Nixons and then watching them. She looked everywhere but at her lover.

She ordered a kir, and he tried to make conversation. She went along with it. None of it meant anything, but at least they were talking. Nixon was talking as well, his wife nodding, bird-like, his daughter and her husband actually listening and occasionally throwing in a remark. But it was Nixon's floor. Marc paid no attention, but Chelsea found herself half listening, and Cox noticed. He touched Nixon's arm and nodded in their direction. Nixon got the hint and shifted conversational gears awkwardly.

"This is interesting silverware they have here, don't you think, Pat?"

When they had ordered, not from the menu but from the captain's suggestions, Marc not caring and passively taking advice, he began to talk.

"This hasn't been easy since Haiti."

"Haiti wasn't easy," she said stiffly, "not for me."

"I'm sorry for that, there were reasons."

"Sure. You didn't want to marry me."

"That wasn't it. I couldn't."

He was still trying to find a way to tell her the untellable. It wasn't coming.

She said nothing, and he was afraid they would slip again painfully into silence. So he babbled.

"How was Christmas? Okay? Your grandfather better?"

"Yeah, yeah, fine. He's okay. Much better."

"You skied."

"Yeah, a lot. Good snow."

"Great."

She knew she had to make an effort, too. Not to offer something herself would be rude, unfeeling. He had hurt her, but he looked so miserable.

"How about you? Stay here in town?" she asked, babbling now herself.

"Yes. Quiet. You know how New York is at times like that."

"I know."

He reached into an inside pocket. "I got you something for Christmas. Just . . . something."

"Oh?" Her face reddened.

He handed her a small package, gift-wrapped. She slid a nail under the Christmas seal. Inside, there was a Tiffany box, pale blue, with a white satin ribbon. Her jaw tightened.

Inside the Tiffany box was a Mickey Mouse watch.

"Oh, Marc, what I always wanted." Her smile was genuine.

She pulled at the chain of the gold watch she was wearing and replaced it with the Mickey Mouse watch, holding it up, admiring it. "It's me," she said.

He grinned. "I knew that the moment I saw it. Cost a fortune, but I said, what the hell, it's *her*."

At the Nixon table they were now the ones eavesdropping.

"I got something for you, too," she said, "for Christmas."

"Hey."

She reached under the table and pulled out the shopping bag. It said "Herman's Sporting Goods." She handed it to him. Inside, wrapped in tissue paper, was a baseball glove.

"Well, I'll be damned." He held it up and then slipped it onto his left hand. "How'd you know?" he said.

"Bobby Swaggerty stole yours once, remember? You said your father wouldn't get you another one because you lied and said you'd lost it."

Nixon was staring at them now, listening to the laughter.

"You remembered that," Marc said in wonder.

They ate dinner civilly, and more than that, even cordially. But they stood a long way from where they had been that night in her bed eating ribs and drinking beer. Her questions still went unanswered. And now, as the plates were cleared and coffee brought, the Nixons rose and went out, the former President giving Chelsea a slight and courtly bow as they passed. There were empty tables now on both flanks, and they could talk. If only he had the words. He was ready to take chances, even risk being thought absurd. He wished silently for a precision of language he knew he did not have to make an explanation that, even to him, seemed fuzzy and half baked.

"I love you. There is no single thing I would rather do than marry you. This last year has been for me the best there ever was. I tried to tell you that in Haiti, and I didn't. I'd hurt you, and no words seemed sufficient to make up for that."

She shook her head, unable to understand. "Then why *did* you hurt me? Why did you let me go on and on about us, while you turned to stone?"

"I didn't turn to stone. Inside, I was being eaten away. What you wanted, I wanted. But just before Haiti I'd learned something that changed things. The situation suddenly was different, terribly different."

There was a silence as the waiter, discreet but still a man with ears, refilled the small coffee cups. Then Marc resumed.

"I'm in trouble. The first hint came just before we flew down there. On the flight, in the hotel, on the beach, a half dozen times I started to tell you about it. I never found the right words. And then that night, when you asked me to marry you, I just froze. I couldn't explain."

She was half turned to him now on the banquette, her broad, placid face solemn, her brow furrowed.

"This is our *life* we're talking about, Marc. I asked you to marry me and you didn't even answer. You said nothing. I think maybe you'd better explain, whether the words are right or not. Whatever it is, no matter how bad, it can't be worse than not knowing."

"Okay," he said, exhaling.

He told her everything, starting with Giordano and going backward in time, about seeing his father on television and learning for the first time what he did for a living, *had* done in Berlin and Paris, told her about his murder, about Carl Lazer and the laundered money.

She listened with the attentiveness of a serious, obedient child. "You should have told me these things," she said quietly.

"I was afraid I'd lose you," he said morosely.

"Does Adam know all this?"

"No, a little of it, but not all. I never trusted him to be discreet. Unfair, probably, but that was how I felt."

"And you didn't trust me, either. After all this time, you didn't trust me."

He was miserable. "I loved you. I couldn't involve you."

She looked at him. "You are so damned stupid, Marc. Don't you know if you really love someone she *wants* to be involved?"

"I do love you," he said. "I always will."

Her hand reached for his, gentle and caring. "Then it's simple," she said, smiling for the first time. "You just go and testify. They're not after you. It'll be all over."

"It's not simple," he said, shaking his head. "I can't do that to Lazer."

She looked stunned. "You owe him *that* much?"

"I don't know what I owe, part of the problem. It isn't all black and white. I'm confused."

"Even though you could have immunity."

"There are no guarantees, just hints. But even if I were sure about not being prosecuted myself, Lazer and I go back such a long way. It would be doing to him what Adam did to me."

"And you won't betray him."

"No, I don't think I will."

He might be confused about what he owed, but there was steel in his voice.

"Then there's you," he said.

She bristled. "I can't tell you what to do about Carl Lazer, but I sure as hell can tell you about me. I don't need protection. Will West isn't going to get all nervous and sweaty and start changing wills or anything else just because my name gets in the paper. You don't know my grandpa if you think that."

"It's a chance I can't afford to let you take."

"Oh, turds. One thing has nothing to do with the other. My grandpa was being subpoenaed by congressional committees when your father was still a schoolboy. And suppose the worst happened, suppose I didn't inherit the West billions. I'm making money on my own, lots of it."

Her self-confidence was genuine. He knew that. But still, he couldn't let her risk everything for him.

"Look," he said, "this could all blow over. Lazer could come in and plea bargain and they'd never even get to me. Or he could flee the country and the case would fall apart. But we don't know that. Next week I'm going to be subpoenaed and then it'll all come out in the papers."

"We're supposed to go to Paris next week, to the collections."

"I know," he said gloomily. Paris was where love began.

"So?"

He had thought it through. He still wasn't sure if it made sense. But now was the time to lay it out.

"I'm going to Paris alone this time," he told her. "And you're going to resign from Majesty Fashions."

"Resign? I'm your goddamned *star*, remember?"

"I know, I know, but it'll get you off the hook. You weren't there when the money was actually laundered, not even Giordano suggests that. You never heard of Seventh Avenue back in those days. And now if you quit it'll prove all over again that you're clean, that as soon as you heard the first rumors that the company was tied in with Lazer, you walked out. You not only won't get involved, you'll be the heroine of the whole mess."

"And where will you be when this stupid scenario is played out?"

"Europe, somewhere. Maybe Paris. Nobody's going to extradite anybody for laundering a little money. Hell, look at Vesco."

"And am I supposed to go back to the ranch and keep house for my grandpa?"

He shook his head. "Chelsea, any one of a half dozen big houses would give you a million-dollar-a-year contract tomorrow. You can write your own ticket. And they aren't all thugs like Baltimore, you know. There are decent firms that would love to hire you."

"I can't believe this is all happening. It's like some corny TV movie. You're going into exile and I'm quitting my job. Am I supposed to tell everyone what a bastard you are to make myself look better? Is that part of it?"

He smiled, grimly. "Not a bad idea at all."

They went back to her apartment and argued some more, and then they went to bed and made love. When they woke in the night, he noticed that she was still wearing her Mickey Mouse watch.

"I love my baseball glove," he said softly.

"What?" she murmured, out of sleep.

"I said, 'I love you.' "

"Good," she said, "me too."

On Friday he flew alone to France.

46

We expect this week's big winners in Paris to be Saint
Laurent, Ungaro, Cardin, and Givenchy. Young Lagerfeld?
Too early to say if he can revive the once great Maison
Chanel.

Mode, January 20, 1982

T here was nothing conspiratorial about his flight. He
packed his bags, slipped in Swaggerty's revolver on a whim,
called a cab to JFK, and strolled through customs. Fashion had
long been an international business; fashion designers and executives and buyers lived in jet planes. If actors could be said to be
bicoastal, the fashion business had become transatlantic.

He had told Heidler nothing of his plans. Why burden the
man? If he was asked questions, he could honestly plead ignorance. Sydney had a little money; for years he'd been threatening
to retire to Miami to sit in the sun and play bridge. Now was his
chance. He'd have to retire: once Chelsea quit, there would be
nothing left of Majesty to manage.

She had argued with him to the last.

"It's quixotic, that's what it is. Do you know what that
means, 'quixotic'?"

"Stupid, dumb? I dunno, tell me."

"Don Quixote went around the country inventing enemies
to do battle. It was allegory, but it was also something else, Cervantes's way of saying that in the most gallant, even admirable
ways, we tend to behave like assholes."

"Cervantes said that? About 'assholes'?"

She smiled. "It's in the original Spanish. If you had any education at all, you'd know that."

When he left, she made no promises. "Okay," she said, "you get the hell out. Maybe it's a good idea. Let things cool off back here. But damn you, you keep in touch and let me know how you are, where you are." Her eyes flashed in loving anger.

"That'll get you in trouble."

"Will not. I'll get a P.O. box number. I'll let Didier know. My grandpa didn't raise any dumb grandchildren."

He dropped the Addison, Burns man a note. That, at least, would be given the protection of the lawyer-client relationship. He apologized for leaving without notice and thanked him for his help. "I just couldn't stand that bastard Giordano any longer. Sorry."

Giordano was frustrated. "Jesus, the son of a bitch could have gotten immunity. He wouldn't even have been an unindicted coconspirator if he'd played ball. Does he think Lazer would have done the same for him, the *schmuck*?"

Marc had talked to Swaggerty before leaving.

"You want me to lean on anyone, Marc? I will, you know, just give me the names."

"No, just if Chelsea needs help, I told her how to reach you."

"She got it. She wants anything, I'm there."

"I know that, Bobby."

He attended the principal Paris collections. People raised eyebrows not to see Chelsea there.

"Press of business," he said, something to do with her jeans and the new perfume.

Fashion people were always vague, and it was accepted that for competitive reasons you lied. No one took it personally. But when the collections had ended and everyone else went home, he didn't. He moved out of the San Regis and into a Left Bank hotel with no phone in the room and the bathroom down the hall. He had money but he would husband it. He told Didier confidentially that he would be staying in France for a time and that if Didier had an idea of a job he could do, he'd look into it. Didier, sober and concerned, promised to make inquiries.

In New York word leaked out gradually that he would not be back. *WWD* ran a story, accurate so far as it went, but incomplete. There was a brief spasm of gossip, and then it died. There was always another scandal along Seventh Avenue to divert interest from last week's.

Nowhere, in the newspapers or among the gossipers, was there any talk of a resignation by Chelsea West. She had not resigned; she and old Heidler were trying, at least for the moment, to keep Majesty going.

"I know you're going to raise hell," she wrote Street, "just because I didn't do what you told me. Well, I didn't. And probably won't. You know why? Because I think that's the worst idea you ever had and because I think I'm smarter than you. So there."

He followed the papers, buying day-late editions at Smith's, the booksellers on the rue de Rivoli. Lazer was indicted, along with a half dozen of his associates. But nowhere was Street mentioned, nowhere was the name of Majesty Fashions printed. Maybe it would blow over; maybe, in a few months, he could go home.

He had reckoned without Stanley Baltimore.

Baltimore raged at Adam, as if it were all his fault.

"I thought you gave that guinea Giordano chapter and verse on your old pal Street. You told me you did. What the hell happened? He beats it out of the country and no one seems to give a damn. Isn't there any law anymore? Any justice? What the hell's happening to this country?"

"Stanley, I told Giordano everything I knew. How can you blame me if the feds don't do their job? Do you think it was pleasant spending all that time down in Foley Square? I hate lawyers. They frighten me."

"Everyone frightens you, Adam," Baltimore said. "If you had any balls you would have relished putting the shiv to Street. Didn't he screw you? Didn't he bring in that dame when you were the king?"

There was more abuse. Adam was becoming inured to it. He hated and feared Baltimore and avoided him when he could. The work itself went well; business was excellent. The trouble was Baltimore. He'd bullied Adam into betraying Marc to the feds. Now he was bullying him because the feds hadn't dragged Marc off in chains. Why did he hate Marc so? Or did Baltimore hate everyone?

Thank God for Luke. He'd moved into Adam's Fifth Avenue apartment. Their relationship was going smoothly. Of course, the boy was a hustler, using Adam to help his career, and Adam was perfectly willing to be used. It was a simple exchange: he helped Luke and the young actor gave him what he wanted.

Baltimore, as he'd told Adam indignantly, had lost all patience with the Justice Department and sought out another appointment with Giordano. The assistant U.S. attorney came uptown to lunch with Baltimore in his office in the GM building, such were the priorities. Baltimore told him of his dissatisfaction.

"That man Street is a criminal. He ought to be in jail."

"Come on, Mr. Baltimore, he was nineteen years old when Lazer began to use his company as a conduit for funds. It's been years since Street broke with the mob. At worst, we could have gotten him fined. The chance of a prison term was never more than marginal. The inconvenient part is that Street could have helped us nail Lazer easier. We'll get him anyway. I feel confident. Street would have helped, is all."

"You don't seem upset that he's run away."

Giordano shrugged. "Annoyed. Maybe a little pissed off. What the hell, Mr. Baltimore, not everyone's a friendly witness. You roll with the punches."

"Not in the America I remember," Baltimore said piously, reminding himself to mention Giordano's slovenly attitude to the attorney general the next time they dined in Washington.

Giordano didn't take it personally. In his experience, the bigger the crook, the louder the outrage at the suspicion that someone else might be getting away with something. And from what Giordano knew of Stanley Baltimore, he was no altar boy. But it was strange, this obsession Baltimore had about Marc Street; more than dislike, it was hatred.

Baltimore raged in frustration. The son of the man who scarred him had evaded justice, had gotten away with his criminality, had escaped. But when his fury at Giordano's incompetence had cooled, Stanley became again the shrewd and calculating man the Avenue feared. If Street was out of reach, his whore wasn't.

He renewed his pass at Chelsea West.

She refused his offer of dinner, and in the end he visited her at Majesty. She was working on the new collection without benefit of French patterns or toiles and without Dufour, let go in an economy move. She wore faded jeans, Levi's rather than her own, sneakers, and a Princeton sweatshirt. Her hair was tied up in a ponytail, and her nose was shiny. She knew how she looked. She was damned if she were going to primp for Stanley Baltimore.

"This company's washed up," Baltimore began.

She laughed. "I'm glad you've decided on the diplomatic approach, Mr. Baltimore, I was afraid you might come on tough."

"Diplomacy wastes time. Majesty was in trouble before. Now that your boyfriend's taken a powder, Majesty is a shell. Heidler's an old man. You lost your assistant. You can't possibly keep this thing going very long. You'll wear yourself out and still end up dealing with a bankruptcy referee in Chapter Eleven. Even if the government doesn't arrest Street, Majesty is finished."

"Don't be wishy-washy now, Mr. Baltimore. Speak right out."

Sarcasm poured off him like water off a turtle's back. He ignored her words and made his bid. Majesty was doomed and she, as its one asset, had to get out now before she ended up holding the bankruptcy bag and having her own assets attached. She had talent, even a competitor could see that. Those Geaux West jeans were a gimmick, but a cute gimmick. If she quit Majesty now, he'd offer her a big contract. Her own studio, assistants, her own label. He'd take over the perfume as well and launch it properly, not in some slapdash manner. Money wasn't a problem. She should tell him what she was getting now. He'd top it. His lawyers could work it out with hers. He had already forgotten his pledge to Adam that he would be the only designer at Baltimore Industries. Baltimore licked his lips over what Street would feel when he learned that his girlfriend had deserted him and gone to work for the enemy. What sweet revenge. Even sweeter, if she took his offer, was the possibility their relationship could mature into something more than a business deal. She wasn't really his type, but even the hint of an affair would humiliate Street, destroy him. All Chelsea had to do was say yes.

She said no.

Heidler shook his head. "Chelsea, that's a bad man. He hates Marc. I hope he's not going to take it out on you. He's a man who doesn't like to be refused."

"The hell with him, Sydney. We Wests don't like to be pressured. We don't take kindly to it."

Sydney sighed. He wished Marc were here.

47

Reaganomics may be voodoo stuff, as George Bush once
said (and since regrets), but interest rates are at last coming
down. Business prospects are brighter.

Mode, March 1, 1982

Marc burrowed into Paris like a worm.

His friend Didier found him an apartment in the rue de
Boulainvilliers, in the Sixteenth, a narrow, winding street that ran
from La Muette to the Seine, studded with chocolate shops,
butchers, stationers, a bakery that sold hot croissants and ba-
guettes fresh from the ovens, and a zinc bar where they sold bundles of kindling and of firewood, split and aged and ready for the
fireplace.

On charges like these, extradition was a rarity. He didn't
need Addison, Burns to tell him that. Still, there was no need to
take out advertisements. It was a season for low profiles.

He had gone to work. A jeans manufacturer who owed something to Didier took Marc on. They were big, with factories in the
South of France, in Italy, and in Flanders. The first few times he
crossed a border and handed over his passport, he tensed. Who
knew how far Giordano's tentacles reached? Nothing happened at
any of the frontiers. But for the first time in his life, he knew how
his father and mother must have felt forty years earlier as they
worked their way across Europe and to America. He knew what it
was to be a Jew in Europe.

The salary wasn't much, but that wasn't the point. The work

attracted him. For the first time in his life he wasn't the boss; he was working for someone else. And he was back in the trenches, working at the most basic level: quality control, vat dying, production-line work, supervising the pattern cutters and the denim industry. For years other men had done such work under his direction. Now he was doing it himself, sleeves rolled up and tie loosened. Had anyone predicted a year ago what he'd be doing, he would have shuddered. Surprisingly, he found himself flourishing. He was working at a trade he knew and loved.

"He knows! he knows," so went the exultation of the men he worked with.

He knew sizing and styling and dyeing and piece goods; he knew price and markup and co-op money; he knew how to judge a sketch and to assess a design, how to cut and sew. He knew what he ought to pay for zippers and what he should get from the dealers in denim scrap. He knew about selvage and he knew about country-of-origin labeling, to satisfy the law. He knew who shipped fastest and who shipped best, who had to be bribed and which models should wear the jeans.

He shrugged off Gallic acclaim and went to ground, pulling work in over his head, ten hours, twelve hours a day, six days, sometimes seven days a week. The work was good, the apartment, in the dank, cold Paris winter, drafty but spacious and homelike. Down the street on the avenue Mozart there was a movie house, a couple of working-class restaurants, a bar, the shops where he could buy anything he needed. No one knew him; he knew no one. But the *concierge* nodded as he swept the sidewalk, the woman who sold firewood wished him good morning, a child thanked him when he kicked back an errant soccer ball. Had Chelsea been with him, he would have been happy.

There were women, of course; this was Paris.

He met them at work, and walked away. He remembered old Heidler's paternal advice: "Never dip your pen in the company inkwell." He hadn't needed Sydney's counsel, not until Chelsea. He'd always known. Sometimes, in a restaurant, sitting alone over dinner, drinking Beaujolais and eating a steak and *pommes frites,* perhaps reading the late edition of *France Soir* or that morning's *Herald Trib,* a glance caught his. Shopgirls, young women who might be students or artists, older women experimenting on evenings their husbands were somewhere else, the occasional *poule,* watching him over the rims of wineglasses, smiled, then looked provocatively away, or fixed him with a stare. He felt the old stirrings. As February thawed into March, he felt them. Chelsea had become not only a lover but a habit. He wanted the chic French girls he passed on the street or saw in the shops or faced across the sawdust-covered floors of small restaurants. But he threw himself into sublimating work, shaking off the dull ache of hunger and loneliness.

If he missed Chelsea, and longed for the taste, the touch, the smell of a woman, he missed home, he missed America.

An American girl won an important ski race at Megeve and he found himself watching her on television and grinning. He enjoyed seeing the occasional big American car tooling heavily through the Paris traffic, past the *deux chevaux* and the Simcas and the Peugeots. The *Herald Trib* was full of stories about the college basketball playoffs. The baseball teams were heading for Florida and Arizona and spring training. The winter book on the Kentucky Derby odds was being debated. Reagan was doing odd things in Washington and what seemed a dozen Democrats were maneuvering for the dubious pleasure of challenging him in '84. Inflation was going down at home, the Oscar nominations were out, there was a late blizzard in the Rockies; the rites of spring. Home.

A man died thirty-five hundred miles away in New York, and suddenly in France, Street was on the run. No one was meant to die; it just happened. In the world of criminals like "Uncle Carl" Lazer, no one shot policemen; least of all did anyone kill federal agents. You tried to avoid them, and if that failed you offered bribes. If the bribe was unavailing, you retained the best lawyers you could afford and set about fixing the jury or finding a pliable judge. It had always been Lazer's way, had always been effective. His people understood this. The problem was that Jocko Collins didn't.

Collins was one of Swaggerty's Westies. "Collins is nuts," Swaggerty once remarked, "and me and him both know it."

Lazer didn't know it. Swaggerty had hired out his people to Lazer. When the heat came down from Giordano and Foley Square, Lazer decided to cut his losses, sending his key men out of town, out of the country until things had cooled off. He himself would stay. He was too old to run and had too much faith in crooked judges to worry. But he didn't want his people being swept up around him. Organizations took years to construct. Men with criminal records, men with outstanding warrants, men who were vulnerable, were given neat bundles of cash and told to get lost. But since a man like Carl Lazer does not go unattended, any more than popes venture abroad without a retinue, other men had to be hired. Swaggerty supplied them. Some of them, like Collins, had criminal records.

Collins had been arrested sixteen times and had served eleven years in various prisons. In his time he had killed a college student–hooker, an ex-pug named Holman, and a Ninth Avenue hoodlum whose name even the police had forgotten. He had never served a day for any of these killings. His jail time had come for convictions on the sale of untaxed cigarettes from North Carolina, hijacking, counterfeiting, weapons possession, gambling, rape, and assault. He enjoyed hitting people, worried about his sexuality and hated women, and carried two guns, a military-issue Colt .45 in a shoulder holster and a .25 caliber Beretta he stashed, detective-style, in his sock. When he was not working, Jocko liked to watch the cop shows on television. Usually he rooted for the cops. The criminals were always such jerks he found it difficult to empathize with them. This despite the fact he was himself a moron.

Swaggerty knew all this. Lazer did not. All Lazer knew, or cared, was that Collins was tough, was experienced, and that Swaggerty had always been a reliable source of muscle.

On the morning of the killing, Collins was a time bomb waiting to detonate. The night before he had picked up a girl in a West Fifty-fourth Street bar, taken her to a hot sheets hotel, and, when she asked him for money, broken her jaw. Then he had stripped her and, ignoring her blubbering, sodomized her bloody mouth. The experience had not been very satisfactory, and Collins was still sulking about it when he reported for sentry duty, with another Westie, at Lazer's office on lower Seventh Avenue. He was drinking Diet Pepsi out of a can when four of Giordano's men, two accountants and two federal agents, came in with a subpoena for still more of Lazer's books.

"Go ahead," Lazer told them resignedly, "take them, you should get eyestrain." The important books had long since been destroyed or shipped out of the country.

Collins did not know this. He resented the intruders. They had none of the smooth of television cops. And when one of the feds, small and pugnacious, pushed Collins out of his way to gain access to a file cabinet, causing some Pepsi to slosh from the can and spill on Jocko's trousers, Collins pulled out the big Colt and shot him three times in the stomach.

They cornered Jocko Collins that evening in an empty lot off Tenth Avenue. Someone had seen him drinking in an Avenue saloon, and when the first prowl cars screeched up, he had run for it, the Colt in one hand, the Beretta in the other. He got off a half dozen shots, grazing one policeman and hitting a passing wino in the foot. He died cursing and choking on his own blood, somehow confusing himself with the girl he had beaten up and wondering why the blood was bubbling from his lips rather than from hers. But by then the federal agent, whose name was Tiel, had died in St. Clare's Hospital.

Giordano went berserk. "Goddamned Jewboy Mafia! Killing my people! I'm going to send up that bastard Lazer and everyone he ever touched!"

A new grand jury was instantly convened, and before the week was out new indictments had been handed up for Carl Lazer as an accessory to murder and for fourteen of his associates on various charges. Among the fourteen, Marc Street.

Chelsea called him the day after the shooting in Lazer's office.

"They must be crazy, killing FBI men like that."

"I never thought Lazer would be that stupid," he said. "Always so smart, so smooth, so businesslike."

"Until now," she said coldly.

He was trying to be businesslike himself, not to panic.

"Look, Chelsea, go see that lawyer at Addison, Burns. Get a quick reading from him. Find out what this means for me. Maybe it doesn't change anything, but I wouldn't bet on it. That guy Giordano doesn't like me very much."

"But you weren't there. You were three thousand miles away. How could it affect you?"

"That won't stop Giordano. As far as he's concerned, I'm Lazer's man, I washed the money that helped kill that cop. That's all he knows, all he cares."

"I'm flying over. I can be there tomorrow night."

"Don't be stupid, Chelsea. By tomorrow night I may be running. Get to that lawyer in the morning and call Didier. Tell him whatever the lawyer tells you. He'll get word to me."

"Darling, you can't run away. That'll just make it worse."

"How can it be worse?" he said bitterly.

Addison, Burns was efficient but slow. Its legal advice was expensive, and the firm preferred that it be right. They waited until the indictments were handed up, studied the charges against Street, and had their people in Washington check the current status of the extradition treaty between the United States and France. Not until then did they offer Chelsea an opinion.

Street had moved again. He left some money in an envelope for the woman who owned the apartment in the rue de Boulainvilliers. She was a countess, and a drunk, who spent her days drinking at the zinc bar next to the butcher shop. The phone was in someone else's name, as was the electricity and the gas. In France you paid taxes on your apparent wealth, and no one's name was on anything. Marc paid everything in cash. The man who came to read the meter didn't care. Why should he? *"C'est la France."* Still, it seemed prudent to move. Not even Didier had the new address. He phoned his boss at the jeans company and told him that he was ill and would not be back. There was an explosion of French indignation. Never had they had such a competent man, and now they were losing him. Marc listened for a time.

"Je regrette, monsieur. Je m'excuse."

The jeans maker was still objecting when Marc hung up.

Didier gave Street the bad news when he called.

"Chelsea says Washington is contacting the French government. They think they can get extradition. Your lawyer agrees. But he says to tell you no one knows what the French will do. The problem is that while they try to decide, they'll arrest you and hold you in jail."

"Can they do that?"

Didier paused. "Marc, the French can do anything."

Marc waited. Then, his voice flat and defeated, he thanked Didier. "You're a good man. I appreciate everything you've done for me. Please tell Chelsea she won't be hearing from me. I'm going to drop out of sight for a while."

"Marc, you're sure? I know some excellent French lawyers."

"I don't trust the law anymore. Tell Chelsea to get the hell out of Majesty. The company's dead. Tell her to forget me."

"Marc—" Didier said. But the connection had been broken.

He found a florist's shop near the Place de Porte-des-Ternes and paid in cash for a dozen roses to be cabled to an address in New York. The card read: "It just wasn't meant to be." He signed it "M."

Rain was falling as he walked back toward the small hotel near Auteuil. The streets were slick and the evening rush-hour traffic sloshed by hardly faster than he was walking. He didn't want to talk, not even to a cabdriver. He had lost his company; his country; he had lost Chelsea; it was likely that he would soon lose his freedom. Everything he had a year earlier was gone. It was a bitter, empty feeling. He had forced the break with Lazer long before Giordano ever started his investigation. He had risked so much to turn Majesty into a clean operation, something of which he, or anyone, could be proud. He'd defied Lazer, he'd made Adam a star, he'd found Chelsea.

Now he was beaten. Back in New York, Nixon might be dining at Le Cirque. But because a crazy gunman had shot a policeman, his life, his work, his everything had been destroyed and he was on the run, a fugitive.

He walked alone through the rain, past warm, lighted windows behind which honest people lived.

48

Must viewing this week over ABC: Barbara Wawa's interview with Adam Greenberg. Will young Adam be polite or
will he tell us what he really thinks of former partner Marc
Street?

Mode, March 8, 1982

Adam roiled in confusion. In a way, weights had
been lifted from him. Street had betrayed him and now was being
punished. He was relieved that he was no longer a part of Majesty
and the vicious wave of rumor and ugly publicity now washing
over it. Chelsea was being paid in full for turning from him to
Marc, for daring to challenge his design supremacy. And yet,
there was the memory of the good years, of the fame and fortune
. . . and the love of two men . . . that had begun over a cup of coffee in a café near the Madeleine.

"Of course I feel sorry for Street," he told Barbara Walters
during an interview for television. "He gave me my chance, my
very first shot. We met at Chanel's funeral. We'd gone to Paris to
mourn the woman who inspired both of us. Her funeral. In the
Madeleine. He'd seen some of my sketches, and the funeral gave
him an excuse to talk. Back in New York, we spoke again. His was
a small house, unimportant, but he sensed that with me it could
become something . . . else."

He paused, smiling sadly.

"It did. The Coty. The business. He saw what I had, what
I would become. Majesty prospered. He was the owner, I was
the designer. I did the work, and he rang up the sales. No, let

me be fair. He worked like hell with me. We were a team."

He hesitated for a moment, effectively, the moment choreographed.

"I can't believe Marc Street is a criminal. He was my friend.
I wish all this were over and he was right back here on Seventh
Avenue, competing with me. That's what this country is all
about, after all: competition."

The interview ran on ABC, on *20/20.* Stanley Baltimore
gave a small party in his townhouse the night it was aired. "Fucking brilliant, Adam, that line about America. You're a goddamned genius."

Adam smiled shyly. He was still afraid of Baltimore. Stanley's pet senator was there, a Broadway actress and her husband,
the one whose name no one could ever remember, an editorial
writer for the *Times,* the man who owned the Kentucky Derby favorite, the owner of a hotel chain, the boy who played opposite
Brooke Shields in her latest movie, and a rich woman who
lunched with Nancy Reagan.

"I'm going to insist that Nancy see your next collection," the
rich woman whispered. "It's time she broadened her horizons
from Galanos and Adolfo and Bill. She'll love your things, I
promise you."

Adam thrilled to think that another First Lady might soon
be wearing his clothes.

This was the way it was now for Adam, he and Marc children again, sharing a seesaw, Marc's end down, touching the
playground's pavement, while Adam was up, high in a sunburst
sky. Nothing could bother him now. Even Baltimore seemed to be
mellowing, falling under the spell of Adam's greatness. A week
before, nutty Charlie Winston had come calling, clutching a
portfolio of sketches and accusing Adam of plagiarism. A year
ago, Adam would have trembled and Street would have sent him
money, anything to avoid a messy scene. This time, Adam
snapped his fingers and Winston was taken by both arms and
thrown out of the office, his battered portfolio disdainfully tossed
after him, landing on his sobbing body.

At the height of the party, Baltimore took him aside. Stanley
had his usual glass of mineral water; Adam was drinking Cristal.

"Adam, we've done pretty well for ourselves."

"Yes, Stanley."

"We can do even better."

"I think so."

"Getting rid of Street was a break. We played that one smart."

Adam said nothing. He wondered where Marc was now, tonight. Baltimore had no regrets, no curiosity about his fellow man, only sour delight that Street had been ruined.

"The boutique plan is moving along. Adam perfume is doing well. Except for those phony French jeans, Majesty is going down the tubes. I talked to that bitch, Chelsea, offered her a job. She said no, damned fool."

"Wait a minute, Stanley. That was what caused the trouble between Marc and me. I was supposed to be your only designer. Remember?"

Baltimore was smooth. "Of course that was the deal. And *is*. But if I got her name on a contract and then just put her on the shelf, who would holler? Eh?"

Adam had to smile. Sometimes he thought *he* was ruthless. Compared to Baltimore, he was a baby.

Stanley went on. "I want you to talk nice with Lincoln Radford tonight. He's a prissy old party, but what he writes is important. John Fairchild didn't come. Call him tomorrow, make a lunch date. Get them all on our side, Adam. I'll take care of the fashion magazines. Who do you know at the *Times*?"

They talked. Or rather, Baltimore talked.

"I'm proud of the way you screwed Street. Couldn't have done it better myself. Of course, we got a break when Street ran. That was lucky."

"Well . . ."

"I know. I mean, it's too bad he got away. But listen, that's life, isn't it? And it sure nails Street. Say, Adam . . ."

"Yes?"

"You got any bad stuff on Lauren or Calvin Klein or any of those other guys? I mean, real dirt? I could lay it off on this U.S. attorney what's-his-name."

"Giordano."

"That's it, Giordano. Wop. If you come up with anything, let me know. I'll pass it along."

Genghis Khan had not been invited. You never knew what he might do or say. All they needed was to have Genghis busted for coke in Stanley Baltimore's house. Luke was there, preening himself and basking in Adam's glory.

"Adam?" he said that night when they were in bed.

"Yes?"

"There were movie people there tonight."

"Yeah?"

"I was talking to them about producing movies, you know, where the money comes from, how it's spent."

"Yes?"

"Adam, you could make movies if you wanted. You have the money, you have taste. It might be fun, like fashion, except even bigger."

Adam laughed. "And they'd all star you, Luke."

"Not *all*, Adam, just the big ones."

After Luke fell asleep Adam lay there staring at the ceiling and thinking.

He'd been thinking about it ever since that trip west. Of course, Luke was thinking only of himself, which still didn't make it a bad idea.

Like fashion, only bigger.

Baltimore had taken several of his guests to Le Périgord for dinner, and now, toward midnight, his limo rolled up to the curb in front of the townhouse. He was alone, and he sat there for a moment, savoring the event. His man Adam had done well. The guest list had been carefully chosen. Barbara Walters had not come, but she had a plausible excuse. Various of his guests had gotten drunk, had said stupid things, had laid themselves open. Baltimore, who never drank, never smoked, never took drugs, and remembered everything, catalogued what he'd heard, what had happened. Who knew? Some of it could one day be . . . useful.

"Sir?" It was the chauffeur, waiting for instructions.

"Oh, yes, you'll have to wait. I have a guest. She'll be going home later."

The new model, the pimples-and-acne girl. Lester was to have her here. Baltimore had considered producing her at the party, his latest "star." But with children, who knew? She might have done or said something unseemly, and he couldn't have that. A big man, moving heavily, he got out of the car, his sharp nose sniffing the night air, imagining that sometime, along this street, a woman might have passed wearing one of his scents.

The girl was in his bed, wide awake and watching Johnny Carson. Lester was reliable.

"Hi," she said, "was the party fun?"

"Great fun. When you're older, we'll have to have you at my parties. There are movie people there. They'll love you."

"Hey, super!"

She was wearing an oversized T-shirt. She looked up at him now, her small, shrewd face alert and expectant. "And am I going to be a star?"

He looked at her. She licked her lips and stared right back.

"You're a star now," he said, his heart pounding in his chest.

"Good," she said matter-of-factly.

He laughed. "You're so young. Yet you always seem to know exactly what you want, what's right for you. Where did you learn all this? Who taught you?"

"My mom, mostly," she said. Then she added, "And boys."

He pulled off his necktie and sat down on the side of the bed.

"Tell me about the boys," he ordered.

She did. In some detail.

An hour later they lay in bed, the girl cradled in his arm, her hair straying across his chest and shoulder, his thick fingers playing with a nipple that was barely there.

"What do you want me to do now?" she asked, her voice concerned and eager.

He thought for a moment. Thought of her legs. And her mouth.

Then, testing the girl, always pushing a thing to its limits, he told her. It was a disgusting thing, and even with all his experience, he was not sure what her reaction would be.

She turned to him and fixed his eyes with hers. "That sounds like fun," she said, a sly smile on her child's face.

In Baltimore's world, there was always a quid pro quo. "And after you do it, what do you want from me?" he asked, still incredulous.

She paused, but only for an instant. "You have a lot of pull, don't you?"

"Yes, some."

"Okay, then."

He waited. She smiled. And then, a child who knew where the candy was, she said, "Make me Brooke Shields."

49

Curious, isn't it, how quickly even the most celebrated
names are forgotten once they vanish from the front pages?
We refer, of course, to Marc Street.

Mode, May 14, 1982

erhaps it was in the blood, the instinct for survival, the resource—the canny intuition that saw French Jake across the
deadly borders of Hitler's Germany and into a Paris underworld—that now surfaced in his son.

At first Marc went into hiding, not in Paris, where he knew
too many people, but in Normandy, where he had once flown in a
hot-air balloon with Malcolm Forbes, high above the châteaux
and the rivers, the tilled ground and the farmhouses, the postage-
stamp villages at the crossings of dusty provincial roads. He
thought of that weekend now, of the fine wine and the lavish dinners, the beautiful women and the celebrated men, the French
horns blaring at morning mass in Forbes's own old stone chapel,
the Norman dancers swirling, the lavish sense of fun and
fête. How different now, a Norman winter, bleak and cold. No
tourists, no bike riders on the winding roads, no one working the
fields, no sullen farmers to greet descending balloonists with
open, grasping hands, demanding payment for crop damage, real
or imagined.

He took a room in a small resort hotel between Bayeux and
the invasion beaches. Business was so slow the dining room was
closed, and he took his meals in a nearby bistro or in the restaurant of the railroad station. He rented a bike one morning and

cycled to the American cemetery. He had never seen it before. And as he stood there regarding the serried gravestones solemnly and with wonder, he remembered hearing a man talking about the cemetery at Forbes's party a few years before, calling it "charming."

At the hotel the maid who did his room watched him narrowly, and in the village old men leaned their heads together as he passed. This was stupid, he realized; a stranger in out-of-season Normandy was to be remarked. The fourth or fifth night he was there he drained off a glass of Calvados, raw and powerful, and decided it was time to run again. Great cities were for hiding. He paid his bill in cash and took the morning bus to Bayeux and the train to the Gare Saint-Lazare in Paris.

In a secondhand shop he bought a gray suit and at Prisunic a couple of polyester shirts, underwear, and socks. He changed in the washrooms of the *gare* and threw his American clothes away. He had money, about twenty thousand dollars' worth of francs and dollars, all cash. Traveler's checks are not terribly useful when you are avoiding arrest. Buying a glass of brandy here and chatting over a drink there in working-class bars, he came up with the name of a man who might know another man who just might be able to fix him up with a French passport. His French was fluent, and when anyone wondered aloud about his accent, he murmured something about Canada, Quebec, and how *"les canadiens"* would one day carve out independence from Ottawa and the damned English.

The man who knew the other man got him a passport. His name was now Gorin, Daniel Gorin. He had been born in Arcachon, on the Atlantic coast between Bordeaux and Biarritz, a good place to be from since it would, to the chauvinistic Parisians, explain his vulgar accent. He was forty years old, close enough, and widowed. That too, sadly, was close enough.

His new identity cost him two thousand francs, about twelve hundred dollars. For another thousand francs he was able to buy working papers and the usual dog-eared documents French workers carry. Armed with French citizenship and a new name, he applied for and got day work as a laborer in a textile mill's warehouse in north Paris, out beyond the Marche aux Puces, a

drab, windswept place that resembled Newark more than the city
of light. His fellow workers were mostly North Africans, Tunisians, Algerians, a few Moroccans, sullen, unhappy men, shivering in the chill dregs of a late European winter, conscious of
French snobbery and racist contempt. Street was bigger than
most of them, and taciturn, and they left him alone. He knew how
fabric was to be stored and worked steadily, and after a week the
warehouse foreman automatically gave him work when he
showed up in the morning, while other men were turned away
and told to try again next day. At one of these shape-ups an Algerian, angered at being told to come back tomorrow, picked a
fight with Street. The two men squared off as the others backed
away, watching. When the Algerian pulled a knife, Marc darted
toward him, knocking the knife arm away, and then, with a short,
hard punch, splintered the man's nose. No one bothered him
again.

Being a fugitive but not a martyr, he moved back to the Left
Bank and a clean, warm furnished room with a bath in the students' quarter near the boul' Mich'. Here there were plenty of
foreigners among whom he could disappear, passing for a superannuated graduate student. The bars and the restaurants were
better here, there were bookstalls and newspaper kiosks, and almost everyone was a transient. Each morning he took the Métro
north to the warehouse. Saturdays and Sundays he read or
roamed the quarter. Except for traveling through it by Métro, he
avoided the Right Bank. If they were looking for him, that would
be their hunting ground.

The work was dull and hard. He liked the hardness of it,
found himself feeling as fit as when he had played football, losing
a few pounds and tightening up the rest.

In May came the true spring, the light and the smell and the
very sound of Paris wakening, and with May came a promotion.
Lionel, the foreman, called him in.

"Gorin, I'm making you assistant. There'll be a weekly wage
from now on. Eight hundred francs. And keep your eyes open.
These Africans will steal your socks without ever unlacing a
shoe."

Marc shrugged and said, *"Tiens."* In the warehouses of north

Paris gentility is little appreciated. Besides, M. Lionel had already turned from him to tend to more important matters.

Each night he bought the *France Soir* and a copy of the Paris *Herald Tribune*. It was important not to rusticate, to maintain interest. And there was always the chance that there would be something about Lazer, something that would tell him inferentially about his own situation. There never was. Garment industry racketeering in New York was hardly the stuff of international coverage. *Time* and *Newsweek* had European editions, and for a while he bought them as well. They were full of Reaganomics and the Middle East. He found he didn't care. His world became circumscribed. He worked, he ate, he slept. And after a time the determination to maintain interest and not to slip into the bovine passivity of his fellow workers began to erode. When he thought too much, he did not sleep. Eventually, he gave up any pretension to intellectual curiosity. He tried not to think. And then he slept. A self-imposed amnesia was better than remembering.

M. Lionel called him in one morning early in June. There were "difficulties." Not the thieving Africans this time. Wherever there is a garment industry, you will find the rackets. In London and Hong Kong and Haiti, in New York and Paris. This time, it was protection.

"Some variety of *salot*," explained M. Lionel, was leaning on the owners of the textile company that owned this and other warehouses and fabric mills. It was the usual ploy. The owners paid the *"salots"* some money or there might be problems. Shipments would be delayed, trucks stolen, workers beaten up; there would be union grievances, fire. When you deal with thousands of yards of fabric, arson is the worst of such threats. M. Lionel was taking it seriously. So were the owners.

"They going to pay up?" Street asked laconically, as if none of this concerned either of them.

The foreman shook his head. He looked unhappy about it.

"Alors?" Marc said.

"I told the owners you were a tough guy, Gorin. I told them about the day you broke the Algerian's nose."

"Punching an Algerian in the face isn't the same thing as taking on a protection mob."

"I know." Lionel sounded unhappy as well.

Marc shoved his hands into his pockets. "I work here. Ware-housing. I'm not a bodyguard or a policeman."

The foreman raised his eyebrows. "You're not a warehouse-man, Gorin. I saw that the first week. I don't know who you are. I don't care. The *patron* says that if these guys come around, we have to chase them. You and me."

"And if I don't?"

"Then you draw your pay and get out. And somehow the word gets around Paris about a guy with a funny accent who calls himself Gorin."

The threat of exposure was hardly subtle. But Marc said nothing.

"If you help me chase these guys, you get another thousand a week."

Marc said he'd think about it. It was Lazer all over again.

That night, as he ate dinner in a smoky little bistro in one of the winding streets between the boulevard St.-Germain and the Seine, he met the girl.

She was a student, in her third year at the Sorbonne, study-ing in the faculty of law, a Norman from Caen, small, dark-haired, brown-eyed, the antithesis of Chelsea West. Perhaps that was what drew him.

"My name is Anne," she said, pulling out a chair and sitting down across from him at the table, without being asked.

"Fine," he said, continuing to eat but looking at her, amused.

"I've seen you here before a couple of times."

"That's possible; one has to eat somewhere."

"*Garçon!*" she called. "A second glass, if it pleases you."

The glass was fetched and she filled it with *vin rouge* from his bottle.

"I've eaten already, thank you," she said.

"Good, but *do* have some wine."

She smiled at the sarcasm. "Of course. I decided the first time I saw you that you were a tragic figure. That your wife had

run away with a banker. That you were a secret drinker. Or a
Russian spy."

He laughed. He had not laughed for a long time, had not
talked to anyone intelligent. Her face screwed up out of conven-
tional prettiness when she laughed with him.

"None of the above," he said. "I'm really a very dull type."

"Sure," she said, drinking her wine and looking at him over
the glass.

She lived in a dorm, sharing a suite with three other women.
She asked where he lived, the suggestion obvious.

"Where's your boyfriend?" he asked. "Studying for exams?"

"Ha! These kids are such a bore. I'm twenty, you know."

"Oh, an older woman."

She laughed again, a nice laugh. They finished the wine and
then he bought them a *fin* and they went back to his place. She
kissed him when they were inside the door and then started to
pull the navy wool sweater off over her head. She wore a tank top
underneath, molded to her small, heavy breasts. Then she sat
down on the side of the bed and kicked off her shoes and began to
pull down her jeans. They had no designer label.

She smelled faintly of sweat and lilacs, and he was glad she
was there.

He flicked off the overhead light and opened the window
and began to undress.

She moved in with him the following weekend. And on
Monday two men came to the warehouse. Lionel called him into
the office.

"This is Daniel," he told the two men, "he works for the
owner."

The two were thugs, but small, skinny men, tightly buttoned
into double-breasted suits. Obviously, they were not worried
about Lionel. When Street came in, they looked at each other.

"So?" one of them said.

Until this moment, Marc had not yet decided what he would
do. Then one of them made a mistake. He turned his back on
Marc and pushed Lionel.

"Enough talk. Where's the money?"

Without thinking, but knowing instinctively what he was doing, Marc gripped both hands together and swung them at the small of the man's back, as if he were hitting a baseball and his twined hands were the bat.

The man screamed in agony and slumped to the floor. Marc wheeled on the second. He started to reach inside the tight jacket. Marc hit him quickly, three times, in the face.

"*Jésu,*" Lionel said, blessing himself.

On Wednesday there was a phone call for Street in the warehouse office.

"M. Daniel?"

"*Oui?*" Whoever it was had gotten his name wrong. Perhaps that was best.

"The two men you hurt work for me."

"So?"

"So, they were not very good at their work, *evidemment?*"

"*Non.*"

"We can use a man like you in our trade, M. Daniel. The pay is good, the hours can be arranged."

The voice was almost friendly, but Marc slammed down the phone.

After that he went no more into the north of Paris to work at the warehouse, and because he was unsure just how genuine was the friendliness behind the voice, he began carrying Swaggerty's gun. Anne had already seen it in a drawer, under some shirts. Like all French kids her age, she had been brought up on American gangster movies, "*policiers,*" and the gun pleased her. No one she knew at the Sorbonne had a gangster for a boyfriend. She became conspiratorial about the gun, assuring him that no matter how many men he had killed, no matter how many banks he had held up, she understood that he must have been driven to it. It was society's fault. Like most French students, she was a revolutionary, or romantically thought she was. She fell in love with her ideal of him.

It was good to have a girl again. She was nimble in bed, experimental and willing. She wrote him love poems and then, histrionically, burned them. He met some of her friends, grave boys in old tweed jackets and long scarves, pretty girls with horn-rimmed glasses and dangling cigarettes, all living out roles of themselves as students. The actual classroom was dour and punishing; it was more fun to play student at the Sorbonne than actually to be one. At night they strolled in the quarter and went to the movies and sat in tiny cafés and drank coffee and *fins* or drank good, cheap red wine and ate pasta in their apartment or in a half dozen apartments like it, listening to American music played over Radio Luxembourg and telling one another, with exquisite delight, how hard life was, how cruel the world.

Sometimes he was tempted to tell them they were all full of shit, that none of them knew anything. Instead, he grinned and listened and enjoyed being young and careless again, and tried to forget why he was living in Paris under another name and carrying a gun, tried to ignore how everything had come full circle again, with the Paris underworld, forty years after French Jake, reaching out now to his son.

50

Majesty glowed, then, like a nova, faded and darkened. No matter. Another star is born every day.

Mode, October 4, 1982

fter a lapse of nine months, Chelsea was surprised to hear from Toy, and surprised at her own pleasure.

"Of course you can stay here in the apartment," she said. "It'll be like when we were starting out."

It wasn't, of course. She knew no one could go home again. But it was pleasant having her around the apartment, hearing her laugh, listening to the stories of her Hollywood adventures and the curious people she met. She liked watching her move around the apartment, a big, beautiful animal, usually undressed.

"My God," Chelsea enthused, "you stay in shape. Do you exercise?"

Toy laughed. "I fuck."

It was a good time to have Toy there. Marc was gone, not forgotten, hardly that, but she was more alone than she could ever remember. Majesty was finished. Whatever she and Sydney Heidler did, nothing worked. Neither of them had realized just what strengths Marc had brought to the operation. Heidler knew the answers; he lacked the energy to respond to the questions. She was still raw, in many ways still a beginner. Seventh Avenue is a hard school where no concessions are made for the well-meaning amateur. Stores canceled orders, textile mills demanded payment in cash, royalties owed by the Baltimore organization on the old deal for Adam perfumes came sluggishly. And when garment industry hoods leaned on them, they lacked the muscle to fight back, lacked the cash to pay off.

She threw up her hands. "Marc was right, Sydney, it's hopeless."

He nodded. "I know. And I'm sorry. I feel I let you down. I let you both down."

She pulled him to her, resting her head on his stooped shoulder. "Never, Sydney. You've been wonderful. It just wasn't meant to be."

She didn't burden Toy with any of this. The girl wouldn't have understood. Or she would have offered to help get Chelsea money in whatever mysterious way Toy herself got money. Toy knew nothing of the West fortune.

Sometimes Chelsea considered asking her grandfather for help. The sum would have been, to him, insignificant. But he had been so proud of her success, had taken such pleasure in her achievements, what she had accomplished on her own, that it was unthinkable now to go to him and confess failure. Old Will wasn't the only proud West.

She and Toy spent their days together, Toy hanging around the studio and the office, occasionally filling in as a showroom model when the last remaining girl was on a break.

"I can't pay you much, of course."

"I got plenty of money, Chelsea. Don't be so worrying."

At night they stayed home and dined on junk food off trays and watched television. One night they went uptown to Elaine's. Woody Allen was there with Mia Farrow, staring down at his plate, avoiding eye contact. Elaine sat with Chelsea and Toy for a while, carefully not mentioning Marc. His name had disappeared from the newspapers. Occasionally there was an item about Carl Lazer. His lawyers had gotten another postponement or the government was subpoenaing some new bundle of documents. The mills ground exceedingly slow. Not an hour passed that Chelsea did not think of Marc. But only Sydney ever pronounced his name. Just before they paid and left, a television producer at one of the good tables along the front wall came over to chat. He'd met Chelsea, he admired Toy, and he and his friend would like to buy them a brandy.

"Thanks," Chelsea said, "but we're leaving."

Toy tripped out after her, looking back to where the two men sat.

"Would have been nice, Chelsea, no?"

"No."

Toy offered to become her lover. "Would be fun," she said, standing at the foot of Chelsea's bed, wearing bikini pants and a sweet smile.

"Take a cold shower, Toy," she snapped.

"Hot showers is more fun, Chelsea. In California I'm always in hot tubs, hot showers."

"I'm sure you are," she said, fearing she was sounding schoolmarmish.

That night she slept badly. Visions of Toy's body wove patterns in her head. It *would* be fun. She knew that. Smoke a little grass, bathe together, and go to bed. She assumed Toy would know precisely what to do, and would do it superbly. She had not slept with anyone since Marc. It was stupid, she suspected. It was hardly credible that after all these months in Paris he had not found someone else. He had told her to forget him. Easy to say; impossible to do. And before her Toy's body shimmered, sleek, graceful, languorous. It might be fun, it *would* be fun. She found herself breathing faster, and she threw back the covers and went to the window, throwing it open. The night air stiffened her nipples and her hands reached for them.

She went into the bathroom and dampened a washcloth and bathed her face with cold water.

In early October Heidler gave the bad news to *Women's Wear Daily.* Majesty would not show a spring collection. Miss West was taking something of a sabbatical. The fiction fooled no one. And in his weekly column in *Mode,* Lincoln Radford meditated on success and failure, the brief lifetime of a falling star.

"For a few brief seasons, first with Adam, then with Miss

West as chief designer, Majesty glowed, showering us with sparks. Now, too swiftly, its light has dimmed. Another brilliant nova has flared up and gone dark, and the universe of fashion is duller for it. But only for an instant. There are always new stars in the firmament."

Even Sydney Heidler gagged. "Such bullshit, Chelsea."

"I know. I threw up this morning when I read it."

"A hard business, Chelsea. Hard."

Her laugh was short and bitter. "Savage, cruel, unforgiving."

"That too, Chelsea." He paused. "And often so wonderful."

She knew he was right. She had tasted the wine, now the dregs.

"What now?" he asked.

"I might go away for a while. Just get away."

She was thinking of Paris. Of the vague possibility that she could somehow find him.

Then came the summons from Colorado. Her grandfather was again ailing. He wanted her, needed her.

She called Swaggerty to tell him where she'd be.

"You mean, in case he gets in touch."

"Yes, Bobby, if he tries to reach me."

Neither of them had to say who "he" was.

Chelsea West flew west toward home.

51

Mardi Gras in Rio, Saint Patrick's in Dublin, New Year's Eve
in Glasgow—they all pale compared to Halloween on
Duval Street in Key West.

                    Mode, October 25, 1982

T
he man who leased the yacht in whose anchor chain the
body had been fouled was a porcelain sink and toilet manufacturer in Ohio. His name was Neale, and he was on deck around
midnight because his wife was watching Johnny Carson on television in their cabin and he did not understand Carson's mono-
logues. He saw the pale mass bobbing at the chain in the dark,
intermittently luminescent water, and he poked at it, out of curiosity, with a long gaff. Then he understood what it was and he
vomited on the deck, soiling his linen trousers and his polished
Gucci shoes.

The initial police reports were understandably vague:
"White male apparently in his twenties."

The genitals, the tongue, the earlobes, the eyes, all the soft
parts were gone, nibbled away by crabs and scavenger fish and
barracuda. The left leg was missing from the knee down. Even in
the harbor, there were sharks. The lights atop the police cruisers
and the ambulance revolved, red and white in the night. Mr.
Neale, tidied up and bolstered by a stiff bourbon, gave his statement. His wife kept sobbing that she wanted to go back to Toledo, that she had known something was going to happen. Mr.
Neale didn't answer her. He was still seeing that eyeless

face. No one knew who the dead man was, and the Key West police put out a missing persons interrogatory. When the police had gone and his wife had disappeared below, Mr. Neale hosed down the deck for a long time, trying to wash away memory.

It was Halloween in Key West, steamy and festive. What had once been Hemingway's town, and a sailors' town, a Cuban town, now was a gay town, punctuated by long-haired boys on motorcycles, in leather jackets. At Halloween, gayness predominated, with costume balls and street parades and men with thick arms and hairy chests in low-cut evening gowns. It was, said someone literary, "San Fermin without the bulls."

Adam, who did not read, missed the allusion.

He had flown down with his entourage for the week, Baltimore again offering his house, with celebrations in order. The first of the freestanding Adam boutiques had opened in a dozen cities, and the omens were buoyant. Baltimore was spending fifteen million dollars between now and Christmas for television commercials starring the lastest teenaged Brooke Shields clone and plugging Adam perfumes and cosmetics. The November collection was virtually complete, and even Adam, who habitually suffered like most designers from pre–first night jitters, pronounced it "not bad." A big new home furnishings contract with Manchester was in the works. *Wall Street Week in Review* had just touted Baltimore stock, citing Adam's contributions. Best of all, to Baltimore if not fully to Adam, Chelsea West had disappeared off somewhere in the Rockies and Majesty Fashions was being broken up by bankruptcy court.

When the story ran in *WWD,* Baltimore gloated. "We kicked the shit out of him," he declared, "just ran him the hell out of business."

"Well," said Adam, "he had some bad luck."

"The *schmuck* ought to be in jail! You call that bad luck? The *gonif!*"

Adam didn't argue the point.

"Having his pals shoot policemen? Jail is too good," declared Baltimore, for whom no triumph over his rivals was complete without humiliation.

"Well . . ." Adam said, and fell silent. He knew Marc, and by now he knew Baltimore.

Key West would be wonderful, away from Baltimore and among his friends, real friends, not those like Marc who had betrayed him. Resentment ebbed and flowed. When Baltimore railed against Street, Adam perversely thought to defend him. Marc had once been his closest friend, his partner, his brother. It would be nice if . . .

Instead, he flew south in the private jet with Luke and Genghis Khan and a French film director and his girlfriend and the usual traveling squad of models and hairdressers and hangers-on. Luke, surprisingly, was moody.

"Snap out of it," Adam urged him as they sunned themselves naked by the pool. "That's a big breakthrough you're getting on television."

One of the ABC soap operas had offered Luke a job starting in January, a minor role but a continuing one. He could do things with it.

"It's a bit part," Luke muttered. "With all the heavies you know at the networks, you'd think they'd give me something better."

Adam laughed. Then, maliciously, "They might have, if I pushed."

Luke scowled. Adam liked that. Luke was even better-looking when he pouted.

As usual, Genghis had scored some good dope, and days and nights passed in a pleasant haze. Adam was back to working out. He looked good, he knew, felt good. Luke, usually wonderful in bed, pleaded that he was exhausted, upset. Adam put that down to nerves about the television job. For all Luke's bluster, there was a core of insecurity. But why complain? Lacking Luke, there were others. Sex, as someone once had it, was always good: "even when it's bad it's pretty good." A Cuban woman did the cooking, and they worked on Baltimore's impressive wine cellar. For a man who didn't drink, he knew vintages. One of the models had a Polaroid camera, and they took comically erotic snapshots of one another, singly and in tableaux, falling about giggling in sophomoric delight.

"Why, you're so good-looking, Adam," one of the girls said in an honest gush, "you should have been a model yourself, not wasting your time designing the stuff." Adam liked that.

When the coke was especially good, he and Khan slept together. Sometimes one of the girls joined them. It was all too frenetic to be very satisfying, but Genghis insisted. Adam would have preferred being alone with Luke. Luke, sulky, self-oriented, demanding, delicious, but now mysteriously distant.

"He's a whore, you know," Khan announced one morning as they swam. He knew about such things.

"Yes," Adam said, "I know." And remembered Peter Feeley, who was not a whore.

Two days before Halloween, with the town already giddy with preparation, anticipation, they broke with their usual custom and went out to dinner, a dozen of them. Khan knew a place.

"Genghis *always* knows a place," Luke complained. "Doesn't he think anyone else has any taste?"

"Oh, shut up, Luke. *Let* Genghis slave over the arrangements. It's too damned hot to argue."

They went for cocktails to Sloppy Joe's. Tourists bought souvenir T-shirts with Hemingway's picture and drank chilled beer straight from bottles in the style of the place. A jukebox blared. Adam danced with one of the models, a girl with an incredible body and a death's head face. Dinner was in what had once been a private house, up the steps and across a porch, where you expected to see old ladies in white dresses rocking slowly back and forth in wicker chairs. Insects whirled around the porch lamps. Inside, the sitting rooms of the main floor had been turned into three or four small, semiprivate dining rooms. The food was southern and extraordinary.

"I hate chicken," Luke said. He was drinking martinis straight up.

One of the hairdressers had come wearing a woman's dress. No one was offended; almost no one noticed. During Halloween week it was terribly disappointing not to create a stir. The hairdresser kept adjusting his shoulder strap to call attention. Adam made a point of not looking. He hated drag queens. The men who attracted him looked like men, like Luke. Like Feeley.

When they brought the Key lime pie and Cuban coffee, Luke resumed his complaints.

"Pie? Don't they have any Brie?"

One of the women said something then, and Luke snarled back.

Khan giggled. "It's that time of month for poor Lukie. Don't take him seriously."

Luke got up, moving suddenly, his chair banging over behind him. "Fuck you, Genghis! This is the dumbest meal I've ever had."

He ran toward the door. Adam started to rise and then, knowing the boy's moods, fell back into his seat.

"Let him go. He's been on edge all week."

Adam woke in the night to find himself alone. Luke hadn't come home. "The little bitch," he thought, and then turned over and slept once more. Nor was Luke there in the morning.

Genghis shrugged it off. "He got drunk and stopped in one of the bars on Duval Street and got lucky. When the money's spent he'll come limping home."

Adam reckoned he was right.

It was Luke's body they found three days later fouled in the anchor chain of Mr. Neale's chartered yacht. Over and over Adam told the police about the events of that last meal with Luke, about the boy's moodiness, the fact that he'd been drinking, about his nervousness over the upcoming television role. There was no indication at all that he was suicidal. Perhaps he'd been killed. He had some money, a good watch (Adam's gift), and a gold chain around his neck. The cops listened and asked more questions. It was Halloween; the town was full of crazies.

"Goddamned fags," a sergeant groused, "they come down here looking for cock in the bars and they get stewed and get rolled and we have to fish out the damned bodies."

Four days later a coroner's jury would issue a verdict of "misadventure." The body's high alcohol content and the traces of drugs, plus the fact that he still wore his watch, convinced them that they could disregard foul play. Adam waited for the verdict and then flew back to New York. Baltimore pounced on him.

"You asshole!"

"Stanley, don't beat up on me. I feel lousy enough."

He got no sympathy from Stanley Baltimore, who waved in his face a fistful of press cuttings compiled by Lester.

"Look at this crap. They're writing about this little fairy of yours like he was an abused child. They mention that I own the goddamned house. They talk about wild parties. Drugs. Orgies. God knows what. My name's all over the papers. Your name. This *company's* name!"

He threw the clippings at Adam, hitting him in the face.

"This could kill the Manchester deal. You think those rednecks want to sign up a designer who gets his face on the cover of the fucking *Enquirer?* What the hell's this going to do to perfume sales? I'm canceling every television gross rating point I can get out of. If I had a morals clause in your goddamned contract I'd hit you with it right now and walk away, you dumb pansy."

"Stanley," Adam said, with some dignity, "a boy is dead. Doesn't that part of it touch you at all?"

"Too bad it wasn't you, *schmuck.* We might have got some sympathy business."

Adam walked out of the office, with Baltimore screaming at him, "Remember Fatty Arbuckle!"

He could not find the limo when he went down into the street, and he hailed a cab. The cabbie had the New York *Post* on the seat next to him.

The *Post* had covered Luke's death in lip-smacking detail. He hoped the driver would not recognize him. When he got to the apartment Mrs. Onassis was going in and he hung back, not wanting to share an elevator and have her staring at him. She wouldn't do that, he knew. She was too well bred. But he imagined she'd be thinking about it.

His manservant was out. The mail, lots of it, was piled in tidy stacks on the table in the foyer. He ignored it and went into the bedroom and undressed. He lay down, exhausted and drained. Luke was dead. He could see him now, not the foul obscenity they'd pulled from the waters of the marina, but the Luke to whom he'd made love in this bed. Oh, he knew it wasn't love; Luke wasn't the sort of person you *could* love. Or who could give love. But he had been . . . important. The November sun sank over Central Park. And Adam lay there thinking and remembering and regretting.

And wishing Marc Street was there to help.

He slept with the help of a few pills. And in the morning, gray and dreary, he took his juice and coffee in bed and flipped through the stack of mail the manservant had brought in with the papers. There was nothing in the morning editions about Luke. Or about him. Maybe it was blowing over. These were sophisticated times, and there was always a fresh scandal to divert people. No one confused fashion designers with Mother Teresa. Perhaps people were already shrugging their shoulders and talking about something else.

He was feeling marginally brighter when he came across the letter, handwritten, and with a Key West postmark.

52

The letter was from Luke, written in Key West the day before he vanished.

"Dear Adam," it read, "You'll get this when you get back to New York. I went to the doctor the other day. Just before we came down here. He says I've got AIDS. I can hear you now, saying 'Oh shit!' or something. I'm sorry. If I knew it before I would have told you. That's why I wouldn't sleep with you, why I was so nasty. I may be a bastard but not that bad. Thanks for everything you tried to do for me. I still think I could have been a star. Remember me like I was. I don't want to get sick and ugly. Love, Luke."

He was wrong. Adam didn't say, "Oh, shit!" He didn't say anything. He dropped the letter on his breakfast tray and began to cry. For Luke, and for himself.

He had no cogent recollection of the next few hours. Or days. He wept, he raged, he fell apart in despair. "Why *me*, God?" Why to him, of all people, had this catastrophe come about? Immediately, he imagined aches and twinges and pains. He examined himself in full-length mirrors and stared into his own eyes, seeking the first ravages of impending death. His manservant came and went, silent and cowed, either shouted for or cursed away. Adam didn't leave the apartment, barely left his bedroom, didn't shave and didn't wash. Phone calls went unanswered. When the mail was brought in, he threw it in his manservant's face. Then, remembering Baltimore, he apologized, and fell again to sobbing. That first night he got drunk, took sedatives, and sank into a tortured, nightmarish sleep.

In his dreams he drowned, with the awful jaws of carnivorous fish tearing at his flesh, gouging away great chunks of him. And when he tried to scream, his mouth filled with seawater that tasted of cocaine, Key lime pie, and Stanley Baltimore's vintage wine, now become vinegar. In the morning he lay there, fatigued and spent, as if he had never slept.

He thought he had known loneliness before, as a child, as a teenager in Brooklyn finding he was "different," then as an adult when love had flown, when he lost Peter. He was wrong. Those days were Times Square on New Year's Eve compared to the vacancy of now, from which all life, all contact, all human connection seemingly had been drained. A new and terrible loneliness pressed down on him, crushing breath from his lungs. He thought that if he cried, it might help. It didn't. Luke was gone. Always before, when he had lost someone, there had been Marc, sensible, sensitive, loving; always, there had been consolation. Sometimes, if the lost love had been a hustler, Marc would remind him of the fact, trot out ridiculous examples of his worthlessness, gently at first and then raucously, in the end making Adam laugh at himself, at his vulnerability. When the relationship had been more substantive, the other man a Feeley, decent and deserving, Marc offered love and support and understanding, listening to Adam's tale of woe, nodding, agreeing, sympathizing.

Now Adam had not just lost another lover. He might be losing his own life. Brooding, he thought of himself histrionically as a Dorian Gray, but without a portrait. And there was no one to tell.

Baltimore phoned. The call was refused. By now Baltimore's anger had subsided. He realized that Luke's death had melted off the front pages, had become, literally, yesterday's news. He was furious with Adam, but he had a hundred million dollars' worth of Adam products on the shelves and in the pipelines. There were license deals worth even more.

"Why do designers *have* to be fagolas?" he demanded of his executives. None of them dared answer. "I'll never hire another fairy. I'm gonna get the football Giants and teach them to sketch. These homos are going to kill me yet. Why can't they be like everyone else and screw women?"

Adam's spring collection was scheduled for November 11 in the Rainbow Room, high atop one of the great old Manhattan skyscrapers, the RCA building. Baltimore considered canceling. Suppose nobody came; suppose, instead of the usual fashion editors with their flowered hats and veined legs, there was an audience of police reporters and *paparazzi* and gossip columnists. Page Six in the *Post*, Liz Smith, the *National Enquirer* had all requested credentials and front-row seats. The damned thing could become a circus, and the negative-publicity fallout potential was enormous. Baltimore loved publicity, understood and manipulated it. But this was different, another dimension entirely.

He flayed the public relations man, Lester, about it.

"Listen, asshole, they could murder us on this thing. I think we just forget it. Postpone. Cancel. Say that dear Adam had a cold. He's got piles, a hangnail. The son of a bitch is in mourning. His pet canary died. I dunno. Something. Anything."

Not for the first time he wished he didn't have to employ people at all, in any capacity. If he could work only with his pictures, his Mirós, his Monets, his Picassos. They caused no trouble, they never talked back, they didn't get sick, they never embarrassed him. They hung there, beautiful and docile. Human beings were nothing but trouble.

Perversely, Lester enjoyed his boss's desperation. The PR man had once, a long time before he became a pimp, been a newspaperman. He still had the smarts. "Mr. Baltimore, you're absolutely right. Like you, I worry about image, the reputation of the firm, the Baltimore name."

"Damn right."

"Exactly, Mr. Baltimore." He paused for a precise second. "Except that this time is different."

"*Different?* How different?"

"Mr. Baltimore, look, you know this business better than any of us."

"Damned straight I do." He was still furious. There was a girl arranged for this evening and it was no good, this upset.

Lester raced in where even angels might hesitate. "Adam's posed a hell of a problem."

"You're a genius, Lester," Baltimore said, the words dripping with sarcasm.

" . . . and a big opportunity."

Baltimore was an opportunist. "What sort of opportunity?"

Lester didn't wait. He dove in, without ever testing the water.

"A fashion show equals a fashion show. Nothing. Some old ladies from the magazines come. A couple of fairy reporters. Some pictures are taken, and maybe they appear the next day back with the want ads. Television doesn't come. The wire services. The national magazines. Does *People* cover fashion shows? Maybe if Jerry Hall is working. Does *Newsweek?* No, none of them. But this time, Mr. Baltimore, this time . . ."

Baltimore listened and said nothing.

"This time it'll be different. Adam is front-page news. Did this guy Luke kill himself? Was he murdered? Did Adam have anything to do with it? Was there an orgy? What the *hell* really happened down there in Key West? That's what they're all asking. That's what they want to know. This collection is going to be a presidential inauguration and Oscar night and the Super Bowl all rolled into one. It can't miss."

"Lester, you're full of shit."

Baltimore didn't really think so. In fact, he was intrigued by the PR man's analysis. But he hated making things easy for anyone. And for once, Baltimore was out of his depth. Had it been suicide? Or had someone killed Luke? What *had* happened in the house on Duval Street? And why wasn't Adam in the office? Why wasn't he taking his phone calls? Baltimore was not accustomed to being ignored by his employees.

"So maybe it's front-page stuff. But is that what America wants in its fashion designers? Sordid behavior? Drugs? Unnatural sex? Don't we want our heroes and heroines on pedestals and not grubbing around in filth?"

"Yessir, you're right. That's what we'd *all* prefer. But when you have an unfortunate situation like this one, there's no use pretending it didn't happen, that we're dealing with Bruce Jenner. Or Jack Armstrong, the All-American Boy. We've only got Adam, for better or worse. And I say, promote the hell out of that fact."

Even Baltimore had to agree it made sense. Making the best of a bad situation. In the end, he gave the okay. "But if it goes wrong, Lester, it's your ass."

Two days before the collection, Adam had still not reappeared and continued to let the phone ring unanswered. Baltimore went uptown in his limo. The manservant, bullied, let him in, against instructions.

"Mr. Adam is sleeping."

"I'll wake him, gook," Baltimore announced, pushing his way past the terrified man.

His first glimpse of Adam was a shock. The handsome face, haggard and unshaven, the eyes sunken and darting, looked up at him from the huge bed.

"What the hell are you doing here, Stanley? I gave orders—"

"I know, I know."

Baltimore sensed a reckless defiance in Adam's voice, as if he just didn't give a damn about Baltimore, about anything. It was the moment for diplomacy.

"Look, fella, I was pretty rough on you the other day. I was upset, you know. I said some things. But look, you and I, we're a team, right?"

"Go away, Stanley," Adam said, his voice a croaking whisper.

Baltimore sat down in a chair, tugging it closer to the bed.

"Listen, Adam, you don't have to do a damn thing. The collection's finished. The girls, the music, the seating, the accessories. All done just as you instructed before you went south." He didn't want to mention Key West, not wanting Adam depressed by memory.

"Just show up. That's all we need. Come out afterward and take a bow. Get the applause. Hurray for Adam! Kiss the editors and pose for a few pix and get the hell out of there and come home. That's how it'll be, I guarantee it."

"Stanley, I'm not going." The voice, just as weak, had unexpected iron in it.

Baltimore shifted gears. "All right, then, I understand. People say I'm unfeeling. That I'm a bully. Not true. I push people. I don't deny that. I push them to achieve their best. Not for myself; I do it for them."

Adam's voice was a croak, but it was distinct: "Bullshit."

Baltimore threw up his hands "All right, Adam, have it your way. But I tell you this, if you're not at the Rainbow Room the day after tomorrow, it doesn't really matter if your collection is great or garbage. If you don't come out, the word'll be all over town. You're sick. You've cracked up. You're on something. You think Lincoln Radford's going to go easy on you? You think *WWD* isn't going to smell a rat? You'll be washed up in this business. Finished. Manchester will find an out. They'll walk away from the license deal. Your perfume's going to go stale on the shelves. All this," he said, gesturing around the room, but meaning much, much more, "goes out the window. You want that? Is that what you want, Adam?"

"Just want you to go away," Adam murmured.

Baltimore stood up. "Okay, then. I've said all I had to say. Stay there in bed and feel sorry for yourself. The hell with your career. Waste your talent."

And when Adam remained mute, Baltimore took his last shot. "That boy who died, what was his name?"

"Luke."

"Luke. That's it, Luke. Did you ever think that maybe somewhere Luke would have wanted you to put on this one, last great show? Just for him? A kind of tribute? A small farewell? A final gesture in his direction? You ever think of that, Adam, or just of yourself?"

Adam stared up at him, hatred in his fevered eyes. "I'm thinking of both of us, Stanley."

In the end, he surrendered.

Women's Wear Daily wrote: "Adam's greatest collection was also a great triumph of the spirit. When he came through the curtains to receive his standing ovation, pale and slim, clearly a man who had suffered, who had known pain and loss, there seemed to be a new maturity. He now stands with the fashion giants, with the Norells and the Galanoses of yesterday; with the Kleins and Laurens of today, a compleat artist, a surer man."

Lincoln Radford led off that next week's *Mode* with his own juicy prose: "As he submitted to the ritual kisses and hugs of his mannequins, I think I saw a tear trickle down his sunken, ravaged face. I know that if he wept, he did not weep alone. I wept with him. For his tragedy. And his triumph."

The next morning Adam awoke with a low fever.

53

Mauve is this season's navy blue.

Mode, November 8, 1982

Τhe specialist had come highly recommended. His offices were bookish, leathered.

"Mr. Greenberg," he said now, his hands forming a small temple, "I'll be frank with you. This is an area of medicine where we are still groping. But before I elaborate, let me assure you that you do not have AIDS."

Adam's breath went out of him as from a punctured balloon. "Thank God," he whispered.

"Not yet, at least."

Adam groaned.

"Here's the situation. I want more tests. You've lived a hard life. You do lots of cocaine; I can tell. The way you live wreaks havoc on your immune system. We don't know yet what causes AIDS, we have no cure. But we do know that if you keep on drinking, snorting, living fast, you'll increase the chance that AIDS could take hold. As Rilke said, you must change your life. If you do that, all evidence shows that you will survive whatever exposure you might have had. But if you go on living hard, taking drugs, doing poppers, then it's plump up the pillows and administer painkillers."

Adam did not smile.

"Look, I know you're scared. I'd be terrified. But you're an intelligent man. Thus, my frankness. I think you are relatively well, Mr. Greenberg, for now at least. Will you submit to additional tests?"

Adam looked down at the carpet. Then at the specialist. "Of course."

"And as to second opinions, I'd not only agree, I'd insist. There are a number of good men working in this field. I can supply the names."

"Yes, thank you."

It was all so polite, so matter-of-fact, so cool and professional, even reassuring. But when Adam came out into Park Avenue in the low, slanting Indian summer sun, he blinked, unseeing, eyes watering, and stood there looking for his limo for so long and in such confusion that the doorman came to him and touched his arm.

"Yes?" Adam said, alarmed.

"Sir, are you all right? Can I call a cab?"

He took the tests over the next several days. His arm was punctured, his urine bottled, his stool smeared onto little sticks; he was prodded and poked while serious men nodded over him and shoved out their underlips. He went through it in a daze, returning to his apartment after each laboratory or office visit. He tried to eat, having been told to keep his strength up, tried to sleep, to avoid madness. Mail came and was left unread. Phones rang, and his servant, on silent feet, answered in hushed tones and took the names. No calls were returned. Not from the press, not from his friends, not from Stanley Baltimore.

And all the while, Adam remembered the specialist's final, cautionary words. "If you have sex, be very, *very* careful. For your own sake. And for the sake of those you love."

It would be exaggeration to say that a world had fallen to pieces—only the small, intimate circle through which Adam revolved. Which did not make him despair any less. His lover was dead. He was told he was healthy, that his T-cell ratio was, for now, what it should be. But everything had changed, changed utterly. Death seemed near, and in the face of dying—soon or some-day—all he ever was seemed worthless: a career it had taken a dozen years to erect, a life that had taken thirty-five to shape. Thirty-five? Half the threescore and ten the Bible promised. He knew the cliché of a man "cut off before his time," but it had never really registered before. Now it did, thudding home, sicken-ing, terrifyingly final, a verdict of capital punishment without appeal. He knew what would have happened to Luke, and what might possibly happen to him. He had read about it in the *Voice*, in gay publications like the *Native*. The decline, gradual and then swift, the fever, the weakness, the pain, the infections that could, in the end, kill. It could be something as trite as flu, an innocent sneeze a death sentence.

He took his medicine. His fever abated.

In spite of the specialist's warning, he also took other things, trying to erase fear, blunt the cutting edge of remorse: he drank, he smoked grass, he snorted cocaine, he knocked himself out with pills. At least then he could sleep, however shattered rest was by nightmare.

Waking was the time for regrets: for time now short, friends betrayed, opportunities tossed aside, for failure to do more with what he had, for knuckling under to Baltimore, for permitting Genghis Khan to lead him by the nose, for drugs taken and loves lost. He thought, for the first time in years, of his mother. He'd sent money, of course, but nothing more. Money solved every-thing, didn't it? Money and fame, magazine covers and talk shows and his name in the columns. The right table at restau-rants, theater tickets on the aisle, name recognition. "Adam" was sufficient. A barman's greeting, a headwaiter's obsequious smile, a doorman's bow, the chauffeur's salute, and an apartment in Jackie Onassis's building on Fifth Avenue. So far from Sheeps-head Bay, so far from obscurity and poverty.

In more rational spasms, he pondered practical matters. He thought about confiding in someone. Surely it would be better to be able to talk about it, to share fear. In sharing, there might be consolation. Comfort.

If he could talk with Marc . . .

But Marc was not there. Desperate, he went to Stanley Baltimore.

"Jesus, Adam, you look like hell, you been on a bat or something?"

"No, just not feeling well. Had a fever."

"You seen a doctor?" Baltimore demanded, suspicious and hostile.

"Yes."

"Well, that's better," he said grudgingly. These goddamned kids in the fashion business never took care of themselves. Drugs, always drugs. Screwing one another in the ass and getting high. That was all they ever thought about. If they took a lesson from him, no booze, no cigarettes, they'd be better off. Instead, they were obsessed by themselves, their own pleasure. Thank God there were a few men like himself who kept the business going, not junkie perverts like this Adam, who sat here now in Baltimore's office high above Fifth Avenue and the park, on one of Baltimore's couches.

"Well?" Baltimore demanded, pacing impatiently.

"Well, what?"

"When are you coming back to work, *schmuck?* More than a week's gone by since your collection. Business is good when it should be great. You ought to be out there beating the bloody drums, doing interviews with the papers, talk shows, personal appearances at the stores. You expect me to be the brains of this operation and on the main floor of Saks at the same time? Do I have to do everything? You get paid pretty well, you know. About time you earned it."

Adam inhaled. This was going to be every bit as difficult as he feared.

"Stanley, sit down and listen to me for a minute. I've got something to tell you."

Baltimore's stomach knotted. Whenever anyone said he had something to tell him, it was bad news. He flopped onto a black leather chesterfield.

"All right, Adam, so tell me."

He told him.

He expected Baltimore to explode. To rant. To curse. Instead, there was a stunned blankness.

"You mean that kid had AIDS. That maybe you're going to get it. That maybe you'll get it and croak. Is that it?"

"Pretty much. The doctors say I'm okay. But they scared the shit out of me. They'll do their best to keep me well."

Baltimore's face changed.

"This thing contagious?"

"Only through intercourse. Or blood transfusions. Not always even then. I can't give it to you just sitting here."

Baltimore was skeptical. Even a bit scared.

"You all right, Stanley?" Adam asked, amused for the first time since Luke's death.

"Of course I'm all right." But he got up and retreated to the window, another dozen feet away from the couch where Adam sat.

"So?"

"So what? What does that mean? 'So?' " Baltimore barked.

"I mean, what are we going to say about it? To the press, to our people? Do we level with them or do we concoct—"

"You just keep your goddamned mouth shut! Nobody knows about this! *Nobody.* I'll fire anyone who even mentions AIDS. How many ounces of Adam perfume you think women are going to buy when they know the guy who put the stuff in the bottle is going to give them AIDS? You kidding me? How many teenyboppers are going to pull Adam jeans up their cute little fannies if they think they're gonna catch AIDS from them? You're not sick; you're fucking nuts! Manchester will fold their tents and go home on that domestics deal if they hear you've got AIDS. No, Adam, you're not going to say a damned thing to anybody."

"I don't have AIDS. But how do we explain that I'm not working? Because I'm not, I've got my own affairs to attend to."

Baltimore began to pace, being careful to keep distance between them. "All right, all right, I agree on that. You're going to take a break. A what do you call it? A . . ."

"Sabbatical."

"Right, a sabbatical. You've gotta recharge your batteries. Greatest collection you ever did, and now you're taking a break and thinking ahead." He rubbed his scar. "That's good. A guy who can walk away from his biggest success to think about doing something even better. I like it. The press'll eat it up."

"But will they believe it?"

"They'd fucking better," Baltimore warned.

When Adam had gone he called in his secretary.

"You see that couch?"

"Yes, Mr. Baltimore."

"I hate that couch. Have it taken out and thrown away. No, have the janitors burn it. I hate that couch."

When the maintenance people had carried it out, Baltimore went to his office sink to urinate. But first he washed his hands very carefully. The little fairy had shaken hands with him when he came in, "the son of a bitch."

54

Our calendar informs us it is Chelsea West's twenty-fifth birthday. A year ago she had New York sipping from her slipper. Where is she now, one asks?

Mode, November 15, 1982

randpa?"

The old man looked up at her from the depths of a big chair set by the fireplace.

"You, Catherine?"

"Yes. How you feeling, Grandpa?"

"Tolerable, Catherine. No more, no less."

He looked so small, shrunken. He had never been a bulky man, but she remembered him as tall, with coat-hanger shoulders. Now even the shoulders were bent, and he seemed to have lost inches in height. She sat down at his feet, on a hassock. He reached out a lean, spotted hand to touch her hair.

"My Catherine."

"Want me to read to you, Grandpa?"

"No, not today."

A man who all his life had loved books, he no longer read himself.

She had been with him for a month now. She spent her days riding or driving one of the four-wheeled-drive vehicles around the ranch. The November snows had come and she'd been skiing a couple of times. Nights they dined together, and sometimes they talked. More often, he was too tired. He asked how things went in New York and she said, fine, they were just fine.

"Good, good, proud of you, girl."

"Yes, Grandpa."

Every week or so she phoned Addison, Burns in New York. She was paying the legal bills now, on a continuing retainer. There was no news. Washington was still waltzing with the French over extradition. Giordano's case against Lazer was nearly complete, and the trial could start anytime. It was likely that Marc would be a defendant *in absentia.* Heidler called to give her the gruesome details of Majesty's dissolution. She worried about Sydney.

"So don't worry, Chelsea. I have some money, a condo in Miami. What more do I need?"

"I miss you," she said. It was true. She missed New York, the people, the competition, the sense of accomplishment. She missed fashion. She should be showing a new collection now, right now, this week. Instead, she was skiing and nursing an old man and trying not to think of Marc Street. Soon, she knew, she would have to come to terms with his absence. Soon, there would have to be . . . someone else.

One night a week, sometimes twice, she drove the Maserati into Aspen for dinner or for late drinks. She still had friends. Sometimes an attractive man was with them or came over to her on his own. She was tempted, as she had been with Toy. She kept saying no, feeling stupid about it, stubborn, mulishly so. Once she saw Raker across a room, leaning against a bar, drinking a bottle of beer. She felt nothing. He must have sensed it, and turned away to talk to a girl. The fact that she could see Raker and not react made her feel less bad. It didn't make her feel good.

Then she met Ingalls. He was there for the early-season skiing, an oil man from Houston.

"Of course we ski in Houston. Haven't you seen that beer commercial?"

She had. And laughed. It was nice to laugh again.

It hadn't been a pickup. Well, not quite. He was sitting with friends at a table in Bentley's saloon and one of them saw her and got up and brought her over, making the introductions.

"And this is Jeff Ingalls, Chelsea. Don't try to ski with him. He's hot."

He was. They skied the next day.

"Wow!" he said, after their first run.

She looked at him. "You *are* pretty good," she said, "nearly as good as me."

He was also very nice—nothing like one of those television Texans—intelligent, amused, sure of himself without pushing it. He didn't push her. Some instinct told him not to, or perhaps her friends had been talking. She didn't care. She loved her grandfather, she missed New York, but she was twenty-five years old and alive again. Over dinner, she found herself talking about fashion, about how the business had gone sour and died. He understood. He was in business.

"I think you and Mr. Heidler did the right thing, folding it. You can always start again. Get new financing. Go to work for another outfit. Down home, people are always going broke and then they hit a new well or the A-rabs start messing around and, bulldog! you're back on top. That's why I'm always polite to bums on the corner. Yesterday they were me. Tomorrow they could be me all over again and I'll be standing there, mooching."

Street would have liked him, she thought.

He told her stories about Texas, and she told him about her grandfather, stories about Toy, about modeling and growing up and Paris. The only thing she didn't talk about was Street.

Shrewdly, he said, "You've got someone, don't you?"

She nodded. "I used to. He went away."

"There must have been a good reason for him to go. He wouldn't have left you without a good reason."

"There was a reason," she agreed, giving nothing more, grasping Marc to herself.

Two nights later, she went to bed with Ingalls.

She drove back to the ranch in the Maserati in the predawn darkness, tiny snowflakes racing toward her in the cones of the headlights, the car windows open despite the cold, trying to clear her head. She liked Jeff; she'd made love to him with a voluptuous recklessness, holding nothing back. Now there were doubts. Not guilt. But unease, wondering, questioning.

When she was still a mile away from the ranch, she knew that something was wrong. She could see the main house and the cottages and dorms where the married men and the single hands lived, all blazing with light. She glanced at her watch. It was four-thirty.

"What happened, Jesse?"

The foreman took her hand.

"Coal mine fire, Chelsea. Up in Doylestown. One of our mines. Looks like a bad 'un. Men trapped. Your grandpa's bound to go up there."

"Hell, he can't travel, Jesse, you know that."

"Tell *him*, Chelsea."

Will West was in his den, fully dressed and smoking a cigarillo.

"Where the hell you been, Catherine?" He didn't wait for her answer. "I'll be back in a couple of days. There's some men in there. We've got to get them out."

"Grandpa, you've got good people working for you. Let them handle it. You can't—"

"Doylestown Number One was my first Colorado coal mine, Catherine. I'm not sending anybody. I'm going myself, and that's it."

She went with him.

Doylestown was 140 miles north of the ranch. His Rolls-Royce got them there in less than three hours in a raging snowstorm. She rode with him in the back seat, a fur rug tucked in around him. She fell asleep briefly. He did not. His eyes were bright and clear in the daylight when they arrived. But he was pale, unsteady on his feet.

It was a typical western mining town, cut between mountains, a narrow stream running through the town, a stream frozen now. An ugly, squalid town, but in the snow with a Christmas village prettiness. The mine was a few miles upstream of town, driven into the hillside. They could smell the smoke even before they could see the mine entrance. Perhaps fifty or sixty men, and some women, stood there in the snow, waiting. They backed away to make a little path when the Rolls came up.

"Well, Rogers, what's the story?" Will West demanded of the manager.

"Bad, Mr. West. We got twenty-two men in there. Down at the twenty-four-hundred-foot level. It began late yesterday. Fire, then an explosion. Soon as we figured no more explosions, we got a rescue crew in there. They're still inside, working down toward them. But it's slow going. Lots of smoke. They're wearing masks and it's slow."

West nodded. There was nothing querulous about him now. He was asking crisp questions, getting answers.

They had radio contact with the rescue team. At noon a second team went in, and in midafternoon the first group of rescuers came out, haggard, sweat-soaked even in the cold, faces blacked around their breathing masks. One of the men stumbled as he came out, fell to one knee, and then, shaking off assistance, got up and went on. A woman ran to him. He put an arm around her shoulder. Her husband was one of the twenty-two still in there.

They got Will West into one of the shacks. An old potbellied stove glowed red, emitting a reeking smoke. He sat on a straight-backed chair behind a battered wooden desk with a black telephone. A girly calendar hung on the wall. Chelsea kept watching her grandfather, wondering if it was worse for him in here with the smoke or out there in the snow. His face looked better, reddened by the cold. Men kept coming in, and the manager gave instructions. Several of West's senior mining executives were here by now. One of them got into miner's gear. He was going in with the relief rescue party. Will West got him aside and talked to him, poking a finger and making points.

"Grandpa? You want anything?" she asked.

"Yes," he said, "hot tea. If you can find it."

They were brewing coffee on the stove and, lacking tea, he took some in a chipped mug. She watched him, worrying about him, worrying about the men in the mine. Ingalls was forgotten, fatigue forgotten. Even Marc.

"Mr. West?"

A workman had slipped into the shack, shaking off snow to whisper to the manager, who whispered to one of the mining executives. It was he who spoke.

"The press has arrived, Mr. West."

Will West smiled for the first time that day, a bitter smile. "Of course they have. Blood's in the water, isn't it?"

Toward dusk, in a half blizzard, Wild Will West stood before the television cameras and the print reporters, in the glare of television lights.

"There are twenty-two men still down there. A third shift of rescue teams is also in the mine. The missing men were reported at the twenty-four-hundred-foot level. The third rescue team is at two thousand feet. They are encountering heavy smoke, but no fire. We are hopeful. We shall press on."

They took their notes. Then someone asked, "Was this mine safe? Were there dangers?"

Will West stared at him. "In a mine, there are always dangers."

West, or his executives, answered all the questions, or tried to. In a tattered semicircle beyond the television lights, the women and the friends of the missing men, and of the rescue teams, stood there, not asking questions, only listening and watching. Hoping.

At midnight a fourth team went in. The third team reported small fires still burning as they reached the 2,200-foot level.

"It looks bad," someone said.

Will West wheeled on him. "Don't buy the flowers yet. These are tough men, resourceful men. It's bad luck to talk so."

They kept the death watch in the small mine shack and talked away the night over Thermos bottles of sour coffee. She had never felt so close to her grandfather, he had never been this confiding, as they spoke low and close, about anything but the men.

"You remember that time I took you to Paris?" he said.

"Yes," she said, "the day after Chanel died I read it to you from the paper and you said we were to go."

He nodded. "I had to go. A long time ago I'd made my first couple of millions and was thinking highly of myself, too highly.

My wife, your grandma, and I went off to Paris on holiday, crossing on *Île de France*. Not easy living with a driven man, and I owed her a trip. We were still in love then, and I wanted to buy her things. We met Chanel at some fancy party, and she said she'd help my wife pick out a few things." He laughed. "I guess among all those French people we looked like a couple of down-home hicks. But Chanel wasn't snooty about it. She was maybe forty then, a slim, handsome woman with eyes that bored right through you. I was thirty, I'd never seen a woman like that. Her English was terrible, and we had restaurant French." He paused, seeing places and recalling times long gone. "But she was gracious to us, selecting just the right clothes for my bride. We got on very well."

She waited, knowing there was more.

"Then after your grandma and I broke up, whenever I had to be in Europe on business, I made it a point of getting to Paris. She was alone then too, Coco. Funny, I didn't call her 'Coco,' it just didn't come off the tongue. I called her 'Gabrielle.' "

"Like you call me 'Catherine.' "

"Yes," he said. There was a hesitation, and then he said, "She and I liked each other, Gabrielle Chanel and me."

He didn't say more, but she understood. "Grandpa?" she said.

"Yes, Catherine?"

"That day she died, when we read it in the paper . . ."

"Yes?"

"I thought I saw you cry."

He looked at her, his thin mouth hard, remembering Paris, a lost wife, a lost lover.

"I never cry, Catherine," he said.

"No, Grandpa."

Finally she got him to go to the hotel. It was a West hotel and there were rooms for them. She put him to bed, knowing that whatever medicines he was supposed to be taking were back at the ranch.

"Don't worry," he said, "I've been through this before."

She fell into her own narrow bed and was immediately asleep.

In the morning, before six, they woke them.

"The men are dead," a man with a face gray and empty told her.

Her grandfather already knew. "It's the gas. The smoke. We had to try. But ..."

The bodies were brought up, one after another. Men stood bareheaded at the entrance with women in worn parkas and long cloth coats. There were no children. The wives of men who work in the mines know enough to keep the children away. The television cameras were there. No discreet rules for them. West made a statement. For once, there were no follow-up questions. People were afraid of Will West, even reporters.

At noon Chelsea and her grandfather drove slowly downhill from the mine and through the town, people lining the way, their faces set and sad. Perhaps hatred would come later. Now there was just an emptiness, like that of the man who had brought news of death.

As they left town a small boy, his face screwed up in fury and tear-streaked, threw an icy snowball at the car. It bounced harmlessly off the hood, and behind them the boy shook his fist.

In the back seat, Will West croaked, "Good boy. I know what he feels. My father died in the mines. I remember the hate I felt."

He fell back against the seat, buried under lap robes, and slept, his mouth open and his breath like the rale of a dying man.

55

Chelsea West is back in the headlines. It is doubtful she will ever be back on Seventh Ave. Gloria Vanderbilt may need money; Miss West apparently doesn't.

Mode, November 29, 1982

Will West died over Thanksgiving weekend. He was ninety years old. The cause of death was given as pneumonia.

A wire service reporter quoted his heir, Chelsea West, as disputing that. "My grandfather died with those twenty-two men in Doylestown Number One. The mine fire killed him as it killed them."

West's photo and obituary ran on the front page of the Paris *Herald Tribune*. Street cabled her his condolences. He would not know that they never reached her, that the protective ring of lawyers and bankers, accountants, company executives, directors, and trustees had already closed in on her, that the hundreds and even thousands of messages received were being handled by Carl Byoir, the public relations firm.

Chelsea was barely mentioned in the *Herald Trib*'s report. It remained for others to correct the oversight.

She was now, tabloids in New York and Los Angeles and Chicago and Fleet Street declared, the third (or fourth or second) richest woman in the world. *People* magazine ordered up a cover story. *Women's Wear Daily* speculated whether she would ever return to the Seventh Avenue where she had, for so short a time, and so brilliantly, shone. The television news shows ran brief clips from her appearances on talk shows. The newspapers ransacked their photo morgues and ran pictures of her with Adam, with her grandfather, even one snapped at Studio 54 in Manhattan "with her close friend and onetime modeling colleague, Toy." There were no pictures with Marc Street.

As if punishing himself, Street stared at all the pictures, read all the stories. Anne noticed.

"You know her?" she asked him.

"Yes," he said, "we once worked together."

Worked together. Banal and incomplete as a description of who they had been and what they had meant to each other. But sufficient for Anne. It was not that he patronized her; only that he disliked explanations. Talking about Chelsea hurt. Perhaps if Anne had known her, but of course she hadn't.

Will West's death had torn it finally and definitely. He was a man on the run and she was the West heiress.

It was over.

"Daniel?"

"*Oui*, Anne?"

"Let's go to the cinema tonight. There is this new Depardieu film I want to see."

"Sure," he said. This was his life now—a pretty university student, a small apartment, and the movies on Friday night. Comfortable, undemanding, marginally satisfying, and emotionally and intellectually empty. And always the fear that someone, the police or the Paris rackets, would find him. He continued to carry the gun.

In New York and Denver and at the ranch, Chelsea met with her grandfather's men. Now, *her* men. Jeff Ingalls was there when he could be. She found herself turning more and more to him. He had common sense, he knew business, he wasn't doing it for the money. How like Street he was. They had not slept together since Will West's death. Jeff hesitated to push her. These were difficult times. When she was ready, she would say the word, make the gesture. He could wait. She was worth waiting for, he knew, remembering their one night together.

She found Will West's advisers impressive men. Old Will didn't suffer fools badly; he suffered them not at all. A blunder, a faulty judgment, a hint of disloyalty and they were out. The survivors were hand-picked men. They served him well. They would, she was confident, serve her equally well. And she needed their counsel. The West empire sprawled across borders and industries: mining in Mexico and Colorado and Utah, banks in California, textiles in the South and in the Far East, cattle in Texas and Florida, a vineyard in Sonoma, land in Mexico, forests in Canada and Oregon, fisheries in Newfoundland, shipping lines, oil exploration, convenience stores, an insurance company, a resort hotel chain. And there was more.

She met with the executive who presided over each, asked questions and got answers. When the answers were vague or unsettling, she consulted with another, inner circle of advisers, tax men and accountants and overseers who summoned the executive back for a second session, grilling him on the points of dispute and, usually, in the end, getting straight answers. There were other advisers, men who worked at headquarters, supervising the whole thing from afar and above. These men had been especially close to Will West. These were the men who told Chelsea how much she had, and suggested what she might do with it. She listened, impressed, and considered.

There *were* things she wanted to do. Things not traditionally done by or within the West organization.

"A New York garment firm called Majesty Fashions, with which I used to be associated, has been liquidated. Please contact a man called Sydney Heidler. He has all the records. There were some people let go in the last year during the belt-tightening, others who were left unemployed by the liquidation. I want equitable severance paid to those people. Heidler will have the names, he'll know the ones to pay."

It was done.

"A cosmetics and perfume firm run by Stanley Baltimore has been putting economic pressure on its competitors. Sometimes legally, other times not. Mr. Baltimore should be taught a lesson. Is there some way through our retail connections that we can cause him discomfort?"

She was told the matter would be explored. And it was.

"Either in Los Angeles or New York there is a young actress, model, whatever, called Toy. Please check into her whereabouts. Don't interfere. My only interest is in keeping informed as to whether Toy is prospering and whether she is being treated decently. If she is well and content, leave her alone. Just keep an eye on her. Is that possible?"

She was assured that it was.

Jeff Ingalls sat in on some of these discussions, shaking his head in admiration.

"You don't forget, do you?"

"Not when it's important."

He laughed. "Hate like hell for you to have something on me."

"Listen," she said, "my grandpa taught me: 'Always pay off, Chelsea.' And that's what I'm doing."

There were three discussions with experts at which Ingalls did not sit in, about which, in fact, he never knew. They dealt with a man called Marc Street.

The first of these sessions was legal. Lawyers with contacts in the Justice Department were to determine, with precision, just how strong a case the government had against Street and what was the status of Washington's efforts to have him extradited from France.

The second, with Will West's head of security, a former CIA man, was simpler, less delicate.

"I want you to find Marc Street," she said. "He's probably in France. I'll give you pictures, descriptions, habits, the works."

"You want him brought back, Miss West?"

She shook her head. "Just find him. And let me know where he is without tipping him off. Understand?"

"Yes, just find him, leave him, and report back. Don't bring him back."

"That's right. If he wants to come back, he will, on his own."

Her third meeting was with an unofficial adviser.

"Bobby," she said, "it was your man Collins who got Marc into this mess."

"I know," said Swaggerty, "dumb son of a bitch. If the cops

hadn't killed him, I would of. You know how bad I feel, Chelsea."

"Yes, Bobby. What's done is done. Now let's try to figure out some way to make it right. You know Lazer, you know what the cops are up to. Let's come up with some ideas. I don't know what. Let's think. There's got to be something we can do to clear Marc."

"Okay," he said solemnly, "I owe Marc for what Jocko done. I'll figure something, I'll figure a way."

"I know you will, Bobby. You owe him a debt."

He nodded solemnly. He knew that. And he knew that this girl, still so young and so beautiful, was a tough customer who would hold him to his promise. Teeth gritted, eyes narrowed to slits, he grabbed her hand and then left. Of all Chelsea's array of experts and advisers, red-headed Bobby Swaggerty was the least credentialed, the least impressive. And the most dangerous.

56

Let Adam get back to work on the next collection. Or hand
in a note from the doctor.

Mode, November 29, 1982

O
f all those who knew her, Adam was the only one
not obsessed by Chelsea West.

A few months ago he would have been jealous of her great
fortune. They were rivals, she had destroyed what he and Marc
once shared, she was beautiful and talented, and for her to inherit
the West billions would have been all too much to bear. Now it
meant nothing. Only Luke's death, the suicide note, and his own
prognosis meant anything. If he now thought of her at all, it was
in glimpses backward. The concern now was his own future.

No one can sustain the extremes of either joy or despair in-
definitely. Adam hit bottom and, as men do, began slowly, ex-
haustingly, to climb back, beginning to hammer out a crude sort
of personal philosophy.

"Look," he told himself, having no one else, "you could get
sick. Baltimore is still paying you, but who knows how long that's
going to last? Word is going to get out about Luke, about your
tests, your withdrawal. It always does. Some son of a bitch will
speculate in print that you've got cancer or AIDS or leprosy or
that you've had a breakdown. You've got to go on living. Not
only that, but to find a reason for living. Without a reason to live,
there's no tomorrow. Nothing. The thing to do is to sum up: What
do I have? And what do I owe?"

He was not talking about money, though money was part of it.

Adam had a money manager named Fred Bernstein, a good and decent man, an accountant who had handled his taxes and his investments since the big money first started to come in. Bernstein charged him 6 percent of the gross, collected his checks and paid his bills, and provided him every month with a statement of his worth. Adam never read the statements. They came by messenger in a large gray envelope marked "Confidential," but he rarely opened them. Now, suddenly, it seemed important to know.

"Fred?"

"Yes, Adam, what's up?"

"Fred, how much money do I have?"

Bernstein laughed into the phone. "Enough, Adam. Don't you read the damned statements?"

"You know I never understand that stuff. Seriously, how much dough do I have? Cash and certificates and stocks and whatever counts as real money. Not houses or cars or the plane."

Fred got the file. "Well, if you had to get away by jet tomorrow wearing a false nose and a wig, you'd have roughly . . . three million two, three million five, something like that. Why?"

Adam breathed a relieved sigh. More than he thought; enough to live on. "You know, a little trouble with Baltimore. I may be taking a leave of absence. I just wanted to be sure I had a few bucks."

"Anything I can do?"

"No, no. It's fine, I'll let you know if I need anything."

"Good, Adam. You're okay. Tips and all, you're breaking even."

On the first of December he flew to Florida to see his mother. Long since departed from Brooklyn, she lived in a flamingo-pink stucco house off Collins Avenue in Miami Beach. He'd wanted to buy her a place in Palm Beach. More suitable, he'd said. She hated it. Miami was the place. She had friends there, they played cards and gossiped and complained about their grown children and wished they were in New York except when the wind blew or when stories about muggers appeared in the paper.

"So, you're all right, Adam? It's been a long time."

"Fine, Mom, just fine."

"So why are you here? You look thin."

He took her to dinner that night at the Palm.

"Such big portions. Will they give us a doggy bag?"

He had not seen his mother for three years. He paid the bills, or rather Bernstein did, and mailed a check every month for spending money. He took very good care of her. There was nothing between them, nothing at all, and there hadn't been for a long time. She accepted this. As a Jewish mother, she complained but accepted it. His name was in the papers, she saw him occasionally on television, her Miami friends knew who he was and were envious. These things were sufficient.

When they went back to her house she wanted to watch Johnny Carson. Although she didn't say so, she wanted him to leave. At a certain age, routine becomes very important. Instead, he made himself instant coffee in her kitchen and tried to talk. She half listened, half watched Carson.

"So do you ever hear from Mr. Street?"

"No. We had a difference of opinion. I work with someone else now."

"I know. Stanley Baltimore. A fine man, they say."

"Yes, Stanley's quite a guy."

They talked some more, the distances and the years between them slowly closing. He left at noon the next day.

"Why don't you come to New York once in a while?" he asked. "You could stay with me. Or I could get you a nice hotel."

She lifted her hands. "No, I'm comfortable here. It would be nice if you came sometimes."

"I will, Mom, I will."

He meant it.

Miami, and his mother, had been a first stop. Slowly, gradually, in a crude way, Adam had begun a trip backward through life, figuratively paging through old photo albums, remembering, reminding himself, and, where he could, settling accounts. He had debts. Perhaps now was the time that at least some of them should be paid. His mother had been a start.

He worried about Peter Feeley. The doctors were so damned

vague about AIDS. Was Feeley at risk for things they had done? Just what sort of incubation period was there? He read about Peter whenever he bought a gay newspaper: Peter Feeley now worked for the Lambda Legal Defense Fund, which was becoming involved in civil rights activity for those afflicted with a curious disease called acquired immune deficiency syndrome. Adam wanted desperately to talk to Peter, to see him, hold his hand, warn him—but too much time had gone by, and after the publicity about Luke, Peter's gentle eyes would ask too many embarrassing questions. Adam was too proud. Instead of seeking Peter out, he wrote a check for ten thousand dollars and sent it to Lambda without enclosing a note, hoping that Peter would see the check and call him. He sent another ten thousand dollars to a new organization called the Gay Men's Health Crisis, which phoned him, delighted. What more could he do for them, Adam asked. Well, he could read to a dying man. Adam shuddered. Then he thought of Peter, heard in memory Peter's measured voice, and said he would consider it. Peter and Marc Street blurred now in his mind, two identical pillars of a new spiritual home he needed to build.

Death focuses the mind, someone said. Even for a man healthy and scared, that was true.

The doctors had warned him of their own ignorance. While he had the time, the money, most of all the energy, he would try to pay his debts. Anything was better than wallowing in self-pity, loneliness, despair.

Charlie Winston was no longer at the Chelsea. Even that refuge of eccentrics had become too grand for him, and Charlie had taken his resentments, his paranoia, his faded dreams a few blocks south to a single-room-occupancy hotel on lower Broadway.

"Charles!"

Winston sat on a narrow bed, sketching. The dresses he drew were doodles now, drawn on stick figures, ideas he and other men had long since discarded. The elegant Winston style of drawing, which once adorned the pages of *Bazaar* and *Mode* and *Vogue,* was now crabbed and childlike. Winston looked up, staring through rheumy eyes.

"It's me, Adam."

"Oh, yes, you're here for the rent. Well, you see, there's a check coming from Bergdorf's. Mr. Andrew Goodman himself is bringing it down. He—"

"No, no, it's not the rent. Look, what do you need?" He pulled out a wallet and began to peel off bills.

"Yes, yes, I'm a few days behind. The stores pay slow, the bastards."

Adam pushed the money into his gnarled, spotted hand. "Here, Charles, it's for your sketches."

Winston smiled, a wild smile, wild and conspiratorial, now recognizing him. "Yes, Adam, that's right. The sketches I did for you. Of course."

A small roach scurried across the wall behind the old man's head. Winston's face became excited, interested.

"I've done some new ones, Adam. Look at these. The marked waist, I sense it's coming back. Forget the hemline. That can always be adjusted later. It's the waistline that's significant. That and the padded shoulder. Your workrooms should do very nicely with these."

He pushed the sketches at Adam. They were worthless scribbles.

But Adam said, "Yes, Charles, I see what you mean. Good stuff. And you're right about the shoulder, lots of padding."

"Yes, yes, don't let them skimp."

Adam took the doodles and carefully folded them and placed them in his jacket pocket.

"You'll be getting paid every week from now on, Charles. Just keep doing the sketches. I'll send someone down if I can't come myself."

Winston, a small, shriveled man, seemed to become larger.

"Yes," he said, "you've got promise, boy. I'll do your sketches. Don't worry, no shortage of ideas here."

They shook hands at the door. In the hallway a black prostitute was leading a man toward her room.

He paid, or tried to pay, other debts. Of several sorts. People to whom he owed money or favors or consideration. Even love. A man with whom he had long before enjoyed a relationship and who was now in an institution. The aging former president of a Fifth Avenue store, a sour, waspish woman with a frost-pitted face, a woman who had never bought herself a meal or a theater ticket in her life, but who had been one of his first customers. A restaurant owner in the Village who had carried his tab for months and then, after success, had been abandoned in favor of places Gael Greene recommended. And others. He went to them and tried, in some way, to settle his accounts. Sometimes he succeeded. On occasion he was told where to shove his money. And his regrets.

There was another variety of account. Old scores, resentments, early snubs, blistering hates. Those too should be paid off. And now he was to have the opportunity, and the justification, for payment.

It was Lincoln Radford, in *Mode,* who broke the rumors of his illness.

Of course there had been rumors. There is a sort of bush telegraph in the freemasonry of the gay that makes it nearly impossible for secrets to be kept. Somehow it got out that he had been seen consulting various specialists. Two and two were put together. A gay newsletter, campaigning for greater public awareness of and federally funded research into AIDS, demanded to know why "a celebrated fashion designer who recently scored one of his greatest triumphs and then mysteriously dropped out of the columns and off the Côte Basque banquettes" did not come forward to admit that even he was vulnerable to the disease and throw himself and his resources into the battle to find a cure.

Radford, though neuter, read all the gay journals, and now he rubbed his hands. His editorial on the matter was a masterpiece of pious venom:

> Cosmetics king Stanley Baltimore is said to be distraught over the inexplicable decision of one of the world's great designers simply to walk blithely away from fame and wealth. What *is* Adam thinking of? What, if anything, ails the boy? When last these old eyes gazed upon him, he seemed to be in splendid form, a vigorous, handsome

young man. Is Adam out of sorts or out of sports? Let him shake off tragic memories of that distressing moment in Key West. America cannot afford to have its great designers lying fallow. I have often tilted with Stanley Baltimore. In this affair, I find myself very much in his camp. Let Adam get back to work on the next collection. Or hand in a note from the doctor.

Baltimore erupted, not caring about personal tragedy or the destruction of a reputation, but about financial loss. Impotently, he raged and did nothing.

Adam traveled downtown by limousine to Radford's mansion, strode past an impressed receptionist through the padded leather doors of Radford's inner sanctum, and slapped him across his simpering face.

"Fuck you, Lincoln," he said, turned, and left.

Radford burst into tears.

That night Adam was sick to his stomach. But the pleasure of that moment in Radford's office remained. Gradually, unevenly, sometimes awkwardly and absurdly, he was paying off elegant debts. There remained, of course, the heaviest—to Marc Street.

57

Nancy Reagan is shopping early this Christmas. Bill Blass
slipped into the White House Tuesday with the new collection, from which the First Lady is choosing at leisure. Nancy
is down to a size six these days.

Mode, December 6, 1982

A rarity among Jews, Street had always celebrated
Christmas. That was his mother's doing, of course. She had grown
sufficiently Americanized to understand about trees, tinsel,
wreaths, turkey, though Santa Claus was still *Père Noël*. His father
went along with his wife's odd notions. No man ever lived who
didn't like electric trains. That was French Jake's contribution,
the toys under the tree in their latest rented West Side apartment.
When he set up his own apartment, Marc didn't bother with a
tree. But he saved Christmas cards from friends and always attached a bit of holly or a small wreath to the door.

Christmas gripped Paris in early December. There was a
brief, unseasonal snow, shopwindows were decorated, the department stores added evening hours, the newspapers ran ads offering
holiday vacation packages to Alpe d'Huez and Megeve and Val
d'Isère and the other French ski stations, people wished one
another *"Joyeux Noel,"* and outside the churches small weather-
beaten *crèches* sprang up. The chic whores of the Faubourg
St.-Honoré and the gaudy whores of Les Halles greeted unlikely clients. Young girls donned boots and leg warmers, stolid
functionaries wrapped scarves around their throats, children
sported rosy cheeks and runny noses, and the smell of roasting

chestnuts hung like fog around every Métro entrance and corner bar.

Anne was going home to Normandy for the university's Christmas break.

"I don't want to, Daniel," she said, her small face solemn and concerned, her pug nose and bright eyes squeezed together in concentration, "I'd much rather spend Christmas with you in Paris. But my family insists. They're suspicious enough about how I carry on. And there's some vile species of local boy who thinks, against all odds, that he's in love with me. You won't be lonely, will you? No, please say you'll be lonely and miss me every minute and seriously consider suicide. But please don't be sad. Yes?"

He promised everything, no matter how contradictory.

They were growing apart. The generation gap, cultural differences, a child's boredom with familiar toys, his own distraction over Chelsea, all played their role. And the "vile species of local boy" was, he was sure, something far more than that, writing her long, weekly letters, to which Anne replied, puzzling over a pad on her dimpled knees late at night when she thought Street was asleep. It was better this way. She had a crush on Marc; she had been, for him, a pleasant companion, a lover, a human being with whom he could talk and share meals and hold close on those nights when it always seemed to be three in the morning. They hadn't hurt each other, and now it was ending.

It would be good for him for a time to be alone again. He took her in a cab to the Gare Saint-Lazare and helped with her bags.

"I love you, Daniel," she said.

"I know." French girls told you they loved you if you lighted their cigarette.

"*Joyeux Noël,* Daniel."

"*Toi aussi,* Anne."

He walked back to the Left Bank, enjoying the crowds of shoppers and the bustle of the great city and the chill wind come down off the North Sea and across Flanders and into the Île de France.

Two days later he noticed that he was being tailed.

At first he thought it was the French police, but he dismissed that. If the French wanted him, they'd simply pick him up, a fugitive with a phony passport. There could be nothing simpler. Then he wondered if it were some enemy, someone from the rackets. It was possible. People resented things, they sought revenge, stupidly sometimes, but they did. It could be one of the men he had beaten up at the warehouse.

Or simply an overworked imagination. Which might have been the most plausible explanation, because eventually the tail just disappeared. It was as if someone had wanted to find him and, having done so, gave it up at that, and went home for Christmas.

Chelsea's Washington connections were equivocal. The indictment in the Lazer case was still outstanding. Desultory efforts to get the French to cooperate were continuing. But, as a source in the attorney general's office admitted to one of the West lawyers, "the government is after Carl Lazer, not some guy who makes designer jeans, for chrissakes."

Swaggerty went his own way, in his own time, consulting only with himself, seemingly vanished into the vacuum of a murky past.

Ingalls sensed her confusion. They were in San Francisco. She was there to meet with the West bankers; he had flown in from Houston for the weekend. They dined together in a joint on the waterfront in Sausalito, self-conscious and picturesque, with banal food. But she was glad to see him. He seemed to want nothing from her but herself. And that was not true of everyone else around her. She was the West heiress, and that seemed to justify all sorts of ridiculous appeals for help, for cooperation, for her blessing. And for money, always for money. She began to understand why old Will had been so crotchety, so snappish, so short and even intolerant of petitioners. Often, as a child, later as a young woman, her heart had gone out to those who approached her grandfather for something and were coldly, curtly, turned away. Now she knew. And she was glad she had never given in to emotion and nagged him about such matters. She had set up, as she suspected he would have done, an anonymous fund for the children and widows of the miners who died in Doylestown Number One. It didn't bring the men back, but it made her feel better. It was, she knew, the right thing to do, a debt to pay.

"Why don't we take some time off and go somewhere?" Ingalls was now saying over coffee. "You've had a rough month of it. I could use a break. Go to the islands. Maui. Or ski."

"It'd be terrific, Jeff," she said, meaning it.

She still didn't know where Marc was. She assumed Paris, less than a day's flight away, even from the Coast. He might be there to be touched, but she didn't know this. She was not even sure if she should reach out to touch him. It was Marc who had broken with her, Marc who had fled. Rejection was never easy to take. And in the mournful, chaotic wake of Will West's death, she hesitated to open herself to further damage. She might be famous, might be wealthy, but she was still vulnerable. Perhaps he had found someone else.

They drove back across the Golden Gate Bridge through the fog into the city. Jeff was staying at the Mark Hopkins, she at the Huntington. They went to the Mark and up to the roof. Here they were above the fog, and far off she could see the Pacific, the lights of incoming planes twinkling in the night. He ordered a Scotch and she had a Calvados. She wondered where Marc was at this very moment. Asleep, probably. Or just getting up in the morning. Maybe from someone's bed. Perhaps that was why she didn't fly to France. Perhaps that was why that night, for the first time in weeks, she made love to Jeff Ingalls.

On Tuesday she was back in New York, trying out the swiveling chair in Will West's Wall Street office, wondering if she would ever really fill this seat, any of his seats. Or even if she truly wanted to.

She was staying in her own apartment in Sutton Place, roaming through empty rooms, wondering where Toy was now, wondering, always, about Street, sometimes avoiding, sometimes purposely standing for a time in front of Chanel's photo above the fireplace, thinking about her, about what she meant to all of them: Marc, herself, even Adam.

Chanel had been Chanel. Let the dead sleep. And as for

Marc, he was gone. Ingalls was a good and decent man who loved her. Why beat her head against the wall of Marc's intransigence? And yet she hesitated, torn between pragmatism and the desolation of a lost love.

In her confusion, a night after she had flown in from Denver, a message came from Boston: Adam wanted to see her.

58

Now that he's withdrawn mysteriously from the scene and we're all being objective, did it ever occur to anyone but me that Adam Greenberg's best work was just slightly . . . derivative? I really must discuss it one day with dear Charles Winston.

Lincoln Radford in *Mode*, December 13, 1982

Adam was in Mass. General, the great Boston hospital. There had been visits and tests in other hospitals before this: Memorial in New York, Emery in Atlanta. There were always new theories, new hope. In New York *People* magazine had smuggled a photographer into his room. The *Enquirer* tattled about his strange malady. Page Six in the *Post* reported authoritatively that he had had a breakdown. His own cover story was ulcers. In Boston he used a pseudonym, Phil Berg, Phil for his middle name, Berg a remnant of his past, the part dropped when he became "Adam Green." Pseudonyms are transparent stuff when you have been as often photographed as he had. When you have been interviewed by Barbara Walters on ABC and profiled on *60 Minutes,* you need more than a change of name. Peter Feeley had been right: Adam swam in a fishbowl of his own design. He wasn't sick. What made him angry was that he was only in for tests, more tests. The doctors were going over his immune system cell by cell, checking for evidence of a virus that some experts felt caused AIDS. So far they had turned up nothing except an ulcer. Adam's cover story was true.

The nurses fussed lovingly, and he invited them to his

next collection. Next collection? A sick joke, literally, he knew.

In one corner of the room a gaudy floral arrangement mocked him. "Stanley Baltimore," the card read. "Get well soon." How like Stanley to rub salt into wounds. He tried to remember the status of their lawsuits. Was he suing Stanley or was it the other way round? Were they countersuing each other? That was probably it. When the flowers first arrived his impulse was to have them thrown out. But they're so lovely, the nurse said. Yes, leave them there. Why argue, why give unnecessary pain. Blessedly, except for the needles there had been very little. Weakness, fatigue, disorientation, especially when they drained pints of blood from him, but almost no pain. How disappointed Stanley Baltimore would have been to know that.

He dreamed. Often the dreams were pleasant, of Paris and Key West and Beverly Hills, of the good, the wonderful times. And there *had* been good times. Not even self-pity could erase them entirely. In cogent moments he attempted to tote up accounts, most settled, others diffuse and inconclusive, not all his fault. Most debts had been paid. A few were still outstanding. Not just a few, he told himself angrily, shrugging off the understandable tendency to be vague. There were still two accounts to be settled, precisely two.

On the sixth day of his stay at Mass. General, with optimistic test results in, without a single specialist peering down at him with grave curiosity (it was a Sunday, and the doctors had gone wherever they went on Sundays), he was forced once again to confront those last two remaining items on the ledger. A photograph of Chelsea West stared out at him from the pages of the *New York Times*. Miss West was in New York on business, she had said very little in response to a reporter's questions, and she planned to stay in the city for a time. Nothing more than that. Probably they had needed a picture of a pretty girl to brighten up the good, gray pages of the paper's general news section. That was all. Then Adam caught himself. Let's be fair. She's news, as he once was, and she was far more than just another pretty girl. He looked at the photo for several minutes. Not even the grainy reproduction of newsprint could blunt those features, the strong, lovely bones of her face, the tall grace with which she stood or walked, the depth of those eyes, the tawny, cascading hair, the appeal of that smiling, generous mouth. He thought of how well they had danced together. In a way, he had loved her.

If they met now would she even speak to him?

That night he slept badly, so badly that he asked the midnight nurse on her rounds for a Percodan. It was better after that. The dreams came fitfully but they were mostly pleasant: a golden beach, a smooth body, a clap of applause from the little gold chairs in the salon of his studio, with every little gold chair filled, the hot Florida sun, a blue-green sea, a champagne toast, a sweet mouth on his. That season's song, "Memory," played in his brain. That, he concluded, half awake now once again, was the trouble. Memory. He remembered everything and forgot nothing. There was so much still to be done and so little time. He thought of Peter Feeley, long lost, and wondered if he was happy.

But there was little point in wishing. He had gone through all of that, empty wishes become despair, and he did not want to experience it again. He forced himself to be realistic, to measure out coldly what he could and could not do. He could sign checks, send notes, use the phone. There were consolations in being rich. He could buy things, buy the services of this hospital and of these expert people, could pay his bills. In the half light of a moonlit night he turned and again saw Stanley Baltimore's grotesque floral jest. Money could insulate him against a Stanley Baltimore. If only it could take him again to Marc.

In the morning, a nurse came in while he was dressing.

"Adam! Mr. Green, may I ask what the hell you're doing?"

He grinned at her, that famous Adam grin. "I am taking a trip, sweetheart."

"But you can't . . . The doctors have more tests. The CAT scan . . ."

He shook his head. "Adam can do any damned thing he wants, nurse!"

As he left, he threw her a kiss.

He and Chelsea met in the grill room of the Four Seasons. It would get out anyway that they had met, why not do it where everyone would see them?

"I wouldn't have blamed you if you told me to go to hell," Adam said when Julian had shown them to their table.

"I nearly did," she said, flatly and without warmth.

He was very thin. The stories about his health must be true, one matter on which she had not bothered to put the West advisers to work. I don't really give a damn, she told herself, and dismissed the rumors as no longer of any consequence to her.

He ordered a *paillard* and barely toyed with it. She had venison and ate it all.

"I've got to see Marc," he said abruptly. "Talk with him. It's important."

"A bit late for that, isn't it? After what you and Baltimore did to him?"

He looked stricken. "Don't beat up on me, Chelsea. I feel bad enough already."

"Why should you feel so bad? You have it all now, you and Baltimore. Marc under indictment, Majesty in Chapter Eleven, all those people who once worked with you out of work. Sydney Heidler is a broken old man. You remember Sydney, don't you? You remember Majesty?"

"I don't blame you for that, Chelsea. But believe me, working for Stanley was no picnic. We're even suing each other."

"I'm delighted to hear it." She was being bitchy and she knew it. It just felt right. He deserved scorn. She felt no guilt, none at all.

"Look," he said, glancing around, trying to ensure that no one at the next table was listening, "this is pretty hard for me. Don't make it any tougher."

She stared straight ahead, not wanting to look at him. "Yes," she said, "you made it so easy for Marc, didn't you?"

He had expected resistance but not open warfare. He had not remembered her as this hard. Maybe it was the West inheritance. Suddenly she had four billion dollars and she could defy anyone. No, he thought, that was unfair. She had always been independent, even when she was living on a Seventh Avenue salary.

It came from family, from background, from the lineage and the blood. He thought of himself, of an invisible father, a mother who preferred Miami Beach canasta to the reality of New York. No wonder he was fucked up, confused, guilt-racked. Chelsea had no such problems, or so he thought.

He knew nothing, of course, of her drunken father, her sluttish mother, her own insecurities. He only knew she was a West, and rich.

"Chelsea," he said, almost pleading, "it's important that I talk with Marc. He's the only person I can talk to, and I don't know where he is, how to find him. You do."

He knew nothing of her investigations, of the tracker assigned to run Marc to earth in Paris. He was making assumptions, based on what he thought was a continuing love between them.

Chelsea turned on the banquette to look at him. Still extraordinarily good-looking, he had changed. Not just loss of weight. He seemed finer, tireder, haggard, almost desperate. Illness? Or was it drugs? He was no angel, she knew. But then, were any of them? She was thinking of Jeff Ingalls, of being in his bed and the things she did with him.

"I don't know where he is," she said, her voice empty and providing no apology.

"I don't believe you."

"So?" She just didn't care whether he believed her, what he thought of her. Adam had abdicated respect. He heard the contempt in her voice, saw it in her eyes. Still, dogged and without options, he pressed her.

"Chelsea, I'm not going to bore you with my problems. They're serious. Not just Stanley Baltimore. I know what you think of me. But Marc and I go back a long, long way, to that day in Paris when they buried Chanel. We both got rich and I got famous, just the way he wanted it. Then you came along." He paused. Then, not wanting to rehash the old enmities, he resumed: "So now I have this serious thing bothering me and Marc is, literally, the only person in the world I want to see, to apologize for what I've done."

"And what's that?" she asked, enjoying his suffering, prolonging and prodding it.

"You mean what I did that demands apology? Well, I went to Giordano down in Foley Square. I don't know if you know that, or if Marc does. I told the feds what little I knew about Carl Lazer and how Marc used to have to see Lazer every so often. I used to ask Marc why the hell this Lazer guy was important to Majesty. He never told me. Maybe he didn't want to implicate me in the money laundering, maybe he just didn't trust me to keep my mouth shut. He was always after me over that. I talked too much, it got into the papers. So I told Giordano what I knew, and it seemed to back up what he'd already learned. Baltimore made me go down there. He had me half crazy with hatred against Marc. Marc was the enemy, the rival, the competition. You and Marc had conspired to destroy me and my work. I know it's nuts, but I resented you so damned much . . ."

This, at least, had a genuine ring to it, and she listened, not saying anything, biting back sarcasm.

"It was as if Marc and I were lovers and you stole him away from me. We never were, of course. Marc was Marc and I was . . . what I am. We could have been brothers. People sometimes said that.

"I resented you. Oh, I heard Marc's explanation a million times, about taking old Abe Goode's idea and putting it to work, a team of designers rather than just relying on me. That didn't wash as far as I was concerned. One moment he and I were partners and then you came along."

His voice fell, defeated. She was unsure if it was a performance or real emotion. For the first time, she gave him the benefit of the doubt.

He pulled himself together, glancing to right and left, lowering his voice. No one seemed to be listening. Life goes on at the other tables too, he told himself.

"Okay, so that was that. I made a mistake going to work for Baltimore. He's a monster; everything they say about him is true. I was wrong going to the feds and giving evidence of something I knew only diddley about. Maybe I was even wrong about you. I thought you got the job because you were screwing Marc."

"Well, I wasn't. And I don't care if you believe it or not."

He turned to her, fierce and hurt. "Well, I didn't know that.

All I knew was I loved this man, and because I was gay and he was straight, I was never going to be able to do anything about it. And along comes this good-looking girl with her long legs and her big eyes and he hires her. No experience, no training, and the ten years I've put in was just thrown away like a goddamned newspaper on the subway. How the hell did you think I felt?"

She looked around the grill room herself now, wondering if they were being overheard. They weren't. She was being made to feel like "the other woman" by a homosexual designer and yet everything was normal.

He waited for her to answer, and when she didn't, he spoke again, drained and pathetic.

"I have to see Marc and tell him I'm sorry. That's all. I'm counting on your decency to let me know how I can reach him."

"Why *now?*" she asked. "Because you and Baltimore had a falling out? Is that it? Marc doesn't have a company anymore, remember? He can't give you your old job back. Majesty is out of business."

He shook his head. "Not that," he murmured.

"Then what?"

He had not wanted to tell her about Luke, about his deadly fear. He didn't know if he could rely on her discretion. After all, she hated him. And it would sound melodramatic, getting to Marc by conjuring up some deathbed yarn. But what choice had he if he was going to settle accounts with the last, and best, friend he had betrayed?

The dishes had been cleared, the coffee brought, and he lighted a cigarette. His hand shook. She noticed that. Then he spoke.

"Because I may get AIDS," he said quietly, trying to maintain control. "I'm all right now, but you never know for sure. My old number, Luke, the one you read about in the papers—he killed himself. AIDS. He sent me a letter. I've been to three or four specialists. They all agree I'm at risk."

"But can't they . . . ?" she started to ask, concerned and caring for the first time.

He laughed. "Oh, sure, they're working on cures. They've given me prescriptions. They say if I live like a nun I'll live as long as Sydney. It's all very optimistic and jolly. Only I can't ever screw again and I might just die. Nice, isn't it? A nice story."

"Oh, Adam," she said, reaching out to touch his hand.

"Yeah," he said, his eyes tearing, "once everything was so perfect."

She swallowed hard, not saying anything.

He went on, talking as much to himself as to her. "Thirty-six years old and I may die."

His eyes glistened, but he shook himself, trying not to disgrace himself by crying in public. It was left to Chelsea to weep.

59

This is the month where you either make your year in cosmetics and perfume or you don't. Preliminary figures indicate one of the best Christmas seasons ever for the industry. One soft spot, Baltimore Inc.'s Adam label products. They're curdling on the shelves.

Mode, December 20, 1982

Two weeks before Christmas Chelsea flew back to Denver to preside over a board meeting of West Industries. It was, despite its apparent splendors, an informal session. There was but one item on the agenda: consideration of the election of a new chairman to succeed the late Will West. The election itself would be by the stockholders, but this meeting was intended to turn the foregone conclusion into as smooth and as seemly a formality as possible. There would be one candidate, the principal stockholder in the company, Catherine West. Walter Felton, for a dozen years Mr. West's right hand as president, had made the arrangements.

"There'll be no difficulty, Chelsea," he said, "old Will made it pretty damned clear what he wanted after he was gone. And the board'll go along with it."

"And you, Walter? You've been the number-two man for so long, don't you want the job for yourself?"

Felton smiled. "Hell, Chelsea, a man always wants to be *numero uno*, the boss. I wanted it when old Will was alive. But listen, this was his company, you're his heir. For me to go against Will now after he went up to Doylestown Number One would be just plain, ornery betrayal. You don't cheat on a man like Will. I didn't when he was alive and I won't now. He'd probably come back and haunt me if I did."

"He would, you know," she said.

"Soooo," Felton went on, "we'll meet with the directors, spell out the succession, set a date for the stockholders' meeting, notify the SEC and the *Wall Street Journal,* and get you elected. I'll stay with you a couple of months, longer if you want, and then I'll go quietly. There are any number of firms out there I can go to as the top guy. They know what I did here. I'll help you all I can and turn in my resignation and go someplace else to get rich. No static, I promise you."

"I know that," she said.

Then Felton smiled broadly. "One other thing. You asked me to check on that old pal of yours, Toy?"

"Yes?"

"Well, she's fine. Least, I guess she's fine. Living with some unsavory character name of Ambrosio, making movies you wouldn't let your old auntie see, but doing pretty well. Seems to be content. That's what our people say. There's even talk one of the major studios wants her to do a real movie."

"Good, that's all I want," she said, "thanks." At least one of the lost children was safe.

She had seen Jeff Ingalls in New York before flying west. He took her to the theater, and then they went downtown to Tribeca to one of the new restaurants for supper.

"I want you to marry me, Chelsea," he said.

"Hey, I thought you Texans were supposed to be shy."

"Not in Houston. Down there we ask on the first date."

They kept it light for a time. She had known this was coming. In San Francisco he'd seemed on the verge of saying something. She had not known then what she'd say, how she'd react. She liked Ingalls, they were good together, she was confident he wasn't after her money, he was a tender, exciting lover, in nearly every way a perfect mate.

If there weren't a Marc Street.

When he became serious and started telling her the reasons, she cut him off. "Jeff, I'm really glad to be asked. I like you very much. Maybe I even love you. But so many damned things have happened to me the last couple of months, I'm just not ready to commit myself. I'm probably a pretty old-fashioned girl. My parents had a lousy marriage; I want a good one."

He nodded. "I'll wait, Chelsea. Not forever, but I'll give you time if you want."

"Yes, I need that, time."

She had also needed time with Adam. She told him she'd think about what he asked and, if she learned where Street was, promised to consider getting to him the message that Adam wanted to see him.

"That's all I want, Chelsea," Adam had said.

"Okay," she said, "I'll be in touch."

"That's all I want," he repeated, "just a chance with Marc, to pay a debt."

She could hear her grandfather, using almost the same words. "Always ante up, Catherine, ante up and pay off. Live by that and you can't go far wrong."

The day after he lunched with Chelsea, Adam met with his attorneys and approved the draft of a letter he was sending to Stanley Baltimore, resigning as his designer and proposing that both lawsuits be dropped and that lawyers for both sides meet to adjudicate the matter of royalties on perfumes and other Baltimore products created by Adam and bearing his label. When he left the law offices, Adam felt as if he had shed a punishing burden.

Walter Felton chaired the Denver meeting, at Chelsea's request. She sat there, at the head of the long, dark wood table, a lone woman with eighteen men, many of them rich and powerful in their own right, a portrait of Will West, thin-lipped and brooding, glowering down on them. There were yellow legal pads and sharpened pencils and ashtrays and water pitchers and glasses on the hard wood. At her place, old Will's place, a brass cuspidor sat on the floor, a West tradition.

"I don't expect to use this, you know," she told Felton before the others came in.

He laughed. "Chelsea, nothing you Wests do surprises me. So if you get the inspiration, spit away."

Now he rapped on the table with his knuckles and told them why they were there. There were some questions, procedural mostly. If any of them objected, and perhaps some did, they knew she held the cards. They knew that whatever they might say, she had the shares. Felton answered the questions, or she did, and then Felton rapped again.

"Gentlemen, that's about it. A February second shareholders' extraordinary meeting here in Denver for the purpose of electing our new chairman. Chairperson," he added quickly, crinkling up his eyes in Chelsea's direction. "Arrangements will be made to have the ballroom of Brown's Hotel available. If there's any problem with that, Mr. Young or I will let you know. Questions?"

There were none. Felton then turned to Chelsea. "Chelsea, Miss West, anything you want to add?"

She thought for a moment. "Yes, there is," she said. She got up and they all looked toward her, this tall, beautiful young woman who had inherited Will West's empire.

"Yes, I'm younger than any of you and obviously I don't know very much about the business of running a company like this one. I've only had one job in my life, and that was designing clothes, putting my label on the rear end of a lot of blue jeans."

There was an appreciative chuckle.

"I don't know mining," she went on, "or banking. Or oil. Or hotels. I know a little about textiles. And there's a hell of a lot more I don't know. My grandfather taught me three things: to read, to think for myself, to play fair. So maybe I could make a pretty good chairman . . . or chairperson, as Mr. Felton put it so thoughtfully . . . of this great company."

She paused.

"But I'm not going to do that. On February two, in Brown's Hotel or wherever we meet, I'm going to cast my shares in the vote for chairman for someone else, for a good man who ought to be running this company. For Walter Felton."

An hour later, after the hubbub and the talk and the hand-shaking and the congratulations, she and Felton were again alone.

"Chelsea, there's going to be a lot of questions about all this. The press, Wall Street, Washington, some of our own people. You gonna be handy for me in case I got to reach you?"

"No, Walter, I won't be around. You handle all that your-self. I've got business elsewhere, things I have to do that won't wait."

"Can I help?"

"No. This is personal stuff. I'm the only one who can do it."

He accepted that and asked no more questions. When she left they started to shake hands, and then he reached out and took her by both arms and kissed her cheek. "Goddammit, Chelsea, have a Merry Christmas."

"You too, Walter. Merry Christmas."

A few days later she flew to New York, just before the season's first blizzard. It was there that word came from Felton that his man in Paris was sure he had found Marc Street.

She hugged the knowledge to herself for a few hours. Then, re-membering a promise, she called Adam. "You have to see him?"

"Yes. I have to."

"All right," she said, making up her mind and praying that she was doing the right thing. "I'm going out of town. If Marc agrees to talk to you, I'll call. Let my office in New York know where you are. If I can do anything, I will."

"Chelsea, you don't know . . ."

"Yes, I do," she said firmly, "and if you betray Marc, I'll kill you."

At the other end of the phone he continued to hold the re-ceiver after she hung up, hearing only the dial tone, tears running down his face.

Chelsea was still unsure about Adam, but her own uncer-tainties were gone. Jeff Ingalls, West Industries, nothing was im-portant now—except to get to Paris before Marc Street could get away again, to see him, to talk to him, to force him to listen.

To love him.

60

House parties, house parties. From Lyford Cay to St. Moritz, from Little Dix Bay to Sun Valley, the beautiful ones gather. If these old eyes are still focusing next week, I shall report who has been doing what where. And with whom. Do have a jolly!

Lincoln Radford, *Mode*, December 20, 1982

She passed up the Ritz and the Plaza Athenée for the San Regis. The little suite on the top floor in the rear where she and Marc had first made love was unavailable, but that didn't matter. She didn't want any publicity, and the airline tickets and the hotel were arranged in another name. When the jet landed at dawn at Charles de Gaulle, there was no waiting limo. She took a cab. It was December 23, and the airport was jammed with travelers. The sky was low and promising rain or snow. There was a nice Christmas feel to everything. Without knowing it, she was reacting to the Paris Christmas just as Marc had done.

She took a long, hot bath, enjoying the lengthy, deep Paris tub, sipping Evian water as the sweat formed on her face and neck, as her body loosened and relaxed after the flight. Then she crawled into bed to sleep, leaving a call for three that afternoon. Outside in the rue Jean-Goujon and at the place François-1er at the corner were the sounds of midday traffic, the horns and the shifted gears, the occasional whine of brakes, a child's cry, a boy's shout, the sound of car doors slamming. She had closed the drapes over the French doors and lay there trying to sleep, trying not to think. If she thought now of Marc, of seeing him again

426

after all this time, she would never sleep and she'd look like hell for him.

Suppose he wasn't there? Suppose, somehow, the detective got it all wrong. Or he'd been frightened and had gone away. No, he had to be there. She'd come so far to see him, an empty apartment was unthinkable, cruel. Finally, she slept.

At five that afternoon she was crossing the Seine in a cab, banking left at the Assemblée Nationale and heading into the boulevard St.-Germain. As she rode, she watched through the grimy windows this lovely Yuletide city where she had found love. Past the Brasserie Lipp, the Deux Magots, the old stone church already floodlit against the gray evening gloom, rolling past shuttered shops and others still open for last-minute Christmas shopping. Traffic was heavy, the sidewalks crowded with shoppers. When the cab stopped at red lights, she caught individual faces, chilled, busy, happy.

God, she thought, I'm nervous as a cat.

The cab turned into the boul' Mich' and then made another, brief turn into the street where Street lived. She had the address written on a piece of paper, and she looked at it for perhaps the hundredth time. The address was seared into memory, but she checked again. She rang the *concierge's* bell, and after a moment a middle-aged woman pulled back the yellowing curtains to peer out.

"M. Daniel Gorin?" she asked.

"Troisième étage, à droite."

She went past the big black garbage cans and through the door into the stairwell. There was a light switch, and she hit it. She mounted the steps, trying to do it slowly, wanting to run but not wanting to reach his door panting and breathless. When she reached his door, she hesitated, trying to frame her first words. She knocked. Knocked again. No answer. She tried to shake off panic. It was only five-fifteen. It was logical that he might still be at work, or on the way home, stuck in holiday traffic. He might have gone shopping, stopped somewhere for a drink. She knew he was not with the girl. The detective had reported that there *was* a girl, Anne, but she had gone home for Christmas. Perhaps there was someone else, another Anne.

She slowly descended the stairs and went out into the street and up the block to the boulevard. There was a large café with a glassed-in porch covered with tables and chairs. She sat down, trying to keep her mind blank, trying not to feel the disappointment. When the waiter came she asked for something, a Coke. She didn't really want it, but she had to order something. She sat there, watching the boulevard through the steamy glass, watching the shoppers and the people coming home from work, hoping one of the reddened, chilled passing faces might be his. From a nearby table a young man looked at her over the rim of his coffee cup and smiled. She barely saw him.

She returned to the apartment at six. Still no response. She considered leaving a message, telling him where she was, almost immediately rejecting the idea. He might panic, run. Then he'd be lost to her again. Maybe she'd never find him. She again retraced her steps. But this time she ignored the café and just walked, looking into shopwindows and not seeing anything. At seven she reached the Seine and started back. This time, she told herself, this time she was going to sit down in the hallway outside his door and stay there all night, if necessary.

"Chelsea!"

"Marc!"

She threw herself into his arms, her face turned up toward his. His head came to hers, and they kissed. He tasted the same, even the slightly stale cigarette taste. He felt the same, big and hard against her. Finally, he broke for air.

"How the hell did you find me? Are you okay? When did you get in?"

She tried to answer everything at once, and failed. Then he started to talk, then she did, and then they stopped and held each other again, their mouths together.

She looked past his shoulder toward the bedroom. But he made no move toward it. It was what she wanted, what she half expected.

"Come on," he said, "let's get out of here. I know a place. Hungry?"

"No. Yes," she said.

The place was a small bistro with sawdust on the floor, a big, old-fashioned NCR cash register, and paper tablecloths. The waiter brought a bottle of Evian and a bottle of Beaujolais nouveau without being asked, and wrote their orders on the tablecloth.

"It's a university hangout," Marc said, "the students come here. But the food is pretty good."

He brought Anne here, she thought.

"God, you look good." Then he stopped. "Listen, I'm sorry about your grandfather. I sent a cable when I heard."

"I never got it, Marc."

"Doesn't matter. I just wanted you to know I was sorry."

Her heart leaped when he said that about the cable. So he hadn't stopped thinking about her. She told him about the mine fire, about the old man's death.

"So now you're rich," he said.

"I suppose so. Yes." Then, swiftly, "But that doesn't matter, Marc. I'm still me. Still the same girl."

He shook his head. "It matters, Chelsea, stupid to say that it doesn't."

"Let's not argue. I just want to look at you. And try to believe that awful mustache!"

He laughed. "Not quite the elegant *boulevardier* you used to know."

"That *is* a dreadful suit."

He shrugged. "It fits."

"Barely."

He looked down at himself in mock hurt.

She frowned. "You should let me do the alterations. I'm very good at it, you know. A man called Marc Street taught me, on Seventh Avenue."

"That man is dead," he said, his voice serious.

She was just as serious. "That man will never die."

They had soup, hot and thick, with chunks of fresh bread and a small tub of creamy butter.

"There goes the diet."

"Hell," he said, "you're a growing girl."

They had steaks and *pommes frites,* and before they were half-way through, the waiter slammed down another bottle of Beaujolais on the paper tablecloth. Around them solid businessmen and shopgirls ate their Christmas Eve dinners, concentrating on the food, reading newspapers, chatting among themselves, shouting cheerfully for the waiters, small, dark men in soiled mess jackets, hurrying through the room, wanting to be home with their own families, eating their own dinners.

"This is the best meal I've ever had." She meant it.

"Sure," he said dubiously. He knew the kind of restaurant she was used to.

She told him about Adam.

"The poor son of a bitch," he said, after a silence.

"He thinks you hate him."

"Hate Adam? I love that kid. We were a team. He was stupid to jump to Baltimore, is all."

"But going to Giordano about you?"

"Come on, he was scared, we were all scared. You get the federals on your case and it's not a joke."

"But you didn't cooperate. You refused to testify."

"I was different. Lazer was my father's friend."

She let that pass. She didn't want to begin her pitch yet, about his going home to testify, to do anything necessary to clear his name with the government. There were other things to talk about, other things to do.

"Adam wants to see you, to apologize, to settle accounts."

"Listen, tell him it's okay, nothing to settle. Tell him I understand. And if I ever get back, he owes me a good meal. Tell him that."

"I will, Marc."

"Tell him . . . I'm sorry. That he ought to do what the doctors tell him. These things . . . maybe they'll find a cure. Maybe . . ."

"I'll tell him, Marc."

How gentle he was. She had expected bitterness, hatred, a hardening of attitudes. Instead, warmth, selflessness, understanding. She knew nothing, almost nothing, of his life in Paris all these months. Whatever had happened to him, had worked on him, had been good. She felt a spasm of jealousy. Anne, the student, whoever she was, whatever she meant to him, had seen these changes in him, had been there as he mellowed, had helped him mellow.

They went back to his apartment. Nothing had to be said. She opened herself to him as if these months of separation were but yesterday.

"I love you," she said, over and over.

Ingalls was forgotten.

At midnight church bells rang, heavy-sounding gongs in the wintry night. Outside in the street they could hear people calling to one another, laughing. "Merry Christmas, Chelsea."

"Merry Christmas, Marc."

They made love again before they slept, not as urgently this time, but slowly, erasing doubt. She had been right to come, right to take the risk, right to walk away from the secure, protective envelope of America and West Industries and Jeff Ingalls's love and old Will's money. Those first moments, here in Marc's place, when he rushed her out to a restaurant to dinner rather than pulling her into bed, had been frightening. She feared that love had died, that the French girl had supplanted her, that she had lost him forever. Those fears were empty; she was sure of that now. There was no way the night's tender passion could have been anything but real.

In the morning, using his bathroom while he still slept, she found the gun in its shoulder holster hung from a hook on the door, behind his terry-cloth robe. She touched it to be sure, feeling the cold blue metal. She pulled her hand away as if it had been scorching hot instead of chilled. She backed away from it, rubbing her hand against her hip as if she could scour off filth.

"Marc?"

He turned to look at her, his eyes sleepy. "Hi."

She shook her head, shaken and angry. "A gun?"

His grin changed. He came awake now. "Sorry."

"You use it? You use a gun?"

"It's a tool."

"It's a *gun,* dammit."

He didn't say anything for a moment. "That's what I've become, Chelsea."

On Christmas morning, she leaned against him, crying into his shoulder while he stared past her, seeing nothing but the faded wallpaper just beyond. It should have been the happiest Christmas morning of their lives.

61

The First Lady looked smashing as she lighted the national Christmas tree in her bright red melton coat by Bill Blass. Adolfo and Jimmy Galanos are trying to be good sports about it.

Mode, December 20, 1982

Stanley Baltimore, half relieved, half furious over Adam's resignation, was passing the holidays in Maui. A half dozen of his favorite pictures had been sent ahead to adorn the walls of the suite. Wherever he went Baltimore insisted that he be surrounded by beauty. There were also two girls. He was into pairs now. It was all apparently respectable; they occupied a suite of their own and one of his female employees accompanied them. Her duties as chaperone were simple: she was to stay out of the way. Lester had found the girls, Lester had arranged things with their mothers, arranged the passage. Baltimore amused himself vicariously now, not actually doing anything himself, but watching the two make love. He supplied the drugs; they supplied the entertainment. They were both thirteen. Lester had promised they would be considered, and seriously, for the new teenaged television campaign. "It all depends," he told their mothers, "just which girl Mr. Baltimore finds most wholesome and appealing, in an all-American way."

On Christmas Eve Mr. Baltimore supplied the two thirteen-year-olds with Quaaludes, suggested they do certain things to each other, and sat back to watch.

The trip was not all pleasure. Baltimore had taken with him a sheaf of sales reports, many of them on Adam-label products. He was a careful businessman, skeptical and astute, a man who knew how to read a balance sheet. The sales reports told an intriguing story. After a very promising start, Adam perfume had tailed off. Even during the Christmas selling season, when more than half the year's total sales of perfume are rung up, Adam had been mediocre at best. The "why" of its failure was obvious to Baltimore: bad publicity. The death of that little fairy down in Key West; Adam's refusal to do promotional chores on the talk shows and with the newspapers after his November fashion show; his "inexplicable" decision to take a sabbatical; the nasty AIDS rumors worming their way through the gay underground.

If Adam products were still booming, if people were still buying, he would have refused to accept Adam's resignation, would hold him to every damned paragraph of every clause in his contract and, if he refused to work, sue him once again for a billion dollars for breach of contract and conspiracy. But the Adam line wasn't booming. It was decidedly "off." Very well, Baltimore was a practical man; he would cut his losses. Let the faggot go, dissolve his division, write off the losses against income, and put an end totally and overnight to the split of royalties still going to bankrupt Majesty Fashions and that damned Marc Street.

He had destroyed Street, had killed his father. Now he would crush Adam as he might a crawling thing on the patio of his house in Key West. He placed a phone call to Lincoln Radford at the offices of *Mode* magazine in New York. When there was no answer, Baltimore exploded. "Try the number again. It's a magazine office. There must be someone there."

"But, Mr. Baltimore," the hotel operator protested, "it's Christmas Day."

Christmas! He had forgotten. The late-morning sun hung over the palm trees just beyond his terrace. He had Radford's home number somewhere. He paged through his address book. Not there. He phoned his secretary at her home on Long Island.

"Go into the office and get me Lincoln Radford's home number. Then call me back."

"Mr. Baltimore, it's Christmas. I'm just—"

He hung up on the woman.

Once he got Radford the thing would be done. He'd tell him the whole story, embellish it—that Adam's lover had killed himself, that Adam had AIDS, that Baltimore had only just now discovered there was a pervert in his employ, that he was going to activate a morals clause in Adam's contract, fire him, and sue for every cent he'd ever paid the homo, sue for back royalties, sue for payment for use of his house in Key West. He couldn't even recall if Adam's contract had a morals clause. So what? The mere assertion that Adam had acted immorally would be enough. It would finish him in this business.

Baltimore rubbed his fat hands. He had finished Street. Now he would finish Adam. Radford's magazine would do it for him.

He went out onto the balcony in his silk robe, feeling the tiles hot under his bare feet. Far below the two teenagers frolicked in the pool in their new bikinis while middle-aged men ignored their middle-aged wives to stare at them. Baltimore laughed aloud. He wondered what the tourists would be thinking if they knew what those two slender, long-limbed young girls had been doing in his bed a few hours before, what they would soon be doing again.

He went back inside the air-conditioned room, stripped to his shorts, and resumed his examination of the figures. He checked and double-checked the Adam division results, losing himself in computer printouts and P & L's. Money and paintings had always been Baltimore's true passion, except that now, increasingly, little girls obtruded on them. Toward sundown, while he was still deep in analysis, one of the two children burst in on him, breathless and wide-eyed.

"Hey, you oughta see her! She looks like a lobster!"

"What? What?" He dropped his fountain pen.

"Sunburn!"

"Oh, shit."

Stanley Baltimore was annoyed. Even in the best of times it took very little to aggravate him, but now, having brought these two kids this far and at such an expense, to have one of them get so painfully burned that there was no way he could touch her, or she could even touch herself, was infuriating.

"I could kill the little bitch," he swore.

Her friend, whose name was Wren, was more reasonable. "She didn't mean it, Mr. Baltimore, we just fell asleep. I had a beach towel over me and she didn't. It was an accident."

The burned girl was in her room, covered with soothing lotions and weeping.

"*You'd* sure as hell better stay out of the damned sun," he warned the survivor, Wren. Where the hell was their damned chaperone?

Wren cocked her head and smiled. "Hey, give me credit for some brains, Mr. Baltimore."

He liked that smile.

"Besides," she said, "I'm lots prettier than her anyway."

His annoyance eased. "No, Wren, you're not pretty; you're very beautiful."

She liked being told that. Baltimore slung a big arm around her thin shoulder, cool under a fresh cotton T-shirt, and led her from his sitting room toward the bedroom.

"And now that there's only you," he said, "you're going to try a little harder, Wren, aren't you?"

"Sure, Mr. Baltimore," she said, meaning it. She knew now which of them would get the modeling contract. Her mother would be so pleased.

Here, as almost everywhere else, people did what Baltimore told them to do, mothers and daughters. Even on Christmas Day.

Perhaps because it *was* Christmas, because he was on holiday, because he was abusing in the most delicious ways this beautiful child, he was distracted, and his keen business acumen for once would fail him. In poring over the figures he had not taken notice that other divisions of Baltimore Inc. besides those bearing Adam's name were less scintillating than customary at this season. Small losses here, discernible failure to grow there, the odd cancellation by a faithful retail customer.

West Industries had begun to wage guerrilla warfare while Stanley Baltimore, working over the nude body of a child called Wren, surrounded by lovely pictures, secure in his wealth and his power, thought himself blissfully at peace.

Adam was not celebrating it at all. Instead, he huddled, shivering, under blankets. He was cold not with illness but with terror. For the first time in years he was spending a holiday alone. But loneliness went deeper than the day. For nearly two months now, ever since Halloween and Key West, he had been alone; he had not made love since sometime in October. Even in feverish weakness, he ached with need. Desire was still there in him, churning and restless. On the bed table, his leather-bound phone book mocked him. How easy it would be to pick up the telephone and call someone. Someone he knew, or a service he sometimes used. How easy. How impossible.

His manservant tiptoed in. "Can I get you something? A drink, some food?"

"Nothing, thanks." He stared at the ceiling, his eyes dull, brooding about what he really needed.

There was nothing from Chelsea. She had promised to convey his message to Marc. Perhaps she had lied to him, perhaps she never intended to talk to Marc. Why should she? She hated him. No, no, he cried out in torment, she *said* she'd help. No one could be that cruel! She promised!

By the side of his bed a silent telephone mocked him.

Bobby Swaggerty had gone to midnight mass on Christmas Eve in Holy Cross church on West Forty-second Street.

"You don't go Sundays," his lover complained as he left their hotel room.

"Christmas is different."

Tonia couldn't understand that. What did Italians know? She was a good kid, for a guinea. She kept wanting them to get a real apartment, with a kitchen, somewhere that she could cook and sew and do housework for him. He was uneasy whenever she talked like that. He felt her closing in on him. It was stupid. With the work he did, he belonged in hotel rooms. This one was in midtown, over on the East Side. But he went back to Holy Cross for midnight mass. It brought back childhood, simpler, more innocent times. She shrugged, not understanding him but not wanting to argue.

"I'll be awake when you get back," she said.

"Sure," he said. He knew she had bought some gifts for him, suspected she would be gift-wrapping them.

He slid into a pew toward the back of the church. By a quarter to twelve the seats were all taken, older people mostly, some teenaged kids, one or two cheerful drunks. At midnight precisely the procession entered, singing "Silent Night." Bobby stood and sang with them, inaudibly at first, then louder, his fine tenor carrying the words. There was a hymnal in the rack in front of him, but he did not need it. He remembered the words. An hour later, to the strains of "Adeste Fidelis," he shuffled up the aisle and out of the church, past old women muffled in scarves and cloth coats wishing one another "Merry Christmas," and dipping fingers into the chill waters of the holy water font.

He and Tonio exchanged presents.

"There's something else," he said.

"Yes?"

"There's five grand in this envelope. I want you to take it and fly down south for a few days or a week, New Orleans. When you get there and get a hotel, call this man. His name is Petitbon. Find a hotel in the old quarter. They call it the Vieux Carré. I spent a couple of months there once. You'll like it, lots of good restaurants and bars, great jazz. Just call Petitbon and tell him where you are. I'll be coming down myself in a few days."

"Oh?"

"Yeah, I've got a job to do."

She knew what his work was.

"Okay, Bobby. But be careful."

"Sure," he said.

After they made love he lay there, smoking a cigarette and thinking just how he was going to make things right for his friend Street, just how he was going to do this last job.

62

Now that Christmas is out of the way, the couture's Marc Bohan, in his twenty-third year as chief designer for Dior, says he senses broader shoulders and a marked waist for spring. Marc shows January 22 in Paris.

Mode, December 27, 1982

In the small apartment off the boul' Mich' in Paris, Chelsea West and Marc Street argued and made love, wheeled away from each other in anger or in frustration, talked and fell silent, turned again to love and to disputation. Disputation with holly leaves.

He ranted at her, urging her to leave and fearing that she might. "What the hell are you doing here in this place when you could be on the other side of the river? The Ritz, the Plaza Athenée, the Georges Cinq? Chelsea, this is nuts. I can't even take you to dinner at a decent restaurant. I can't go to Maxim's, to La Coupole. But you *can*. All the places we once had, I've lost them. But not you. And you hang out with me, in this?"

"Marc, I didn't come to Paris to sample the three-star restaurants in the *Michelin*. I came here to find you, to be with you. You're just being stupid."

"The stupid thing was coming here in the first place. I told you it was finished, that I was finished. You've got everything, Chelsea. You had it before and you have it even more now, since your grandfather died. How many billions have you now?"

"Oh, Marc, what bullshit! Did I ask you how much money

you had when we met? Did I give a damn? I'm not H. & R. Block. I'm the woman you used to love!"

He stalked the small apartment, angry, frustrated. "How can I get you to understand? You're a famous woman. One of the richest people in the world. You can have, you can do anything you want. I'm a bankrupt, a fugitive, an indicted man. I'm nothing. I'm dirt, compared to you. I'm a big boy, I know I lost."

She shook her head, the blond hair flying. "Oh, Marc, why won't you understand?"

"Forget me, Chelsea. I'm dead."

They argued like this. Even in argument, he could not remember her being this beautiful, this desirable.

"I love you. I want you," she told him.

"I know," he said despairingly, "and I want you, too."

And they made love again.

She went back to the Right Bank and the hotel each day to change her clothes. He couldn't come with her, of course. The manager, the *concierge,* even the bellmen at the San Regis knew him too well; even with the mustache, in his ill-cut French suit, they would know him.

They took lunch and dinner at local student hangouts and workingmen's bistros, at the place where he had met Anne. Because of the holidays, most of the students were away, and there were always tables. They took walks when it wasn't raining and when the wind off the Seine didn't whip through the narrow, winding streets. She dragged him into print shops and old bookstores and junk shops boasting of antiques. One afternoon they went to the movies. They drank endless cups of bitter coffee in tiny sooty cafés. It was like having Anne only better, and that was the wrenching part. He knew it was not going to last.

"But why not?" she demanded. "Do you owe so much to this gangster that you'll give me up, throw your life away?"

He realized how stubborn he was being and hung his head, responding in words that rang dull and dumb, even to himself.

"It isn't just Lazer. Testifying against him would just be the beginning. They'd turn it into a circus, with every two-bit garment district graft and hijack in the last twenty years. They want to know about them, too. I saw it happen to my old man. Now it's going to happen again if I let it."

She looked into his face. "Marc, your father was a racketeer. You're not. There's a difference."

Anger flared near the surface. Even from her, it hurt to hear. Especially from her. "I don't want to talk about my father."

But *you* brought him up, she wanted to say. Miserable, she bit off the words.

At night, after making love, they slept. Sometimes. Other times he lay there with her head cradled against his arm and shoulder, listening to her breathe, watching her face, her throat, the slow, easy movement of her chest in sleep.

"Chelsea," he said without making a sound, "you're a good girl."

Three days after Christmas she sat up in bed, drinking coffee heated on a hot plate, wearing one of his T-shirts and watching him dress, watching him strap on the shoulder holster.

"You have to take that?"

"Yes," he said, "protection."

She watched as he slid the .38 into the worn leather, hating it, trying to hate him for his stupidity, his mulishness. But she couldn't.

"Be careful."

"Sure," he said, "this is Paris. Not Dodge City."

"Okay. I'll change and be back."

He didn't answer.

"You want me back, don't you?" she said.

"Yes, Chelsea, I want you back," he said hopelessly.

They kept saying good-bye, but neither of them left.

She phoned Adam in New York and told him he was forgiven, that Marc said to forget it, that it was okay. But it wasn't good enough for Adam.

"He insists he's got to see you, to tell you himself," she said. "He sounds desperate."

"Jesus," Marc said, feeling Adam's pain himself.

"I lied," Chelsea said, "I told him I didn't know where you were anymore."

"Oh, hell, Adam isn't Baltimore. He wouldn't turn me in."

"I don't know, Marc. I can't take that responsibility."

He took a deep breath. "Okay, call him. Tell him to stay at the Plaza and you'll call him there. Keep it vague as to whether I'm in Paris or just in touch."

She made the New York call. Two days later Adam was in Paris. At the Plaza Athenée there was some confusion with the *concierge,* and she hung up without giving a name. Marc paced the apartment, restless. She was afraid he was going to do something impulsive like going to the hotel, putting himself at risk. She could not permit that. She had done too much already in bringing Adam to Paris. Then she made the call again, and this time she got through.

"Chelsea!" Adam half shouted. "Will he see me? Does he agree?"

"Just shut up, Adam. Marc is in enough trouble without hysterics. Are you okay?"

"Sure, sure, just tell me where he'll meet me."

She lied then, assuming he would know she was lying. "*I'll* meet you, Adam, and if everything's cool, I'll take you to Marc. Let's just not screw up, okay?"

There was a pause, and then he said, shyly she thought, or was it slyly: "How about the Madeleine? Where we first met."

When they'd made the arrangements, Marc nodding silently as she spoke, he shook his head.

"He has a talent for drama, that boy. Nearly twelve years since Coco died and that's where he wants to meet."

But it wasn't a bad place, not at the evening rush hour, bustling and disinterested, as safe as any place, he supposed. When the cab let them out a block away, Marc hurried inside the church by a side entrance and Chelsea strolled past the flower vendors to the front porch, where she stood, halfway up, watching the evening traffic bending around the *place,* headlights in the gloom.

Then Adam was there, slowly coming up the steps toward her.

"Thanks," he said, "I love you for this, Chelsea."

"Save your speech for Marc," she said.

"Yes, Chelsea."

She had never known him this docile.

"I'm going inside to pray," she said. "You're to wait here."

There was no one with him, Marc assured himself before emerging into the evening chill at the windswept top of the great stairs. Then Adam saw him, wheeled, and ran toward him, Marc letting him come, just waiting. If he were really sick, making those few yards on his own might mean something. Now he was there, his right hand out, his face split in a grin, a little thinner perhaps, tireder, no longer as full of hope and arrogance, no longer as young, no longer innocent and unburdened. But still Adam.

"Hello, Sundance," Marc said, taking the hand.

It took Adam an instant to bring the words:

"Hello, Butch."

His arms were around Marc now, they at least still strong. Adam always had strong hands, a craftsman's hands, and Marc could feel them gripping his arms through the heavy coat. Marc led him inside the vestibule of the church, to an old stone bench worn smooth by the years and the generations of worshipers. He could see Adam's face was slick with sweat. It was a good place, quiet and out of the wind.

Inside the Madeleine, in a small chapel off to the side, Chelsea knelt with a few old women in black who mumbled and ran beads through their fingers, and she watched the votive candles flicker in the dusk and tried to remember how to pray.

63

Sears, J. C. Penney, and Macy's all report Christmas sales 4 to 6 percent higher. Perfume, small appliances, and accessories were the big winners this season.

Mode, December 27, 1982

Adam and Marc just sat there for a moment, not talking. Then Marc said: "How are you? How are you feeling?"

"Okay. Just tired. Weary."

"Swell."

Adam pulled himself up straighter, his face wet with emotion, his eyes bright.

The two men talked for a time, Adam saying all the things he had wanted to say for so long, apologizing, asking to be forgiven.

"Sure, kid, it's okay. Things happen."

Adam nodded. "I got everything mixed up. Business and life. And then when they told me about . . . dying, it all started to straighten out again. I began to recognize the difference. Business isn't life. It isn't love."

"Well, that's a start. That's something we all have to learn."

But he wasn't thinking of Adam; he was thinking of Chelsea and himself.

Then Adam brightened. "You hear about Stanley Baltimore? He's finished, you know."

"No, I didn't. What happened?" Marc leaned forward, eagerly now.

"They caught him with one of his teenyboppers in Hawaii. The kid OD'd on something and ended up in the hospital. She told them Baltimore gave her the stuff. She was only thirteen or fourteen."

"No."

"Day before yesterday. It was in all the New York papers."

Marc exhaled. Baltimore wasn't important now. Chelsea was important. And Adam.

"Look," he said, "you just get yourself *balanced* again. Understand? Nothing else matters. Just do what they tell you and remember how *good* you are."

"Sure, Marc. I was good, wasn't I?"

Street grabbed his arm. He smiled. Good old Adam.

"We'll be in touch. Through Chelsea. I've got to be careful."

"I understand. That's why it means so much, that you came. Chelsea's a good girl, Marc. I was all wrong about her. About everything."

"No, we both made mistakes, you and me both. But you're right about her."

Adam tried to smile. "If I hadn't lost Peter, if Feeley had stayed with me, I guess I wouldn't have screwed up. If you have love, you can handle just about anything. If you have someone, nothing else matters."

"I guess so," Marc said; then, thinking of what Chelsea was offering to give up for him, he said, "I *know* so."

Adam said nothing, and Marc wondered if he was wandering off.

"Adam?"

"I'm okay. Just thinking. About the old days, about you and me, about me and Peter. Most straight people can't understand how it is with us, how a gay man can fall in love and really mean it, how it's not just sex, how it can be so much more."

"I know, Adam, I understand." He meant it.

Adam brightened. "You remember Max Mannerman, the coat and suit guy? *Women's Wear* used to call him 'America's Balenciaga.' "

"Yeah, I remember."

"I worked for him once for about fifteen minutes, before

Majesty. He paid me peanuts, but I learned. On a whim I went to see him the other day out in Arizona. Max retired. He made a fortune and he and his friend Jack just retired, walked away from Seventh Avenue."

"I remember Jack," Marc said, "the designer."

"Yeah, Max picked him up when he was a kid. They said Jack was a boxer. Or that he was pumping gas. Anyway, old Mannerman picked him up, gave him a job, taught him the trade. They became lovers. Jack did the sketches and Max tailored the clothes. They were a great team. Like us, in a way."

Street was silent.

"Max manufactured the coats and Jack did the sketches. Max paid him a fortune. Not only that, he paid Jack's taxes. Ten years ago they were in Paris for the collections and Jack said he'd always wanted a Rolls. Max and he flew over to London and Max bought him the Rolls. Paid the tax on it, too. I don't think Jack ever spent a dime. He was making a million a year and Max still paid for everything." He paused. "I guess he really loved Jack."

Marc could feel the chill swirling through the church, but Adam, absorbed as he was, didn't seem to notice.

"Max is maybe eighty-five or ninety. Really old. Jack is maybe sixty or so. And you know how they live?"

"How?"

"Max's senile, like a child. He wears a diaper now. This elegant, brilliant, genius son of a bitch is wetting his pants and wearing a goddamned diaper. He can't walk anymore, couldn't even feed himself, and he and Jack are living in this big fucking mansion near Phoenix with a pool and everything and servants. But every morning Jack just picks up Max in his arms and carries him out to a chair by the pool so he can feel the sun. And he feeds him with a spoon at lunchtime, feeds him and wipes his chin where he dribbles things, and then after he's had enough sun Jack takes him back inside and changes his diapers again and puts him to bed. He does it himself, won't let the servants help."

Marc said nothing.

"They're just a couple of fairies," Adam said, "that's how people thought about them. A couple of rich old fairies. That's all they are." Adam fell silent for a moment.

"Yes, Adam," Marc said, "I'm listening."

A tear ran down Adam's face. "But the thing is, they have each other. They have love. And that's why Jack stays, why he's still there even after Max couldn't work anymore, couldn't screw anymore, couldn't pay the bills anymore. Jack and Max. I think of them sometimes, now."

Marc said nothing.

"When I think of me and Peter, I think about that," Adam went on. "Peter was right. I should have come out of the closet years ago, and to hell with public opinion. I told him he was crazy, that I wasn't a politician or some nut-case martyr. I was just a guy selling dresses."

He was crying now, and shivering in the cold, as if for the first time he could feel it.

"Adam," Marc said, "you were never just a guy selling dresses."

Adam looked up then, seeing Chelsea hurrying toward them. "Don't lose her, Marc," Adam said, his voice level, "don't screw up the way I did."

Marc threw an arm around him and they went slowly down the long flight of steps, Chelsea falling into stride with them. There was a rank of cabs, and they helped Adam into one.

As the cab pulled away Adam watched Marc through the window. He put a hand to his forehead. It was cooler now, or it felt that way. He slumped down against the plastic seat and smiled, watching the lights blinking on in the Paris dusk.

Marc and Chelsea talked about him that evening at a tiny table in the corner of a stone cellar on the Left Bank, smoking cigarettes and drinking *fins* and listening to a thin girl in a black turtleneck sing old Charles Aznavour songs.

"Yeah, I feel pretty good. I'm glad you got him here. I feel better."

"I knew you would."

"I hope the poor bastard doesn't get sick."

She nodded. "I think maybe you made him well."

"That's something," he said, "just walking out on Baltimore

like that. All on his own, and being so scared. That took guts."

"Just like it took guts for you to forgive him, Marc."

"Well, we go back a way." He toyed with his glass, listening to the singer, watching Chelsea's face in the dim, smoky light, thinking, remembering.

"It all began here in Paris. Right in that church. Adam knew what he was doing when he met me there today. You were probably wearing braces on your teeth and just killing the boys in the eighth grade. Were your legs as long then?"

"Almost. I jumped center on the girls' basketball team. All arms and legs. I kept wondering if I was ever going to grow breasts."

He laughed. "You can stop wondering," he said.

It was pleasant, even cozy, sitting together with the music and the brandy, her knee lightly touching his. But they were settling nothing. The chasm of disagreement still yawned between them, deep and unbridged, no matter what Adam had said so hopefully.

"Marc," she said.

"Yes?"

"While you and Adam were talking, I snuck back into the church, into that little chapel near the front door. There were just a couple of old women inside, kneeling down and lighting candles. So I knelt down, too, and prayed. I haven't ever prayed before, except as a kid. Grandpa wasn't much for churches. But I was there and so I knelt and I prayed. I prayed for you and I prayed for me, I prayed for Adam."

"Yes?" he said.

"And I prayed for *us*."

He nodded, silent.

"Marc, I'm going to ask you one more time."

"I know you are," he said, breath held.

She inhaled deeply. Then: "Marc, come home with me. Now."

"Chelsea," he said, his voice dead, "I don't have a home."

"The hell you don't. I got Sydney to pay rent on your apartment. Dust balls and all. The landlord's been warned if he lets a maid in there, it's his ass."

He looked at her in a sort of wonder. "You did that?"

"Yes, Marc."

He sat there for a moment, not moving, not saying anything, a man at a crossroads, thinking of his lousy apartment, thinking of one man who had come all this way to say he was sorry.

Then, abruptly, he shoved a few crumpled hundred-franc notes onto the table under an ashtray and took her arm. "Come on," he said, "there's something I want to do."

She grabbed her coat from the back of the chair and hurried after him.

Outside, the raw wind caught at them.

"Come on," he said again, urgency in his voice. She slid into her coat and ran after him, down the winding, cobbled street toward the Seine. It had begun to snow, large, wet flakes coming at them in the light of the streetlamps. They crossed the quai Malaquais to the stone parapet that bordered the river, and stood there staring down at the black flow of the Seine, rushing toward Normandie and the sea.

Then, without saying anything, he reached inside his jacket and pulled out Swaggerty's gun. He held it for a moment and then, with a backhand flip, tossed it out over the river. She could just hear the splash, see a brief glint of foam, and then the river was again smooth and black, erasing the moment, erasing the past.

"I still won't testify against Lazer. And they'll crucify me for that."

"Yes?"

"But I'll go back. With you."

She said nothing but slipped an arm through his. They walked slowly back up the street away from the river toward the boul' Mich', feeling neither the snow nor the year-end wind.

64

The designer label will be bigger and better than ever in 1983.

Lincoln Radford, *Mode,* January 1983

In the morning she went out for fresh croissants and the papers while he slept, feeling like a little girl on Christmas morning, knowing that they had crossed the last bridge of doubt, that whatever happened back in New York in the courtrooms and the law offices, they would be there together. Now and forever. Thank God she'd come, that she'd shucked off logic and made this foolish, quixotic flight. Half to herself, she laughed, remembering when she'd lectured him about Cervantes. It was a wonder he put up with her, that he didn't break her neck.

In the chill morning streets early risers were already on their way to work. *Revillon,* the day before New Year's. She found herself grinning inanely at passersby. One man turned to watch her rear as she passed, wondering why a *poule* would be working the sidewalks this early on a cold, snowy day, especially a pretty one like this. She didn't care. At the bakery she shook the clerk's hand, babbling terrible, enthusiastic French. She thought that she had never encountered such a courteous salesperson as the man who sold her the newspapers, had never seen such a bright array of magazines and papers.

She considered making a snowball and taking it back to Marc as a gift, the season's first snowball. But as she thought about it she opened the *Herald Trib* to see whether all the world was celebrating too, and if not, why not.

The story was on the front page.

"Marc, Marc!"

She came into the apartment running, her face glowing from cold and excitement.

He pulled himself up in bed, staring at her in sleepy confusion. She shoved the newspaper at him.

"There, on the front page. Lazer's dead, Carl Lazer's dead. He was shot. It says the federal case'll be dropped."

He grabbed at the paper.

Lazer had been shot in his office in midtown Manhattan by parties unknown. He died in Bellevue Hospital without ever regaining consciousness. He had been out on bail of a million dollars on racketeering charges in connection with the murder of a federal agent by one Jocko Collins.

The assistant U.S. attorney was quoted: "These gangsters are always knocking one another off. There was some sort of feud with another gang, the Westies." He added lugubriously: "The case? There is no case. Lazer was the case."

The assistant U.S. attorney was named Giordano. Marc could see his small, angry face.

He put down the paper. "Swaggerty," he said.

"We don't know that," Chelsea said.

Marc didn't say anything. He was thinking of Lazer, "Uncle Carl," and of Bobby. On the run again. But not before settling accounts.

Chelsea had crawled into bed next to him, sitting there, reading the paper over his shoulder.

"Yes," he said, not so much to her as to himself, "it was Bobby. Paying off. Maybe in some crazy way he thought Lazer owed him for Jocko Collins. Maybe because he thought he screwed me up by getting Jocko into a situation where he blew his cool. I dunno." He shook his head, wondering about the world and its curious ways.

"Marc?" she asked, huddling against him.

"Yes," he said. "Sometimes you get lucky."

She was thinking of the Madeleine, of the gloomy moments she had spent there on her knees, praying without really knowing how to do it, praying as a stranger in a strange place while Marc and Adam murmured nearby in the darkness. Had someone listened, had those few moments in the candled dark really made a difference? Or was it, as Marc said, simple luck?

"I don't care," she said aloud, "I don't care."

They held each other close, he naked and she still wearing her coat, the newspaper splayed across their laps, talking, as lovers do when it is real love and not only sex, making plans, exchanging promises, remembering yesterday and shaping tomorrow. Together.

"Children," she said, remembering Denver, "I want a kid, right away. A child of our own."

"Oh, yes," he said, knowing what it was like to be a child alone. "Kids, lots of kids."

Soberly, she said, "Some people have houses. They make love and have children at home."

He pulled her to him again, kissing her mouth.

"A house. We'll get a house. I never owned one, never had an upstairs, or a cellar. Never had a front lawn. We need a house. We can't live in that apartment of mine."

"Won't you miss the woollies?"

"The hell with 'em. With you, who needs woollies?"

He would work again. "Start up small, nothing like Majesty in full flight but like it was in the beginning. A couple of patternmakers, a few tailors, some seamstresses. Hire some bright kid fresh out of FIT. Get old Sydney to leave his bridge game in Miami and come back to run the shop."

"You'll need a model," she said, teasing.

"Yes," he said seriously, "pregnant women rarely show the collection."

"Toy," she said, "we'll get Toy." She giggled. "And Adam," she said, "you'll bring Adam back to work with Sydney, to teach the boy."

"Yes," he said, remembering their afternoon in the vestibule of the Madeleine, "we'll get Adam back, the best designer on the Avenue."

"He'll be fine," she said, speaking quickly, "he doesn't have to die."

"Of course he won't die," Marc said, his voice a shout. "And you can't let a man like Adam slip away from us. We lost him once. We *need* him. We'll get him back!"

"Yes, yes," she said, meaning it.

"Maybe I'll have to borrow a few bucks from you, seed money. But it's got to be a loan."

"I'd insist on it," she said. "I know you Seventh Avenue hustlers."

It had all begun a dozen years before here in Paris at Chanel's funeral on a winter's day. Now, on another winter's day, it was ending and starting anew, a long and lovely time-warped crescent of memory and incident curving across the years, across the settling of so many accounts, across the payment of debts, his own and Adam's and Bobby Swaggerty's.

He slid an arm around her shoulder, pulling her toward him, feeling her strong young body relaxing against his, not making love but simply drawing close as the account book of their lives opened to a fresh page, still to be filled.

Outside, snow continued to fall, muffled and crystalline, over Paris.